PRAISE for…

Hit & Mrs.
If you're in the mood for a cute chick-lit mystery with some nice gals in Montreal, Hit & Mrs. is just the ticket.—Globe and Mail

Crewe's writing has the breathless tenor of a kitchen-table yarn.… a cinematic pace and crackling dialogue keep readers hooked.
—Quill & Quire

Ava Comes Home
She expertly manages a page-turning blend of down-home comedy and heart-breaking romance.—Cape Breton Post

Relative Happiness
Her graceful prose…and her ability to turn a familiar story into something with such raw dramatic power, are skills that many veteran novelists have yet to develop.
—Halifax Chronicle Herald

Shoot Me

LESLEY CREWE

Shoot Me

Vagrant
PRESS

Vagrant Press is an imprint of
Nimbus Publishing Limited
PO Box 9166
Halifax, NS   B3K 5M8
(902) 455-4286

Printed and bound in Canada
NB1586
Interior Design: Margaret Issenman, MGDC
Cover design: Heather Bryan
Author photo: Nicola Davison

Library and Archives Canada Cataloguing in Publication

Title: Shoot me / Lesley Crewe.
Names: Crewe, Lesley, 1955- author.
Description: Originally published: Halifax, N.S. : Nimbus Pub., ©2006.
Identifiers: Canadiana 20210117532 | ISBN 9781771089630 (softcover)
Classification: LCC PS8605.R48 S56 2021 | DDC C813/.6 — dc23

Nimbus Publishing acknowledges the financial support for its publishing activities from the Government of Canada, the Canada Council for the Arts, and from the Province of Nova Scotia. We are pleased to work in partnership with the Province of Nova Scotia to develop and promote our creative industries for the benefit of all Nova Scotians.

For John, who taught me everything I know
about being in love.

Prologue

Gaborone, Botswana

Hildy took a sip of her tea. It was cold. How bloody irritating. Placing the teacup back on the china saucer, she reached for the hotel phone and dialed room service.

"I'd like a cup of very hot Earl Grey tea please and if it isn't produced right away, I will speak to the manager. Room 218." She hung up without waiting for a reply, choosing instead to lean her head against the back of the armchair and gaze out the open window.

It was early evening and Hildy was tired. After being on safari for the last ten days, she desperately needed the welcome rest this luxury resort provided. Her fellow travellers were surprised she kept up at all, and most of them wondered why an old lady would want to bounce around in a jeep day after day. But at the age of ninety-one Hildy was used to being underestimated and she certainly didn't give a hoot about the opinions of these strangers.

The last rays of the sun gave the room an orange glow and Hildy felt its warmth seep deep into her bones. The light made all the sharp edges of the room disappear. As she watched the branches of a tree sway easily in the soft breeze, she remembered the tree outside her bedroom window when she was a child. Was it still there, on the other side of the ocean? She knew that African plains spread out beyond the courtyard, but just then the wind-swept grass looked like undulating waves. And waves brought back thoughts of home. And memories of him. She closed her eyes and let the past wash over her.

The fog and the damp and the sound of a lighthouse, moaning. The street with its broad graceful trees in that city by the sea. A big beautiful house with leaded windows, wide verandas and ornate trim, with a gabled roof and widow's walk. A house with nooks and crannies and wonderful places to hide. A glorious shelter from any storm.

How did a Maritime girl get so far from home? What was she doing away from the salt air and water? Away from the August gales that roared up the coast and left tree branches strewn over gardens and wet pavement. Away from the sight of billowing sails approaching the harbour. Away from the boom of the noon-day cannon.

Hildy sighed and looked down at her hands, and was startled for a moment. These weren't the hands of the girl who lived and laughed in that house. They were the hands of a very old woman. She rubbed the parchment-thin skin that stretched over her enlarged knuckles. She was almost transparent. Well, well.

"The sun was setting in the West, the birds were singing on every tree. All nature seemed inclined for to rest, but still there was no rest for me."

A knock at the door brought her out of her reverie. She quickly wiped her nose with a hankie.

"Come in."

A piping-hot pot of tea was produced by a nervous-looking waiter. As he stepped away from her desk, Hildy raised her hand. "Stop."

She rose from her chair, went over to the desk and opened one of the small drawers. Taking out some coins, she placed them in his hand. "Thank you for the tea."

"Thank you, Missus."

When the door closed behind him, instead of reaching for the pot, Hildy pulled out the desk chair and sat down rather heavily. Her heart hammered in her chest and she rubbed the front of her sweater before reaching for some writing paper and an ink pen. Her hand hovered over the creamy white paper. She started to write.

Chapter One

Dearest Elsie. I'm coming home to die.

Elsie shivered in the hot bath water. Was this a joke? It had to be. Aunt Hildy was always one for pulling pranks. Elsie rapidly scanned the rest of the letter, looking for the punch-line.

I will ship my belongings by freight. And would you be kind enough to arrange for a safety deposit box? My banker will be in touch with details about transferring funds. I will give you a shout when I've made my travel arrangements.

Yours,

Hildy

Elsie flipped the letter over. There was nothing written on the back. Dripping water over the side of the tub, she reached for the envelope to see where it had originated. She'd ripped it right over the post mark.

"*NO!* This can't be happening!" she howled, waving the letter over her head as if it were on fire.

"Mom?" Lily's muffled voice reverberated from the other side of the wall. "What's wrong?"

"We're expecting company," Elsie shouted back. "But not for long."

Elsie threw the letter on the floor and watched it soak up the spilled water like a paper towel.

The bathroom door flung open and Lily roared in. No matter how many times the girl stood before her, Elsie was always shocked to see that beautiful brown hair a flaming flamingo pink.

"Oh goody," she said. "Who's coming?"

"Do you mind?" Elsie sunk lower in the tub. "I never get any privacy in this house."

Her daughter sat on the throne and shrugged. "You should learn to lock doors then. Did you know an unlocked door means that psychologically you want people to barge in on you?"

"Thank you, professor." Elsie leaned over to turn on the hot water tap so she could put her feet under the faucet.

"You're an exhibitionist at heart," Lily continued. "Mild mannered by day, but with a secret desire to show yourself to all and sundry. Next, you'll be getting ready for bed with the blinds open."

Elsie looked at her. "An exhibitionist? You should talk. A nose ring, an eyebrow ring…"

"…and pink hair. I know, I know. God, Mother, get over it."

"Fine. Now tell me this, smarty-pants. What's your explanation for why Aunt Hildy wants to come home to die?"

Lily's big brown eyes widened. "Really? She actually said that? She wants to die here?"

"Apparently."

"Hmm." Lily looked out the bathroom window and stroked her chin.

"Stop that. You look like Sigmund Freud."

"Why *does* the great prune want to come home?"

Elsie turned off the hot water. "Don't be rude."

"Rude! You just had a hairy fit and screamed at the thought of her coming. Isn't that rude?"

"She's coming to die, Lily. Normal people come to visit."

Not that Aunt Hildy had ever been normal. She'd return to Halifax from the far corners of the earth every few years when Elsie's mother was alive, to "check in" with her Nova Scotia relatives. After about a week, she'd decide they were all mad and leave. Elsie and her sisters dreaded the visits. Their aunt never made any bones about her opinions and never kept those opinions to herself, casting a critical eye over their clothes, their rooms, their friends, and their behaviour. Elsie never understood why her mother didn't step in and stick up for them. "Life can be cruel, Elsie. Some people need as much kindness as you can give them," was all she said to explain.

Now the woman wanted to die in the house she'd been in only two or three times in twenty years.

The front door banged open downstairs and Flower the bulldog barked on cue.

"*MOM!? LIL?*"

"Up here!" they hollered together.

Steps pounded up the stairs. Dahlia rushed into the bathroom, followed by the dog.

Elsie never could figure out how her daughters, created in the same womb and raised in the same home, could be so different. They were born exactly a year apart, and when they were very young they were sometimes mistaken for twins, but it didn't take long for it to become abundantly clear that they didn't have a lot in common.

Dahlia grinned at them before plunking herself down on the creaky rocking chair next to the old dresser covered in seashells, candles and books. Flower scampered over to Elsie for a pat.

The best thing about this rambling old house was the huge bathroom. The worst thing was that the whole family fit in it.

Dahlia flashed her fabulous smile. "Guess what?"

"You've been chosen for *America's Next Top Model*," Lily scowled.

Dahlia pushed her long blonde hair back with her open fingers and gave her sister a look. "That was last week." She turned back to her mother. "Guess."

Elsie, now frozen despite the additional hot water, refused to leave the tub. Her forty-two-year-old body was not something she bragged about, or showed off too often. It was the one thing about the separation that was positive — she didn't have to be naked in front of a man anymore. So much for Lily's theory.

"You've been selected as hairdresser to the stars?" Elsie guessed.

"Nope."

"You've won a part in a movie?"

"Nope."

Lily slapped her hands together and looked incredulous. "You're engaged, aren't you?"

"Yep."

Elsie jumped out of the tub and spilled water everywhere. She tripped over Flower as she grabbed a huge towel to cover herself. The girls screamed at her for dripping on them.

Once wrapped, she turned to Dahlia. "Are you insane?"

Now it was Dahlia's turn to scowl. "No."

"You're twenty years old!"

"So?"

"*So?*"

"Yeah. So."

Elsie turned to Lily for support. "Tell your sister she's insane."

"You're insane," she confirmed. "Certifiable."

"Well, this is great," Dahlia cried. "I come home with fabulous news on the happiest day of my life, and this is the reaction I get. Why am I not surprised?"

Elsie wanted to throw her hands in the air but couldn't for fear of losing the towel. She also wanted to wring Dahlia's neck but her towel would fall off if she did that too. So she yelled.

"Why would you marry a guy you've only known for four months?"

"Because I love him," Dahlia pouted.

"Just because he looks like Brad Pitt doesn't make him a suitable husband. He rubs bodies for a living, for heaven's sake."

"Yeah," Lily said. "And he's stupid."

Dahlia quivered with indignation. "I'll marry Slater if it's the last thing I ever do. We'll never be parted." She looked down at her diamond. "Don't you even want to see the ring?"

Lily grabbed her sister's hand and pulled it toward her. In spite of herself, Elsie leaned over for a closer look too. She had to admit it was a doozy.

"Holy guacamole," Lily whistled. "I think the boy means business."

"What did he do, rob a bank?" Elsie asked. "How can he afford this?"

Dahlia drew her hand away and gazed at her emerald-cut diamond ring with a moony expression. "He ate Kraft Dinner for three months."

"I told you he was stupid." Lily sat down on top of the toilet lid and examined her nails.

Dahlia stamped her foot. "Mommy, tell her to shut up. She's just jealous because she's never had a real boyfriend."

Lily stood again. "Excuse me? I've had a boyfriend."

"You mean that geek lab partner of yours?" Dahlia laughed. "The guy who strapped the block of nails to your arm and pumped it up with a blood pressure cuff?"

"For your information, it's called psychological research. It's called making sure I don't end up a hairdresser like you."

"I'm sure you'll make a fortune as a shrink, sister dear. All you need is yourself as a patient."

Elsie joined the fray. "You'll be a client too, young lady, because if you marry Slater you're off your rocker."

"Well, everybody in this house is a loony anyway, so why not join the club!" Dahlia shouted as she paced up and down, stepping over Flower with every turn. "I suppose it hasn't occurred to you Mother, or to you Sister, that the reason you're both yelling at me is because someone loves me but nobody loves you two!"

Lily stormed out.

Elsie followed her. "This is shaping up to be a great day. I've gained three pounds since yesterday. I have Aunt Hildy coming home to die on my doorstep, and now my baby girl wants to marry a great hulk at the ripe old age of twenty."

Dahlia yelled at her retreating back. "Okay then. You're not invited to the wedding."

"Good."

"Fine!" Dahlia cried. "See if I care." She slammed the bathroom door. And then opened it again. "What do you mean Aunt Hildy's coming home to die?"

Elsie didn't answer. She raced to her room, flung herself onto her unmade bed and threw the duvet over her head. She wanted to lie there until the neighbourhood crows realized she was ripe for the picking and pecked her to death. It was her favourite brooding fantasy. She wondered what Lily would think of it.

Naturally, the girls made up almost instantly. Elsie could hear them nattering away in the hall about Aunt Hildy and Slater, and then about whether there was pizza in the freezer. Footsteps, then silence.

Elsie uncovered her head and stared at the ceiling, then slid over the side of the bed and reached for her emergency shoe-box. She pulled it out, dragging an enormous dust bunny with it.

"Sorry. You're not invited." She poked the silent creature back into its lair and opened the box. Inside was an old pack of cigarettes, a lighter, a dozen Halloween-sized chocolate bars, wrappers, and a worn copy of *Playgirl*. She reached for a Coffee Crisp, tore it open and popped it in her mouth. Before she even swallowed, she took a smoke, lit it, then held it between her teeth while she shoved her arms into a tattered bathrobe. Dry as the dust critter it lived with, the cigarette flared and sputtered and disappeared rapidly.

Elsie hopped around, looking for some kind of receptacle in which to fling the tiny firework before it dropped on the floor and ignited the litter at her feet. She stubbed her toe on the bedpost in her haste.

"Ow!" Elsie danced a jig of pain before she grabbed the flaming filter and stuck it into an open jar of Nivea Cream. She collapsed on the bed once more and screamed into a pillow.

The phone rang.

It was Graham's ring. She could always tell. Unbelievably, it sounded like a fed up, sighing kind of ring. Whenever she admitted that to others, they gave her a fed up, sighing kind of look. Kind of like the look she got when people asked her why Graham still lived in the basement. Weren't they separated? That question irritated her to no end, mainly because she didn't have a reason, other than the fact that since the house was so large, they could go for days without seeing each other.

The phone rang again.

She grabbed the receiver and proceeded to knock the phone off the table with a crash.

"*What?*" she hissed into the mouthpiece.

"Are you all right?" Graham asked.

"No, thank you very much, I'm not." Elsie bent over to pick up the phone, which caused her bathrobe to open and reveal her soft belly bulging over the top of her thighs. "And it's all your fault."

"What did I do?"

"Do you know what a total of seventeen pounds of baby does to a woman's stomach?" Elsie shouted.

"Dear God. The girls are two decades old and they're still to blame? Have you ever heard of sit-ups?"

Elsie took the receiver and whacked it against the mattress several times. Then she put it back to her ear.

"Stop hitting me on the bed."

"No."

"Dahlia just told me she wants to marry that guy. Did you know about this?"

"I've kept it a secret for weeks."

"Thanks a lot."

"Don't be stupid Graham. As if I wouldn't tell you. I only found out myself five minutes ago."

"Well, what do you think?"

Elsie snorted at him. "What do you think I think?"

"I know you. You've just stuffed your face with a Coffee Crisp so you don't have to think."

"Sod off, Graham."

She slammed the phone down.

And waited.

The trouble with Graham living in the basement was that it only took him a minute to run up three flights of stairs. She started to count. Twelve was his best time. She saw in her mind's eye the neat-as-a-pin basement digs he'd fashioned for himself. That irritated her — not the fact that he lived there, but the fact that it was neat. She visualized him taking the stairs two at a time to reach the rec room, then up another flight before he emerged through the kitchen door, rubbing Lily's head quickly as he ran through the kitchen. She imagined Flower jumping off the sofa in the sunroom at the sound of her master's steps.

Through the sunroom, past the library, down the wide hall with the grandfather clock, man and dog would turn right at the French doors and start up the wide staircase, right again at the first landing to emerge on the third floor of the great house and into the corridor, with its branching bathroom and bedroom doors. He'd rush past the door that led to the attic and arrive at her door, a little out of breath. He'd give Flower a couple of slaps on the rump for a job well done.

Knock. Knock.

"Who's there?"

"Guess."

Elsie was reminded of the fact that Dahlia and her father

were two peas in a pod. Both airheads. Both unambitious. Both irritatingly carefree.

"A spendthrift?"

"No."

"The perpetual good guy?"

"How about a worried dad?"

"Enter."

Graham walked in. As much as she wanted to throttle him, her stomach always gave a bit of a lurch when she saw him. It used to be from attraction. Now Elsie put it down to jealousy. He'd kept in good shape, the miserable beast. That's what being a plumber will do for you, all that stretching under sinks and reaching around toilets. She even resented his hair. It was still thick and caramel-coloured, curling around his ears like it did back in the eleventh grade when she fell in love with him. Why didn't it just turn grey already?

He sat in the deep armchair by the window and eyed her crummy bathrobe.

"Don't you dare," she said.

"I didn't say a word."

She slumped into the pillows behind her back. "You didn't have to."

He sniffed the air. "Did you have a bonfire in here?"

"As a matter of fact I did. I burnt your love letters."

"What love letters?"

She folded her arms. "My point exactly."

"What is it with you?" Graham shook his head. "You've got to let go of crap like that."

Elsie closed her eyes and pressed her fingers against them to ease the pressure that pounded from within.

"Say what you've come to say and go home."

"Yes, I must run before the traffic gets heavy."

"She wants to get married, Gray," she whined. "Aren't you worried? You said you were worried."

"I am worried. About *you*. I know you Else. You'll wring your hands and howl at the moon, but she's in love with him, and it's obvious he adores her."

"She's only twenty."

"So were you when we got married."

She knew he'd play that card. She looked around her chaotic bedroom in despair and then back at him. "And look what happened." Her hands flopped to the mattress.

"What happened? We're separated. You make it sound as if we grew up to be serial killers. At least we're still civil to each other."

She screwed up her face. "Are we? You could have fooled me."

Graham leaned toward her, his large, calloused hands clasped in front of him. He gave her a steady look with his blue eyes. "I'm not happy about this either. She *is* young. But I won't stop her because I know it won't do any good. She's always been headstrong and if you tell her how to live her life, she'll bolt. Mark my words, Elsie. Is that what you want?"

"But a massage therapist?"

His voice became dangerously low. "You say that like he's a plumber."

Elsie felt her insides knot. "Don't turn this into you and me. This isn't about us."

He didn't say anything for a good minute. "If it's going to happen, it might as well be with him. He's a nice kid…good and kind, with a steady job. We should thank our lucky stars he's not a biker type. He could have been a drug dealer."

She shook her head and peered at the cobwebs draped around the ceiling fan. "Slater? A drug dealer? He's too stunned to be a drug dealer." She knew that was harsh but she didn't care.

"He's an innocent. He's not stupid."

Elsie was starting to feel bad about the remark. "He reminds me of an overgrown puppy."

"I thought you loved puppies," he smirked.

"Not when they jump in your lap and lick your face." She gave him a solemn look. "Don't try to jolly me out of this, Gray. I need to grieve. My baby girl wants to marry a boy who outweighs her by a hundred and thirty pounds. The thought of them together is like…a St. Bernard with a Chihuahua."

"Oh for the love…"

Elsie started to cry.

"Will you please control yourself? It's not the end of the world."

"My *baby* wants to get married," she choked. "How am I supposed to react?"

"Slightly better than this."

"Go jump off something."

"I think you're menopausal. That has to be it. Or mental."

She threw a pillow at him. "Go down to your dungeon and leave me in peace. Why do you always have to make me feel stupid?"

He stood and walked to the door. "Get a grip, my dear. This is Dahlia's moment. It's about her. Not you."

With that, he opened the door and shut it in her face. And as usual, made her feel like she was the spoilsport ruining everyone else's good time.

Graham could hear the girls in the pantry reading the pizza box ingredients. He pulled up to the table and waited for them to stop their argument about trans fat, mad cow disease and the evils of dairy products. Finally, he couldn't stand it any longer.

"If frozen pizza is the poisonous concoction you say it is, why don't you eat celery?" he shouted from his chair.

They emerged from the pantry holding the object in question.

Dahlia stated the obvious. "Celery doesn't taste like pizza."

"And you have to wash it and cut it up." Lily opened the oven door and threw the pizza on the middle rack.

Graham tried not to stare at Lily's hair. He knew his daughter very well — any hint of disapproval, and she'd keep it that colour forever. But after six months with the new do, he was desperate for her to get rid of it. Perhaps if he tried reverse psychology.

"You look very pretty today, Lily."

"Nice try, Dad."

"Girls, sit down a minute. I want to talk to you."

He saw them glance at each other before they sat opposite him at the old pine harvest table Elsie loved so much. He'd brought it home for her years ago, after coming across it in a farmer's cow barn. The old fella was thrilled to get rid of it, in lieu of a plumbing bill. When she saw it, Elsie jumped up and down before smothering him with kisses. As he recalled, they'd had a great night.

They used to have a lot of great nights in this big old South Ender. They were surrounded by large, attractive homes on Cambridge Street, but their house stood apart. Elsie's grandfather had been a sea captain and his travels all over the world shaped the look and beauty of the house. There were shutters and trim from Norfolk, England, and wrought-iron fencing from Italy. A massive oak door that he'd shipped from France graced the front entrance. He even brought home a bronze dragon-shaped door-knocker from Thailand. Family lore had it that his wife had a hard time explaining the creature at her IODE meetings.

The first time Elsie brought Graham home, he was overwhelmed. His family lived in an upstairs apartment off Robie Street. Few of his neighbours had a yard — their porch steps and front doors were smack up against the sidewalk. And even if they had a small back garden, it was usually filled with old cars, bikes, and dustbins. He and his friends hung out on The Commons, a large expanse of grass that filled up on summer days with kids horsing around and people walking their dogs. In the winter months, he played hockey and tobogganed on Citadel Hill.

The young Graham didn't recognize Elsie's world. He remembered not being able to eat his dinner for fear of spilling gravy on the cloth napkins. He knew better than to mention the cloth napkins to his mother, but his fascination was such that he bought her some for her birthday one year. She thanked him with a tight voice and put them away. Maybe she threw them away. He never saw them again, in any case.

He realized Dahlia had spoken to him. "Sorry...what?"

"I said, you're not mad at me too, are you?"

"Of course not," Graham assured her. "And your mother's not mad at you. She's frightened."

"Of Slater? That's ridiculous," Dahlia frowned.

"It's not about Slater. You'll always be three years old to your mother. You know that."

Lily picked at her thumbnail before she chewed it. "She treats everyone like a baby, which must be exhausting. When you mother the whole world, you're an enabler, in psychological terms."

"How about 'crazy,' in ordinary terms," her sister said.

Graham folded his arms in front of him. "Your mother's not crazy, but I think she is tired. Do you girls help out around here?"

They gave him indignant looks.

"Y-e-s-s-s," they said together.

Graham beckoned with his hand for more information.

"I clean my room and wash my own clothes," Lily huffed first. "I'm not helpless. But I do have piles of assignments. You don't want me to flunk out in my third year, do you?"

"And I'm not responsible for my schedule," Dahlia informed him. "They'd have me down in that salon day and night if they could. Did you know they sprang three perms on me at the last minute yesterday? I didn't get home until eight o'clock."

Dahlia looked at her sister and Lily tsk-tsked at her sympathetically. Graham recognized the tactic. It was called "confuse the old man with senseless information until he stops the interrogation." He was about to call them on it, when the girls burst forth with "Guess what? Aunt Hildy's coming home to die!"

Graham was always spooked when they spoke in tandem like that. Their news didn't help either.

"Excuse me?"

"It's true," Lily squealed. "Can you believe it? Mom got a letter."

"How sick is that?" Dahlia cried. "I don't want her to die in my house. Why can't she die somewhere else?"

"Because we're her family."

All three of them jumped.

Graham turned to look at Elsie in the doorway. In that old bathrobe with her damp curls gathered on top of her head she looked just like Lily. She seemed vulnerable and sad, the weight of the world on her shoulders. He didn't know whether to shake her or give her a hug. "You can't be serious, Else. You're not going to let her stay, are you?"

Elsie got herself a glass of water before joining them at the table. "Of course I am. She's my mother's only sister. I can't throw her away."

"You're hardly throwing her away," Graham said. "She has enough money to buy her very own old folks' home. Not to mention an entire hospital wing, should she need it. Why on earth does she want to push her way in here? I know this house is big, but it's a hovel to someone like her."

Elsie took a sip of water. "What business is this of yours?"

His head jerked back. "Pardon me. I forgot I'm not supposed to care what happens to you anymore."

"No. You're not. Do me a favour and let me sort this out myself."

"You have enough on your plate as it is…"

"Graham. Listen to me. I can't let my elderly aunt die alone. She's ninety-one years old. I'm all she's got."

Graham stood and chose to ignore the girls' worried looks.

"That's nonsense and you know it. You have two grown sisters who are perfectly capable of shouldering some of the responsibility. But of course, that would mean you'd have to get out of the way and actually let them do something."

Elsie stood too. "Excuse me. Why am I being yelled at in my own home by someone who's not really my husband anymore?"

Graham wiped his hands down his pants in a deliberate effort to calm himself. He didn't want to be sucked into another fight in front of the girls. "Don't let this miserable old woman do this to us again. She comes here, turns the place upside down and then goes on her merry way."

Dahlia raised her hand. "Apparently after this visit, she's off to the funeral home, so maybe it'll be easier this time."

Everyone looked at her.

"Well, it's true," Dahlia sulked.

"Where's she going to sleep?" Lily asked suddenly.

"She asked for her old room back," her mother shrugged. "What can I do?"

"You can't be serious. Why my room? Why not the guest room?"

Elsie shrugged again.

Dahlia stood and put her hand on her hip. "Hey, wait a minute. This will seriously affect my wedding. I don't want her to die while I try and plan a reception. I mean, that would totally ruin the mood, don't you think?"

Graham took a step back. "I can't believe you just said that."

"Well, think about it, Daddy." Dahlia grew teary-eyed. "What if someone throws me a surprise shower and wrinkly old Aunt Hildy just sits in the corner and moans about death? I mean, that would be so unsexy."

"What about my room?!" Lily cried. "Isn't anyone else besides me bummed about that?"

Elsie put her head in her hands. "Will everyone just stop? I can't think."

Graham reached over and put his hand on Elsie's arm. "This is nuts. You work long hours at the hospital and now you have a wedding to plan. Besides which, that leech upstairs sucks you dry at every opportunity. Do you really need this? Think about how this will affect us."

Elsie raised her eyes and looked at him. "That's the second time today you've said, 'us.' But there is no 'us.' Remember?"

She might as well have slapped him.

Just then the phone rang. Elsie jumped and made a dash for it. "Hello? Yes, I'll accept the charges."

She turned away and he knew in an instant it was Aunt Hildy.

"Yes, it's me!" she shouted. "Hello, dear. Where are you?" There was a pause. Elsie stared at the ceiling. "Where?… Botswana! Why on earth are you there?"

She turned to look at the girls and mouthed "Africa."

"Well, that's wonderful." She twirled the cord and looked uncomfortable. "Yes. I got your letter. No. No trouble. We can't wait to see you. When's your flight?"

Graham noticed Elsie's body stiffen. There was another long pause. "All right. Yes, don't worry. We'll be there." She nodded several times. "I'm losing you dear. I better go. See you soon. Bye."

She hung up slowly and kept perfectly still.

"Elsie?"

"What?"

"When?"

She didn't answer him.

"When?"

Elsie put her index finger to her temple and pulled an imaginary trigger.

Chapter Two

Faith sat at her desk in the attic. It was late — the best time to write. The only time really, since Elsie and the girls had a contest earlier in the evening to see who could slam a door the loudest. Little did they care if creative genius was being interrupted.

She stretched her arms over her head and cracked her knuckles. Picking a lit cigarette off the overflowing saucer she used as an ashtray, she took three deep drags for good luck before stubbing it out. Finally she was ready.

Her hands hovered over the keyboard. Deep breath. Slow exhale. Now.

She typed.

"It was…"

A mouse scurried across the floor.

"Oh, for the love of…" Faith picked up a slipper and threw it in the critter's general direction. Jumping up from her desk, she grabbed the broom she used for just such occasions. She knelt down and picked up the flowered, rubber-backed slipcover that was draped over the old couch in front of her.

"Come here, you little bastard," she said through clenched teeth, sweeping the broom from side to side until her forearm cramped. All she managed to unearth was an old *TV Guide* and an empty pack of gum.

"Nuts to this." As she rose from the floor, her knees cracked in unison. "God, it sucks to be old."

Back at her desk, she started again.

"It was a dark and stormy night."

Shit. That's been done to death. Okay then. Highlight. Hit delete.

"It was a bright and sunny morning."

Shit. Doesn't sound spooky enough. Okay then. Highlight. Hit delete.

"It was a drab and dreary afternoon."

Shit. Sounds as dull as dishwater. Okay then. Highlight. Delete.

"It was dusk and pissing rain when the sex-starved creature came storming into town."

There. That at least held the promise of excitement and danger.

She looked at her watch. She'd been at it for what…five minutes? She glanced at her wall calendar. September's sexiest fireman looked back at her, holding out his suspenders, begging her to jump right into his pants.

Sorry. Another time perhaps. She had things to do because becoming a famous writer was really hard. So hard in fact, she decided to take a break and lit another ciggy. She gazed at her familiar surroundings, her shoulders drooping as she blew out the smoke with a long slow sigh.

It wasn't that the attic was a dump or anything. Elsie did a fine job fixing up the joint. She'd painted the beams and walls white, and even harangued Graham into building two window seats on either end of the vast room, so Faith could gaze over the tree tops. Her best view was Elsie's back garden, and the gardens along their street, but she had to admit, a good pair of binoculars certainly added to the overall charm of the place.

Her musing ended abruptly with a knock on the door. It was awfully late for the gang downstairs to be up. She heard slow footsteps climb the stairs.

"You better not be a robber because I'll sic my guard mouse on ya."

"It's only me."

Elsie's pale, tired face was visible through the railing before she reached floor level.

Faith took a puff. "Can I ask you something?"

Her sister collapsed on the crappy couch. "Not if it's hard."

"How much do social workers make?"

"Not enough, why? Do you want my job? If you'd like to kill me and assume my identity, go for it. Do it with a knife though…I don't want the obituary to read 'gnawed to death by an attack rat.'"

Faith smirked. "As much as the thought of killing you cheers me up, I only ask because I need to know why you insist on wearing the world's ugliest housecoat. Are you broke?"

"It's not ugly. It's comfy."

"It's vile. It looks like it's been mauled by a cat in a rage of self pity."

Elsie burst into tears. Faith crushed the cigarette into her pyramid of butts and ran to her sister's side.

"I'm sorry, I didn't mean it. Please don't throw me out. I promise I'll clean up the joint more often. I'll find a job…"

Elsie snuffled and reached in her pocket for a Kleenex. "Don't be silly. That's not it."

"Thank God." Faith went back to her computer and reached for another smoke.

"Well, aren't you going to ask me what's wrong?" Elsie sniffed.

Faith nodded while she inhaled, then shook out her match before she sat back at her desk. "Sure. Sure." She threw the match on the floor. "So. What's up?"

"Dahlia's getting married and Aunt Hildy's coming home to die."

Faith reached for a piece of tobacco on her tongue. She looked at it before she spoke. "You know, that makes a pretty good country music lyric." She pretended to strum a guitar and sang, "My Dahlia's gettin' married and that ol' Hildy's fixin' to die."

This time Elsie burst out laughing. She laughed so hard Faith thought she was hysterical.

"So. Why are you letting the old hag come back?"

"That's what Graham wants to know."

"Well, you know how I hate to agree with that man, but this time he's probably right."

Elsie slumped even further into the pillows. "I have no choice. What kind of reputation would I have if people found out the wonderful social worker at the hospital wouldn't let her ninety-one year-old auntie come home? And this was her home. Aunt Hildy was born in this house, in case you've forgotten."

Elsie's goody two-shoes routine irritated Faith. "My dear girl. Aunt Hildy isn't a sockeye salmon. She doesn't have to return to her spawning grounds…which is a good thing, because I'd worry about the black bears cavorting along the river looking for their dinner. She'd jump out of the rapids and kill them with one chomp of that very big mouth of hers."

Elsie gave a weak smile.

"When does she get here?"

"The day after tomorrow."

Faith shook her head at Aunt Hildy's nerve. And then remembered something else. "I take it our girl's marrying that gorgeous creature Slater, or has she moved on to someone else in her usual fashion?"

"No. It's Slater."

Faith looked at her baby sister's long face. "Cheer up, Else. You're lucky she wasn't whisked off her feet at the age of thirteen. She's had every male from here to Montreal salivating at her door for years."

"That's true. I forget she's almost grown up."

"Almost?" Faith sang, "She's a woman. W-o-m-a-n. I'll say it again."

Elsie stood and smiled at her. "Thanks. You always make me feel better. I'll let you get on with your writing. How's it going, anyway?"

"Margaret Atwood just had me on the phone, begging for advice about goal, motivation and conflict…I mean, I do what I can for her, but she's a real pest."

Elsie dismissed her with a wave of her hand. "You're a nut. Goodnight sis." She shuffled down the stairs.

"Good night."

Finally. The goings-on downstairs with her sister's family were enough to drive Faith to drink. Thank God she was smart enough never to have married and had brats. Men and kids drained a woman's creativity to the point of extinction. Phooey on that.

Faith looked at the screen again and suddenly realized Aunt Hildy would certainly want to read her novel, now that she was coming home. She conceded the best course of action would be to avoid words like *pissing* and *sex-starved*. She wanted to be included in Aunt Hildy's will, after all.

Okay then. Highlight. Delete.

She typed.

"It was a glorious dawn when Sister Agnes prayed for world peace."

Smarten up Faith. You're forty-four years old. A writer doesn't compromise her art.

"It was dusk and pissing rain when the sex-starved creature stormed into the nunnery herb garden and loomed menacingly behind Sister Agnes as she prayed for world peace."

Faith read it over a couple of times. It was a start. She'd call Juliet tomorrow and read it to her. Juliet liked Faith's stuff, although she always complained about the lack of explicit sex in the love scenes. Poor Juliet. She was beyond frustrated. No wonder, with Robert as a husband.

But Faith didn't like to write about sex. She didn't want anyone to guess she was still a virgin.

❧

Juliet was just heading out the door the next afternoon when Faith called and invited herself over for dinner.

"Tonight?"

"Yeah, why? Do you have somewhere you have to be?"

"I think so, just a minute." Juliet made faces at Robert who was reaching for his car keys by the front door. "Do we have anything going on tonight? I'm sure we do." She tried to mime the word Faith, point to the phone and shake her head all at the same time so Robert would get the message, but no such luck.

"No. *The Apprentice* is on tonight. You never miss The Donald."

Faith overheard him. "I love that show. We can watch it together."

"Great," Juliet sighed. "Faith, I have to run. I'm late for an appointment." She hung up before Faith could say goodbye.

"Thanks a lot, Robert."

"What did I do now?" he frowned.

"I couldn't think of an excuse to tell her to stay away. You never catch on, do you?"

"Apparently not. Let's go."

"Kiwi! Come to Mommy." Juliet's teacup poodle came running and jumped into her arms. A quick cuddle and kiss and Kiwi was deposited in Juliet's straw shoulder bag before they left the house.

It was a beautiful sunny day, unusually hot for September, so Robert put down the top of his MG. Juliet reached for her silk scarf to keep her hair from blowing every which way and put on her 'Jackie O' sunglasses. As they drove down their street in Clayton Park, she waved to a couple of her neighbours. They didn't wave back.

Robert headed out towards the MacKay Bridge. "Where are we going exactly?"

"The Mic Mac Mall. Dahlia works at the new hair salon there and I promised her mother I'd drop in and give her some business."

"Didn't you have your hair done yesterday?"

Juliet ignored him. She pointed to the cruise ship in the harbour. "Why don't we go on a cruise?"

"We just got back from the Mediterranean, that's why."

"That was last month."

"Exactly."

"You're no fun."

Robert geared down as he approached the toll booth. "I'm no fun because I spend every waking minute working my butt off to keep you in hair appointments."

"Do you hear the way Daddy talks to me, Kiwi? He's a bad, bad man." Juliet gave her baby a quick scratch under the chin. Kiwi yipped her appreciation.

Robert tossed three quarters into the toll net and threw his car into gear so he could pass the slow poke in front of him. Juliet held onto her scarf and looked the other way. Finally she said, "Who's prettier? Me, Faith or Elsie?"

Every so often his wife came up with a question that gave him ulcers. And it usually had to do with her sisters, especially the youngest. Robert knew Juliet was jealous of Elsie because Elsie could have children and she couldn't, but if he were being honest, he'd say it was because Elsie was a beauty. Her older sisters were very pretty, certainly, but Juliet's comeliness was bought and paid for, while Faith had a tragic, withering vine kind of look.

"Now what do you think?" Robert winked at her and hoped that would suffice.

"I don't have a clue. You haven't answered me."

"Juliet, you are the fairest of them all."

Juliet reached over and gave his knee a pat. "I know. I was just checking."

Thankfully they reached the Mic Mac turnoff and all conversation halted until Robert manoeuvred his way into the parking lot and found a spot close to one of the entrances. Juliet opened the car door and swung her long legs out in one swift motion. With her baby carrier tucked under her arm, she sashayed between the parked cars.

"Do hurry up, Robert."

Robert hurried.

They found the salon and Juliet made a great fuss as she marched over to Dahlia's station. "Hello, darling. I do hope you know what you're doing."

Dahlia looked horrified. "What's that supposed to mean? It's just a wash and a blow dry. Even I can't mess that up, if that's what you're insinuating."

Juliet heaved a great sigh. "Calm down, sweetheart. I'm not insinuating anything. Don't you know a joke when you hear one?"

Dahlia pointed to the four eager young men in the waiting area. "If you'd like to go, it's okay by me. I've got plenty of customers."

"Keep your hair on." Juliet turned and passed the doggie bag to her husband. "Take Kiwi and wait over there. If she wakes up give her a cookie."

Robert did as he was told, but not before he smiled at Dahlia. "Hello dear, how are you?"

"I'm fine, Uncle Robert." She gave his balding head a quick look. "I'm good at men's haircuts, if you want an appointment. I'll give you a discount."

"I'll do that," he smiled again, but stopped when Juliet gave him an elbow.

At the sinks, Juliet was forced to concede that Dahlia gave a great shampoo, although she didn't tell her so — the girl's ego was big enough.

Back in the chair, swaddled in small white towels, she let her niece pump her up like an old tire. This was the part she hated most — when hairdressers took the towel off her forty-something wet head. Suddenly every wrinkle and saggy eyelid was magnified a hundred times over, or so it seemed. Juliet was desperate to distract herself. "So. What's new?"

Dahlia gave her a dreamy smile. "Did you hear the good news, Aunt Juliet? I'm engaged." She held out her hand.

Forgetting about her hair, Juliet grabbed Dahlia's fingers and examined the ring closely. "Mother of God! It seems you're smarter than you look."

Her niece wrinkled her brow. "What's that supposed to mean?"

Juliet pushed her hand away. "I mean, my dear, it's a clever little minx who gets a ring like that."

Dahlia attacked her hair with a comb. "I didn't choose it."

"Ow. Watch it."

"I would've been happy with a crackerjack ring."

"Leave me with a bit of hair, for heaven's sake. I didn't mean anything by it. You're a lucky girl, that's all."

Dahlia looked mollified. She put her hand on the roots of her aunt's hair, before tugging at it with the comb.

"No doubt you want a big wedding?"

"Well, why not? I mean, it's once in a lifetime, so why skimp."

"True. Of course, I'm sure your mother disagrees, knowing her. Don't you let her bully you into a cheesy affair. You come to me if you don't get anywhere with her. I'll make her see the light."

"Mom wouldn't want cheesy. She wants what I want. But I know it will be expensive, because I have to have six bridesmaids…Lily of course…but Jillian for sure and if I have Jillian, I have to have Megan, and if I have Megan, I have to have Amanda, and if I have Amanda, I have to have Samantha and if…"

"Fine. I get the picture," Juliet said quickly. "By the way, I understand Slater works here too. How did that happen?"

"When I got the job, he applied and they hired him. It was simple."

"Isn't it a distraction to have him roam around all day?"

"A little," she grinned. "But he's really popular. His massage clients are pretty much one after the other. I don't see him a whole lot. Just at lunch hour."

"I can see why he'd be popular. He's built like a brick shithouse."

Dahlia's mouth gaped open. "*Aunt Juliet.*"

"I'm only stating the obvious."

Dahlia reached for the blow dryer and turned it on, shaking out her aunt's expensive auburn hair. Grabbing a fat round brush, she took a section of hair at a time, and rolled it around the bristles, drying as she went. Juliet was impressed. So far so good. She started to relax.

"Oh yeah, did Mom tell you? Aunt Hildy's coming home to die."

Juliet bolted up in her chair. "Are you kidding me? That old boot? When did this happen?"

"Just last night. Mom got a letter asking us to take her in, apparently."

"I know Aunt Hildy. She didn't ask your mother anything. She *told* her. Well, I hope your mother sent an urgent telegram with a big fat NO written across it."

"You know Mom. She's welcoming her with open arms."

Juliet practically spit. "Your mother should be put in a loony bin. Who welcomes a tyrant into their home? Your father can't be happy about this…but no…I suppose it's none of his business any more."

Dahlia rolled her eyes while she brushed. "Whether it is or it isn't, he's still fit to be tied."

"When's he moving into his own digs, anyway? It's mighty odd that he's still hanging around."

"I think he's there because he's afraid Mom can't cope with the house on her own. The expense and repairs, I suppose."

"That's an excuse," Juliet grunted. "He's always been a tick on her backside…"

Seeing her niece's face in the mirror, Juliet realized she'd gone too far. "I mean that in a nice way."

"A tick on your backside is nice?"

She had to backpedal. "No. You're right. I think it is the house. That place is a monstrosity. I should know. I was born there." She shivered for Dahlia's benefit.

"Hey, it's a nice house. A little messy maybe…"

"Your loyalty is admirable, but I thank God every day that I escaped, unlike poor old Faith."

"Did Aunt Faith ever live anywhere else? She's been a permanent fixture for as long as I can remember."

"Yes, she did for a time. But she got sacked for accidentally setting fire to the bookstore she worked in. Your mother naturally felt sorry for her and said she could stay with you guys until she found her feet again."

"I guess her feet are still missing. How did she cause the fire anyway?"

"Three guesses."

"Smoking?"

"Bingo."

Her niece shook her head. "It's scary to think an arsonist is living in our attic."

"She's hardly an arsonist, Dahlia. An absent-minded feather brain, maybe, but she didn't intend to cause a four-alarm blaze."

"Why can't she stay with…"

"You're insane if you think I'd have Faith live with me. She's a total bloodsucker. At the risk of repeating myself, your mother belongs in a loony bin, but I don't intend to join her."

Out of the corner of her eye, Juliet watched the approach of Slater, a blonde surfer-boy Adonis with muscles on his muscles. No wonder his day-planner was filled to capacity. Just the thought of his hands on her flesh made Juliet want to crawl out of the chair and jump on his bones.

He grabbed his girl from behind. "Hey baby. I need some lovin'."

Juliet wanted to raise her hand to volunteer for the assignment.

Dahlia giggled and turned around. They kissed each other with as much abandon as humanly possible in public. Was that allowed? It must be. No one stopped them.

After what seemed like forever, Juliet had had enough. If she wasn't getting any, neither was Dahlia.

"Do you two mind? I'm in the middle of a hair appointment."

They parted reluctantly. That's when Slater realized who was in the chair.

"Hey Mrs. W. How's it shakin'?"

"It's not shaking at all, thanks to my plastic surgeon."

Slater gave her a funny look and shrugged. Then he got the joke. "Wicked. You rock."

"I'm thrilled."

"I think you're done." Dahlia picked up a round mirror and held it up to the back of Juliet's head. "What do you think?"

This time she really was thrilled. Her sleek pageboy never looked better. Never one for over-enthusiasm, she tempered her comments. "It's very nice. Thank you. I may even come back," was all she said.

Dahlia pursed her lips. "Sure. I'll pencil you in."

"You should come for a massage, Mrs. W. You look tense. See how your shoulders are all hunched up." Slater reached over and started to massage her neck. She became a pool of liquid jelly. This was better than an...

"Juliet...are you finished?" Robert appeared out of nowhere with Kiwi popping up out of the straw bag at three-second intervals. Naturally. It was too good to be true. Her husband always showed up at the wrong moment. Slater stopped to reach over and grab Robert's hand in a gripping finger-grab ritual that passed for a handshake.

"Hey, Mr. W. Long time no see. How's it goin' dude?"

Robert stared at Slater with alarm. "Fine. I think."

"You look like you could do with a massage as well." He reached out, but Robert held him off.

"No thank you. I golf. That's as relaxed as I want to be."

"Cool man. Whatever turns you on." Slater gave Dahlia a dazzling smile. "And I know just the girl who does that for me. Come here, babe." He pressed her against him once more.

Tired of not being the centre of attention, Juliet barked her command: "Come Robert. Kiwi must be ready to go home." She got out of the chair, grabbed her baby and marched out of the salon without paying. She heard her husband say goodbye, but no one answered him. He followed her outside.

"I like your hair. She did a good job."

"Mmm."

"Don't you think so?"

She wanted him to shut up, so she could concentrate on the feel of Slater's hands around her neck. She definitely needed to make an appointment with that boy.

The wind had picked up in the interim, which made for less conversation on the way home. As they crossed back over the bridge, they saw the Dartmouth ferry plow its way across the harbour with a boatload of commuters. They took a right and followed the Bedford Highway back to their own neighbourhood. Juliet always hated to go this way because the container terminal reminded her of a Hollywood set. One designed for a sleazy gangster movie. It was always a relief to turn up Bayview Drive and get back to the tonier parts of the area.

Juliet loved her home on Lady Slipper Drive. It was a modern cube style, clad with mahogany stained wood, built into the hillside. Large windows looked out over the street, but because the living room was on the second floor, it was private, and needed no curtains.

Naturally, when Elsie and Faith first saw it, they just wandered around with their mouths open. Faith asked her if she liked the idea of living in a museum of modern art. Juliet replied it was a lot better than living in a stinking attic. That's when Elsie suggested they all go out to dinner. Her treat.

They turned the corner and there was Faith's tin can of a car in the driveway.

Juliet rolled her eyes. "Oh, great. She's early."

"Be nice," Robert said.

"I'm always nice."

They pulled alongside Faith's rusting Tercel. Faith got out of her hunk of junk as Juliet emerged from the sports car.

"Hello, darling," said Juliet, kissing the air beside Faith's left and right ear.

"I thought I might as well come over. There's nothing going on at home."

Juliet rooted through her purse for house keys while she walked to the front door. "Great," she said vaguely.

"I think Dahlia did a nice job on your hair. Don't you think so, Robert?"

He mumbled something.

Juliet told her sister to go sit by the pool while she went upstairs and changed into the new silk lounging pyjamas she'd bought the day before. She admired herself in the full-length mirror while looking at her silhouette for any unsightly bulges. Satisfied, she joined Faith on the back deck.

It was Juliet's favourite space. The decking around the heated pool was enclosed with expensive fencing, which in turn was covered with beautiful clematis, wisteria and honeysuckle vines. The Virginia creeper was just starting to turn a glorious red. Juliet paused to admire it.

"I'm so glad I decided to add this to the mix." She pointed to the newest plant, then grabbed a lounge chair and pulled it up beside Faith, who handed her a glass of red wine from the small wrought iron table between them.

"Thank you," Juliet smiled. "Boy, do I need this." She sat down and took a long sip.

Faith put her hand up to shade her eyes from the late afternoon sun. "Isn't Robert going to join us?"

"He's cooking dinner."

"Don't you ever cook?"

"Do you?"

"Not if I can help it."

"Ditto."

They both took another gulp of wine. Juliet tried not to stare at the faint grease stains on Faith's T-shirt, but it was nearly impossible.

"Did you know the arrow on your 'I'm with Stupid' T-shirt points north?"

"Well, duh. That's why I got it on sale for a buck."

It wasn't the first time Juliet wondered if her sisters were foundlings.

Faith handed her a folded piece of paper. "What do you think of this?"

Oh goody, Juliet thought, another horrible opening sentence. She reached over and gave it a quick glance. "It seems fine, although maybe he should grab her boob from behind or something."

"You have to build to the climax, you ninny, not have an orgasm right off the bat. That ruins the sexual tension. It's obvious you know nothing about structure and nuance. You want your audience to turn the page."

Juliet shrugged and took a big gulp of wine. "Exactly. I'd turn the page if he grabbed her boob. Have you ever thought that maybe that's why you're not published?"

"You're a horny old woman, did you know that?"

"It takes one to know one." Juliet noticed the wine bottle was almost empty.

"Ro! Get us another bottle please," she yelled at the open kitchen window.

"In a minute."

"Now, Ro."

"What a bossy boss." He marched out with a dish towel draped over his arm, and leaned the bottle against it for their approval. "Will that be all, madam or may I get back to grilling my Portobello mushrooms?"

"You may."

He put down the bottle and they watched him return to his culinary duties. Juliet shook her head slightly. Robert definitely needed that butt tuck she'd booked for him.

Faith read her mind. "Have you ever noticed Robert has a…?"

"Of course I have. And he's getting it fixed…not that he knows anything about it yet, so don't breathe a word. I have to pick my moment carefully."

"Do you actually love him? I mean, he looks like he's been pulled too tight."

Juliet filled her glass before she offered the bottle to her sister. "Does that go for me as well?"

"No. You must have a better surgeon."

"I do."

"Why do you call him Ro, by the way? It's stupid."

"So he can pretend his name is Romeo."

Faith stuck her finger down her throat and pretended to gag.

"Hey. I've never had a better lap dog, so back off. You're just jealous."

Her sister sighed. "No. I don't think so. No one's attractive to me anymore."

"I can think of someone."

"Who?"

"Slater." Juliet lifted her eyebrows. "It was all I could do not to rip his clothes off today."

"He is perfect, isn't he? Can you imagine him in bed?"

They didn't speak for a moment. Juliet didn't want to ruin the steamy images coursing through her brain. She assumed that was the reason for Faith's silence as well.

Finally Faith leaned over to her and whispered, "I heard them once, when they didn't think I was home. Girl…it went on for hours."

Juliet fanned her face with the nearest coaster. "God. Stop talking or change the subject. I have to go to bed with Ro later and I don't want to set myself up for disappointment."

"Elsie was pretty upset last night. She thinks Dahlia's too young to get married."

"Would you wait if you had someone like *him* chase you? Damn. It's so unfair. A whole lifetime of…that…waiting for her. I can't stand it."

"Settle down. He might be built, but he talks like someone's used him as sparring partner once too often."

Juliet brightened slightly. "That's true."

"Hey. You'll never guess who's coming to town."

"Aunt Hildy."

"Geez Louise," her sister frowned. "I never get to tell anyone anything. You could pretend you didn't know. I suppose Dahlia told you?"

Juliet nodded. "What's it all about, anyway? She's coming home to die? The old trout will outlive all of us."

"I daresay."

"Who does she think she is, Queen Muck? The way she carries on, you'd think she was born in Buckingham Palace instead of that old house. I don't know how Mom stood it all those years."

"Not only that. She wants her old bedroom back."

"Typical behaviour, ordering people around." Juliet knocked back another mouthful before hollering, "Hurry up Ro. I'm starving."

Chapter Three

An airport employee whose name tag read 'Antony' rolled Hildy Chamberlin up to the gate at Heathrow.

"Here we are madam."

"And about time too. A drugged sloth would have had me here sooner. If I miss my plane to Canada young man, your head will be on a chopping block."

"You have plenty of time before you board, madam. Have a safe trip."

Hildy looked at him as she heaved herself out of the wheelchair. "I intend to have a journey. Whether it is safe or not is up to the employees of this airline and if your shoddy performance as a chair pusher is anything to go by, I have a feeling I'll be nose-diving directly into the Atlantic before the North American continent comes into view."

And with that Hildy, in a flowing North African gown and headdress and carrying an ancient carpetbag, an umbrella and a fertility mask, took her leave.

The chair pusher turned his rig around and hightailed it to his pal at the next gate. He held his hand up to his mouth and said under his breath, "Whoever's working business class to Halifax today will be up on murder charges by the time they land. That, or jumping out of the emergency exits."

Finally the announcement was made for anyone with small children or those requiring assistance to proceed to the gate. Hildy sat firmly in her chair, with her nose in her book—*The*

Finest Hour by Winston Churchill. One of the ticket agents approached.

"Would you like to board now, ma'am? Before the others?"

Hildy removed her glasses from her nose and let them dangle from the silver chain around her neck. "If I wanted to board now, young lady, I would have done so."

"But it goes a little faster if…"

Hildy shut her book with a bang. "It goes a little faster if the old dear is put on first and out of the way of the galloping hordes of important businessmen…is that what you're suggesting?"

"I only meant…"

"I'll have you know I've just crossed the Sahara on the back of a camel, thereafter joining another party to go on safari through the plains of Africa. Lions and tigers and elephants are to be respected. Not insipid, dull and dreary men in suits, who, if they can't wait the extra thirty seconds needed for me to plant my generous behind in a seat, can feel free to off themselves in the john after we've reached a flying altitude."

The young woman bit her lip and unfortunately turned a bright shade of red.

"Oh do buck up, girlie. You can't let an old thing like me put you off your dinner. Where's your backbone? You're more than a pair of breasts in a tight uniform. Be proud of yourself. And the next time a mouthy old dame gives you a blast, tell her to get stuffed and be on your way."

"Get stuffed."

"Jolly good. Keep it up."

Business class was announced next. Hildy gathered her possessions and headed for the gate. Eight men in three-piece suits rose from their seats as well, but gave her a wide berth. Sound carries in open airport terminals.

❧

Meanwhile, on the other side of the Atlantic, Elsie waited in agony for the elevator to inch its way upward to her office. At this rate, Aunt Hildy would be in Canada before she got to the fourth floor. It never failed to amaze her that an elevator would be this slow in a hospital. Surely the seconds saved rushing around for a code blue were a wasted effort if the poor schmuck had to get to another floor. A patient would be better off strapped to a gurney and pushed down the laundry chute to surgery. Maybe she'd suggest it at the next board meeting.

But it wasn't just the elevator that had her in a lather. She carried a plate of homemade cupcakes in one hand and a thermos of tea in the other, which normally wouldn't have been a problem but for the fact that her huge purse, gym bag and leather satchel were sliding down her shoulders and digging into the crooks of her arms.

Finally the elevator doors slid open. She burst forth and very nearly knocked over an elderly man with a cane. He shook it at her.

"I'm so sorry," she apologized over her shoulder, rushing to get to her office. By the time she reached it, she looked like a gorilla lumbering through the jungle.

"Crys...for God's sake...grab this, will ya?" She shoved the thermos and cupcakes at her assistant.

Crystal reached for the offered items, cracking her ever-present gum. "Why don't you just push a wheelbarrow in from the parking lot? It'd be a whole lot easier."

Her hands finally free, Elsie dropped her stuff on the floor. "And have one more thing to drag? I don't think so."

"What are these?"

"Carob cupcakes with cream cheese icing."

"Healthy but fattening…they are so you…no, I meant these things." She pointed to the toothpicks that stuck out of the cupcakes and held up the plastic wrap.

"Those are miniature marshmallows, so the toothpicks don't poke through."

Crys cracked her gum in double time, which Elsie knew from long experience was Morse code for "you're a lunatic."

Elsie picked up her belongings. "Never mind the sarcastic remarks. Just do me a favour and take those to the ward clerk on third. If I have to get in that elevator again I'll scream. Of course I should take the stairs, since Graham continues to nag me about my lack of exercise, but I refuse to do that, just to make the point that he can no longer…"

"You're rambling. Answer the question. Who are these for?"

"Someone on third is having a little do for…I forget who… and I forget why…but I said I'd bring something."

"So you don't actually know this person?"

"I don't *know* if I know this person."

"I suggest you don't know. I suggest you have no flipping idea who this person is, which means…"

"…*we* eat them. You're brilliant."

She turned to go when she looked back for a second. Crystal was already hiding the plate in her left drawer.

"Crys…are those earrings?"

She shook back her frizzy red hair to reveal her lobes. "You like?"

"They're dream catchers, aren't they?"

"Yeah. Great eh?"

"They're the size of a pancake."

Crystal folded her arms. "My life is a nightmare, as you well know. Better safe than sorry."

"Perfect. Buy me a couple of dozen on your lunch hour. I'm going to need them."

With that, Elsie disappeared into her office.

❧

The beleaguered flight attendant hurried over to seat 4B and switched off the blinking call light. "Yes, madam?"

"I've had better food in the slums of Calcutta," Hildy barked. "And the wine is swill. Take it away and bring me a glass of tomato juice. That, at least, can't be messed with."

She scurried off and came back with the juice. Her passenger took a sip and grimaced.

"Apparently I'm mistaken. Right then. I'll have a glass of ice water please, with a slice of lime. And if you foul that up, I'll have no choice but to worry about the future of mankind."

The attendant, accompanied by her migraine, went back behind the curtain to collapse into the arms of a colleague. "I can't take it anymore. I give up. She wins. I'm quitting as soon as we land."

Her friend patted her back. "We only have a few more hours."

"Where's a tailwind when you need one?"

❧

Mrs. Abernathy was upset. "I think I still love the rat."

Elsie pressed her lips together to keep from smiling. She reached for the box of tissues on her desk and passed them to Mrs. Abernathy. "By rat, you mean your husband?"

The woman sighed as she took a tissue and dabbed her nose. "Is there any other?"

Graham. Oh God, did I say that out loud?

"I told him to get out….I told him to leave…."

Elsie leaned towards her. "But now you think you've made a mistake?"

Her head bobbed up and down. Tears fell down her cheeks. "Is that wrong? Am I being stupid?"

She smiled at her. "Of course that's not wrong. And you're not being stupid. Everyone has doubts about changes in their lives. Change is frightening. And none of us can turn off our emotions just like that. What you have to decide is whether your life is better with him or without him."

"Oh, I've already got that one figured out…it's a whole heck of a lot better *without* him, let me tell ya."

She blinked. "But you're still having doubts?"

"I love the creep."

Elsie looked at her watch. She picked up her pen and scribbled something on the woman's file, something she did whenever she was uncertain about how to help. It gave her a few seconds to think. The poor woman was obviously not ready to strike out on her own. It saddened her when a client didn't know her own potential.

She pushed her chair back from her desk. "I tell you what. I think it would be a good idea if you took a piece of paper and put a line down the middle. Write all the reasons you want him to come home on one side and all the reasons you want him to stay away on the other. I think you'll find it helpful in sorting out your emotions."

"The bum drinks. He smokes. He gambles. He plays around. He hasn't bought me a birthday gift in twenty years…"

Elsie held up her hand. "That's a start. You write it all down and then bring it to me for our next session. We'll figure it out together. How's that?"

Mrs. Abernathy rose from her chair and smoothed down her drab coat. "Thank you dear. You're a sweet girl. I have no one else to talk to."

"You can always talk to me. I'll see you in a couple of weeks, okay?"

The poor woman nodded and left her office. Elsie flopped back into her chair, put her elbows on the desk and rubbed her temples with the tips of her fingers. Then she picked up her pen and drew a line on her blotter. She wrote "bossy know-it-all/ good with a hammer."

It was so maddening, the things men got away with. Really! What nerve. Who do they think they are…telling her to do sit-ups…

"Elsie?"

She snapped her head around. Crystal was in the doorway.

"Sorry. I did knock."

"That's okay."

"I hate to tell you this, kiddo, but they've called an emergency meeting and orders are 'Everyone show up.'"

She threw her pen on the desk. "Wonderful. Just what I need. I'm supposed to pick up Aunt Hildy at the airport."

"Can't someone else go?"

Elsie reached in her purse for her cellphone. "I guess so. Or let me put it this way. I sure *hope* so. Otherwise my life won't be worth a plug nickel."

The phone rang.

Juliet lay on her deck chair, baby-oiled to the hilt, wearing a green facial mask, terrycloth turban and not much else, taking advantage of another heavenly day. A pitcher of margaritas and a dish of salted cashews were placed beside her by the ever-faithful Ro. Kiwi slept at her feet on a suede doggy cushion.

"Get that. My face is frozen."

"We have an answering machine, you know."

"I forgot to tell you. Kiwi knocked it off the table. It's broken. Scared her to death, poor little poopsie."

Robert looked to the heavens as he reached for the cordless phone. "Worthington residence."

"Robert, it's Elsie."

"Oh, hello Elsie."

Juliet groaned.

"Is Juliet there?"

He looked at her. She waved her hands back and forth in front of her, as if to ward off a cloud of blackflies.

"No sorry, she isn't. She's off doing her usual charity duties. No rest for the wicked."

"Oh, I see." There was a moment of silence. "You wouldn't want to do me a favour, would you Robert?"

He hesitated. "Ah…"

"I've been called to an important meeting, and I'm supposed to pick up Aunt Hildy from the airport. You wouldn't be a doll and go for me?"

He slapped his hand to his forehead. "Gee Elsie…any other time. I've got a client coming to sign some papers for a major deal and it's too late to back out now. Gosh. I'm awfully sorry."

"That's okay, I know it's last minute. I'll figure it out. See you later."

"Yeah, see you."

He hung up and wiped his brow. "That was a close one."

Juliet gingerly brought the iced glass to her lips and took a big sip. "What did she want?"

"To go to the airport and retrieve Aunt Hildy. Frankly, I'd rather walk on hot coals."

"What cheek asking us to do it. I'm staying away from that miserable old bat as long as humanly possible. This is her problem. She brought this on herself. Besides, you have no idea how mean Aunt Hildy is to me, Robert. You have no idea."

"Actually I do. I've seen her schtick before. She better not start when I'm around or I'll tell her a thing or two."

"No Ifs Ands Or Butts Plumbing Company. How may I help you?"

"Hi…is that…?"

"Bunny."

"Oh yes, Bunny. Is my husband…ah…former husband… God…is Graham there?"

Bunny's heart fluttered a little. "I'm sorry, but he's not here right now."

"Oh darn. His cellphone's turned off and I'm not sure where

to reach him. You don't know what job site he's on by any chance?"

"Sorry, I don't. But if I see him I'll tell him you called. Is there any message?"

"No. Never mind. Thank you."

Bunny no sooner hung up when she saw Graham walk toward the office from the back shop. She loved to watch him. He had a smile that melted her toffee in a big way. Not that he ever looked at her, but a woman could dream. Especially now, for heaven's sake…Graham was *divorced*? Why hadn't someone told her that before? She didn't have a moment to lose.

She grabbed her make-up bag out of the bottom drawer of her desk and ran to the bathroom. She applied a little blush to her cheeks and a smear of lip gloss. She bent over and whisked her hands through her hair before swinging her head back up and fluffing her blond mane with her hands. That's when she noticed a coffee stain on her blouse. Rats. She reached for a roll of brown paper towels someone had left on the back of the toilet and tore a piece off, quickly dipping it under the tap and tried wiping at the stain. That didn't work, so she opted to leave one more button undone. That solved the problem. She high-tailed it back to her deck just as Graham came in holding a bunch of invoices. He looked annoyed. Then dismayed.

"Ah…"

Bunny licked her lips. "Can I help you Graham?" She leaned forward just a tad.

He backed up a little. "Ah…yeah. These figures are totally messed up. The client's having a fit and I don't blame them."

"Well, let's go over them item by item, shall we? I'm sure I'll be able to fix you up in no time. I have a real head for figures."

Graham hesitated, then pulled up a chair beside her. "I guess so."

She thought she'd faint. He smelled so good, in spite of his messy overalls. Reaching over, she took the invoices out of his hand, and felt a jolt of electricity.

Then she remembered the phone call. Should she tell him? If she did, he'd leave. His ex said there was no message, so it couldn't have been that important. She decided not to waste this wonderful opportunity. Who knew when Graham would sit by her again?

Faith typed away like a madwoman. She was on a roll. The muse had hit.

"Agnes leapt up from her prayers when she saw the sex-starved creature and opened her mouth to scream but suddenly remembered she'd taken a vow of silence and so couldn't make a sound. Well, that was a bummer. Then she remembered that as a nun she shouldn't be grumpy, let alone violent, so hitting him with a rake wasn't much good and of course, there was the vow of chastity thing, so she really couldn't be of much use to him there but she had no way of letting him know that. And because she just stood there, getting really wet and not doing anything, the sex-starved creature wasn't sure what to do either. No one had ever just stood there before. So they stared at each other...and the longer they stared, the more understanding passed between them, until finally they lunged together and started rolling around in the oregano and parsley. But Mother Superior spied them from the chapel and came running out with the entire nun population behind her and —"

Ring.

Ring.

Ring.

"Blast it to hell. Hello?"

"Faith, it's me. You wouldn't do me a really big…"

"No!" She hung up.

"— everyone ended up rolling around in the mud and that's when the bus tour arrived…"

Lily was worried. She looked at her human guinea pig with alarm.

"Are you okay, Habib?"

"I think so," he said weakly.

"Is the blood pressure cuff too tight?"

"It's not so much that. It's the nails that are a little uncomfortable."

"Oh gosh." Lily looked around for her dumb lab partner, who really was a total jerk for letting her do this experiment by herself. "Perhaps I better stop pumping this up." She looked at the cuff and Habib's blueish arm.

He whispered, "I don't mean to be nosy, but is this incredible agony absolutely necessary?"

Lily wrung her hands. "I'm so sorry, Habib."

"I mean, I don't mind helping out, but I'd really like to get back to my fish and chips."

She was desperate. "I'm measuring pain thresholds between males and females. I shouldn't mention this, but we tell some of the guys that girls are better at this, because when we do suggest it, we find they try to outdo the girls' results but when we don't tell them…"

"Please…I'm a card-carrying wimp."

Just then her cellphone went off. She would have ignored it but she thought it might be her stupid lab partner and she wanted to give him a blast.

"Excuse me Habib. I won't be a moment."

"A moment…an eternity…"

"Hello? This better be you Martin and I'm going to kill you if it is."

"Lily?"

"Mom?"

"Hi honey…"

Lily looked at Habib's arm and decided enough was enough. She shrugged the cellphone against her shoulder.

"Look, Mom. I can't talk right now. Oh dear…" She fumbled with the gauge and in her hurry, turned it up.

"The other way!" Habib screamed.

"Hello? What was that? Are you all right dear? Who's that crying in the background?"

"Mom, I can't talk. I have to take Habib to the nurses' office." She threw the phone across the table and tended to her victim.

Dahlia pulled strands of hair through a plastic skull cap.

Her client made a face. "This reminds me of my daughter's Play Doh machine — you push down on it and the stuff sprouts up like spaghetti."

Everyone laughed, so Dahlia didn't hear the receptionist tell her she was wanted on the phone. She only looked over when the girl whistled and pointed to it. She turned to the hairdresser next to her.

"Would you mind pulling Mrs. Brown's hair out?"

Mrs. Brown grinned. "I like to pull out my own."

Dahlia smiled. "I'll be right back." She crossed the salon floor. "Hello."

"Hi honey. I'm sorry to call you at work."

"That's okay. What's up?"

"I'm in a real bind. I can't get to the airport to pick up Aunt Hildy and apparently everyone I know and love can't pick her up either and I'm desperate…"

"Sure, I can do it. Slater won't mind. What time?"

There was silence on the other end.

"Mom?"

"I'm sorry. I'm momentarily stunned. I can't believe someone said yes."

"It's no problem. I want her to meet Slater anyway. The sooner the better."

More dead air.

"Mom?"

"Sorry. Can you be there by five? It's the flight from London. Air Canada."

"Yeah sure. No problem."

"Thanks, honey. I hope to be home by the time you guys get there. Tell Aunt Hildy I'm sorry I was delayed."

"Will do."

"And Dahlia?"

"Yeah?"

"Is your sister involved with someone named Habib?"

"Habib? You're kidding? How exciting! When did this happen? Why didn't she tell me…"

"Never mind, dear. I've got to go. Thanks again."

"See ya."

Dahlia hung up and went to the back of the salon, where the

massage cubicles were. She popped her head in the first one and saw Slater organizing his room, piling clean towels for the next day's clients. He whistled under his breath and it made her smile. Her friends assumed it was his body that made Dahlia swoon, but that was only part of it. How could she not love someone who was so cheerful all the time?

He turned around and noticed her in the doorway. He threw her a thousand-watt smile. "Hey baby...you finished?"

"No. I still have Mrs. Brown. But once I'm done, Mom asked if we could go to the airport to pick up Aunt Hildy."

"Groovy baby, yeah."

Dahlia went up to him and gave him a big kiss. "You're so sweet. I can't wait for her to meet you. She'll love you as much as I do."

"Cool."

"And guess what? Lily's involved with some Arab guy."

"Far out, man."

❦

They searched among the faces of those coming through customs.

"What's she look like?"

"She's...hard to describe."

"Hey, babe. Look at that old crone. The one carrying a head or something."

Dahlia got up on her tiptoes to see. The crowd parted to reveal Aunt Hildy in all her glory.

Her African costume was so colourful, it made her look like a stooped peacock, but the headdress did give her the illusion of height. Nike running shoes completed the outfit. She was even more wrinkly than Dahlia remembered. Her mom told her it was from years spent under the desert sun. Aunt Hildy, an archaeologist and a complete renegade, pooh-poohed the idea of sunscreen, saying it smacked of feminine whimsy.

"Aunt Hildy!"

Hildy looked around. Dahlia ran up to her. "Hi Aunt Hildy. It's me, Dahlia."

"Dahlia?"

"Yes. Elsie's daughter."

"Oh yes, of course. Such a silly name. Were you conceived in the back garden?"

"I'm not sure."

"You must have been with a name like that."

"Lily too."

"Who's Lily when she's at home?"

"My sister, remember?"

"Merciful heavens. I'd forgotten. You may kiss me."

Dahlia leaned over and gave Aunt Hildy a kiss. Her cheek was incredibly soft, considering it looked like a piece of chewed leather. And she smelled like the outdoors. Not a fresh laundry detergent outdoors, but a musky, dusty, wild outdoors. She smelled of smoke and leaves and sunshine. Dahlia hugged her so she could keep her nose pressed against her skin. She wanted to cry and she had no idea why.

"Dear heavens, child, what a reception." Aunt Hildy held her at arm's length. "How old are you now? Fourteen, if I remember correctly…Great Scott. Who's this incredible specimen?" She jerked her head toward Slater, who hovered close by.

Dahlia grabbed his arm and pulled him over. "This is my fiancé, Slater Peach."

"You're marrying a large fruit at the age of fourteen? How interesting. You may kiss me too."

"Welcome home Aunt Hildy." Slater reached over, grabbed her around the waist and lifted her off the ground, giving her a big hug before placing her gently back on the floor.

"Where were you when I was hiking in the Himalayas? You would have come in handy."

"Cool, man."

"I find it distressing that you think I'm a man, young man."

"He didn't mean you're a man, Aunt Hildy, it's just something everybody says now."

"I will never say it, so that's an inaccurate statement. Perhaps Mr. Peach will be so kind as to hold my belongings. I'm rather tired."

"Hey, no prob Mrs. ..." Slater looked to Dahlia for a clue.

"C...C for Chamberlin."

"No prob, Mrs. C."

"Mrs. C" held her baggage closer to her heart. "Unless you address me as Miss Chamberlin or Aunt Hildy, I will not acknowledge your existence. Is that clear?"

"Sure. Yeah."

She waited.

"Ah. Sure Aunt Hildy. Whatever you say."

She thrust her belongings at him.

Dahlia thought about it. "Why aren't you called Hildy Macdonald like the rest of the family?"

"Chamberlin was my mother's maiden name. I have my reasons for disowning my family name and someday I may tell you about them, but not here. Come and take my arm, I'm starting to fade."

They walked to the luggage carousel, where Aunt Hildy's bags stood out from the rest. Hers were enormous old leather valises, completely battered and fastened with belts. No hidden handles or rollers on these babies. Slater heaved them off the carousel and piled everything into a baggage cart.

"I'll go get the car." He sprinted off.

"I'm not sure about his brains but his bum is quite something."

Dahlia hit her lightly on the arm. "Aunt Hildy, you're awful."

They walked slowly through the throng. "Not awful my dear…just honest. Now tell me, what does this boy of yours do for a living?"

"He's a massage therapist."

"At a brothel?"

"Of course not. At the place where I work."

"Please don't tell me you work at a massage parlour."

"I'm a hairdresser."

"Quite. And what does the other flower do?"

"She wants to be a shrink."

"A shrinking Violet. How quaint."

"Her name's Lily."

"Oh yes. I forgot. And what does your mother think of you marrying at fourteen? If you were mine, I'd beat you with a stick."

"I'm twenty. Almost twenty-one."

Aunt Hildy stopped and looked her up and down. "Are you quite sure?"

"Quite."

"Oh, well, that's all right then. By the time I was twenty, I had just about that many lovers."

"Really? How exciting!" Dahlia laughed. "I think Lily's having an affair with a sheik."

"How nice. I've met a few of them in my day. Lovely chaps. Always trying to give you things."

They pressed on, taking their time, oblivious to the glances being thrown their way. Suddenly Aunt Hildy spoke quite sharply.

"Where's your mother anyway? I expected her to be here."

"She's stuck in a meeting."

"Is she still trying to save the world?"

"Yes."

"And is she successful?"

"No."

"Useless occupation then, isn't it?"

Dahlia agreed with her, but out of loyalty said, "Mom's very good at her job. She helps a lot of people."

"Admirable, I'm sure. But a chronic do-gooder is the first to die a slow and painful death."

Dahlia wasn't sure how she should respond to that, so she kept quiet.

"I'm afraid to ask how Juliet and Faith are. They always were a handful for my poor sister."

"They're as weird as ever. Faith is writing a novel in our attic and Juliet spends her days buying designer clothes for her little dog."

"How positively revolting."

They eventually made it to the entrance where Slater waited with his souped-up Mustang. The trunk was ajar, tied together with a rope.

"How is this going to work? You'll need a crane to get me into that front seat. Camels I can do. Sports cars, I'm not so sure."

"Dee, you crawl in the back and I'll lift her into the front seat."

Dahlia scrambled in.

Hildy remained unconvinced. "I'm not a piece of furniture you can toss into…"

"Get a move on lady, you're holding up traffic," a taxi driver yelled from the lineup behind them.

She turned and marched over to his cab. "What's your number, you impertinent oaf? I'll see you're fired on the spot…"

"Let's go, Aunt Hildy." Slater scooped her in his arms and placed her firmly in the passenger seat, before he ran around and jumped behind the wheel. They laid rubber as they left the airport behind.

Hildy adjusted her headpiece. "Well, I never."

❧

The endless meeting finally came to a close. Elsie raced back to her office, grabbed her things, and took the cupcake Crystal handed her as she flew by her desk.

."Thanks!"

Crystal waved her goodbye. "Have fun tonight."

"Yeah, right."

She didn't dare wait for the elevator, choosing instead to run down four flights of stairs. The cupcake was gone by the time she left the QEII. Throwing files into the back seat of the car, she peeled out of the parking lot onto University Avenue and made her way to the Superstore in the middle of five o'clock traffic.

What vegetarian dish could she serve Aunt Hildy for dinner? Maybe she'd settle for a cheese pizza, but somehow Elsie doubted it. She had to pull down the visor while she waited at a red light because the late afternoon sun shone directly into her eyes. She loved these early September evenings, when the air was cool and refreshing, but not when she was rendered blind at the intersection.

Time was of the essence, so Elsie galloped into the store and headed straight for the bakery. She grabbed two whole wheat baguettes and then marched directly to the frozen food section, throwing a large vegetable lasagna, two McCain Deep and Delicious Chocolate Cakes and a carton of Breyer's Vanilla ice cream into her cart. Dinner was served.

When Elsie got home, she struggled out of the car with the groceries and pushed the door shut with her hip. The cats were turning themselves inside out along the driveway while Flower drooled on her shoes as a sign of her deep affection.

"You guys hungry?"

"Yoo hoo. Elsie!"

Elsie turned and smiled at her crazy old neighbour, who waved frantically from the porch next door.

"Hey, Mrs. Noseworthy. How was your day?"

"Terrible. Terrible. Someone stole two of my cucumbers. Can you imagine the nerve?"

"Oh dear. Two?"

She shook her tiny wrinkled face. "Yes. I had thirty yesterday morning and today I have twenty-eight."

"What did you have for supper last night?"

"Cucumber salad. Why?"

"No reason. I have two I can spare. Shall I bring them over later?"

Her crinkly friend clapped her hands. "You're a sweet girl, Elsie. A sweet girl."

"I better go, Mrs. Noseworthy, my arms are falling off."

Elsie grappled with her keys at the back door while twenty furry paws surrounded her ankles. Once the door opened, Flower and her feline friends charged in. Elsie threw everything on the kitchen table since the counter was crowded with breakfast dishes. She shrugged off her jacket and fed the critters, then ran upstairs, opened the attic door and waved away the cloud of smoke that billowed out.

"Can you come down and help me get dinner ready? I'm running late. Aunt Hildy should be here any minute."

"Aunt Hildy can kiss my big fat…"

Elsie slammed the door. It wasn't worth it. She tore off her clothes, threw water on her face and put on a pair of old jeans. Then back downstairs to empty the dishwasher, fill the dishwasher, set the table, turn the oven on and look for a dining room tablecloth that wasn't stained.

The back door slammed and she jumped. They were here already?

But it was Lily, looking very unhappy. Elsie went over and gave her a kiss. Lily held on for dear life.

"Did you have a hard day, sweetie?"

"You have no idea."

"What's wrong? It's not that Arab boy, is it? Trust me, sweetheart. No man is worth it."

She lifted her face off her mother's chest. "Are you on drugs?"

"I wish."

Lily snuggled into her arms again. "I take it you're referring to Habib?"

"Have you known him long?"

"About three hours."

Elsie pushed her away with her arms. "My God. You can't be in love with someone after three hours."

Lily's jaw dropped. "In love? The guy hates my guts. After the nurse put his arm in a sling, he said if he ever saw me again, he'd have me committed."

"Goodness."

She started to bawl. "I seem to get that response from every male I come across."

Elsie pulled her back and hugged her. "Don't be silly, Lily. You're a perfectly wonderful girl. There must be a million guys just dying to meet you."

"They're dying all right."

Just then a horn blared in the distance.

"What's that?" Lily sniffed.

Elsie ran to the kitchen window just in time to see Slater's red Mustang round the corner and careen up the street.

"Oh God. She's here."

Chapter Four

Elsie had nine for supper that night. It didn't surprise her. Everything about her life was out of control these days: her marriage, her children, her relatives and now her dinner table.

Lily ran upstairs to repair her blotchy face while Elsie watched from the window as the kids got Aunt Hildy out of the car and escorted her up the back stairs. They were laughing, which was odd. She was sure Aunt Hildy would be hitting Slater with her umbrella by now.

Hildy teetered into the kitchen. "Elsie dear. Come and kiss me and tell me why you look like a wet noodle."

"Perhaps it's because I'm cooking lasagna for dinner," Elsie said diplomatically. She kissed her. "You look marvellous. How was your flight?"

Hildy put down her carpet bag. "Frightful."

"Turbulence?"

She pulled off her turban. "The water was undrinkable. And the *service*. If I didn't know better I'd say the flight attendant had a mood disorder. You'd think they'd weed out that sort, now that flying is such an iffy business."

Elsie smiled in spite of herself. Aunt Hildy's wispy pure white hair was a swirl of fluff around her head. As her bony, blue-veined hands swept over her hair in an attempt to tame it, Elsie's eyes suddenly watered. This woman seemed so tiny and faded. It was hard to believe such a huge life force was now contained in this vulnerable package.

Elsie blinked back her tears. "Would you like to go upstairs and change?"

"Into what, my dear?"

Slater grinned. "Far out. You rock."

"Yes, Peaches, I've rocked plenty in my lifetime. I'm sure I've sifted through tons of rocks in the course of my career. I've unearthed a few unexpected gems too. I have a feeling I'm looking at one right now."

Slater beamed at her and looked around the kitchen. "Where?"

"Perhaps not."

Peaches? She must be hallucinating out of pure exhaustion. "Come and sit, dear. I'll pour you a lemonade."

Hildy made her way to the rocking chair by the window. "Make sure you put plenty of gin in it."

Slater threw his hands on his head. "You drink? Wicked! Did you hear that, Dee?"

Dahlia nodded and looked impressed.

"Of course I drink. You're a fool if you don't. Hang onto your hat, but I've even smoked up on a few occasions. Bedouin tribesmen can be a pretty persuasive lot."

"*Awesome.*"

Elsie shouted, "Slater, will you please go get Aunt Hildy's bags out of the car and take them upstairs."

"Okay…sure." He left in a hurry.

Both Dahlia and Aunt Hildy gave Elsie a quick look, so she turned around and went to get the gin. She retrieved the ice cubes and slammed the tray on the counter to loosen them. It felt good, so she did it again. She mixed the drink, threw the spoon into the sink with a clatter, and nailed a smile on her face before emerging from the pantry.

Elsie passed her the drink. "Here you are."

"Thank you my dear. So. When are the others coming?"

"Others?"

"Your sisters. I assume you invited them for dinner. A welcoming committee, as it were."

Elsie's pulse raced. She never even thought of that. The matriarch comes back from overseas for the first time in years and Elsie's efforts involved throwing a frozen dinner in the oven. If her mother were alive, she'd be mortified. She had to do something.

"Of course," she smiled. "They'll be along in about an hour. I believe Robert had an important meeting today. That's why they aren't here at the moment."

Slater came into the kitchen carrying all the bags at once. "Where to, Mrs. B?"

"Take them to Lily's room, please."

"Righto," he said cheerfully. And out the door he went.

Elsie looked around and saw Aunt Hildy's carpet bag. "Just a minute. You can take this too."

She dashed out the kitchen door, grabbed Slater's arm and whispered, "Tell Lily and Faith to get their fannies down here now. Faith's to call Juliet, and make sure she and Robert come over for dinner, pronto. It's very important they be here."

"Got it." He turned to go but she held on to him.

"And I want Juliet to go to the liquor store and pick up some champagne and liqueur."

"Right." He tried to leave but she grabbed him a third time.

"And tell them to run to the florist and buy a bouquet of flowers on their way over."

In her panic, she didn't notice the beads of sweat along Slater's upper lip.

"Okay." He started up the stairs with the luggage.

"One more thing."

Slater slowly turned around.

"Juliet needs to bring some more vegetable lasagna. If everyone's coming, I won't have enough."

Slater nodded and climbed only one stair. "And Slater?"

He stopped but didn't turn around.

"Thanks, honey."

He looked at her and smiled. "Anything for you, Mrs. B." And he was gone.

Elsie dashed back to the kitchen.

"Do you always run like a chicken with its head cut off?" Hildy asked.

Dahlia, who sat hugging her knees on a kitchen chair, nodded. "Oh, she does. Don't you Mom?"

Elsie was stung. "I try very hard not too, but sometimes things come up out of the blue. You know how it is."

Hildy took a large swallow of her drink. "Actually, I don't. Life is not something that needs to be tamed. It's messy. Always was, always will be."

Elsie stood by the window and gazed at nothing. "That may be true. But I'm sure it's different when you're a single woman with no family responsibilities. You don't have to answer to anyone."

"Of course I do."

Elsie looked at her. "Who?"

"Me."

Just then Graham's van pulled into the driveway. He hopped out and started for the side entrance.

Dahlia's voice sounded unnaturally high. "Daddy's home."

Hildy looked out the window. "Goodness me. That boy never changes…always was a handsome devil."

And before Elsie could stop her, she leaned over and rapped on the glass. Elsie saw Graham give a startled jump and look up as Hildy gestured for him to come inside.

Elsie's stomach churned — Aunt Hildy didn't know about the separation. This was something else that needed to be revealed. Maybe she could waylay him, but it was too late. Graham came through the back door.

"Hi Daddy," Dahlia squeaked. "How was your day?"

"Fine. Just fine. Well, hello Aunt Hildy." He crossed the kitchen to bend down and give her a peck on the cheek.

"Hello yourself. I see you're still slopping about in sewage."

"Just lucky I guess." He smiled and rattled the change in his pocket. He finally turned to Elsie. "Is there a beer in the fridge?"

Oh, good thinking. "Yes. I'll get it for you."

"No, no, that's okay. I'll get it," he said in a hurry. Once he had the can in his hand, he stood in the middle of the kitchen, looking uneasy.

Elsie glanced at the stove. "We're having vegetable lasagna for dinner tonight, Graham. Your favourite."

"My favourite?"

"Yes, don't you remember?" Elsie gave him a wide-eyed look.

"Right. Can't wait." He took a large swig of beer and turned back to their visitor. "I hope you're well, Aunt Hildy."

"Really? I always thought you couldn't wait for me to cash in my chips."

"I've waited a long time, but you're just too stubborn to die," he chuckled.

Hildy held her glass in the air as if to toast herself. "You're so right."

While Graham and Aunt Hildy taunted each other, Elsie took the opportunity to grab Dahlia by the arm and lead her into the dining room.

"Dee, be a sweetie and take these dishes off the table and reset it with the good stuff."

"And just where would the good stuff be? I've never seen the good stuff."

"Are you joking? You've never seen it?"

"No."

Elsie sighed. "I need a life."

"Mom, this is silly. Is all this really necessary? Aunt Hildy seems pretty laid back to me. She's not as scary as she used to be."

"Don't let her fool you. She's a charming fox."

Dahlia shrugged. "Well, she likes Slater, and if she likes Slater then she's okay by me."

"That is so weird," Elsie said under her breath.

"Pardon?"

"Nothing. Hurry now."

"Do you have any idea how much this evening has cost me?" Juliet griped to Elsie in the pantry.

"Well, why on earth did you buy so much liquor?" Elsie took a bottle of rum out of the paper bag. "What else is in here?" She picked through the parcel. "Vodka. Whiskey. Vermouth?"

"Faith said to get liquor. She didn't say what kind."

"Liquor? I said *liqueur*."

Juliet opened a jar of maraschino cherries and stuck her fingers in. She pulled two out and popped them in her mouth.

While she chewed, she said, "Well, don't blame me. That bone-head son-in-law of yours told Faith liquor. Speaking of bone-heads, do you mind telling me why you've dragged all of us to a love-fest for the world's most irritating old broad?"

"Jules, will you just shut up and go play nice? If for no other reason than to hone your social skills."

Juliet sucked her fingers. "They're wasted on Aunt Hildy. She's got a hide like a rhino. She wouldn't know repartee if it jumped up and bit her on the ass."

Faith joined them, holding cigarette ashes in the palm of her hand. "There's something sinister about people who don't own an ashtray." She threw her ashes in the sink.

Elsie let out a screech. "Fay…you idiot! My lettuce is in there."

"Crikey…have a fit why don't you. It'll wash off." She reached in the sink to retrieve the dusty romaine hearts, but Elsie grabbed her shoulder.

"Go away." She pushed Faith right out the door.

Juliet gave her a filthy look. "You asked us here to help and now you're kicking us out? Are you off your nut?"

Brandishing a vegetable peeler in Juliet's face, Elsie said, "If you value your life, you will go in that living room and enter-tain Aunt Hildy until dinner is served."

"I can't believe you have a career dealing with the public," Juliet huffed over her shoulder before joining Faith in the de-serted kitchen.

She pointed her thumb at the pantry. "Can you believe that?"

Faith shrugged her shoulders. "She wants to kill Aunt Hildy. She just doesn't know it yet."

Juliet gave a grunt. "I *know* I want to kill her, but you don't see me being rude."

"SHHH. She's in the living room."

"Who cares? She doesn't scare me."

Faith looked at her. "She should."

"Excuse me?"

"She's rich and she's old and she can leave her money to whoever she wants. Put on a happy face and you may get some."

Juliet adjusted her skirt. "Sometimes I forget you're not stupid."

"Charming."

"Let's go butter up the old girl."

At last the family gathered around the massive dining room table. It was a far cry from the original effort Elsie had thrown together. The table looked beautiful with its Irish linen tablecloth, lit candles and flower centrepiece. Elsie's heirloom Spode china and Waterford crystal adorned the table and shone in the light of the large chandelier and a roaring fire.

When Graham sat down at the head of the table, Robert leaned over to Juliet. Elsie heard him whisper, "What's up with this?"

"We're in the twilight zone," she whispered back.

Elsie gave them a beady eye and raised her glass of champagne. "A toast. Welcome home Aunt Hildy."

"Welcome home," everyone echoed as they lifted their glasses.

Hildy acknowledged them with a nod. "Thank you. It's good to be home. I must say, this table looks very nice, Elsie."

Elsie smiled.

"Unlike the rest of the house. You should hire a housekeeper."

Elsie frowned.

"You have far too many animals. There's fur everywhere…"

Graham suddenly spoke up. "Why were you in Africa, Aunt Hildy?"

Hildy looked at him in confusion. "Africa? Who said anything about Africa?"

"I did."

Hildy buttered her roll. "Well, that's my business, isn't it? Tell me Graham. Are you still with that silly company…what was the name? Butt and Sons?"

"No Ifs Ands Or Butts."

Hildy shook her head before taking a sip of champagne. "I can't imagine a more ridiculous moniker. I do hope you had nothing to do with it."

"No, as a matter of fact, I didn't."

"If you had bought the company when you had the chance, you could've renamed it," Faith observed.

Graham stabbed a cherry tomato with his fork. "Is that right?"

She kept it up. "That's right. But why own a company when you can drive a van for a living."

"What's this?" Hildy asked. "Did I hear correctly?"

Dahlia grabbed a plate of salad and passed it to her. "Would you like some?"

She took the plate. "Yes, thank you."

"Faith, would you help me bring in the lasagna, please?" Elsie intervened. "Robert, pour Aunt Hildy another glass of champagne." She jumped up from the table with Faith following on her heels into the kitchen.

"*What?*"

"Are you trying to make my life more miserable than it already is?" Elsie spat, taking the lasagna out of the oven.

"What the hell do you care what I say to Graham?"

Elsie shook off her oven mitts. "He's in there pretending we're together. Do I need him with a bee in his bonnet?"

"I'm only repeating what you said, in case you've forgotten. Anyway, why is he here?"

Elsie hacked the lasagna with a knife. "I'll tell Aunt Hildy about the separation later."

Faith nodded and kept it up until it was Elsie's turn to say "*What?*"

"You two are pathetic."

"Is that so?"

"Why don't you just admit you made a mistake?"

Elsie scowled. "There's only one mistake I made. I let you live here." She grabbed the casserole dish and walked back into the dining room, Faith trailing behind her, just in time to hear Aunt Hildy say, "Your sister tells me you're in love with a sheik, Violet. Is this true? Personally, I can't see it. You're not exactly their type. They like girls with bracelets on their wrists or ankles, not stuck in their faces."

Lily looked at her sister. "A sheik?"

"Well, that's what Mom said."

Elsie put down her dish and served dinner. "I said no such thing."

"If not a sheik, then who?" Hildy persisted. "Who are you in love with?"

Lily turned several shades of purple. "No one. I refuse to be trampled by convention. And pardon me, but I don't have to be anyone's type. I'm my type. Case closed."

Slater gave her a clenched-fist salute. "Whoa Lily pad...you sound just like Judge Judy."

Everyone looked at him. He grinned.

"Mr. Peach," Hildy remarked. "Do you do anything more with your day than handle flesh as though it were bread dough?"

He looked confused. "I don't make bread. I can't cook worth a darn."

Hildy gave Dahlia a sly look. "I'm sure he can cook when he wants to, can't he?"

"Gosh no. He burns water."

"You two deserve each other."

Robert snickered. Hildy turned her attention to him.

"And what do you do for a living, Robert? I draw a blank where you are concerned."

"I'm in real estate."

"And do you have swamp land in Florida I might be interested in?"

"As a matter of fact…"

Juliet poked him in the ribs. "He's a businessman. And a very good one, I might add."

"Doesn't he speak for himself?"

"Of course he does," Juliet snipped. "Speak, Robert."

"Yes, Robert," Hildy instructed. "Do speak. There's a good boy."

He got red in the face. "Now see here…"

Hildy ignored him. "What do you do all day, Juliet, besides buy pyjamas for your four-legged child?"

Juliet sputtered. "I take good care of Kiwi…"

"Kiwi? As in fruit? As in a tiny ball of brown fuzzy skin?"

Slater clapped his hands and startled them. "Awesome, Auntie Baby. That's just what that dog is. You are one cool dame."

"It's so reassuring to know I have your approval, Slater."

Hildy looked at Faith. "So. When will you let us read your novel?"

"It's a work in progress. It's not finished."

"No," Graham said, "and at the rate she's going we'll all be dead a hundred years before it is."

Faith paled.

"Is this true?" Hildy asked.

"Of course not. I've already finished chapter one, no thanks to the endless interruptions I get all day." She glanced at Elsie.

"What's your story about?" her aunt wanted to know.

"Two star-crossed lovers thwarted by the prejudices of their families and society and how innocence dies in a harsh and un-forgiving world."

"Very ambitious. If I didn't know better, I'd say you've just accurately described one of Shakespeare's greatest works… *Romeo and Juliet.* Your mother's favourite play."

"Oh, it's better than that, Aunt Hildy," Slater chimed in. "Before dinner Mrs. W. told us it's about this nun and a horny monster who do it in a vegetable patch."

Faith turned to Juliet with her mouth open.

Juliet shrugged. "I thought it was. Pardon me."

Hildy put down her knife and fork. She dabbed her lips with a napkin before placing it back on her lap. Faith started to say something, but Hildy put up her hands, as if to ask for silence.

"Let me get this straight. Your lovers are a nun and a creature?"

"It's symbolic," she explained quickly. "You know, piety ver-sus animal instinct."

"You're about as subtle as a runaway train."

Faith's utensils fell on her plate. She pointed her finger at her aunt. "Listen here, you miserable…"

"Faith…" Elsie rushed in. "Would you like another roll?"

Juliet spoke up. "WILL you pass me the butter, Faith? I WILL give it back as soon as I'm done."

Faith looked around as if coming out of a daze. "Yes. I WILL pass you the butter." She gave Juliet a grateful glance.

"Why is everyone talking like a robot?" Dahlia wanted to know.

"Who'd like dessert?" Elsie smiled around the table.

Everyone looked at their platefuls of lasagna.

"I believe it's customary to let your guests eat the main course first," Hildy said.

"Oh dear, silly me," Elsie laughed with a tinge of hysteria. "Dig in everyone."

Graham threw down his napkin. "OK, enough of this non-sense." He turned to Aunt Hildy. "Elsie will have a nervous breakdown if I don't say something."

"Gray, please…"

"No." He shook his head. "This has got to stop. We don't appreciate the fact that you come here and pass judgment on our family, Aunt Hildy. We love and respect you as the eldest member of the tribe, but we won't change who we are and what we do, just to satisfy you. We all know you're an accomplished woman who's done great things with her life, but you've no right to measure us by your yardstick."

"I'm…"

"No. Let me finish, please. This will come as a bit of a shock, but Elsie and I are separated. Yet here we are, pretending we're still married just so we don't meet with your disapproval."

"If you're separated, then what on earth are you doing here?"

"I live downstairs."

"I see you're handling your separation as well as you handled your marriage."

"Who do you think you are?"

"An ex-relative, obviously."

Elsie stood up. "Maybe you better go, Graham."

"Yes," Juliet joined in. "I think it's about time you returned to your cave and stopped this harassment of our darling aunt."

"This has nothing to do with you anymore," Faith added.

He slowly rose. "Of course, you're right. What was I thinking? I hope you have a pleasant stay, Aunt Hildy." He looked at Elsie. "Thank you for dinner. If you'll excuse me." He turned and left the room.

Elsie sat. Hard. Eventually she said, "Please. Eat everyone. Before it gets cold."

Lily threw down her napkin. "I don't feel very well. I'm going to my...upstairs." She left the same way her father did.

Dahlia sniffed. "I can't eat either. Sorry." She rose from her chair. "Are you coming, Slater?"

He looked around in a panic. "Can't I eat my dinner first?"

"*Slater.*"

He got up quickly, grabbed three rolls and left with Dahlia. Elsie smiled weakly at those left at the table. Hildy dug into her lasagna. "More for us."

Later that night, when Faith went upstairs, she smoked four cigarettes in a row before she had the courage to sit at her computer and reread the first chapter.

Shit.

Highlight. Delete. She cried herself to sleep.

Juliet and Robert headed for home as soon as dinner was over. They didn't say much as they drove down Oxford Street toward Bayers Road.

Finally Robert sighed, "What a lousy evening."

Juliet groaned in agreement. "I can't believe I spent a fortune and got nothing but heartburn in return."

"Is all this really necessary? I mean, how rich is the old bitch?"

"So rich we have to lick her boots."

"Well, that's just wonderful. Talk about indigestion."

Dahlia and Slater sat on the front porch swing. The street was quiet and the house was dark. It was a warm, velvety night, perfect for curling up together. Dahlia sighed and cuddled up closer to her man. "That was a disaster."

"Total bummer."

"Why do adults argue all the time? They ruin everything. Aunt Hildy was great with just us."

"I totally get her."

She squeezed his arm. "I know she likes you. She said your bum was quite something."

A worried look crossed his face. "That's sort of gross."

She smiled at him. "She didn't mean it like that, you big dope."

"Hey, I knew that."

Dahlia shivered. "Gosh. I better go in. It's late." She kissed him goodnight. "I love you."

"I love you too, baby doll. I'll pick you up in the morning."

Dahlia watched him sprint across the lawn, hop in the car and gun it down the street. He blew the horn a couple of times. The grouch across the way opened his window. "Will you tell that knucklehead to knock it off with the horn? Some of us are trying to sleep."

"Sorry Mr. Mooney."

Dahlia whistled for Flower, who charged up the stairs from the front hedge she liked to root around in. Once inside, Dahlia locked the door and went upstairs to her room. She forgot Lily would be there.

"This is weird," she said to her sister.

Lily lay on her bed and stared at the ceiling. "Tell me about it. You have so much crap, there's no room for my stuff."

"Why not go in the guest room then?" She waited for an answer but Lily stayed quiet.

Dahlia pulled off her sweater and kicked away her jeans, then rummaged in her drawer for a pair of pyjamas. "Don't worry. I'll put a lot of it in the sewing room. I have to pack some things anyway."

"You don't have to remind me. I know you're leaving."

The misery in Lily's voice made Dahlia stop and go sit with her sister. "Don't be sad, Lil. I'll always come back. We won't go far."

Lily sat up. "I don't want to be here in this house by myself. I'll be lonely."

Dahlia reached out and held her sister's hand. "I'll miss you too."

Lily looked down.

"Is there something else? Besides me leaving? Is it Mom and Dad?"

She still wouldn't look up.

"Out with it."

Lily raised her head and chewed the side of her thumb. "How come nobody likes me?"

Dahlia was astonished. "Everyone likes you. You have friends."

"And not one boyfriend."

"True."

"See! I'm a loser."

"Don't be ridiculous. You just need to…"

"To what?"

She looked at her sister's bubble gum hair and the four silver rings in her ears. "Be more approachable. You need to glam yourself up a bit. The pink thing doesn't work obviously. But it's more than that. You've got to stop wearing skater clothes and start wearing lycra."

"That is such a load of garbage. Why should I tart myself up so someone will notice me?"

"Okay then. Whatever," Dahlia sighed. She started to leave but her sister pulled her back.

"I can't believe I'm saying this but…can you dye my hair?

"Not if you want green or orange."

Lily smirked. "How about burgundy?"

She smiled with relief. "That's better. Thank God. I didn't want to walk down the aisle and have to compete with your head."

Just before turning in, Elsie snuck downstairs and knocked on the basement door. Graham took his time before opening it.

"I'm sorry," she said.

"It doesn't matter."

"I don't know what to do."

"I can't help you. You're on your own. Remember?"

She pulled her bathrobe belt tighter. "Fine. I only came…"

"I know why you came. To make sure I know you're the victim in all this."

"You are such a *creep*."

He laughed. "So you always say. If you'll excuse me, I have to go to bed now. Unless you'd like to join me? You might want to work off a little of that frustration."

She reached out and shoved him. "You jerk."

He regained his balance and put his face next to hers. "Why do you keep finding excuses to come down here in your bathrobe, night after night? So I can pull it off?"

She was horrified. "I don't come down here night after night."

"Have you got anything on under that?"

She looked down and grabbed her robe, feeling her own nakedness. "Of course I do."

He put both hands through his hair. "Listen Elsie, it's over. Let's just get on with our lives because I can't stand this. I've got to move out. This arrangement's not working."

"No kidding. I come down here to apologize for my aunt and you turn it into something else. Go then. It'll be a relief to bring a man back here without you hanging around."

Graham stood very still. "Is that right? Well, if that's the case, I'm sure you won't mind if I entertain a few lady friends before I go. It may take a few weeks before I can find a new place."

She fumbled for a balled-up wad of Kleenex in her pocket. "Entertain who you like. I could care less. I'm sure they're lined up down the block as we speak."

He pointed at her. "You have no idea. If I made a call this very minute, I'd have a woman in my bed so fast your head would spin."

Elsie felt her throat close over. She swallowed a few times before she finally said, "I don't believe you."

He walked to the phone, took a scrap of paper out of his pocket, and dialed.

"Hi. It's Graham…yeah, I'm sure…I know it's late but would…half an hour? Where? Okay. I'll see you then."

He hung up and looked at her.

"Goodnight Elsie."

She turned on her heel, stomped up three flights of stairs. When she shut her bedroom door, off came her robe and on went an equally tatty flannel nightgown. She threw herself in the old armchair by the window and hugged her knees to her chin.

"You are one stupid bastard, Graham Brooks. I could care less who you take to bed, just as long as it's not me."

While she stewed, she stared at her toes. They were a mess. "I don't even have time to go for a bloody pedicure. And what's worse, I'm sitting here talking to myself." She got up and went over to the bedside table, yanked open the drawer and rooted around for her nail clippers. Bouncing back on the bed, she grabbed her own foot and started to clip. "I don't know why I'm bothering. It's not like anyone's going to even see my stupid feet. When do I ever get to go to dinner with pretty sandals on?"

The question hung in the air. She stopped clipping. What was to stop her from going out to dinner wearing nice strappy shoes? It wasn't against the law. If stupid Graham could rendez-vous with some bimbo in the middle of night, she was certainly allowed to go to a fancy restaurant and show her toes. But with who?

She threw the clippers across the room and yanked the duvet over her head. She kicked her feet as hard as she could and had her own private temper tantrum.

Graham was furious with Elsie. Here he was at midnight sitting in the living room of a woman he barely knew. All he wanted to do was go to bed — and if Bunny got her way that's exactly what would happen.

He loved sex as much as the next guy, but frankly he was out of practice and not in the mood. He found Bunny's note in his jacket pocket that morning at work. Bunny Hopkins, emphasis on the Bunny Hop.

And now here he was, necking up a storm with a woman whose gigantic breasts made it nearly impossible for him to reach around her. It amounted to too much work, not to mention the fact that her lip gloss smelled like apricots.

Bunny purred. "I can't believe you called me."

"I can't believe it either."

She traced a line down his face with her three-inch nail. "You're just so unbelievably sexy."

He hoped she wouldn't stab him in the eye. "Really?"

"Oh yeah." She pressed her finger against his mouth. "I just want to…"

He had a cramp in his thigh. Needing to get her off his lap, he pushed her away as politely as he could.

"I'm sorry. It wasn't fair of me to call you at such a late hour. We both have to work in the morning."

Bunny reached out to run her fingers through his hair and cooed, "Well, why don't you just sleep here?"

Graham removed her hands. "We don't have to rush things."

She looked puzzled. "Why did you call if you don't like me?"

Ah, geez. He blurted, "I do…we'll get together soon."

Her face lit up. "Oh, Graham cracker. I'd love that."

He stumbled out the door when she finally released him from his goodnight kiss, and into the unfamiliar hallway. He looked around to get his bearings. Which way had he come in? He couldn't remember and that pissed him off. Going to the left, he hit a dead-end, so he doubled-back, making sure he didn't look at Bunny's door as he hurried by. He was running by the time he got out of the building, his throat dry and his pulse racing. The key wouldn't fit the truck door. What the hell was going on? Then he realized he was trying to use his house key.

Finally in the truck, he slammed his fist into the steering wheel, not once but twice. She called him Graham cracker. Only one girl had ever called him that, the very first time she nibbled on his ear under the gym bleachers, the first time he knew he wanted the world to stop and let him live in her arms and against her body for the rest of his life.

He'd never forgive Elsie for this.

Hildy opened her diary, and settled herself into the pillows. Her eyes burned, with that sandpaper sensation caused by lack of sleep. She blinked several times and looked around. Despite the Johnny Depp posters, it was still recognizable as the room of her childhood, with its gabled windows and view of the garden. Tomorrow she'd make a start and put it right, unpack her belongings and surround herself with her dearest possessions, gathered after a lifetime of adventure.

She put on her glasses and took the top off her favourite pen. This nightly ritual of scribbling down random thoughts was a way of staving off loneliness. As a spinster, Hildy didn't have the luxury of lying next to a loved one, telling them about her day before she fell asleep.

She wrote, "*It's difficult to be here. Harder than I imagined. It seemed like such a good idea when I was separated from this place by an ocean, but now that I've returned, I wonder if I've done the* right thing. Memories crowd me. People haunt me, especially in this room.

"The house is the same as it always was, a keeper of secrets and sorrows, love and heartache. I see it all in the family who live here now.

"Elsie and Graham are twisting in the wind. The girls are beautiful but spoiled, like all youngsters. Dahlia's young man is the only one who tells the truth. I'm afraid Juliet and Faith are the same as ever and Robert is a male counterpart to his wife, all of them totally self-absorbed.

"Oh dear. What a silly little family to be involved with. Forgive me, sister dear, if that sounds harsh, but it makes my job more difficult.

"What am I going to do about the treasure?"

Chapter Five

Dahlia banged on the bathroom door. "Slater will be here any second. If you want to do this, we leave in five minutes...do you hear me?"

"The whole street can hear you," Lily yelled back. "Give it a rest. I'll be right down."

"This was your idea, remember."

Lily heard her sister march down the stairs. She gripped the sink with her hands and leaned into the mirror.

"Coward."

She liked pink hair. So why change for some stupid boy? How weak-minded did one have to be to conform to the norm? She was better than that, surely.

"Yeah. And lonely," she admitted to her reflection. Not that she didn't have a few offers from guys. Just not *the* guy.

"Lily livered. You're doing it for all the wrong reasons."

There was a sharp rap on the door. Her Aunt Faith shouted, "No wonder psychology is your major. You and your split personality get out of this bathroom. Some of us have old bladders, ya know."

"Ewww." Lily pushed herself away from the sink and jerked the door open. Her aunt stood there with a pink shower cap on.

"God. Can't a person have a little privacy?"

Faith pushed her aside. "Not when you hear voices in your head." She shut the door in her face.

Lily hit it with the palm of her hand. "Your latent hostility is a sign of unfulfilled desire!"

Faith yelled out, "You're so right. My desire to pee."

Outside, a horn blew three times.

She stormed down the stairs. "Hold your horses. I'm coming."

Lily was in a much better frame of mind later when the tin foil came off her head. She turned one way and than the other to look in the mirror at her new do, ignoring the self-satisfied smirk on her sister's face.

"Huh? Huh? What did I tell you? It's a thousand times better."

Lily had to admit she was right. "It's sort of a rich eggplant colour, wouldn't you say?"

Slater stood behind Dahlia. She'd called him over to see the final result. He grinned at Lily. "Whatever it's called, it's hot."

"Do you think?"

"I'd do ya."

Lily giggled but Dahlia's jaw dropped. "Slater...she's my sister!"

"She asked my opinion."

"About *colour*."

"Just trying to be helpful."

Dahlia pointed her finger at the back of the salon. "Go."

Slater leaned toward Lily. "Call me." He laughed and ran off but Dahlia still got him on the back of the head with a wet towel.

The moment of truth had arrived. As she walked toward the psych lab, Lily's mouth was dry. This ticked her off — it meant she had too much invested in this little experiment of hers, one planned night after sleepless night, one that involved getting Eli Stanton to notice her.

She knew all the girls in psych class would give their eye teeth just to have Eli look in their direction, let alone talk to them.

Every female she knew was mad about him and that fascinated her. How does a person do that?

He wasn't classically handsome like Slater. He wasn't built. He wasn't even that tall. But there was something about him. The way he sauntered into class, with that rumpled just-out-of-bed look, his brown hair messed up and sort of spiky and those gorgeous brown eyes giving everyone a sexy sideways glance. He never seemed to wear anything but a baggy white T-shirt and faded jeans but somehow he looked better than anyone.

The thing Lily loved the most was his smile. And his white teeth. And his lips. And the way his cheeks always looked like he'd just come in from the cold.

She knew she had it bad.

He looked at her sometimes, but of course that was usually because she was staring at him. Odds were he was bound to turn his face in her direction once in a while. He even asked her for help with an assignment once, but she didn't dare think it was because he liked her. Everyone knew she was the smart one in class.

Well, she'd soon find out.

She held her breath and walked through the door.

Eli Stanton was doing his usual schtick at the back of the lab — charming the birds right out of the trees. It would've thrilled most guys to have every female within a ten-mile radius vying for attention, but Eli couldn't count on just his saucy smile as the reason for their ardour. He knew there were rumours floating around about his old man and his money.

The only girl he hadn't been able to impress was Lily, the clever one with the pink hair. He admired her spunk. And the diamond in her nostril turned him on, big time. Sometimes he saw her looking at him, but whenever he flashed his pearly whites at her, she stuck her nose back in a book. She was the only one he wanted to know.

His lab partner, Tiffany, poked him with a pencil. "Oh my God, freak girl has joined the dark side."

Eli looked up. And his heart stopped.

It was Lily but it wasn't Lily. He couldn't take his eyes off her at first. She was the most beautiful creature he'd ever seen. He was thoroughly rattled and unsure about what to do, so he sat there and pretended to ignore her.

Tiffany persisted. "Do you see her?"

He shrugged. "Yeah, I see her."

"I suppose she thinks she looks good," Tiffany sniffed. "But she's still a freak."

Tiffany could be a bitch. "How would you know?"

"Because she is, everyone knows that. She never goes out with guys. She's a lesbian."

"No way."

"Don't believe me? Go ask her out."

Eli ignored her.

Tiffany poked him again. "I bet you a hundred dollars she won't go out with you."

Eli leaned back in his chair and folded his arms. "Don't be stupid."

"You heard me. A hundred bucks."

Eli shook his head in disbelief. "Are you sure you want to risk it? What happens if she not only goes out with me, but falls madly in love with me? What then?"

"I'll owe you two hundred bucks," she laughed.

"Get a life, Tiff."

"Coward."

He looked at Lily again. This was crazy. He was dying to go over to her before the professor walked in but if he did, Tiffany would think he was playing along. Screw it. He got out of his seat. "We do not have a bet. Got that?"

"Got it," she smirked.

He walked right up to Lily's desk and willed his hands to stop shaking. "Hey there."

He groaned inwardly. You're a smooth operator, Stanton.

Lily looked at him, almost with contempt. Two seconds in and this wasn't going well.

"Hello."

"You're Lily, right?"

"You know that."

"Well, I wasn't sure. What with the pink hair missing-in-action." He gave her a half-hearted laugh.

"Excuse me?"

He wiped his upper lip. "Listen. I'm Eli, by the way."

"I know that."

"Oh yeah, right." He mopped his forehead and rubbed his hands on the back of his pants. "Well, thank goodness for that — now I'm not a stranger and you'll be more apt to have lunch with me when class is over."

"I will?"

He tried his standard move — a dazzling smile. "I'm buying."

"Why would I suddenly go to lunch with you? You've never asked me to lunch before."

He nodded and pulled on his earlobe. "There's always a first time, right?"

"And it just happens to be when my hair is a different colour." She looked away and opened her book. "That tells me everything I need to know."

"Need to know about what?"

She pushed her hair back off her forehead with her fingertips. It fell like silk over her shoulders. He broke out in a cold sweat.

"About why I have no intention of having lunch with you."

"Oh."

"Class is about to start. You better get back to your seat."

He'd never been rejected before. It didn't feel too good. "Right. Okay then." He tossed his head towards his chair. "I better get back."

She nodded.

"To my seat."

"Bye."

He turned around and walked back to the lab table. He didn't dare look at Tiffany.

She was laughing. "I told ya. You owe me a hundred bucks."

"Shut it."

The prof walked in and they settled down to do their work. Well, some of them did. Eli spent the entire time rehearsing what he wanted to say to Lily at the end of class, but the minute they were dismissed, she jumped out of her seat and took off before he had a chance to do anything. He panicked and ran after her.

He caught up with her by the Coke machine. Putting his hand on her arm, he stood in front of her. "Please, Lily. Can I just talk to you?"

"About what?"

"Are you mad at me or something?"

She averted his gaze and looked at her books. "Don't be stupid. Why would I be mad at you?"

"Because I didn't ask you out when you had pink hair?"

"Don't flatter yourself." She pulled out of his grip and walked away. He'd blown it. But suddenly she turned and marched back to him.

"It's a little suspicious when a guy only sniffs around me after I've changed something as superficial as my hair colour."

He put his hand on his heart. "Hey, that's not fair. I've always noticed you. But you've never given me the time of day. Why have you ignored me?"

Lily started to open her mouth, but he pressed on. "And yes. I have to say I did notice you today because you're freakin' beautiful. I love your hair this way. I hated it pink. There, I said it. If that makes me a creep, so be it."

She seemed shocked. He didn't know if that was a good thing. She looked at him for what seemed like a very long time. He wanted her to say something.

She finally did. "Tell me this. Are you impressed with the package or the girl?"

He went limp and pretended to stagger backwards. He looked her up and down and gave her a big smile. "Oh, definitely the girl...but I have to admit...the package is heavenly."

She blushed.

"Please say you'll have lunch with me?"

They talked for four hours in the cafeteria. People came and went at their table but they never noticed. They didn't even realize they missed all their afternoon classes. It wasn't until the guy who cleaned the tables gave them a dirty look that they realized it was so late.

Eli walked her to the exit. She stood there and looked everywhere but at him. Finally, she said softly, "I guess I better go."

He couldn't wait anymore. "Then I must kiss you goodbye." He gathered her in his arms, covered her beautiful mouth and was lost.

After an eternity, he pulled back and looked at her. "You're delicious. You taste like strawberries."

She just looked at his mouth.

"Let me taste you again."

They ended up at his place, a top floor apartment on Maynard Street, but afterwards neither of them could recall how they got there. They took the stairs two at a time and Eli had a hard time getting the key out of his pocket, what with Lily trying to take off his shirt and him glued to her lips.

The lady who lived next door opened the door with a bag of garbage in her hand.

Eli waved when he came up for air.

"Mrs. Minelli...how's tricks?" He went back to unbuttoning Lily's jeans.

"Not so good. My hip, my back, my rotten doctor. It's a nightmare, he's a butcher, that's what he is....He doesn't know from nothin'..."

"Gotta go, Mrs. Minelli." Eli and Lily fell into the apartment and rolled around on the floor, Eli trying to shut the door with his foot.

"You crazy kids. Here...allow me." Mrs. Minelli reached inside and shut the door for them.

"I love Mrs. Minelli," he confessed, sliding off his belt, before he helped Lily pull her top over her head.

"I'm so glad." She reached behind her back to undo her bra and threw it over his head. "But you have to love me first."

He pulled her on top of him. "I love it when you're bossy."

Lily had to be dreaming. She wanted to explode and it was all she could do to raise her head off the mattress that lay in the middle of Eli's living room floor. They were side by side on their stomachs. She ate chocolate pudding out of a cup while he watched her.

"How come you don't have any furniture?"

"I'm never here, so why bother."

"True." She took her spoon and scooped out another bite from the plastic container she held. "You don't have anything in your fridge, either."

"I'm never here, so why bother."

She licked the spoon, sliding it out of her mouth slowly. "I'm starving. I've burned a lot of calories this afternoon because of you. I think I love this diet."

He gave her a wide grin. "You'll be skin and bones before the week's out."

Lily looked at him, so close beside her. She knew she was on fire. She put down her cup, reached over and folded her arms around his neck.

"I've never felt like this before. Is this what love is? Do you feel it too?"

He pushed her back onto the mattress, reached over and held up the container of pudding and let it spill all over her. Then he lowered his head and held his tongue against the soft skin of her belly. He licked her slowly and softly at first, then harder and deeper, until all the pudding was gone. He pulled himself up and over her, whispering in her ear.

"Do you honestly think I'll love anyone else, after having my chocolate and strawberry girl?"

"Oh, Eli."

"Baby, you're the only recipe I'll ever need."

***

The sisters met on the stairs that morning as Faith shuffled up with a mug of coffee and Elsie ran down with a toothbrush in her mouth.

"Mmm."

"Morning to you too. Do you know that crackpot auntie of ours woke up around five and started to bang things around in her bedroom? Now she's out in the garden bending the ear off poor Mrs. Noseworthy."

Elsie put her toothbrush in her cheek. "Make her something for lunch. I'll get more groceries on my way home."

"I'm sure she won't starve. She's got the poor soul out there picking all her cukes."

Elsie started to leave but Faith held her arm. "Do you think I can write, Else?"

Her sister hesitated only a second but she noticed it.

"You can write. Of course you can. You just need a good story."

She turned to go. "Gee, thanks. I never thought of that."

"Ask Aunt Hildy. Her whole life's been an adventure. Mom said she had more secrets than the CIA."

Faith's ears perked up. That was actually a good idea. Too bad it required being outside and sitting with two old broads. Oh, well. Maybe writing a book required some personal sacrifice. Perhaps if she suffered for her art, she'd get a book deal.

Fifteen minutes later she found herself out in the garden. The old dears sat in Adirondack chairs under the oak tree, deep in conversation. Never in a million years did she think her aunt would find anything in common with their neighbour, but there they were, as thick as thieves.

Aunt Hildy put her head back and laughed at something Mrs. Noseworthy said. Faith felt a chill for an instant. She looked just like Mom, or what her mother would've looked like had she lived into her nineties. A deep loneliness engulfed her. It wasn't fair. Her mother was soft and Aunt Hildy was hard. The wrong sister had lived as far as she was concerned.

She joined them and listened to them prattle on about everything under the sun. She took notes while they talked. After a while her aunt looked at her.

"Am I that interesting, that you must write down every word I say?"

"Oh, you should," Mrs. Noseworthy said. "Your auntie is very clever. Very clever indeed."

"I want to write down some of your stories. Something to pass along to the family when..."

Hildy put up her hand to shade her brow. "I croak?"

Mrs. Noseworthy slapped her knees. "That's a good one, Hildy. Don't croak too soon. I have to find out what happened in Ethiopia."

Faith leaned forward. "Ethiopia? What about it?"

Hildy sat back in her chair and looked up into the tree. "Those were some of the best digs of my life. Ancient worlds. Treasure. Secrets. Everything a mystery. All the best digs solve mysteries. Who they were, how they lived and died. It's fascinating stuff."

She wrote furiously. "Did you ever find treasure?"

"I found lots of treasure."

Faith looked up to see if she was teasing. "Really?"

"Really. There are all kinds of treasures in one's life. People, places, experiences. It's everywhere."

Disappointed, Faith said, "Oh. I thought you meant jewels and coins and stuff."

"That too."

Mrs. Noseworthy clapped her hands. "What fun. Imagine knowing someone who has a treasure chest."

"I'm sure she doesn't have a treasure chest. She didn't bring it with her in her luggage, at any rate."

Hildy brushed away a fly. "I have a treasure chest. It's hidden in the house."

"Okay. Whatever you say."

"You're free to believe it or not. It doesn't matter to me."

Faith's scalp tingled. "Are you serious?" She squinted at her aunt and again tried to guess if she was joking.

Their elderly neighbour wrung her hands. "You should be careful, Hildy. Someone might come and take your treasure."

Aunt Hildy spoke to her as if she were a child, instead of her peer. "I don't think so, dear. And even if they did, they'd never find it."

"And why's that?" Faith asked.

"My whole life's been a game of hide-and-seek. I play it very well."

After the ladies went indoors, Faith stayed where she was, hardly believing what she'd just heard. What luck. Elsie thought Aunt Hildy's stories might be worth something but what Faith discovered was even better. What was her aunt thinking, talking about a fortune hidden away in the house? She must be senile, or as daffy as Mrs. Noseworthy.

Faith sat outside for a long time and pondered the situation she now found herself in. No one else knew about this treasure or they'd have said something by now. Her aunt clearly didn't need it because she was rich already.

Come to think of it, how *did* she get so rich? Archaeologists don't make a lot of money. Maybe she kept some of the priceless items she unearthed. Maybe the great Aunt Hildy was just a common everyday thief.

Faith had a decision to make. Live the rest of her life in someone else's attic, go nowhere and do nothing, or take a chance and find this treasure and use some of it to better herself. If she had her own place and could afford new clothes, maybe she'd be able to meet a man. And once she met a man, she'd be happy enough to write a book and then she'd be famous. Since Aunt Hildy probably stole this treasure anyway, what harm would it do to have something good come out of it?

One thing was sure: She wouldn't tell Elsie. She'd be horrified and get all holier than thou. But she'd tell Juliet because this was too big to keep to herself. Juliet would help her find it and wouldn't be judgmental. Of course, she'd have to give her some of it, but that was okay. They needed to stick together. They'd been left out of their parents' will, the house going to Elsie. True, Elsie had uprooted her own family to move in and nurse their parents through separate bouts of cancer, but it still hurt to have been so overlooked.

Faith put her head back against the lawn chair and let the breeze wash across her face. Hopefully, the winds of change were finally blowing her way.

At about the same time Lily walked into her classroom, Elsie and Crystal walked down Spring Garden Road on their lunch hour. It was a blustery day. Hair whipped around the faces of people as they walked down the street, some striding quickly, obviously on a mission, while others meandered, window shopping or checking out the menus on the doors of the restaurants that lined the street.

Elsie always loved to see the day-care workers escort their small charges up the sidewalk. Each child held on tight to the communal rope as they headed toward the Public Gardens. It seemed like only yesterday the girls were that age. She and Graham would take them to feed the ducks and stop for gelato on the way home.

All those precious days disappeared when she wasn't looking.

Despite the brisk wind, they stopped for fries at the local chip wagon, and sat on the stone wall that ran along the sidewalk amid a legion of sparrows and fat pigeons. She had no business eating greasy fries, but if ever a day called for fattening food, this was it.

"So," Crystal said with her mouth full. "How was the first night with Aunt Hildy?"

Elsie shook her head and swallowed before she attempted an answer. "Terrible."

"Let me guess. She gave everyone a mouthful and nobody ate the great dinner you made."

She looked at her friend. "You're psychic."

"I'm not psychic. You're just predictable and your aunt's a tyrant."

Elsie dipped a fry in her ketchup. "I can't win. No matter what I do, nothing ever changes."

Her friend snorted. "And nothing ever *will* change unless you stand up for yourself."

"Oh, brother. Not you too."

"Graham's right, Elsie. You never should have let her move in."

She threw her cardboard container in the nearby trash can. "*Don't* talk to me about Graham."

Crystal threw her container too. "What did he do now?"

"Can you believe he made a date on the phone right in front of me?"

She threw her hands up to her cheeks. "Oh my God. You mean a forty-two-year-old man had the audacity to make a date? Call the *National Enquirer*, this is news."

Elsie stuck out her tongue.

"Fight fire with fire, then. There's no reason you can't date too."

"Oh, don't worry. I plan on bonking the first guy who walks down the street."

Crystal looked behind her and burst out laughing.

"What?"

"Don't look now, but here comes Harry Adams. He's wanted to get in your drawers for years. Guess it's his lucky day."

She turned and, sure enough, there was Harry strolling down the street in his cop uniform, bigger than life. She'd known him since high school and often ran into him because of work. He was a great-looking guy but he knew it and that had always bugged her.

"Jesus," she yelped. "Hide." She threw her purse up over her face but it was too late. Harry had spied her and was barrelling over.

"Hey there, Miss Social Worker. How's it going, now that I hear you're sort of a free agent? Graham's one stupid guy to let you out of his clutches."

There was nothing for it. She couldn't run down the street. That would be too obvious.

"Hello Harry."

Crystal gave him a big smile. "Hi Harry. Don't tell me you're still single? A nice-looking guy like you?"

He literally preened and winked, "Have to keep the ladies happy, if you know what I mean."

Oh barf. Elsie tried to get Crys to look at her, but she refused, content to smirk up a storm.

"Well, now that Elsie's available, maybe you should call her up."

Elsie wanted to beat the face off her.

Harry put his hand through his dark hair. "I think that's a great idea. I'd love to take you out for dinner Elsie, or even for coffee. We can catch up on old times."

She prayed the sidewalk would open up and swallow her. She wasn't sure who to kill first, Crystal or Harry. She looked at them with desperation and tried to think of an excuse to leave, but then remembered how Graham had humiliated her the night before.

This was the solution. Harry was a nice guy, in spite of his showing off, and at least she knew him. Who better to go out on a date with? She didn't want to cruise bars and pick up a stranger. Yes. Harry was just the ticket. Graham wasn't the only one who could make a new life for himself.

"Sure Harry. Call me."

Elsie was pleasantly surprised when she got home from work

a few hours later and found Faith humming in the kitchen while she made vegetable soup.

"Whose house it this?" she teased. "Where's my sister and what have you done with her?"

Faith opened the fridge and looked in the vegetable crisper. "Oh, hardy har har. Do we have any mushrooms?"

"They're in a paper bag."

"Oh yeah, here they are." She took them out and shook them into a colander.

Aunt Hildy and Dahlia were at the pine table. One browsed through a bridal magazine while the other did the *New York Times* crossword puzzle with a pen. Her daughter pushed the magazine across the table. "What do you think of this?"

Hildy held up her chin to look down the end of her nose at the picture. "Merciful God. Does that say eight thousand dollars?"

Dahlia sighed and touched the picture with her finger, outlining the dress "But isn't it beautiful?"

"It's obscene. Eight thousand dollars, for a piece of cloth?" She took off her glasses and looked at Elsie, "You wouldn't be foolish enough to agree to such nonsense, surely?"

She picked up the mail. Nothing but bills. "Of course not."

Her daughter pouted. "*Mom.* I have to have something nice. I'm not saying it has to cost that much, but..."

Hildy spoke up. "Why not wear your grandmother's wedding dress? It's in one of the trunks upstairs. It's ivory lace if I remember correctly. Very tiny. Very pretty."

Faith tossed the cut up mushrooms into the soup. "I'll look for it, if you like."

Dahlia flipped through more pages. "Well, I'm sure it's lovely, but I'd really like my own."

"I saw the most beautiful dress of all."

They turned to look at Aunt Hildy.

"Whose was it?" Dahlia asked.

"A girl. She never married though."

"Why not?"

"Her young man didn't come. He couldn't."

"That's awful."

"Mmm."

"What did the dress look like?"

"It was simple. It's about the love, my dear. Nothing else."

The three of them exchanged glances. Unbelievable. Aunt Hildy talking about love.

They were brought back to earth when the screen door slammed.

Elsie called out. "Is that you, Lily?"

Dahlia squealed. "Oh my gosh, I forgot to tell you. I coloured Lily's hair today. Wait until you see it."

Elsie went weak with relief. "Bless your heart."

Lily floated into the kitchen. "Hello."

She shone, as if light poured out of her skin.

No one moved.

"Lily?" her mother finally croaked.

"Yes."

"Honey, you look wonderful. I love your hair."

"Yes."

Aunt Hildy piped up. "Who is he?"

"A boy."

Dahlia squealed again and clapped her hands excitedly. "Who? Don't tell me you've found someone already. I must be really good!"

"Eli," Lily whispered as she continued to float across the kitchen, down the hall and up the stairs.

Faith stirred the soup. "For God's sake, let's invite him to dinner. This one, I've got to see."

It was a rare and wonderful thing to see Lily so happy. The women in the family were anxious to see the boy who'd worked such a miracle. So a week later, Eli came for dinner.

Elsie rushed through her day, bought some nice wine and hurried home to help prepare the meal. Once again, Faith was in the kitchen cooking up a storm.

Elsie laughed. "Has a culinary fairy cast a spell on you?"

Her sister looked up from mixing an apple crisp. Her thick salt and pepper hair was caught up in an elastic and one roller sat on the top of her head. Her cheeks were dusted with flour. Elsie thought she looked better than she had in years. Maybe she was coming out of her depression. Elsie had prayed long and hard for that to happen.

"I'm hiding in here so I don't have to haul furniture all day. Aunt Hildy has Lily's room in a complete tip. Do you know more packages arrived this morning? As well as a couple of crates. She's probably got a mummy in one of them."

"Nothing would surprise me."

"She talks to herself," Faith confessed. "Did you know that? I hear her all the time. It's spooky."

"She is over ninety," she said, grabbing a piece of apple and popping it into her mouth. "We think of her as invincible, but there's been a big change, don't you find?"

Faith looked pensive. "You don't think she's off her rocker… you know…imagining things?"

"I can't possibly know. She hasn't been here long enough. I'm sure we'll find out soon enough."

Just then the front door opened and Flower gave an obligatory woof.

"We're here," Lily hollered.

Elsie clapped her hands. Faith threw the dish towel she had wrapped around herself on the counter and started out the door but Elsie held her back. "Your roller."

Faith clawed it out of her hair as they beat it down the hall.

"Mom, Aunt Faith…this is Eli."

A boy not much taller than Lily stood in the doorway wearing a pair of black slacks and an open-collared white dress shirt. The minute he smiled Elsie knew right away why Lily had fallen for him. His face lit up and his grin was infectious. He shook their hands and gave them both a rose. "Ladies. It's lovely to meet you."

Dahlia had Aunt Hildy by the elbow as they hurried down the stairs.

"And this is my Aunt Hildy and my sister Dahlia."

Eli reached over to hand Dahlia and Aunt Hildy their roses. "More beautiful women. I love this house."

"It's so nice to meet you Eli," Elsie smiled. "Lily talks of no one else."

"*Mom.*"

"Well, it's true," Dahlia chimed in.

Eli turned to Lily and took her hand. He brought it gently to his lips and kissed it. "It makes my heart happy to know that."

"Well, young man," Hildy said. "I'm sure it will come as no surprise when I tell you we've just fallen in love with you ourselves."

"You can't have him," Lily murmured. "He's mine."

They had a very jolly dinner. Eli cracked them up with stories about being raised on a hippy commune with his middle-aged parents, who, it turned out, weren't hemp farmers after all, but a wealthy stock broker and brain surgeon having simultaneous mid-life crises that miraculously disappeared when he was twelve. And so he spent his fragile teenage years trying to cope with living in a penthouse condo in mid-town Manhattan.

Elsie was so happy for Lily. She looked at her face watching Eli's every move as he chatted and gestured and laughed with them all. Her girls were incredibly fortunate. It was obvious they were both in love. She turned to look at Slater, who'd joined them before dinner, and could see that he was shy around this sophisticated charmer. He laughed at all the jokes and yelled "Far out," every few minutes, but he looked worried, as if somehow he didn't quite measure up to the new guy in the family. He seemed vulnerable and, for the first time, Elsie wanted to protect him as one of her own.

Dahlia must have sensed his uncertainty too. She turned to him, took his chin in her hand and mouthed "I love you." The look of gratitude he gave her for this sweet gesture made Elsie suddenly excuse herself, saying she'd get the tea. She rushed out of the dining room and into the pantry, where she picked up an apron and held it to her face to keep from sobbing out loud.

Later that night, when all was quiet, she climbed the stairs with a mug of hot milk — something her mom used to do when she was out of sorts. As she tip-toed down the hall, Aunt Hildy's bedroom door opened.

Elsie crept across the hall. "Are you all right?"

"Why are you whispering?" Hildy asked.

Elsie slipped inside the bedroom. "I don't know. You looked like you were going to tell me a secret."

Her aunt laughed as she shut the door. "I have lots of secrets. Don't you?" She motioned for her niece to sit on the bed, while she took the armchair next to it.

"Secrets?" Elsie held her mug against her chest and thought about it. "Not really. I don't have time for secrets."

Hildy shook her head. "Oh dear. That's not very wise. That means you have no mystery, and where there's no mystery, there's no magic."

"That's all well and good, Aunt Hildy, but in this day and age who has time for such things?" Elsie heaved a great sigh and looked around the room. It had been transformed. Masks, embroidered silk throws, lamps and candlesticks dotted the room. There were pieces of sculpture and paintings from all over the world. Black and white pictures in elegant frames of people she didn't know stared at her from every vantage point.

She put her mug down and wandered over to a small music box that sat on Aunt Hildy's bedside table. It was covered with gemstones in a pattern of flowers and butterflies. "This is beautiful."

"If you look closely you can see the moon and stars as well. Open it."

Elsie lifted the lid and a haunting melody began to play. Hildy put her fingertips together and held them to her mouth as she listened. When it wound itself down, Elsie closed the box.

"One of my most precious possessions."

"How wonderful."

"Would you like to have it?"

She spun around. "Oh, no. I can't do that. It's too much." She put it down as if it were on fire and sat on the bed.

Her aunt didn't say anything. Finally, Elsie couldn't stand it.

"Did you want to talk to me about something? Are you comfortable here? Is there anything I can get for you?"

"My dear girl. I make my own comfort. I don't rely on anyone else to give it to me."

Elsie's eyes welled up.

"You're not a maid, child."

That's when the dam broke. She cried for a long time while her aunt watched her, never making a sound. She reached for the Kleenex in her bathrobe pocket. "I'm sorry. I don't know what came over me."

"I think you do."

Elsie hit her knees with her fists. "I miss Mom. I wish she were here. I need to talk to her."

Hildy shrugged. "So talk to her."

She wiped her nose. "You know what I mean."

"Yes. I do. Your mother's with you forever, so whatever you have to say, you should say. She'll hear you."

"You make everything sound so easy. Is it really?"

"Of course."

She balled up her tissue. "You've had such an interesting life. How did you get so brave?"

Hildy put back her head and laughed. When she did, Elsie had a brief glimpse of what she must have looked like as a young woman. Striking.

"I wasn't brave. Your mother was brave."

"Really?"

"I ran away. Your mother stayed. Which was more courageous?"

Elsie shrugged.

"Does an ordinary life have less value than an exciting one?"

Elsie looked down at her hands. "No."

Hildy continued with her endless questions. "What do you love?"

"My children. This house."

"Graham?"

Elsie's eyes once again filled with tears. She struggled to speak but couldn't.

"I thought so."

Desperate to change the subject, she said, "Why did you run away?"

Suddenly her aunt looked very old. Elsie was sorry she asked.

"Because of my father."

"You didn't get along?"

She looked away. "I've loved only one man in my life. It wasn't him."

"Oh."

Hildy sat up a little straighter. "I've also been loved by many men," she announced matter-of-factly.

"Gosh. I didn't know that. You never seemed the type to… you know…want a man."

"I didn't want them. I used them."

Elsie was taken aback. She didn't know what to say.

"Does that shock you?"

"No-o."

Hildy said wearily, "It should."

"You look tired dear. I'll let you get to bed."

"Yes, you're right. I am tired. You may kiss me goodnight."

Elsie walked over and kissed her cheek. "Please don't die. Not yet."

"I'll die when I'm good and ready, thank you, and not a minute before."

As Elsie turned to leave, Hildy got up and went to the bedside table. She picked up the music box and placed it in Elsie's hands.

"I want you to have this. Someone I loved very much gave it to me. It's a little treasure."

Chapter Six

Faith was at the kitchen sink when she heard the back screen door open.

"It's your lucky day! I'm back!"

It was Juliet. Oh, thank God.

Faith came out of the pantry with cookie dough on her hands as Juliet came around the corner. They stared at each other in shock.

"Is that a new nose?"

"Is that you in a kitchen?"

Faith grabbed her and gave her a big hug.

"You have no idea how much I've needed you these past few weeks." She pushed Juliet away so she could be looked at. "Do you like it?"

"Are you saying you don't?"

"No. No. It's very nice. But what was wrong with the old nose?"

"It was old. Now tell me what on earth you're doing in here. Not baking, surely?"

Faith motioned for her sister to follow her, looking around to be sure they were alone.

"Have you lost your mind? What's going on?"

Faith ran her doughy fingers under some warm water and grabbed a handful of paper towels to clean them off. "I damn near lost my mind while I waited for you to come home. I've been cooking up a storm ever since you left."

"Why, for God's sake?"

"Looking for treasure in the kitchen."

Juliet turned to leave. "Now I know you've lost your mind."

"Come here," she hissed. "You haven't heard everything."

Juliet turned back. "So tell me already."

"Aunt Hildy told me she has a treasure chest in this house. You're going to help me look for it, and when we do, we won't tell a soul and when we find it the whole thing will be ours."

Juliet stared at her. "I don't believe you. Why on earth would she tell you?"

"Listen. I don't think she really meant to, but she didn't exactly keep it a secret either. She just matter-of-factly told me she had one and I could believe her or not."

"Well, what kind of treasure?"

She shrugged. "Treasure treasure. If it's treasure it has to be worth something. All I know is that it's in this house and we'll find it eventually. We'll pretend I want to fix up the attic...decorate...so you have to be over here a lot and that's when we can search. Isn't that a good plan?"

"But if she's already told you it's here, won't she know who took it if she looks for it? Did she tell Elsie or the girls about it?"

"I don't know. But if she does happen to wonder where it is, we can say we don't know what she's talking about."

Juliet chewed her finger. "I'm not sure."

"If she plans to die anyway, we don't have to worry. Maybe she'll do us all a favour and go quickly."

"Life gets so damn complicated when she comes to town. I wish she'd just bugger off and leave us alone."

"So will you help me?"

"I guess so, but if we get in trouble, I'll deny everything."

Faith put her hands on her hips. "Well thanks. You're a pal."

"Oh nonsense. Put the kettle on since you're such a Suzy Homemaker. I bought you something."

"Oh goody."

The tea made, Faith opened her gift. It was a book. *How to write a Book in Seven Days and Make a Million Dollars* by Jerry Quakenbush. She tsked. "Oh great. As if I need more pressure. I'm surprised Graham didn't buy this for me."

"It's the thought that counts."

"By the way. Did Robert get his…you know…tucked?"

"Tucked, scraped, stretched and stitched."

"Lord. Sounds horrible. Where is he now?"

"In bed on a rubber doughnut. I had to leave. All he does is moan and groan."

"Was it worth all the agony?"

"Who knows. It's so huge and puffy I can't tell."

"Oh yuck." Faith finished off her tea and put down her cup. "You know, we should start right away. There's no one here and Aunt Hildy naps for hours."

Juliet looked down at her tailored pant suit. "I can't search for anything in this outfit. It cost me a fortune."

"I have stuff…"

"No thanks."

Faith rolled her eyes. "Heaven forbid, you might get cooties. Fine. Go home then and hurry back. We have a few hours at least, before Elsie arrives."

"Righto."

With not a moment to lose, Juliet sped home as fast as she dared. She burst through the front door and wasn't inside for more than five seconds before a pathetic voice rang out.

"Juliet? Juliet, is that you? What took you so long? I thought you were supposed to come right back?"

She screamed up the stairs. "What in the name of God do you want now?"

Robert's pitiful voice pleaded from above. "Can I have an ice cream float, sugar lump? You know…with ginger ale? The kind I make for you."

Juliet stomped off into the kitchen with Kiwi at her heels. "He's become the biggest pain in the butt. Get me a drink. Get me something to eat. Get me, get me, get me. It's all about him."

She threw some ginger ale and a blob of ice cream in the blender and hit puree. The high pitched whine sent Kiwi running for cover. She immediately turned it off.

"Oh mama's little baby. Come here sweetheart." She reached down and Kiwi jumped in her arms. "That mean old Daddy shouldn't have scared my baby girl."

The still lumpy mixture went into a glass, and Juliet thumped upstairs and delivered it to her helpless husband, stranded on the bed.

"You almost scared Kiwi to death."

"I did?"

"Yes. You did. Here's your stupid drink." She held it out so quickly it spilled on the bed sheets. "Now look what you made me do. Honestly Robert. You're such a pain."

He eased one butt cheek out of his doughnut for a second, then settled back into the float with a groan. "I'm not a pain. I'm in pain. If it wasn't for your harping about a tight ass, I wouldn't be in this predicament." He took a sip. "This is lumpy. How is it possible to make an ice cream float lumpy?"

Kiwi bounced up and down in her mamma's arms. "You

shouldn't drink those anyway. You'll have a fat ass again in no time. Won't he Ki? Won't he Wi?"

Robert sulked. "I will not. Don't be so mean. I'm not mean to you."

"Oh all right. I'm sorry." She put Kiwi down and went to her walk-in closet. "Mommy has to change."

"Are you going somewhere? You just got back."

"I am if I can find some old clothes. God, there's nothing here. I'll have to use one of your shirts."

He took another big sip. "Why do you want old clothes?"

She came out of the closet and went over to his dresser. "Because my dear, I'm treasure hunting."

He looked up. "What did you say?"

She rifled through his drawers. "Treasure hunting. Treasure hunting. You heard me."

"May I ask where?"

She held up a possible choice.

"Not that one."

"Why not?"

"I like it."

"Typical." She threw the shirt back in and picked another one. "I'm going to Elsie's, if you must know."

"Elsie's? That old dump? There's no treasure in there."

Juliet threw off her blouse and put on Robert's gym shirt. "According to Faith, Aunt Hildy has a treasure chest in that house, and Faith and I are going to find it."

"Hey! And leave me out of it?"

She pulled off her linen slacks and found her jeans. "We'll pretend to decorate the attic...wallpaper and stuff. It would look pretty weird if you hung around."

"Well, why can't I go over there for supper and visit Aunt Hildy? I'll chat her up and maybe she'll be nice and leave us some money." He sucked up the last bit of float. "What kind of treasure are we talking about?"

"Knowing her it could be anything...jars or something stupid from some boring old civilization. But we can't take any chances because it might be gold. She dug up a tomb or two in her day. Don't tell me those archaeologists don't pocket a few doodads from time to time."

"Well, I'm coming with you." Robert tried to get out of his doughnut, but couldn't do it lying down, so he rolled off the bed and planted his feet on the ground. He was bent over with his butt in a halo of hot air, fingertips scraping the ground in front of his feet.

"Help."

"Oh, for God's sake Robert. Look at you. You're pathetic."

Kiwi rushed over to her daddy and licked his toes.

"Get away from me you miserable mutt," he warned as he hurried away at a snail's pace. "Don't just stand there. Get the dog."

"I wish I had a video camera." She walked across the room and picked up Kiwi. Then she grabbed the doughnut and yanked it off his tush.

"*Ow!* Not so hard." Robert stood up slowly. "Oh my God. I'm dying. Why did I let you talk me into this. Now I know what it's like to sit on a bed of nails."

"When you stop moaning every hour on the hour, you'll feel better. Now if you insist on coming, let's go."

She rushed ahead of him with the dog under her arm as he brought up the rear.

Faith wasn't exactly thrilled to see Robert. She made a face and took her sister aside. "Thanks a lot. This is just what we need. How can he help? He can hardly move."

"What could I do? I'd never hear the end of it if I left him alone again."

"Stupid men."

"Tell me about it. Now where do we start."

Faith took them upstairs to the attic. "We might as well begin here, since this is where we're suppose to be working. Look, I got the ladder out of the basement."

"I'll get on it," Juliet said quickly. "I don't weigh as much."

"Bite me."

They got organized. Two minutes later Juliet stood on the ladder while Faith held it.

"Robert, do hurry up and pass me that thing."

"What thing? There are forty-two things in this tool box."

She shook her fingers at him as if that would make him respond faster. "The thing that pries things open."

"By thing, do you mean a hammer, a screwdriver, a chisel, a…"

"Crowbar," Faith sighed. "Give her the damn crowbar."

"I can't see a crowbar." He bent down to take a better look. "*Owww.*" He grabbed his buttocks. "Why am I the one bending, when I'm not supposed to bend?"

"Jesus. Hold the ladder," Faith yelled. "I'll get it."

He rubbed his butt and did as he was told. Faith threw stuff out of the tool box until she found the crowbar and passed it up. "Do you see anything up there?"

"It looks like there's a few loose floorboards in this crawl space." Juliet coughed. "It's so frigging dusty I can't imagine anyone being up here for the last hundred years."

"Aunt Hildy didn't say she hid the treasure since she's been here. She's probably been hiding stuff for fifty years…every time she came home to visit."

"Just a minute. I think I see something." Juliet climbed the last two rungs of the ladder and crawled over to an open spot in the ceiling and peered in.

"What do you see?"

"I definitely see something."

Before she knew it Faith and Robert had pushed their way in beside her, elbowing each other until they were all wedged into a space fit for one.

"I can't see anything. Robert, get off me."

"There…" Juliet pointed with the crowbar. "Do you see that lump in the dark? Maybe that's a chest."

Robert groaned. "It's a heating duct."

"Well, how did I know?"

Just then they heard the door to the attic open and Aunt Hildy call out, "It's only me."

Juliet looked at her husband and her sister. "Holy shit, it's Aunt Hildy. Everybody down." They shuffled on their knees backwards toward the wedge and in his hurry Robert knocked the ladder over. It landed with a quiet thud on the carpet. They stayed perfectly still, six feet up in the air.

"Hello?" Aunt Hildy called out. "Faith? Are you in here?" There was a long pause. "That's strange. I could have sworn you were up here." They heard her sigh and go back downstairs.

Three backsides looked out over the room.

Juliet couldn't believe it. "Way to go Sherlock. How do we get down?"

❧

Harry proved to be nicer than Elsie originally thought, in spite of the gold chain around his neck. They met for coffee several times over the course of a few weeks and even went to lunch. Finally, he asked if he could take her to dinner at The Five Fishermen.

She gathered up some papers off her desk. "I don't know Crystal…what do I do?"

"Go to dinner. At least you don't have to cook. I'd go out with just about anyone if they sprang for a lobster."

Elsie laughed as she shoved files into her briefcase. "You do. That's why your life is a nightmare, remember?"

"Thank you."

"But what do I do if he wants to kiss me or something, at the end of the evening?"

"I'd definitely call 911."

Grabbing her jacket, Elsie gave her supposed friend a wave as she left her office. "Goodnight. You've been a great help."

"I try. See you tomorrow."

Her sisters and brother-in-law were in the kitchen when Elsie got home.

"Hi guys. How was your trip? Did you…" She stared at Juliet. "You look different. Did you cut your hair?"

"Nose job."

Elsie did a double take. "Again?"

"What can I make for supper?" Faith interrupted.

"That's not my problem tonight, thank goodness. I have a date."

"You're kidding?"

She threw her stuff on the kitchen table. "Is there something wrong with that?"

Faith grinned. "Wow. I can't believe it. That'll tick Graham off."

"Good."

Faith opened the freezer door. "But it might make his girlfriend happy to know you've moved on. Gosh. There's nothing here. I'll have to make macaroni and cheese."

"What did you say?"

Juliet piped up. "Graham's got a sexpot downstairs. We saw him bring her back after work. Who knows what they're up to down there."

Elsie knew she was red as a beet. "Right." She marched up the stairs, took a shower and was ready to go the minute Harry turned into the driveway. She never even gave her sisters a chance to see what he looked like. She ran out the door, jumped in the car and said, "Drive."

Harry was worried. If he didn't know better, he'd say Elsie was drunk. He ordered a bottle of champagne and before they even finished their appetizers, it was gone.

He glanced around and wondered if anyone else noticed her knocking back the bubbly.

"I want more champagne."

"Maybe you've had enough."

"Oh, I've had enough all right." She hiccuped and nodded her head violently. "And I'm going to do whatever I want, from now on."

Harry couldn't believe it. The queen of proper was slurring her words. Maybe this was a good time to ask her a few things.

"Why did you and Graham break up, anyway?"

She shrugged her shoulders right to her ears and left them there. "You tell me," she grinned, raising her palms to the sky.

"He's crazy?"

She pointed at him. "That's it. He's crazy."

"I could never figure out what you saw in him. I thought you'd end up with a college guy. You were always so smart."

"Graham *was* a college guy," she shouted. "For about three months." She waved her hands about. "But *no*…hated it." She hiccupped again. "You should have seen my father. Whoa. He was *really* impressed when Graham went into his uncle's toilet business."

"Your father was a big-time lawyer, wasn't he?"

"He was a big-time jerk, that's what he was." She stopped and covered her mouth. "Oops. That wasn't very nice. Shame on you, Elsie. Shame on you."

Harry could see she looked flustered. "How about we get out of here?"

"How about we get out of here?" she mimicked. "How about we don't? How about you order me some more champagne? There's a good lad." She reached across the table and patted his hand.

"I've got champagne at home," he lied. "We'll have some there."

She grinned at him. "You are so bossy, did you know that? I like a bossy man…I think….No, maybe I don't….Anyway…"

Harry got up quickly and took Elsie by the arm, holding her closely against him, for fear she was going to fall in the middle of the restaurant.

"You're big. Much bigger than Graham."

"Why don't you forget about Graham tonight? I'm here now."

She giggled. "Yeah…what do I need him for? I've got you and your chain."

He looked at her. "Pardon?"

"You know…"

"My handcuffs?"

"Oh my, you are a naughty boy."

He couldn't believe this was mild-mannered Elsie. "Ah, maybe later…"

She put her finger on her lips. "Shhh. You talk too much."

Somehow he paid the bill and got her into the car. As soon as he was behind the wheel, she shouted, "I don't want to go home…way too many people there."

So he took her back to his apartment.

She slipped out of her sweater. "This is messy. I love mess. Graham's a neat freak. Did you know that?" She turned around too quickly and he caught her before she fell.

"Do I have to call 911?" she whispered.

"What are you talking about?" She looked adorable, all soft and sweet with her arms around his neck. And her perfume was incredible. He'd had a crush on her in high school. All the boys did, but Graham was the only one she'd look at, a kid who couldn't afford a pot to piss in. And now he'd thrown her away. Harry wrestled with his conscience. This was bad. She was drunk. He should do the right thing and take her home.

"You're supposed to kiss me," she giggled. "That's what they do in the movies. I love kissing. Did you know that? I could kiss all day and all night. Graham and I…"

"There's only one way to shut you up about Graham."

He kissed her.

Graham was on a bucking bronco hanging on for dear life. Bunny was a force to be reckoned with in the sack. He didn't know what to do first because she seemed to want to do everything at once.

"Come on baby, light my fire," she groaned.

Little did she know he was attempting to put her out, afraid she'd eat him alive before the evening was over. He knew one thing: He'd have no hair left if she kept this up.

"Do me, hurt me, throw me, *take me*," she screamed in his ear. Graham was terrified they'd end up in the emergency department if she didn't stop throwing herself around. His back already felt the effects of her strenuous workout. And with his luck, one of Elsie's colleagues would be on call.

"Tell me you like it, Graham," she demanded, raking his back with those claws of hers.

"Ow."

"You do?" She licked her lips. "Oh, yes. I could just do this for hours, couldn't you? Yes. Yes."

He didn't answer. This was exhausting. He wanted to call it a night, so he summoned what little energy he had left, flipped her over and rode like hell for the barn door, finally saying what he'd wanted to say all evening.

"Oh Elsie."

Everything stopped dead for a good ten seconds. Then Bunny got up on her elbows. "Tell me you didn't just say Elsie."

"I didn't just say Elsie."

Another ten seconds went by.

"You're a real piece of work, did you know that?"

Elsie opened her eyes. She was in a strange bed with a strange man feeling very strange indeed. Then she remembered.

"Oh, my God," she groaned.

Harry leaned over her. "You dozed off. Was I that bad?"

"Oh, my God." She covered her face with her hands. "What happened?"

"You're a tiger. That's what happened."

She opened two fingers and peeked out. Harry grinned at her. This couldn't be true.

Her head ached. "What time is it?"

"Midnight."

She sat up and was instantly sorry. "I've got to work in the morning," she moaned. She threw off the sheets and threw them right back on.

"Where are my clothes?"

Harry smirked. "Well, your shoes are in the living room, your dress is in the hall, your bra is on the door knob and I've got your panties." He picked them up off the bed and twirled them around his index finger. "And the handcuffs are behind you."

"*Handcuffs?*" She groaned and fell backwards. "Oh my God, what have I done?"

Harry stroked her forehead. "Elsie, you haven't done anything. You've had a bit of fun, that's all. Aren't you allowed to have fun? If it makes you feel better I think you're wonderful. And very beautiful."

Elsie looked at him. "I'm not like this," she finally said.

"Like what?"

"You know."

"No."

She turned her head away. "I don't...go to bed with men."

"How do you explain your children then?"

She tsked and punched his arm.

"That hurt."

"Shut up, Harry. I'm all mixed up. Just because you do this on a regular basis, doesn't mean the rest of the world does."

"Lighten up," he frowned. "You're allowed to have sex, you know."

"Look, I'm not good at this. It's new to me, as you well know. And my head is splitting, so if you don't mind, I'd like to leave."

Harry turned away from her and got out of bed, reaching for the pants and dress shirt that were crumpled on the floor. "Fine. Get dressed. I'll take you home."

"Don't be mad at me. I've got a hangover and it's not even morning yet."

"It's always a good idea to eat before you drink. That way, bad men can't take advantage of you."

The drive home was silent. Elsie peered out the side window, chewing her knuckles as the empty streets slipped by.

He finally stopped the car in front of her house. She waited for him to say something but he didn't. She looked down and fiddled with the hem of her sweater. "Look, Harry, I'm sorry. I know you didn't ply me with liquor or anything. I'm just…"

"Ashamed and sorry you went to bed with me. That's okay. I won't ask again."

"No, that's not it."

Harry looked straight ahead. "Don't worry Elsie. I'll live. See ya around."

He wouldn't look at her so she had no choice but to get out. "Thank you for dinner…and everything."

He stayed quiet.

She needed to leave. "Well, goodbye then." She got out of the car, shut the door and was halfway up the driveway when she heard him call out her name. He hurried over.

"Look, I'm sorry too. I don't usually care this much, that's all."

Elsie smiled at him. "I do like you Harry..."

She stopped because she heard a door bang shut behind her. Out of the darkness Graham approached them with a chesty woman in tow. Even in the dark, Elsie could tell she wore too much make-up.

They stared at each other.

"Graham," said Harry.

"Harry," said Graham.

Elsie didn't open her mouth. Bunny looked at Graham and said out of the corner of her mouth, "Who are these people?"

"My...nearly ex-wife and her..."

"Date. He's my date. We've just had a fabulous meal and a fabulous evening."

Bunny stood on one foot with her hand on her hip. "Let me guess. Is your name Elsie by any chance?"

"That's none of your business." She turned to Harry. "Thank you. I had a nice time."

"Me too."

She gave him a quick kiss. "Good night."

Then she ran into the house and promptly threw up.

৵৬

The next morning, they left for work at the same time. Graham noticed Elsie looked pale. They stared at each other and neither said a thing. Elsie started toward her car.

"So. Did you have fun?"

She unlocked the car door. "Did you?"

"I asked first." He realized how childish that sounded.

She threw her bags onto the passenger seat, then looked at him with sad eyes. "Does it matter?"

"I guess not."

"Did you like kissing her?"

"Does it matter?"

"I guess not."

She got in the car and started it up. He stood in front of it until she looked at him, then he approached her window. She rolled it down.

"Look, if we're supposed to be getting on with our lives, we can't make each other feel bad when we date other people."

"Who says I feel bad? You're a big boy. You can screw anyone you like."

Graham nodded and rocked back and forth on his heels. "You see? You do this all the time. Say you have no problem with something and then make it abundantly clear that you do. I've put up with this crap our whole married life."

Elsie gripped the steering wheel. "Stop accusing me of judging you. That's all you ever say."

Graham pointed at her. "Because that's all you ever do! I don't have the right job…."

"Shut up Graham. I'm sick of you hounding me about that. I just want you to realize your potential…"

"Maybe this is it, lady. Maybe this is as much potential as I can stand. Has it ever occurred to you that I might be happy just the way I am?"

She brushed her hair out of her face. "No, because you look

about as happy as I feel." She glanced at her watch. "I've got to go."

"Fine. Who's stopping you?"

"You are. And it's really nice of you to bring this up when I have so much else going on in my life, what with Aunt Hildy —"

"Aunt Hildy is here because of you. Everyone else thought it was a lousy idea, but guess what? We were all outvoted by Elsie the Good."

Her eyes started to blur with tears.

"I'm sorry. I didn't mean that."

She blinked a few times. "Don't forget the girls' birthdays are this Thursday."

"As if I would. I'll never forget those days as long as I live."

She rolled up the window and drove off in a hurry. Graham was rooted to the spot.

What are we doing? he thought.

❦

Hildy was outside in the back garden. She reached up and pulled the wooden pegs off the line to release the few towels that hung there. It was coming on evening, and the air was damp. A thick fog rolled in, and made everything grey and very quiet. Her fingers were numb but she ignored the cold. She loved this time of day. And she loved the fog. It made her invisible for a time.

She took her small wicker basket and went inside. No one was about, so she continued on, climbing the stairs to the top floor. The hallway was full of shadows, the mist pressed up against the window at the far end of the corridor. Everything looked exactly like it did the day she realized she'd leave this house forever.

She walked to her room and opened the door.

Her father rushed at her.

"*Hildy.*"

"Yes?"

"Wake up, Aunt Hildy." She felt a hand on her shoulder. She blinked awake and the fog lifted.

"What time is it?" she grumbled.

"It's almost seven," Faith said. "You remember. It's the birthday dinner tonight. Everyone's here."

She sighed. "I'm sure that's a diplomatic way of saying, get your skates on. I'll be right down."

Faith didn't move. "Are you all right? You were moaning when I came in."

Hildy wanted to be alone. "Must have been the beans you gave me for lunch."

"Fine. We're downstairs when you're ready." Faith shut the door behind her.

Hildy sat still and was aware of her heart. It beat like a drum. It was time. She'd tell them tonight, birthday dinner or not.

Juliet sidled up beside Elsie to refill her glass of wine. "So, I want to hear all about your date last Saturday. Did you have a good time?"

Elsie nodded and continued to ice the birthday cake at the kitchen table. This year it was a lupin. Every year she made the girls a flower cake, but she was running out of flowers.

Juliet nudged her arm, ruining the "a" in Dahlia. "And…?"

Elsie held her icing bag in mid-air and gave her a look. "If you must know, I got drunk and shagged him while wearing handcuffs."

"Oh ha, ha. Seriously. Did you have fun?"

"It was a blast." She went back to the task at hand.

Her sister leaned against the table and drank her wine too quickly. "God, if only that were true. What I wouldn't give for an evening like that."

"You have sex on the brain. Change the record."

"Oh, shut your gob." Juliet waved her glass around and looked down at the cake. "Jesus. Is that a penis?"

Elsie looked at the cake with dismay.

"Faith, get in here," Juliet hollered.

She walked into the kitchen. "You yelled, your highness?"

Juliet pointed at the cake. "What does that look like to you?"

"A purple penis."

"*You guys!* It does not. Don't be so mean. It took me all afternoon."

Faith crossed her arms. "Okay then. What's it supposed to be?"

"A lupin."

They pressed their lips together and didn't look at her. She stared at the cake. "Oh my God. What am I going to do?"

"Eat it," Juliet snickered, before draining her glass.

Faith was more helpful. "Put some lettuce leaves around the top. It'll look like a palm tree."

"Lettuce? With a birthday cake?"

"Well, it's better than presenting your daughters with an iced phallic symbol, isn't it?" she pointed out.

"Okay."

Elsie and Faith chopped some lettuce into strips and placed them artfully at the top of the cake. There was a slight knock and Graham emerged from downstairs. Elsie glanced at him. He held two small gifts in his hands.

"Hi. Where are the birthday girls?"

She straightened up. "In the living room with the boys. You're staying for dinner, I hope?"

"Well…"

"The girls want you here. They're yours as much as mine."

"Do you want me here?"

"Not really," Juliet answered for her.

"Yes, of course. Juliet, mind your own business."

"Okay then." He crossed the kitchen to peek at the cake. "What's the flower this year?"

"Well?" drawled Juliet.

He hesitated only slightly. "It's a lupin with a head of lettuce."

Elsie squeezed her eyes shut to keep the ache in her heart from showing. When she opened them again, he was gone.

Everything was finally ready, so she told the family to sit at the table. The girls looked sweet. Both of them had their hair back, to show off the diamond stud earrings their father had given them.

"What a beautiful gift," Elsie smiled, after they showed her close up.

Graham looked pleased. "It's not every day my girls turn twenty and twenty-one."

Dahlia held out her wrist. "Look what Slater got me. It's a Pooh Bear watch."

Juliet coughed into her glass of wine.

"That's lovely," Elsie said quickly. "Isn't that lovely?"

Everyone murmured how lovely it was.

"And I'm sure Eli gave you something nice too," she smiled at Lily.

"Oh, he did. A gift from La Senza and tickets to see The Emergency!"

"That's wonderf…sorry?"

"The Emergency!"

"La Senza?" Juliet cried. "Well, aren't we all grown up? But tell me, what the hell is an emergency? Sounds like a queer gift."

"Joel Plaskett isn't queer," Slater replied. "He's a dude."

"Who the hell is Joel Plaskett?"

"I told your mother to wash your mouth out with soap when you were a little girl, Juliet," Aunt Hildy interrupted. "She declined, and I believe she would rue the day, if she were alive."

Juliet downed her drink. "Well, she's not, is she? We're stuck with you."

"Yes, more's the pity."

This was going downhill fast.

"Remember how we had to celebrate Dahlia's first birthday party in a hospital room, because Lily insisted on being born two weeks early?" Elsie laughed.

Graham picked up the story. "Your mother had chocolate icing all over her hospital gown in the delivery room Dahlia, because you were a mama's girl and you didn't want her out of your sight."

More childhood stories were trotted out to the delight of the girls and the emergency passed. When the time was right, Elsie brought out the cake and it was devoured in spite of the lettuce. Everyone was enjoying their first cup of tea when Aunt Hildy spoke up. "Now that the party's nearly over and everyone is here, I wonder if I could have your attention."

Elsie held her breath. The last thing she wanted was another scene.

"As you are all aware, I have come home to die."

No one said a word.

"I know that some, if not all of you, will be mightily relieved when I go."

Slater yelled, "No freaking way."

Everyone joined in with indignant "nevers" and "not-at-alls." Aunt Hildy ignored them.

"I'm the last surviving member of my family."

They nodded.

"Which means you're no doubt interested in my will."

There was silence.

"I thought so. And you think I'm worth a fortune."

No one moved.

"I am."

Excited whisperings.

"And you're wondering if you're in my will."

Expectant faces all around.

"You're not."

Everyone froze.

"I'm leaving my estate to the Archaeology Department of my alma mater. Great things will be done with the resources at their disposal. I've already informed the chancellor of the university and the board is ecstatic."

Hildy looked down the table.

"That being said, I also want you to know that each of you will receive a gift. I've given these gifts a lot of thought and hope you'll be pleased with my choices."

There was a slight defrosting of the air around the room.

Folding her hands together in front of her, she continued, "I've led an exciting and unorthodox life. An unexpected life.

And so it doesn't end there."

The family gave each other puzzled looks.

"There's a game to be played at the end of my life."

"A game?" Elsie said.

"A game. A game of hide-and-seek." Aunt Hildy paused. "I've spent my life looking for things, things hidden away from all eyes. It's a wonder and a mystery when these things are uncovered and more often than not, the treasure one finds is the treasure one deserves."

She stopped then, and looked thoughtful before she continued. "This house is full of treasure. How I acquired it is my business and why I hid it here…let's just say I had my reasons. Some of it will be found and whoever finds it is welcome to it. Some of it won't be found. That's the way the world works. So that being said, good luck to you all."

Everyone was speechless.

Aunt Hildy got up to leave the table. "Oh, yes. One more thing."

They waited.

"I'll never speak of this again." And with that, she walked out the door.

All hell broke loose around the table.

"That woman is off her rocker," Graham shouted. "What does she mean, 'there's treasure all over this house?' We live here for God's sake. Wouldn't we know if there was something here?"

"Do we get this treasure before or after she dies?" Juliet wanted to know.

"What if someone finds a lot of treasure and someone else finds nothing?" Faith asked. "Is that fair?"

Robert was indignant. "I'll tell you what's not fair. It's not fair that you people live here and we don't. You can search all day. We can't."

"She's just opened a huge can of worms," Elsie worried. "I don't know what she's thinking."

"When she said 'everyone,' did she mean me and Eli, too?" Slater wondered.

"Of course, baby," Dahlia reassured him. "Why not?"

"Of course not," Juliet contradicted her. "He's not a member of the family."

"He will be soon. He's entitled as much as you are."

"I'm just new," Eli said. "I don't need anything. Slater can have my share."

"No way," Lily yelled. "Why should you be left out? Aunt Hildy really likes you, unlike some I can name." She glanced at her Uncle Robert.

"He's not going to be left out of anything," Graham said, "because knowing that insane woman she'll have the last laugh when we stumble on a box of chocolate coins."

"You won't be stumbling over anything," Juliet laughed. "You don't belong here."

Elsie stood. She didn't even know she was going to.

"Shut up!"

Everyone did, clearly stunned at this turn of events.

"I will not have this family turned upside down by an eccentric old woman. And Aunt Hildy is nothing if not eccentric. I'll not put up with people tearing each other to pieces to find things that probably don't exist."

She took a deep breath. "There's no need for everyone to get greedy. Aunt Hildy's left each one of us a gift. That's more than I expected. Who are we to be entitled to her inheritance? If —

and it's a big if — there *is* something in this house, then the only fair thing to do is to share it with everyone. Robert has a good point. He and Juliet don't live here. If we don't share it equally, everyone's going to be at each other's throat. I see it all the time at work. As soon as money is mentioned, even the best of families go insane. And I'll not have that happen to us. We're better than that. And quite frankly, I think that's what Aunt Hildy wants us to find out. How we live up to this little game of hers, this experiment. And as much as I love her, I could strangle her at this moment for putting the cat in with the canaries."

Elsie sat as suddenly as she stood. Everyone snuck peeks at each other and looked humbled by her outburst. There were a few moments of embarrassed quiet.

"Is it agreed?" Elsie asked them.

"Agreed," the group muttered.

"Fine. Would anyone like more tea?"

There were no takers. Everyone seemed to be in a hurry to push themselves from the table. But Elsie wasn't stupid. "Before you all start to look for this treasure, I need help with the dishes."

The table was cleared in ten seconds flat. When the last of the cutlery was put in the dishwasher, Graham yawned and said he'd call it a night. He kissed the girls and went downstairs. The four youngsters disappeared as well.

Juliet nudged Faith. "He's down there by himself. Someone should be with him."

"You're right."

Elsie sat at the kitchen table and picked up the paper. "You better hurry girls, before he finds the Fabergé Egg in Mom's hope chest."

"Don't be so superior," Faith tsked. "You know you want to look for this treasure as much as the rest of us."

"Well, if we're all going to share, I've decided to let you guys do all the work. I'll be here when you divvy it up. Fair enough?"

"There's nothing fair about that," Juliet piped up. "Why do you get off scot-free?"

"For pity sake, go find your treasure. I'm not interested."

Juliet, Faith and Robert hurried after Graham. They were downstairs for exactly two minutes when they re-emerged with their tails between their legs.

"No luck?" asked Elsie.

"That man is a menace to society," Juliet huffed. "He went after Robert with a wrench."

"It was a hammer."

Elsie rose from the table. "I wonder if Aunt Hildy is up there laughing her head off. I'm going to bed. Goodnight."

And up Elsie went. At the top of the stairs, Aunt Hildy's door was opened a crack and she stood behind it in her nightgown.

"What were you thinking?" Elsie sighed.

Aunt Hildy tapped the side of her nose with her finger. "Enough said." She closed the door.

Elsie tried to sleep, but couldn't. Too many problems crowded in. Aunt Hildy was a nightmare. Harry called her that day hounding her for another date. She'd gone to her bank manager in the morning to hear the sad truth about the state of her finances, which meant Dahlia would have to elope. And now it was pretty clear Lily was growing up in a hurry. She needed someone.

She knocked on Graham's door. He opened it. "What took you so long?"

She entered his sitting room/bedroom/kitchen, everything as straight as a pin. It calmed her somehow.

"What am I going to do about Aunt Hildy?"

Graham rolled his eyes. "She's off her rocker. There's nothing here. I know every inch of this house. Didn't I tell you this would happen?"

Elsie plunked herself down on his sofa. "Don't start saying 'I told you so.' It doesn't help."

"Why would she have *treasure* here? No one in their right mind even uses the word treasure anymore."

She pulled her hair back. "You're right. I know you're right. I just don't know what to do. Bad enough she's living here, but now this? She's got everyone all in a tizzy."

"Kick her out."

She got up off the sofa. "If that's the best you can do, I might as well say goodnight."

"Fine. Goodnight."

She looked at him and then closed her eyes. "Never mind. I don't want to talk about her."

"You just said you did."

"Listen." She tried to stay calm. "About Harry…"

He turned away. "It's none of my business anymore."

"It drives me crazy when you say that."

He turned back. "You say it all the time."

"I know. I know. But I don't mean it."

"*Huh?*"

She wanted to scream. "I miss you being my friend, that's all."

He looked her up and down. "Have you got anything on under that?"

"Stop it. Just stop it."

He came right up to her, his breath in her face. "Are you do-ing this on purpose? You wanted this separation, so I gave you one. Why keep coming here?"

"I miss talking to you. I'm not here just because you're irre-sistible to women…"

"I know you…"

She was furious. "And I know you. You get to swan in and give the girls diamond earrings for their birthday. Did you ask me to go in on it, so it could be from both of us? No. That would take away some of the glory. Guess what I gave them?" She began to cry. "Sweaters."

He stood so close to her, she felt her energy seep away. He grabbed the back of her head with his big hand, brought his mouth down on hers and kissed her the way he'd always kissed her. Totally, completely and with great skill.

It went on and on. The two of them together again. It felt so good. He gathered her closer, groaning as he did. She wanted to give in, until a small voice inside her head warned…*this is what he always does when you try and stand up to him.*

She couldn't fall for it. She needed to be strong. She put her hands against his chest and pushed herself away. Breathless now, she struggled to say, "I need a hug, Graham. Not sex."

He dropped his arms. "Of course. You've got Harry for that."

She felt the blood drain from her face. "I'm sorry. I won't bother you again." She turned and was almost out the door when he said, "Elsie, wait…"

She didn't.

Chapter Seven

The next morning Hildy went out into the garden as usual, to sip her green tea, which she'd acquired a taste for during her travels to the Orient. She never could go back to the Maritime custom of tea with plenty of milk.

Since it was Saturday, there was plenty of noise from the surrounding neighbours — the clatter of dishes and radios through open windows, the drone of a vacuum cleaner, kids shouting and dogs barking over the incessant buzz of a lawn mower.

She enjoyed it as an observer. Sitting there as part of the scenery, no one would guess that Hildy left the world a long time ago — ever since the night Nikolai disappeared. It was her body that insisted on staying, which was fine. She'd found a way to spend her days. To be truthful, archaeology wasn't so much a passion as a necessity. She stopped living her life and immersed herself in the lives of others.

That was her career. Making men pay was her hobby.

But now, at the end of her life, she realized it left her with a silly dilemma, which brought her to the events of last night. She had a momentary lapse of uncertainty about what she'd done when she saw Elsie's face as she came up the stairs. Perhaps this little family wasn't ready for what awaited them. She knew there was more than enough to share if her relatives worked together, but somehow she doubted they would. She really didn't care if they did or not. Their lives were still to be lived. Hers was over and she was tired.

She only came home to start the game. They could finish it. She didn't need to know who won.

Mrs. Noseworthy waved from her porch. Poor old soul.

"Good morning, Hildy. How are we today?"

"We're perfectly fine, dear."

"Has it begun?"

"Indeed it has."

"Can anyone play?"

She looked so earnest and eager, Hildy didn't have the heart to say anything but, "The more the merrier."

Mrs. Noseworthy laughed and laughed.

Since it was Saturday, Slater came over after lunch. Dahlia beckoned him to follow her into the library. "I think if Aunt Hildy hid treasure, it would be in here."

"Right on." He paused. "Why?"

"Because Aunt Hildy's a smart lady. I know she roamed around ruins and stuff, but she lectured at university too. I bet she has a map in one of these books and it's up to us to find it."

Slater looked around the room. "We'll be here all day then."

The library was smaller than the living room but it too had a stone fireplace, perfect for cold winter nights. The walls were taken up with floor-to-ceiling bookshelves. Only the fireplace wall was panelled in dark mahogany. Two leather club chairs faced each other in front of the fire, with a large tufted ottoman between them.

A rolltop desk was beneath one window, while two embroidered wing chairs took up space by the second window. This was where Elsie and her mother would sit and read on rainy

Saturday afternoons, her mother with a cup of tea and Elsie with hot chocolate. They would indulge themselves and eat Pantry cookies or Milk Lunch and a bit of old cheese.

Faith would be there too, but she was always curled up in one of the chairs by the fire. Inevitably though, she'd storm out and go read in her room because of Elsie's habit of reading passages out loud to her mother.

Juliet never set foot inside the place.

Dahlia motioned to the first shelf. "Let's start here." She pulled out a book and shuffled through the pages.

Slater did the same and sneezed instantly. "Holy cow, man. I'm going to need an antihistamine if I keep this up." He sneezed again.

"Great. We just got started." Then she remembered the scarf around her neck. "Here. Put this over your mouth. You won't breathe in the dust." She placed it over the lower half of his face and tied it behind his head.

"I feel like the Lone Ranger or something." He raised his thumb and pointed his index finger at her. "Stick 'em up!"

She held her hands in the air, playing along in a sing-song voice. "Don't shoot. I can't pay the rent."

"But you must pay the rent."

"But I can't pay the rent."

"Then I'll…"

The door opened and Aunt Hildy walked in. She looked at the cow- poke and his girl.

"Do carry on." Aunt Hildy walked out.

Since it was Saturday, Lily and Eli lounged on the mattress that served as bed, couch and chair, instead of rushing to class.

They enjoyed a homemade linguini picnic thanks to Eli's nosy neighbour.

"This is fabulous. Mrs. Minelli is like, the best cook in the world. How come she keeps feeding you?"

Eli shrugged. "She tells me I'm too thin."

Lily shoved in another mouthful. "You won't be, if she keeps this up."

"Your father will kill me long before I get fat. Why on earth did you tell everyone I got you something from La Senza?"

"Dad wouldn't know it's a lingerie store, but maybe I subconsciously wanted everyone to know I'm not a little girl anymore."

Eli put his plate aside. "Or there's always the other theory."

"What's that?"

"You're a blabbermouth."

"You asked for it." She shoved her plate away too and attacked him. They rolled around on the floor, trying not to make too much noise, with not much success.

There was a knock at the door.

"You okay in there, Eli?"

"Yes, I'm fine, Mrs. Minelli."

"Is Pansy with you?"

"Yep, and Lily too."

Lily tried to cover his mouth with her hand.

"Mama mia," she said from the hall. "You kids today…I don't want to know."

"They've ganged up on me, Mrs. Minelli. You have to help me."

"Santa Maria. I make you some nice tortellini, to keep up your strength." Her voice faded away.

"Eli! You're terrible."

"She loves it. Now get over here before I decide I like Pansy better."

Lily giggled. "Pansy doesn't have access to Aunt Hildy's treasure, buster, so you better be nice to me."

He grabbed her around the waist. "Oh, I intend to be very nice to you. But don't tell your dad."

Since it was Saturday, Juliet and Robert were in the attic with Faith, all of them brooding.

"I can't believe my lousy luck," Faith griped. "Just when I find out about a treasure chest, Aunt Hildy announces the fact to the whole damn family. I mean, can you believe it?"

Robert balanced on a cushion. "Oh, I believe it. The way my life's going, I'll have a plague of locusts in my yard before nightfall."

"Oh, do shut it, Robert. As if you have anything to complain about. You're married to me aren't you?" Juliet didn't wait for an answer, but instead pulled a compact out of her bag and touched up her nose in the mirror. "Do you really think we're any worse off, now that everyone knows? No one's here most of the time. We have loads of time to look." She shut the compact with a resounding click. "Besides, the girls will never find anything. The family jewels they're interested in don't belong to Aunt Hildy."

"Juliet, don't be…"

"What? Vulgar? It's the only excitement I get, Robert. Don't be such a sap."

Faith lit a fag. "Will you two knock it off? We're wasting time. We'll stick with our decorating story because it can't be blatantly obvious we're on the hunt. Otherwise, everyone will be on our tails and we'll have to share everything."

"So where do we start?" Robert asked. "I mean, do we just stand around and wallpaper all day and wait for the coast to clear?"

Faith pointed to paint cans piled in the corner. "Just grab one and take it everywhere you go. Carry a brush and a tape measure too. Make sure people see them."

Juliet sighed. "This is all so irritating. Why don't we just gang up on Aunt Hildy and make her tell us where it is?"

"Are you serious?" Faith cried. "You'd beat up an old lady?"

"Given the right circumstances, I wouldn't put it past her," Robert nodded.

"The both of you are being ridiculous. I mean we can just wear her down. Persuade her to change her mind."

"Hello. We're talking about Aunt Hildy." Faith said.

Juliet made a face and picked up a paint can.

Since it was Saturday, Elsie stayed in bed as long as possible, even though it looked like another sunny day. This, of course, made her feel guilty. There were all sorts of outside chores that needed her attention. Barring that, she could get off her duff and go for a walk, but all she did was gather her pillows behind her and reach for her notebook. Lily had given it to her, to write down her dreams. Most of the time she just used it to make lists:

deodorant
dry cleaners
60-watt light bulbs
stamps
get Graham out of my life.

She doodled flowers around his name and tried to think of

something constructive she could embark on. What she needed was a sign. That's when the phone rang.

"Hello?"

"Hi Elsie. It's Harry."

She crawled out of the covers and lay on her stomach. "Hi."

"You busy?"

"No."

"What're you doin'?"

She wrapped the phone cord around her finger. "Lying in bed."

"Want some company?"

She turned over on her back and felt vaguely ashamed of the instant stab of heat this question generated.

"Just remember. You and Graham are not together."

She smiled. "I'm sorry I'm such an idiot."

"Hey, don't say that. I think you're wonderful."

"No, I'm not. I made a fool of myself the night we were together."

His voice got deeper. "I hope you remember some of it. I know I'll never forget a single moment."

This felt nice. Girly and silly, but nice. Was there something wrong with that?

"I remember," she said softly.

"Then let's do it again."

"Do what again?"

She heard him chuckle. "Drink champagne. It has a pleasant aftereffect."

She laughed out loud and suddenly felt much better. "Okay, but you have to buy me lunch first."

"It's a deal."

After she hung up she sat on the bed and bit her nails. She wasn't sure if this was the right thing to do, but knew if she could distract herself for even an hour from the madness in her life, she'd be doing herself a favour.

"Even I deserve some happiness. Right Pip?"

Pip, the newest stray cat in the family, gave her a happy purr-meow and snuggled back into the duvet to sleep.

Elsie bounced out of bed, took off her nightgown and grabbed her bathrobe. She held it to her chest as she dashed to the bathroom for a leisurely soak. She let the bathrobe drop as she shut the door. Robert was behind it, holding a can of paint.

"AAAHH!" she screamed.

"AAAHH!" he screamed back.

Elsie grabbed the bath mat hanging over the tub and tried to hide herself.

"You scared me to death, Robert. Get out of here!"

"I'm sorry, I'm sorry…"

"What are you doing here, anyway? No. Never mind, don't answer that. Just go."

Robert held the paint can over his face and backed away from her, trying to grab the doorknob.

"Do you want me to tell Juliet you're a perv?!" She grabbed a face cloth and threw it at him.

"I'm not stalking you, if that's what you think." He finally got the door open. "I'm decorating."

"Well, go decorate someone else's bathroom." She shut the door behind him and leaned against it while her heart thumped in her chest. "God. What an idiot."

"I'm sorry," he said from the other side. "If it makes you feel any better, you've got great tits."

Incredulous, she got ready to fling the door open and slap his face, when she heard a new sound in the hall. She put her ear to the door.

"Who has great tits?" Juliet demanded to know.

"No one. I didn't say tits."

"Well, what did you say then?"

"I'll see if it fits."

"See if what fits?"

"Crikey, Juliet. Do you have to know everything? Elsie asked me a question, that's all. Go find something else to do and leave me alone."

Elsie heard footsteps. She opened the door slightly. Juliet stood there with her arms crossed.

"So let's see these famous tits of yours."

"Why are you here?"

"We're decorating."

"You're decorating my house but you didn't think to ask me first? Who do you think you are, Debbie Travis?"

Juliet leaned in to whisper, "I'm helping Faith, okay. And you, for that matter. If I left it up to her, she'd hang a velvet Elvis in your foyer. Is that what you want?"

"Fine," she sighed. "Just keep a leash on your husband."

Elsie banged the door shut and turned on the faucets full blast. "I'm drinking *two* bottles of champagne."

Since it was Saturday, Graham thought he'd take a look at the dryer and see if he couldn't fix it. He'd heard the girls talk about their mom having to call a repairman, and this seemed like a good way to try and make up for his big mouth.

He'd bitten his tongue the minute he mentioned Harry.

Why didn't she bring up Bunny? At least then they'd be even. He also felt awful about the earrings, but it never entered his head to ask Elsie if she'd like to contribute. Of course, that's what she always complained about — him not thinking.

The simple thing was to fix something. Anything. He gathered up some tools and headed for the dryer. He thought he could smell smoke, so he ran to the mud room and pushed open the door, which in turn hit Faith on the backside, causing her to fall forward flat on her face.

"For the love of Christ. Was that necessary? Look what you did to my ciggy."

"What the hell are you doing?"

She got to her knees. "I'm decorating if you must know."

Graham noticed the can of paint beside her. "Do you seriously want me to believe you're decorating the dryer? Is it a mural you have in mind or just a touch-up?"

"You're so incredibly clever." Faith rose to her feet and put her hands on the small of her back. When she gave it a twist, it cracked.

"You're in a small, closed room, surrounded by paint fumes, yet smoking like a chimney. Talk about clever."

She threw her hands in the air. "Okay, okay. I don't need this aggro."

"Aggro? You have about as much aggro in your life as a bowl of fruit."

She took a piece of gum from her pants pocket and popped it in her mouth. "Want one?"

He shook his head.

She proceeded to stand, hand on one hip, and chew her cud for awhile. Then she pointed a finger right in his face. "Do you know what your trouble is?"

"Enlighten me."

"Ever since the day you laid eyes on my baby sister, you've made her pay."

Graham snorted. "For what?"

"For everything. You've been jealous of her from day one. So you make her feel stupid, make her second-guess herself constantly. You laugh at her because she lets me live here. You get mad at her because she can't turn Aunt Hildy away. You think she's a pushover."

"She is."

"Where would you be without her? Where would any of us be without her? She took you in, but you can't stand it when she does it for someone else."

Graham wanted to smack her.

"There's only one difference between thee and me, dearie. *Graham*, I *know* I'm a loser."

He couldn't think of anything to say, so he just stood there. She picked up her paint can and patted him on the shoulder as she went by.

"Do her a favour, Graham. Let her go."

And out she went.

Was it true? Was he jealous of Elsie's life when he first met her? He couldn't remember. There was only one emotion that stayed with him from those early years. It started the night she told her father they wanted to get married. The night her old man looked at him with utter contempt. Anger.

And that's what he felt now. He went back to his room and called Bunny. He was a bomb ready to go off and she was an easy and safe way to detonate.

Later that afternoon Eli invited Slater to join him and his buddies from Dal in a game of Ultimate Frisbee. Slater was thrilled to be included with this university crowd, but he didn't say yes until Dahlia told him to go ahead. Lily rolled her eyes.

When the boys drove off in Slater's Mustang, she and Dahlia decided to go to the Halifax Shopping Centre and buy make-up at the MAC store. They took the bus, since their mother had taken off with the car and they'd rather not shop at all than drive their father's company van. When they arrived, there were about ten other women in the small space.

Spotting a consultant who looked free, Dahlia made a bee-line over to her, but another girl pushed in ahead and started talking.

"Excuse me," Dahlia said. "I was just about to ask her something."

The girl ignored her. Dahlia's mouth dropped open and she looked around for Lily, finally catching her eye. She waved Lily over.

"This chick pushed in front of me," Dahlia told her. "Can you believe how rude that is?"

"So tell her." Lily held up an eye-liner. "What do you think of this colour?"

"It's nice." Dahlia reached over and tapped the girl on the shoulder. "Excuse me."

The girl turned around and glared at her. "Get lost!"

Dahlia's head went back. "Are you kidding me?"

"Wait." Lily tugged on her sister's sleeve. "I know you. Tiffany, isn't it? From Psych lab."

Tiffany gave them both a filthy look. "Look, I'm busy here."

"You pushed in front of my sister. There's no need for that," Lily told her.

Tiffany sighed. "Tell your sister, freak girl, that she has to wait her turn like everyone else."

"What did you call me?"

Tiffany smiled. "Didn't you know that was your nickname when you had your Bazooka hair? Even your precious Eli used to call you that. But that was before he and I made our bet."

Lily was suddenly ice-cold. "What bet?"

"I bet him two hundred dollars he wouldn't ask you out. Looks like he'll do anything to make a buck."

Dahlia pushed her. "You nasty little tramp. Take that back."

"Why don't you ask him, freak girl?"

Lily was numb. "Why are you doing this? What did I ever do to you?"

"I don't have time for this shit." Tiffany pushed past both of them and walked away.

Dahlia screamed after her, "Whoever does your hair should be arrested!" She turned back to her sister. "She's lying."

Lily put her hand over her mouth. "I think I'm going to be sick. What if it's true?"

Dahlia put her arms around her. "I'm going to kill him if it is."

"I need to get out of here, Dee. Take me home."

"Okay. Frig the bus. I'm calling a taxi."

❧

To go to bed with Harry in the middle of the night while drunk was infinitely easier than to do it in the middle of the afternoon while sober. Try as she might, Elsie could not get a buzz on at lunch — due, at least in part, to the fact that Graham's best friend and his wife were eating lunch just three tables away, giving her the hairy eyeball every time Harry grabbed her hand or stroked her arm.

"Let's get out of here."

"The lady can't wait," Harry winked. "Your wish is my command."

Elsie squirmed. "Excuse me a moment. I'll be right back." She ran to the bathroom, flew into a cubicle and locked it behind her. "Help."

"Do you need some toilet paper, dear?" an elderly voice said through the wall beside her.

"Oh…yes. Thank you." God. Now she'd have to pee.

Things didn't improve. As they walked to the car, Harry put his arm over her shoulder and bent down to give her a great messy kiss in the middle of the street. When he finally came up for air, who was walking down the other side of the street but Graham's uncle. He gave her a dirty look and a curt nod and continued on his way. She yanked on her skirt, a subtle hint to indicate it hadn't been over her head in the last half hour. She was a lady.

She wasn't in the best of moods when they landed back at Harry's apartment because it dawned on her that this was her new reality. Welcome to the single life.

"Relax," Harry whispered. He tried to remove her clothes, but she was as stiff as a mannequin. Her limbs would not budge.

"I'm sorry. I'm just not…"

"Cooperating."

She pinched him. "No. I'm just not in the mood, if you must know."

"But…"

She wiggled out of his arms. "Look, Harry. You're a very nice guy, but I'm not good at this."

He let her go. "I'll say."

She stood on one foot and gave him the same pose the girls used when she asked them to vacuum.

"Is this what dating is? A Caesar salad and a glass of wine buys you an hour in bed?"

Harry gave her a funny look. "You were up for it on the phone just a couple of hours ago, in case you don't remember."

She turned her back on him and plunked down on the first chair she saw. She cupped her chin in her hand. "I know. I'm losing my mind."

Harry gave her a smirk. "Yes, you are."

"Listen mister. In my own defence, I'm so out of touch, I didn't know condoms came in different colours. You could have warned me."

"Poor little Elsie. She's having such a hard time. But can you resist me?" He pranced around and pretended to be Ricky Martin, singing *Living La Vida Loca* until she laughed in spite of herself. He grabbed her hands and pulled her out of the chair, holding her close. "Think of this as therapy. Let yourself go. What are you afraid of?"

"Everything."

He kissed her nose. "Close your eyes then, and let me do all the work."

Oh, whatever. The only other thing she had to do today was defrost a pound of ground beef.

"Fine." She went limp. "Do your worst."

Harry drove her home afterwards, on his way to work. She

had to admit she liked the look of him in his uniform, but she could do without him asking her four times how he rated as a lover. She finally gave him a ten, just to shut him up.

When they rounded the corner of Elsie's street, a crowd of kids stood in front of her house. Mrs. Noseworthy jumped up and down in the middle of them.

"What in the world?"

"Looks like a party," Harry laughed.

She couldn't believe her eyes. Slater and Eli were on the front lawn yelling up at the girls, who threw Beanie Babies at them from their bedroom window. A pile of stuffed animals lay at the boys' feet.

Elsie got out of the car. "What's going on? Is this a joke?"

Lily threw an octopus out the window. "It's no joke when someone you love makes a laughing stock of you in front of your entire class."

"You have to believe me, Lil. I didn't pay her two hundred bucks."

"Pay who two hundred bucks?" Elsie hollered.

Slater filled her in. "They're saying Eli made a bet with a blonde slut, Mrs. B."

"It's the only reason he asked me out!" Lily wailed.

Elsie looked at the boys. "A blonde slut? What does her hair colour have to do with anything?"

"She's a big fat liar," Eli pleaded with Elsie.

She was confused. "Who's a big fat liar? Lily or the slut?"

"He is!" Dahlia pointed down at Eli. "He's just wants to cover up his guilt." She pitched a gorilla, which just missed Slater's head.

"Hey. I'm the good guy, remember?"

Lily cried, "Then why are you sticking up for him?"

"Because he knows I wouldn't do something like that, would I, Slater?" Eli pleaded.

"I don't think so. But then again, I haven't known you that long."

"Thanks for the help, big guy." Eli held his hands out in front of him. "There is no one else for me and there never will be. Tiffany is just some…"

"Just a minute," Elsie yelled. "Just a minute!" A dolphin sailed past her.

"I'll 'pink freak' you, Eli Stanton!" Lily warned.

Suddenly another upstairs window opened and Aunt Hildy stuck her head out. "In all my considerable years on this earth, I've never listened to such a moronic conversation. And the fact that it's being conducted in the middle of the street for everyone to hear is beyond ridiculous and if you don't all keep quiet, I shall be forced to…"

The attic window opened. "For Christ's sake, will you keep it down!" Faith screamed. "I can't hear myself think."

By this time, Harry was out of the car. He walked over to her.

"Oh goody," observed Aunt Hildy. "We're to be arrested for creating a major disturbance and carted off to jail. Well, I for one will be first in line. Perhaps a jail cell will afford me the peace and quiet I so desperately lack in this madhouse."

Elsie was mortified. She looked at Harry. "My entire family appears to have gone off their rockers."

He looked up at the windows. "Hello ladies, I'm Harry Adams. Nice to meet you."

As soon as he spoke, Aunt Hildy was charm itself, notwithstanding the fact that she hung out a window.

"Officer Adams, how lovely to meet you."

The girls waved. Faith did too, with a pair of binoculars across her face.

"These are my daughters' boyfriends. Well, they were their boyfriends. I have no idea what will happen now that world war three has broken out."

Harry nodded to them. "Hi guys. It might be a good idea if you took your discussion indoors."

The boys hesitated and looked at the girls in the window, still in possession of their furry ammunition.

"Girls, I'm sending the boys in. If you don't want to speak to them that's fine, but we need to get off the street. Stay in your room please until you can act with civility. You two make yourselves a sandwich."

"Thanks, Mrs. B," they said together, before slinking indoors.

Harry looked around at the crowd. "That's the show for today folks. Everyone can go home."

"Even me?" Mrs. Noseworthy asked. "I'm Miss Chamberlin's best friend."

Elsie sighed. "Even you dear. It's getting late."

Mrs. Noseworthy shuffled across the lawn. "I always miss the good stuff."

Elsie turned to Harry. "I better go and find out what's going on. I'll see you later, okay?"

Harry nodded, and then grabbed her arm. "A ten, eh? Are you sure I'm not a twelve? I've been told I'm a twelve."

"Yes. You're a twelve. That's the number. Bye Harry." She didn't wait to see him off.

Once indoors she assembled the outraged parties in the living room. Elsie folded her arms. "I want this sorted and I want it sorted now. I don't care how you do it. Do you understand me?"

The kids nodded.

"Of course, I don't suppose anyone's thought about what we might have for dinner since you were all too busy entertaining our friends and neighbours with this ridiculous spectacle."

They looked at the floor.

"Perfect. Thanks a bunch."

She left them as they stood and eyed one another. The minute she shut the French doors, the yelling started. She took her weary bones to the kitchen.

Later that night, Eli and Lily rocked on the porch swing.

Eli stroked her face. "So you forgive me?"

"I guess so."

"Wait till I get my hands on that chick."

Lily snuggled under his arm. "Don't react at all. That's what she wants. It'll bug her to no end if she thinks her little bombshell went unnoticed."

Eli smiled down at her. "I can tell you'll get an 'A' in psych this year."

When she looked up at him she frowned. "Hey, your nose looks a little swollen, did you know that?"

He touched it gingerly with his fingers. "That's because Slater tackled me."

"I thought you were playing frisbee, not football."

"He didn't understand the rules at first."

"Oh brother. What did your friends think of him?"

"They liked him. I like him too." He whispered in her ear. "But he's a bit of a dope."

She hit him. "Don't say that."

"Well he is. The other day Aunt Hildy talked about a sand-storm and Slater thought she meant it rained sand. Can you believe it? You should have seen the look on her face."

She rubbed Eli's hand absent-mindedly. "That is pretty dumb, but smarts aren't everything. Last year he picked up a dog that had been hit by a car and ran all the way to the vet's. He saved its life."

"Ah crap. Now I feel bad."

She hugged him closer. "He's a great guy, but I know one thing. With his brains, he's never going to find the treasure."

"That doesn't matter, if we're to share it."

She gave him a quick look. "Yeah, right, like that's going to happen. I trip over Aunt Faith everywhere I go. She was in the linen closet the other day when I went to get clean sheets. She scared the life out of me. I asked her what she was doing and do you know what she said?"

"What?"

"'Nothing.' She said 'Nothing.' She's in a dark closet with a pen flashlight. The woman's bonkers. As if I didn't know she was treasure hunting. Like, excuse me. I wasn't born yesterday."

"Do you realize how ridiculous this sounds? The people in this house talk about treasure as if it were a pair of socks. 'Oh, I think I'll go look for the treasure now' or 'I wonder where the treasure went,' and 'Pardon me, have you seen my treasure?'"

Lily pouted. "Fine. When I find the stupid socks I'll make sure I don't tell you."

"You don't have to go that far."

As Lily and Eli made up on the swing outside, the great dope and his girl were in the library, still only on their third shelf.

"I shouldn't have tackled Eli like that. I feel bad about it."

"Well, they should've explained the rules better. That's not your fault." Dahlia crouched down to retrieve another book. "But it was my fault that Eli got in trouble today. If I'd just let that stupid girl go ahead of me, Lily would never have known about all this. Me and my big mouth."

Slater came up behind her and put his hands on her hips. "Your mouth isn't big. It's just right."

She dropped her book, turned around and put her arms around his neck. She giggled, "You sound like baby bear."

He lifted her onto the edge of the desk. "This porridge is too hot."

She grabbed him around the waist with her legs. "This porridge is too cold."

"But this porridge mama is mmm-mmm, just right," he growled as he bent down to nuzzle her neck. That's when he saw Aunt Hildy in the doorway.

"GEEZ." He jumped and pulled Dahlia off the table with him. "Sorry Aunt Hildy, we were just…"

"I know what you're in the middle of young man and it distresses me that you feel the constant need to carry out juvenile fantasies in order to make love. I mean, really. The Three Bears? I suggest while you're in this library you read a copy of the Kama Sutra I left here years ago. Now that makes for an interesting read. Goodnight."

Dahlia sighed at the closed door. "That woman has managed to ruin our sex life."

Slater tapped his temple. "Yeah, but you know what just occurred to me? Why does she always come in here?"

She gave him a thoughtful glance. "You're right. Why is she

always in here? Hmm…I think we're on to something Slater. But don't tell anyone. That way, if we find the treasure, we can keep it."

He shook his head. "No way. Whatever we find, we share, just like Mrs. B said."

She stamped her foot. "Oh darn. Why do you have to be so honest? Couldn't we keep one little thing and share the rest?"

Slater folded his arms and gave her a look.

She raised her eyebrows. "What if one little thing was enough to pay for a wedding?"

He stood there like Mr. Clean.

She threw her hands in the air. "Oh, all right. Forget it. Whatever we find we share. But you can bet everyone else in this house runs around and looks for stuff. And they don't tell us about it, either."

Still, he didn't move.

She finally smirked, "You look just like that big genie in that Aladdin movie. Do I get three wishes, big boy?"

"That I can do." He picked her up and continued where they'd left off.

Chapter Eight

Finally Robert's nether region made enough progress to warrant his return to work. He couldn't wait to get back to it — wandering around Elsie's house all day bumping into his nieces and their boyfriends became mighty tiring. It was too cruel that the little girls he used to push on a swing now swung from the chandelier with these guys. It made him feel old.

He sat at his desk and went through the accumulated paperwork. At first glance everything appeared normal, but as the hours went by a nagging thought kept running through his brain. Things weren't quite adding up. He turned over file after file and tried to put his finger on it.

His mouth was dry. He cleared his throat and had the first fluttering of panic as he added up the figures again and again with exactly the same result. Pushing himself away from his desk, he gripped the arms of his chair.

Nah. Couldn't be.

Rolled back to his desk and pressed the intercom.

"Charlotte, get Russell on the phone."

"I'm sorry Mr. Worthington. He's out of town."

Robert tried to breathe deeply. "*When* did he go out of town?"

"Just after you left for your…holiday."

"Did he say where he was going?"

"He didn't tell me. But he said he left you that information in the safe."

Robert blew out his cheeks in relief. "Thanks Charlotte."

He walked over to the safe, turned the dial and opened the door. He reached in and pulled out a red lollipop. "What the...?"

Then he got it.

Sucker.

Faith and Juliet were in Juliet's pool atop air mattresses, their chins resting on their fists as they bobbed along.

"Did I tell you I saw Elsie's cop last week?"

Juliet yawned. "Only about a hundred times. Daffy Duck looks good in a uniform, so don't get your drawers in a knot."

"You don't get it. I zoomed in on him with my good old spy glass."

"You don't say..."

"...and I swear he looked like Tom Selleck."

"Yesterday's news."

"Pardon me. Like Robert's such a great catch."

Juliet floated along, not saying a word. A few minutes went by before her sister grumbled, "You're so lucky. A great house, a nice pool, his-and-hers MGs. *And* you don't have to work. God."

"And you do? For heaven's sake, you're like a broken record. Why don't you find a nice rich sugar daddy for yourself? You're still a good-looking woman. Sort of."

Faith raised her head. "What do you mean, 'sort of'?"

Juliet dipped her hand in water and flicked some at her sister. "Oh, don't be so touchy. All I mean is, you should spend some money on yourself. Get a new hairstyle. Colour your grey."

"I don't have any money. That's the problem."

"Ask Dee to do your hair."

"And walk into that snotty place? Not a chance. All I need is for Aunt Hildy to open that mean mouth of hers and tell us where the treasure is. I swear to God, I'll kill her if this is a joke. It's gotten to the point where if I don't find something I'll shoot myself."

"You're so dramatic." Suddenly Kiwi yipped. "Oh dear. Daddy's home. I wonder what's for dinner?"

Robert burst out of the sliding screen door and ran over to the edge of the pool. He gestured wildly. "Juliet! Come here, quick! Faith, you have to go home now."

Both sisters straddled their air mattresses and disappeared into the water.

"Stop messing around and get out of the pool!" he screamed at them.

"Don't yell at me," Juliet hollered.

"Me either," Faith chimed in.

They watched in horror as Robert started down the steps of the pool in his three-piece suit. He waded over to them as fast as he could, getting shorter and shorter. "*Get out of the pool! Get out of the pool! Get out of the pool!*"

"Have you gone crazy?" Juliet heaved herself off the air mattress and paddled like a mad woman away from him.

Faith wasn't fast enough. The mattress covered her face, and she ended up paddling straight into him. Juliet watched him pull her off the float and drag her out of the water. She threw a noodle at him. "Let go of her."

Robert still had Faith by the arm. "I'd appreciate it if you'd leave now. I've asked you nicely, but if you continue to struggle I'll throw you out on your ear."

Pulling her arm out of his grip, she said, "*Okay*. You don't have to go on about it. I'll leave. I wouldn't stay here if you paid me." She picked up her towel and stormed out through the screen door.

Juliet swam over to the edge and he hauled her out too. "What in the name of God is wrong with you? What is…"

"*Shut up!*" He sat her on a patio chair and pulled one up beside her.

Her lip quivered. "Robert, you're scaring me."

"It's bad. It's so bad."

She was frantic. "What is it?"

"Russell's left the country with all our money. We're broke."

Juliet jumped up and screamed. She ran over to the noodle, picked it up and started to beat him over the head with it. Then she fainted dead away.

When she regained her senses, Juliet sat with her head between her knees and a cold cloth on the back of her neck. Robert was on the other side of the patio table in exactly the same position. Kiwi frolicked between them.

"I hate you," Juliet told her Romeo.

He turned to look at her through the table legs. "Did I leave town with all the money? Did I?"

She looked back at him. "You might as well have, because you can't go to the police, can you? You and your shady schemes."

"My shady schemes kept you in luxury madame, so don't you dare blame me for everything."

She snorted. "I can blame you for everything. If you were half the man you're supposed to be, you'd never have been involved with that two-timing skunk."

"Say that again!"

"If you were half…ohhh." She sat up suddenly and held her

head to stop the dizziness. "Oh my God. What are we going to do?"

Robert sat up as well. "Whatever we do, we can't let anyone know about this. No one. Especially not your sisters."

"Why shouldn't I tell them? They're my sisters."

"Listen to me. I know you think I'm stupid but I do have a few smarts. And one of those smarts tells me that if we're in this much trouble, we'll need *all* the treasure. We've got to find it before Faith and everyone else does. We can't let on to anyone that we've no intention of sharing it. Do you understand?"

She thought it over. "But what if this is just Aunt Hildy's idea of a joke, and there is no treasure? What do we do then?"

"It won't matter, because after I shoot the old bitch, I'll shoot myself and I won't have to worry about it."

Juliet glared at him. "Wonderful. How thoughtful. Leave me and Kiwi to die of starvation."

He glared back. "Fine. I'll shoot you and Kiwi before I shoot myself. Does that make you happy?"

"You're a bum." She picked up the dog and marched into the house.

"No, I'm not. Thanks to you I don't have one, remember?"

Robert left the house early the next morning, telling Juliet he'd try to pull in a few favours from some business types. As soon as he was gone, she took off for Elsie's. The back door was open, so she barrelled in and ran up the stairs, pushing past Elsie in the upstairs hallway.

"Why are you here? Is something wrong?"

"Shut up, no time to talk." She threw open the door that led to the attic and slammed it shut in her face.

"Love you too," Elsie yelled from below.

Faith was at the front window with her binoculars.

"Stop spying on the neighbours and sit down."

"Hey, quit being so bossy. Why are you here anyway?"

Juliet sat on the couch. "Will you shut up and sit down? I have to talk to you."

Faith set the binoculars on the window sill and did as she was told. "I take it you're here to apologize for your husband's behaviour yesterday?"

"Faith, you and I have got to stick together."

"We always do."

She took her sister's hands and said, "Yeah, but this is serious."

Faith scrunched up her face. "Oh great. You want a kidney. Am I right?"

"You won't need a kidney if you don't shut up because I'll kill you if you don't keep quiet."

She kept quiet.

"Robert's lost all our money."

"*What?*"

Juliet squeezed her hands. "Shhh. Keep your voice down. His stupid business partner, who I never trusted, left the country with all our money and there's not a damn thing we can do about it because Robert's always operated just a shade on the wrong side of the law, if you get my drift."

"Are you serious?"

"Is that all you can say? Do you think I'd joke about this? We're broke. We have to sell everything to make ends meet until we can figure things out."

"Wow. That's awful. What are you going to do?"

"You and I will find this miserable treasure and get the hell out of this Godforsaken place. We were screwed out of one inheritance. Not again."

"But what about Robert?"

Juliet finally let go of her sister's hands. "That weasel didn't want me to tell you. He wants to take all the treasure for ourselves."

"That creep. So does this mean…"

"Yes. If you and I find this treasure, I'm gone for good. He's so stupid, he let someone walk off with our money, and he'd probably do it again given half the chance."

"But what if there is no treasure?"

"I find that very unlikely," Juliet assured her. "Aunt Hildy's just sneaky enough to do something like this."

Faith nodded.

She looked around the room and beckoned her sister closer. "And if there's no treasure, there's still treasure."

"What do you mean?"

"I mean, sister dear, she has a fortune in her room alone. All those art pieces and jewellery and tapestries. That stuff would fetch a bundle on eBay. Not that we can use it, but you know what I mean. We'd sell to private dealers."

"But how do we…you know? She's always in her room."

"Not always. You told me she's in the garden every morning. That's the perfect opportunity to go in there and maybe take a few things."

"Okay, I understand. But what about when we look for the real treasure? Robert will be here if he's so desperate to find it."

"That's okay. We'll use his muscle, but it should be easy enough to keep him away from anything interesting. We may have to sacrifice a few pieces, to keep him off the scent."

"Okay. I'll do it."

She gave Faith a thumbs-up and congratulated herself on covering all her bases. If Robert found the treasure first, she'd leave with him. If Faith found it first, she'd leave with her. And if she found it first, God willing, she'd wave farewell to the whole damn lot of them.

❦

While Robert ran around town chasing down business associates who didn't return his phone calls, his brother-in-law lay on Bunny's bed with his arms behind his head. It was the first time Graham had stayed overnight. He knew Bunny was thrilled and was taking it as a sign of his blossoming affection for her.

She hopped out of the shower and bounced on the bed, then threw off her towel and crawled over to him. "Sugar bear. Isn't this nice? How about a little morning delight?"

Graham was amused by the fact that while his body was agreeable to the suggestion, his mind yawned. This was a woman who was incredibly easy to please. It never occurred to him before how boring that was.

"Sorry, I can't stay."

Bunny pouted as she straddled him and rubbed his shoulders. "That's all you ever say."

"I stayed last night, didn't I?"

"It's probably because you had too much beer."

He didn't deny it.

"I have to go because I promised Lily I'd take her to lunch."

Bunny sighed and got off him. She sulked, "Your stupid family ruins everything. Why don't you move?"

Graham shrugged. "I haven't had time to look for another place. Besides, even if I did, I'd still see my girls. That won't change."

She got off the bed and put on a slip. "How come we never go anywhere?"

He laughed. "Because you only ever want to…"

"Well, so do you. How about tonight we go somewhere expensive? I want champagne and caviar."

"I'm not made of money, believe it or not."

"All you do is mouth off about that old biddy's treasure. Why don't you find it and we can go on a nice Caribbean holiday." She gave him a smouldering look and flicked a strap off her shoulder. "You'd like that wouldn't you?"

He got up and put on his jeans, then reached for his shirt on the floor. "Sure. Who wouldn't? But if you want me to find this elusive treasure, I have to stay in the house, don't I?"

"That's true. Maybe I can help you look?"

"I don't think so."

"Why not?"

He went over and gave her a kiss. "I'll see you later." He left before she could say anything else.

❦

Elsie and Crystal were in the hospital cafeteria sizing up the new batch of residents. Crystal jerked her head toward the one who stood in front of the cash register. "Look at that yummy specimen."

Elsie sipped her java. "He's too young."

Her friend gave her a queer look. "What's that got to do with the price of eggs? I can look, can't I?"

"Well, if that's the case. Hello there!"

"Oh, no you don't. You've already got a guy. Don't hog them all."

Elsie put down her cup. "Would you like to have him?"

Crystal gaped at her. "You need your head examined. You've got a great-looking guy who chases you all over the city and you're still not happy."

Elsie didn't say anything.

"What's wrong with him, may I ask?"

"Nothing."

"That's the perfect reason to dump him."

"It's not that. But I'm always expected to stroke his ego. He constantly asks me if he's a ten in bed. I mean, come on."

"And is he?"

"Sort of. He's a cop, so he's a ten-four."

"Huh?"

She grinned. "He thinks he's a ten. I think he's a four."

"Ouch."

"I seriously don't know what's wrong with me," Elsie sighed. "One minute the thought of Harry cheers me up and I'm happy he's around, yet the minute he wants to be intimate, I can think of a hundred reasons not to be."

Crystal wiped her mouth with a napkin. "That's because you're still in love with Graham."

She shook her head sadly. "Graham and I are in the habit of loving each other, that's all. He was my first and only love, so it's a hard habit to break. But you know how unhappy I was. He always judged me, always disapproved of everything I did. Why should I live like that?"

Crystal reached over and held her hand. "There's only one thing that keeps you two apart."

"What's that?"

"Everyone else."

It was all Elsie could think about for the rest of the day. She wondered if it was true. When Graham came into the house after work to drop off the backpack Lily left in his truck at lunchtime, she startled them both with an invitation to dinner.

"Are you sure?"

"Of course I'm sure. This is ridiculous. Why can't we eat together as a family from time to time. You like to hear about the girls' day just as much as I do."

"All I heard from Lily at lunch was how wonderful Eli is."

"He's a nice boy."

"He's too experienced for my liking." Graham sat at the table while Elsie went to the fridge and got him a beer. They smiled at their old ritual. Then she continued to bread the haddock for their dinner.

"You forget, old man. You were just as 'experienced' when you were his age. And I should know. I was there at the time."

"You sure were."

They laughed together. Elsie opened her mouth to say something saucy, but before she could get it out, there was a rap at the back door and in waltzed Juliet and Robert. Elsie realized Crystal's observation was right on the money. She and Graham were never alone. The temperature in the kitchen fell about ten degrees.

"It's just us," Juliet announced needlessly. "Mind if we stay for supper? We brought dessert." She held up a box of Tim Horton doughnuts.

Elsie wanted to tell them to get lost, but it looked as if Juliet had been crying, and that never happened.

"No, I don't mind," she said as she turned away from Graham's exasperated look.

Once again, the entire mob sat around the dining room table. There was always a place set for Eli and Slater now — they never seemed to go home, and she wondered if anyone missed them.

Juliet was like a flea on a hot stove. She yammered on from the minute they sat down and only picked at her dinner. "You would not believe how much work there is to do upstairs. Faith and I can't possibly get it done by ourselves."

Robert jumped in. "I've taken a little hiatus from work. We think we should step up our renovations in the attic. Get it done lickety-split. Since you people are good enough to let Faith live here, I feel it's only right that Juliet and I help out in other ways."

Graham nodded. "Well, that's thoughtful, isn't it Elsie? I'm sure this has nothing to do with the 'T' word."

"What are you insinuating? That my wife and I are only interested in being here because of the treasure?"

Aunt Hildy took a small bite of haddock. "That's exactly right and he's done it very well, don't you think?"

"I resent…"

"Keep your teeth in, Robert," Graham interrupted. "It's not exactly a secret we're looking for it. Apparently no one's found the treasure, as nothing's been mentioned. Does anyone want to confess anything?" He looked around the table.

"I do."

All heads swivelled in Elsie's direction.

"I much prefer the fish done this way. Thanks for the suggestion, Aunt Hildy."

Her aunt laughed. "You're very welcome, Elsie."

"Brother," Juliet sneered. "It's not hard to tell who your favourite niece is."

"Is that so?"

"That's so."

Aunt Hildy gave Juliet a stern look. "How would you know what I think, since you never talk to me?"

"I talk to you."

"And what do you say, other than 'brother' and 'that's so'?"

Juliet stood up. Elsie put out an arm to stop her.

"Why should I talk to you? You dare to come here and drive us bonkers with your silly game of hide-and-seek. You hear us talk about treasure and wonder about it. You trip over everyone searching for it, but you act as if you've no idea what we're up to. If you were any kind of a decent human being, you'd stop this nonsense and tell us where it is. If you don't want us to have it, then why don't you wrap your precious treasure in a pillowcase and throw it off the MacKay Bridge and then maybe I'd want to talk to you."

Juliet sat and cried. Elsie handed her a napkin.

"Would you like a glass of water?" Slater asked. She shook her head no.

Aunt Hildy stared at her for a few moments. "You're quite right, Juliet. I should throw it away. It would make your lives much easier, I'm sure. But I'm not prepared to do that, because I believe each one of you has an equal chance of finding what you're looking for. I don't want you to miss out on that opportunity."

Faith spoke up. "What in heaven's name *are* we looking for? Jewels? Coins? Gold? What is it? And why is it here?"

"That's for me to know and you to find out."

Faith screeched. "You're impossible."

Hildy laughed and turned back to Juliet. "I'm sorry, my dear, if I appear heartless. I certainly don't mean to be. You three girls are my beloved sister's children and because of that you have the same place in my heart. Each of you has something of her in you. And I hope you find that something before your lives are over."

Aunt Hildy stopped for a moment. She touched her hand to her wrinkled brow. The arm of her knitted cardigan was loose around her frail wrist. It seemed to Elsie that she was smaller with each passing day.

She took off her glasses. "I cannot tell you what you want to know. The reason this treasure is here is my secret. It doesn't concern you. It doesn't matter to anyone but me. What matters is what you do about it. What matters are the obstacles in your way. Your lives are easy. You have no experience with desire because things are handed to you on a platter. Is it wrong to make you work for it? I want you to get your hands dirty. Believe me, it's the best therapy there is." Her shoulders drooped suddenly. She tapped her hands on the table. "I'm sorry, I'm afraid I'm a little weary. I shall retire early." She stood and bid them goodnight.

When she was gone, everyone was left to stare at each other. Robert spoke first. "This is nuts. She's a madwoman, that's all there is to it."

Dahlia folded her arms in front of her. "She always talks about the treasure, but never actually says what it is."

"Yeah," Slater agreed. "Everything seems to be parables and philosophical jargon. What's up with that?"

They turned with opened mouths to stare at him in amazement. He looked embarrassed. "Well, it's true."

Dahlia suddenly said, "Slater, could you come to the library for a moment? Excuse us everyone."

They got up and walked sedately out of the dining room, then took off like scalded cats for the library door. Once behind it, she jumped into his arms and kissed him passionately. "Oh, baby. You have no idea how hot that made me."

"Awesome," he muttered against her mouth. "I have no idea where that came from. Maybe the library's messing with my head. I'm being invaded by words."

She kept her lips on his. "Babe, quit while you're ahead."

The conversation at the dinner table continued. Juliet pointed her tear-soaked napkin in everyone's face. "I think that bonehead's on to something. Maybe she has no real treasure here. She talks about 'finding your treasure,' 'being one with your treasure,' 'the treasure you find is the treasure you deserve.' It's all total bullshit."

"Gosh. Sounds like something my parents used to say," Eli volunteered.

She turned on him "Who gives a fig what your parents used to say?"

Lily gasped. "What gives you the right to talk to him like that? Haven't you made enough of a spectacle of yourself?"

"That's enough," her mother warned.

Lily threw her napkin down and glared at everyone. "I think you grown-ups are pathetic. Why don't you just kill Aunt Hildy now and be done with it. Pick over her bones and see if you can find something that'll make you happy. Because you know what I think? None of you will ever be as happy as she's been. If she's left this so-called treasure for us, that means she's never used it herself…and what does that tell you? Come on Eli, I've got to get out of here."

She left the table and waited by the door. Eli stood. "Thank you for dinner Mrs. B." They walked out hand in hand.

Elsie looked at the others. "Aren't you ashamed of yourselves? Do you see what you're doing? Even our kids know something we don't. This isn't about treasure. It's about us."

Faith stood too. "Spare me the violin music. This is about an old bitch who's got some jewellery hidden in a secret safe and she gets off watching us grovel for it. Nothing more. Nothing less."

"You're right," Juliet rose from the table as well. "And I for one won't let her get away with it."

The two women walked out.

Robert pushed his chair back. "The same goes for me. If there's something here, I'll find it." With that, he left.

Graham looked at her. "I sure as hell won't let that greedy bastard find anything." He took off too.

Elsie was left once again with Flower and Kiwi. She leaned on her elbows and looked at them. "This really stinks." They thumped their tails. She knocked the bread basket off the table. "Have some treasure, girls."

By the time Elsie finished the dishes, she was in a fury, and she knew why. She and Graham had been interrupted and it was all thanks to people who wanted that stupid treasure.

She stormed up the stairs. There was a light on under her aunt's door, so she hurried over and knocked on it.

"Enter."

Aunt Hildy was in bed, with her inevitable book. She looked like an elf wearing flannel pyjamas. Elsie walked over and sat beside her.

"I'm so angry with you. I could spit."

Hildy put her book down. "Oh dear."

"Why are you doing this?"

"Doing what?"

Elsie folded her arms and stared at her.

"Oh, you mean the treasure."

"Tell me. Because if I don't get an explanation…"

"What will you do? Shoot me?"

"I just might."

"How romantic. It would be more thrilling to be shot by a jealous lover of course, but one can't have everything."

"I honestly think you're crazy, Aunt Hildy."

"Of course I am. Was there ever any doubt?"

"So this is a joke?"

She shrugged and gazed at the rings on her hand, not looking up.

"Is it a joke?"

She raised her head. "Sure, it's a joke."

Elsie looked at her and no words came.

"Sorry."

"You're sorry? Guess what? I don't believe you are."

She laughed. "You're quite right."

"I think this is despicable. Does it give you some kind of perverse pleasure to play everyone for a fool?"

Her aunt clasped her hands together in front of her. "I wanted to find out for myself who you people really were. There's nothing like greed to bring one's true character to the surface. Money's a powerful motivator…almost as powerful as love."

Elsie stood. "You have no right to come into my home and create havoc."

"The havoc was already here, my dear. Didn't you know that?"

Elsie's stomach clenched. "You think you know everything. You think because you've lived this eccentric and crazy life, everyone else's is lessened somehow. That we're so inconsequential, it doesn't matter if you use us like rats in a cage. Well, it's not on, Aunt Hildy. I think you owe me an apology. You came back here and I didn't even blink, because I thought it was your right or something. But it's not. You gave away this house a long time ago. This is my home now. I don't owe you anything. You're here by my good grace alone. If you don't stop this nonsense immediately, I'll be forced to ask you to leave. You can die somewhere else and see if strangers aren't better subjects for your cruel games. We don't deserve to be."

The door slammed on her way out. She went downstairs, making sure no one saw her go down to the basement. She knocked softly on Graham's door. He opened it.

"What took you so long?"

She closed the door and leaned against it. Her heart raced a mile a minute. He was gorgeous. He'd always been gorgeous, with that shaggy hair and strong jaw covered with stubble, those big dimples and the scent of him. She needed that on her skin again.

"Crystal said something to me today that made me stop and…"

"When Juliet and Robert walked in on us tonight, I wanted to kill them."

She tried to swallow. "Really?"

"Have you got anything on under that?"

"No," she whispered.

"I want you so bad." He reached out, grabbed her wrist and pulled her to his chest. He put both his hands up through her hair. "I need you, baby." He kissed her then, a deep searching kiss that made her ache. His mouth opened hers and he took her in, made her come closer to him. She didn't want to wait anymore. She pulled him back with her until they banged into the door.

"I want you now," she groaned in his ear. "Do it now."

He reached down and slid his big hands up her legs until they were under her robe, encircling her ribs. As he kissed her, he reached around and lifted her off her feet. He pressed himself against her. In only a moment, he'd have all of her again.

"Oh my God," she moaned. "Hurry."

She was completely unaware of anything except Graham's body moving against hers. So it came as such a shock when she heard Bunny say, "Isn't this cozy?"

Her head flew up and the beads of sweat on her forehead turned cold. Graham suddenly stopped panting and looked around too. There was Bunny, a bottle of champagne in one hand and a jar of caviar in the other, in a dress three sizes too small.

"Put me down."

He did. The three of them stood there for a moment, but it felt like hours.

Bunny smirked at them. "I know you like kinky sex, Graham, but I'm a good girl. I won't do it with you and the missus, so don't even ask me."

Graham buttoned his jeans. "Don't be disgusting."

"Disgusting? We had a date, remember? We made it when you crawled out of my bed this morning." She turned to Elsie. "But I don't recall you being invited."

He looked at his wife. "It wasn't like that…"

"It's okay," Elsie said hoarsely. "This is my fault. I'm sorry." She turned and fumbled with the doorknob.

"He might forgive you, but I won't. Stay away from my man."

Graham ran after Elsie and grabbed her arm.

"Don't, Gray. Just don't."

"But…"

"Please."

He released his grip and let her slip away.

Numb, he turned around, walked over to Bunny and grabbed the champagne bottle out of her hand.

"Do you have the slightest idea what you've just done?"

She stood in front of him and quivered with righteous indignation. "I could ask you the same thing. Don't you dare get snotty with me. You can't use me like Kleenex and then throw me away."

Her counterattack took him by surprise. He was in the right, not her.

She pointed at the door and then back at herself. "She's supposedly not your wife anymore. I was under the impression that you and I were dating. How do you think I feel when just this morning you said you'd take me down south…"

"I didn't. You did."

"You treat me like a prostitute. Did you know that?" Bunny threw the jar of caviar in the sink, smashing it to smithereens.

All the energy drained out of Graham's body. "Just leave, please. I can't deal with this."

"You think you can get rid of me that easy?"

"Apparently not."

Bunny started to cry. "You're so mean. I've only ever been nice to you."

This was worse than her anger. Now he felt sick. He held his head in his hands and took a few deep breaths. That's when he thought of something. "How did you get in here?"

"The door was unlocked. I thought I'd surprise you."

"No it wasn't."

"Yes, it was. Oh, this is rich. Now I'm being accused of breaking into your house." She grabbed the champagne bottle out of his hand. "I'll take this, shall I, and don't you dare come near me unless you intend to apologize."

She stormed out into the night and left the door to bang in the wind. Graham walked over and shut it. He was sure it had been locked, but maybe he was crazy. He threw himself on the sofa and stared at nothing, oblivious to the tears that streamed down his face.

Chapter Nine

Life continued and things calmed down, as things usually do. Elsie took a week off to try and sort herself out. It was fall, Elsie's favourite time of the year, so she spent most of her days out in the garden. She enjoyed the work involved in making sure her plants, bushes and shrubs weathered the winter. Every year she planted more bulbs and gathered the fallen leaves to use in her compost. By the end of every day her hands were raw with cold.

Aunt Hildy didn't exactly apologize, but Elsie knew she was contrite. She made an effort to help with any small task, and liked to sit on the iron bench under the dogwood tree and polish Elsie's gardening tools. She told stories about her mother and what plants she grew to help her family through the harsh Maritime winters.

Sometimes the girls joined them, Dahlia usually with a *Modern Bride* magazine in tow. She'd fill out the wedding quizzes and grill her mother on proper etiquette for every nuptial occasion.

"How can you be the mother of the bride, if you don't know how to do it?"

Aunt Hildy finally spoke up. "What codswallop. Your mother is the mother of the bride. End of story."

"Well, she's suppose to know stuff."

"Like what, pray tell?"

"Like who sits where at the head table and who stands where in the receiving line."

Aunt Hildy slapped her hands on her knees, creating a puff of dust. "That's ridiculous. Do you want to strangle every bit of joy out of your big day?"

Dahlia looked resentful. "I'm not."

"I beg to differ. You make this ceremony sound about as much fun as a funeral march."

Dahlia stuck out her chin. "Have you ever organized a wedding?"

"That's none of your business, missy." Aunt Hildy stood and walked quickly to the house.

She looked at her mom with big eyes. "I only asked a question."

Elsie stuck her pitchfork in a mound of dirt. "Well, don't."

Inside, Robert was on his hands and knees behind the cupboard of the sewing room, attempting to pry off a piece of moulding with a butter knife.

He whispered to Juliet, who was keeping watch. "What room adjoins this one?"

"The bathroom. The far wall I think but I'm not sure."

"Because there's a hole behind this board. Maybe it's a hiding spot."

"I bloody well hope so. I'm tired of doing nothing but crawl around and ruin every pair of pants I own."

"Where's Faith? I don't want her here."

Juliet reassured him. "She's in the laundry chute."

"And the others?"

"They're out in the garden."

"Good." He grunted. "I've almost got it. Just one more nail." The moulding popped off in his hand. "Pass me the flashlight."

Juliet looked in the pocket of her sweater. She took out

a small torch and turned it on. It didn't work. "Damn. The battery's dead."

"Oh, typical."

"It's not my fault. I told you to get more."

"Fine. Never mind." Robert got down on his stomach and gingerly put his hand into the opening.

"Do you feel anything?"

"Just a lot of grit. This is disgusting work. If I get bitten by a spider, I might sue."

His fingers felt around. Suddenly he touched something cold. It felt like a hand. He screamed and bucked around on the floor as he tried to get his arm out of the hole.

On the other side of the wall, Faith did the same, hitting her head against the sink as she tried to get away from the hairy hand in the wall.

The two of them ran out of the adjoining rooms at the same time, screaming like children. Juliet hopped up and down. "What happened?"

Hildy hurried up the stairs, brandishing a cane. "Who died?"

Faith gasped and held her chest. "There's a hand behind the wall in the bathroom."

"I felt it too." Robert slumped against the door jam. "Behind the sewing room cupboard. A dead body."

Hildy stood still for a moment and processed the information. Then lowered her cane and said with exasperation, "Do you always shake hands with Faith through a layer of drywall?"

No one said anything.

"The sooner I die and get away from you people, the happier I'll be." She marched into her room and slammed the door.

They looked at each other. Juliet shot daggers at them equally. "I don't know who's more stupid."

"Next time Robert," Faith fumed, "When I'm upstairs, you stay downstairs. I don't need any more grey hair."

"If you'd stayed in the laundry chute, none of this would've happened."

"I'll send you a detailed report of my future whereabouts from now on. How will that be?" She stomped upstairs to the attic.

A couple of days later, Juliet phoned Faith to tell her that she and Robert had a bad case of the flu, so it was up to Faith to continue the search by herself. "An opportunity," she whispered, "to find something without you-know-who around."

What Juliet didn't know was that it occurred to Faith that she'd like it if neither one of them showed up for a while. They'd been breathing down her neck and it annoyed her, especially after the bathroom incident.

With Elsie back to work the next morning, Faith thought she'd have the opportunity to nose around at her leisure, but almost instantly there was another snafu. Aunt Hildy declared she had a sniffle, so rather than venturing down to the garden, she spent the morning in bed. Disappointed she wouldn't be able to snoop in her aunt's room, Faith tackled the girls' room instead, making sure to check on her dear aunt first.

She knocked lightly on the door.

"Enter."

Faith walked in. Aunt Hildy sat in bed with what looked like an army jacket on, surrounded by books of all sorts, scribbling in a journal.

"I thought I'd write this morning, Aunt Hildy, so I wanted to know if you needed anything before I get started. It's annoying to be on a creative roll, only to be interrupted."

"I know all about interruptions, Faith. I'm enduring one now."

"Sorry. So you're okay then?"

"Yes, thank you. I'm fine. Toddle off."

Faith stole a glance around the room. Talk about treasure. There were hundreds of items that would fetch a hefty sum. Surely, a few trinkets wouldn't be missed. Hopefully her cold would be over soon.

The door closed, she snuck across the hall into Dahlia's room. What a disaster times two — more clothes on the floor than in the closets or drawers. The bureau tops resembled cosmetic and jewellery counters.

If I were a treasure, where would I be? Probably right out in the open because with all this stuff thrown about, you'd never see it.

Faith picked her way across the room, throwing clothes about. Surely the girls had searched this room already, but maybe they'd found something and kept it from the rest of the family. She rifled through some of their bureau drawers just to be on the safe side, but that proved fruitless. There was nothing there but a fortune in pretty underwear. God. She'd worn bloomers at their age. Life was so unfair.

The makeup table that belonged to her mother was in the corner, its beauty lost, hidden under a mess of twisted cords attached to blow dryers and flatirons. Faith went over and sat on the upholstered bench in front of the mirror. She and her sisters had loved to watch their mother brush her long wavy brown hair before she twisted it into a bun at the nape of her neck. The silver brush and comb set she used was made in Vienna, a gift from her sister Hildy. Her mother would touch the engraved initials, and put it to her cheek.

Don't think about Mom.

Moving quickly to the other side of the room, Faith felt around and looked in obvious spots, the back of the radiators, under the beds, and the window seat. She even used a chair to search the top of a large wardrobe. Finally she rifled through the closet, throwing things behind her in an attempt to expose the deep recesses of the space. That's when she noticed an interesting mark on the wall — a square of newer paint applied over old.

She reached to touch the spot.

"Aww…I see you."

Faith whipped around, her heart aflutter. She was busted.

"Do de do."

"Who's there?"

"Me no like."

God. This was insane. Then she saw it. A stupid Furby come to life. She grabbed it.

"Whoa," it protested.

Faith threw it against the opposite wall. A muffled "Again," came from a pile of jeans.

"Shut up."

It did.

"God damn toys they make nowadays," she muttered. She turned her attention back to the wall. She felt around the square, tingling with excitement. The wall was softer in the middle. She pushed hard, and the square bit of gyprock fell into the hole.

She didn't know what to do first: scream Hallelujah or pass out. She put her hand inside, mindful that if she bumped into something this time, she was in deep trouble.

Her hand touched something and she held her breath. If this was it, a new life beckoned. She lifted her prize out of its hiding spot — it was an old jewellery box. She closed her eyes and crossed herself. Even a Baptist needed help at a time like this. She opened the lid and squealed.

Inside was a pile of jewellery, just like in the movies or on a cartoon, all heaped together, apparently dumped in at the same time. The baubles looked more real than real. There had to be hundreds of thousands of dollars' worth of stones in the settings alone.

"Thank you God," she whispered to the closet ceiling. "I'll never ask you for anything again."

Realizing she better scram, she reached into the hole to retrieve the square bit of wall. It took a few moments to manoeuvre it back into place. Just as she threw Furby and a pile of stuff back in the closet to hide the evidence, Flower barked. She ran across the room and out the door. She had almost made it to the attic when Lily ran up the stairs.

Faith hid the jewellery box behind her back and inched toward her escape hatch.

"Hi. Have you found the treasure today, Aunt Faith? You wouldn't keep something from us, would you?"

"Don't be crazy. As if I'd do something like that."

Lily started for her room when she turned. "What's behind your back then?"

"There's nothing behind my back!"

"Gee. What a grouch."

Faith tried to recover. "It's a box of cookies if you must know. I'm on a diet and it's embarrassing to be caught, that's all."

Lily shrugged. "It's your body."

"That's right. It is. So if you'll excuse me." She backed into her open door and disappeared.

That night the four kids were up until the wee hours playing 45's at the kitchen table. It was slow-going, with Slater confused about the "thirty for sixty" rule.

"Why didn't you bid, Slater?" Dahlia grumped.

"You told me not too. Don't do anything, you said, unless I have every-thing. Well, I didn't have everything. I didn't have the ace of hearts."

"No, I had the ace of hearts. You have to rely on your partner sometimes, you big lug."

"Hey. How did I know you had it?"

"When your back's against the wall you have to risk it. These two creeps are only five points away from winning. You have to keep the bid away from them."

Eli rubbed his hands together. "I can't wait to whip your butt, Dee. You're the world's biggest whiner when you lose."

"How on earth would you know?"

"Your sister told me."

Dahlia frowned. "Does my sister tell you everything about me?"

"There's not that much to tell," Lily laughed. "You lead a pretty boring life."

Dahlia shuffled the cards. "Is that so? Well, there are a few things you don't know about me. I'm not that boring, am I, Slater?"

"That's for sure. You should see what…"

"Slater! Keep your mouth shut!"

Lily leaned across the table. "What? What did she do?"

"It's none of your business," Dahlia insisted.

"Then why did you bring it up? Is it something you're ashamed of? Something you don't want anyone to see?"

"If that's the case you better get rid of it," Eli said. "Someone might find it when they're looking for the treasure."

Dahlia and Slater looked at each other. He smacked his own head. "Where'd you put the pictures?"

Lily shoved Eli's shoulder. "My god, you're right. What about that thing you bought me."

"What thing?" Dahlia and Slater asked together.

"A none-of-your-business thing." Lily put her hand over her mouth. "What if Uncle Robert found it? Ewww!"

Eli jumped up. "What if your father finds it?"

"I told you to leave it at your place, but nooo. Wonderful Mrs. Minelli might stumble across it. You guys take off. We have to go thing hunting."

"Don't forget the video," Slater whispered as Dahlia pushed him out the door. Eli ran back to get his cards but Lily stopped him. "Never mind. Get them tomorrow. Go."

The girls took the stairs two at a time and zoomed into their bedroom, both of them in a panic to remember favourite hiding places. Everything was rearranged because of the sharing of rooms and nothing was where it should've been.

"I can't believe this," Dahlia sobbed. "I can't wait to get out of this nut house and into my own place, where I can put my pictures on the wall if I want to."

"You want them on the wall? Not if you want me to come over."

"Oh, shut up." She threw things out of a trunk. "Pictures are at least normal. What's a thing when it's at home?"

Lily reached under the bed. "In today's world, it's normal."

"If it's so normal, why are you in a frenzy to find it?"

"Because it's mine."

They frantically scrounged around but were interrupted by a small voice.

"Whoa. Whoa. Me scared."

The two looked at each other.

Lily crossed the floor on her knees and opened the closet door. "Wow. It's so tidy." She grabbed Furby by the ear.

"Yippee. Party."

"Go see Aunt Dee." She tossed Furby over to her sister.

"Hee Hee."

"Hard to believe it still talks after six years. Kind of spooky really."

As Lily rummaged around, she remembered how guilty Faith had looked when she caught her in the hallway earlier. "Wait till I get my hands on that woman. She has no right…."

"What?"

"Come here."

Dahlia crawled over to the closet.

Lily pointed to the back. They stared at the cut-out square Faith had tried to replace. They looked at each other and burst out laughing. They laughed so hard they couldn't breathe, so hard they couldn't see because of their tears.

"Oh my God. This is too good to be true," Lily wheezed as she lay on the floor. Dahlia wiped her eyes with her sleeve. "I forgot all about it. Can you believe it?"

"I forgot about it too. Can you imagine the fun we'll have, now that Faith thinks she's found the treasure?"

Dahlia leaned against the wall. "It was Faith? How can she

believe a bunch of costume jewellery is the real thing? I mean, how dumb is she?"

"Remember when we hid it? What...nine years ago? I forget."

"All I know is that I can't wait to see her face when we tell her."

Lily nodded. "But we won't tell her too soon."

Dahlia looked at the time. "It's three in the morning. Time to find our treasure and hit the hay."

Faith gazed at the jewellery box for two days, waiting for Juliet to feel better. The stomach-turning excitement had worn off, but the idea that it was even there and in her possession caused a small shiver of anticipation every time she thought about it.

A pair of dangly emerald earrings caught her fancy right from the beginning, and she had a great time waltzing up to the calendar, where Mr. October squatted by a fire truck, his big hose dangling across one knee.

"Do you like?" she asked him. "I put them on just for you."

Apparently he didn't care. Oh well, what did he know about jewellery?

It was time to try on the ruby necklace. This is what she'd wear to the Oscars when her name was announced as the winner for Best Screenplay. Glancing at the popcorn bowl to the right of the couch and acknowledging the applause from the dirty glasses on the left, she leapt up and blew kisses to the crowd. Reaching for a bottle of hand lotion, it was time to thank the academy for this magnificent award. A big grin and exit stage right.

Faith flopped on the bed.

For God's sake, Juliet. Hurry up and get well.

Two days later and still no word from Juliet. Faith didn't dare call her, knowing darn well Juliet would scream or jump up and down and Robert would be alerted that something was up. With nothing better to do, it was time to spy on the neighbours. She wandered over to the back window and reached for her binoculars.

Hmm. Mrs. Noseworthy and Aunt Hildy were standing by the hedge but kept moving every so often, a few feet at a time. What were they up to? From the looks of it, deadheading flowers along the fence. Perfect. This would be a good chance to sneak into her aunt's room for a moment. She knew the girls were gone — she'd seen the breakfast mess in the kitchen when she went down to raid the fridge.

She snuck to the second floor and listened. The house was quiet, so she tiptoed over to the door and opened it carefully. She didn't close it behind her in case she needed a quick escape.

It was impossible to know where to start. Aunt Hildy's possessions overwhelmed her. The room was ablaze with colour; it spoke of history and stories, adventure and mystery. Imagine having such a life.

Faith gulped. "How come it's never me."

A collection of frames sat on a bookshelf, black and white pictures of Aunt Hildy as a young woman. She stood with groups of men and held up artifacts in front of excavation sites. They smiled for the camera, proud of their accomplishments. In most of the pictures, she wore pants, a tall slender figure, who, except for the kerchief around her hair, looked like one of the boys.

Faith noticed a small photo in an ornate frame on the bedside table. She picked it up. It was a girl, her face half hidden by a shadow, and a young man who kissed her hand. It was the look on the girl's face as she watched him that captivated Faith. It was beautiful. Was it Aunt Hildy? It was hard to tell. They were outdoors. Someone must have caught their image at a picnic or a garden party, a brief moment in time years and years ago, but alive in the picture Faith held. She felt the love between them.

Who was he? Faith traced her finger along their silhouettes. Imagine being that girl. Imagine knowing their story. What a story it would be.

"Yes. That's me."

Faith swung around. Aunt Hildy stood in the doorway looking amused.

"I wasn't snooping," she said in a hurry. "I thought I heard one of the cats in here, so I came to look."

"You're welcome to come in here. My doors aren't locked."

"How old were you in this picture?"

Hildy crossed the room and took the frame from her. "Seventeen."

"Where was it taken?"

"Point Pleasant Park."

"Who was he?"

Her aunt gave her a quick glance. "A friend."

"A boyfriend?"

"A boyfriend?" She shook her head. "No."

Faith was disappointed. "Oh. I thought he might be."

"He was more than that."

"Really?"

"Maybe. Maybe not."

"Why don't you ever give anyone a straight answer? It's so annoying."

Aunt Hildy put down the picture and sat in her armchair. "Have you ever heard of a secret, Faith? Do you know what it is? It's when something happens that's so private, you don't want to share it with anyone." Her hands gripped the arms of her chair. "The only ones who do know the story are dead. I am the only one left, and I intend to take my secret to the grave."

"This story has something to do with why the treasure is here?"

The old woman gave a little smile. "Maybe, maybe not."

Faith thought of the jewellery box upstairs. To deflect suspicion, she said casually, "I don't believe there's anything here. And I think it's really silly to pretend there is."

"There's plenty of treasure for you, Faith. You just have to know where to look."

She was tired of this mumbo jumbo. "Look. This is ridiculous, Aunt Hildy. You're manipulating us like puppets on a string. You can't do that to people. You've no right." Faith crossed the room and paused at the door. "It's not fair."

After her niece had gone, Hildy looked at the picture and touched the young man's face. "Life isn't fair. Not fair at all. But I'm almost home, Nikolai. I'll be with you soon, my love."

❧

"Robert, give me that ice pack." Juliet grabbed it from him.

"I'm sick too, ya know," he moaned.

She pushed him over to his side of the bed. "You're not as sick as I am…God. Must you hog all the space?"

"I'm not hogging all the space."

"You are so. Isn't he Kiwi?"

Kiwi jumped up and bounced on Robert's stomach. "Gawd. Get this demon from hell off me."

Juliet looked furious. "How can you talk to Kiwi that way? I'm glad we never had kids. You would've shipped them off to boarding school in the blink of an eye."

"No, I wouldn't. I'd ship you off instead." Robert coughed, sneezed and farted all at the same time.

"That's it. That's it. I don't care how sick I am. I'm not lying around with a sniffling disgusting pig," Juliet said, and leaped out of bed.

He belched. "Don't forget bankrupt."

"Fine. A bankrupt, sniffling disgusting pig." She stormed into the bathroom. "I'm going to Faith's. I need to get out of here."

He took a coughing fit. "Great. Just great. Leave me here to languish on my own."

His wife stomped back in the room. "Are you completely stupid? I'm sacrificing my health to go over there and try to find that damn treasure so we can get out of this mess you created and all you can do is complain about how selfish I am. Do you realize what I'm sacrificing? I may end up with pneumonia. How do you like them apples?"

She marched out of the room once more and turned the shower on full blast.

Robert reached across the bed to grab more Kleenex from Juliet's bedside table, along with the TV remote, painkillers, cough drops and heating pad.

He sat up and let one go, just for dirt.

"I heard that!"

"Good."

Kiwi's nose went twitchy. She scurried off the bed.

A few minutes later, Juliet was back. She rushed around, grabbing some clothes.

"You're in an awful hurry for someone so desperately ill."

"There's no time to lose. I've had it. I refuse to skulk around anymore. I'll take a sledgehammer to that place."

He watched her and suddenly had a horrible thought. "You'll take off with all the money, won't you?"

She dressed as she talked. "Don't be stupid."

"I'm not stupid. It just dawned on me that since you hate me so much, you'll do a runner."

"You're delusional. Stop whining and let me out of here. The sooner I find the stuff, the better off we'll be."

He leapt out of bed. "I won't let you go alone. I don't trust you."

Her mouth dropped open. "You actually think I'd take it all myself?"

He gave her a beady eye that turned into a staring match; neither one of them blinked. He wasn't going to let her win this time. He'd stay like a statue forever if he had too. But she looked frozen, and Kiwi was circling his legs, and it was creeping him out. When Kiwi crouched and peed on his foot, he exploded.

"You little shit!" The chase was on.

"Leave her alone, you big bully." Juliet grabbed a bottle of Rolaids and whipped it at her husband's head. It missed by an inch.

"I've had it." He turned and chased Juliet around the bed. She jumped on the mattress and tried to crawl away but he grabbed her pant leg.

"Get off me." She kicked at him with her free leg.

"Stop kicking me."

"I'll kick you all I want." And she did, until Robert let out such a howl of pain, she stopped instantly.

"What's wrong?"

Robert's face screwed up in agony, beads of sweat on his forehead.

"Are you having a heart attack? God, Robert, thanks a lot. That's all I need."

"My ass," was all he said through clenched teeth.

"Your ass? What about it?" She looked behind him. Kiwi hung off Robert's rear end, her razor sharp teeth planted firmly in his pyjama bottoms.

"Oh, isn't that cute. She's protecting her mommy." She reached over to pry Kiwi off. Robert screamed again.

"Don't be such a baby. Give me a second." She gave it another try and yanked Kiwi away from him.

His head flopped on the mattress. She took a peek under his pyjamas. "There's no blood. It's not that bad."

Robert said in a low voice, "Take that fluffy piranha and get out of here."

Juliet hopped out of bed and held her baby. "She didn't mean it. She thought you were trying to kill me. It's her instinct to go after someone who wants to hurt me."

"And at this moment, it's my instinct to kill you both, so I suggest you go and leave me alone."

She grabbed her purse. "You don't have to be nasty, Robert. She's only a little dog."

"But you're the bitch."

"You horrid man. If you don't watch it mister, I may just take everything for myself." She turned to go.

"Your whole family can rot in hell as far as I'm concerned. You're all idiots."

"You should know. You've been one your whole life."

Juliet drove to Elsie's, with every intention of staying until she found something. Anything. She'd pilfer Aunt Hildy's room if she had to. She was desperate. She hadn't had a manicure in a week and it was driving her to distraction. She couldn't figure out why things never went her way. There was always disaster behind everything she did. She felt cursed.

How come the old bag had such a great life? Who was she to deserve everything? Aunt Hildy was born in that house too. She wasn't anything special, yet she always held herself above the rest of them. It made Juliet sick.

She carried Kiwi out of the car and saw Mrs. Noseworthy head her way. Great. That's all she needed. That old fruitcake.

"Hello Juliet. Are you here for treasure?"

She looked down her nose at the tiny woman. "Of course not. You don't believe that stuff, do you?"

Mrs. Noseworthy grinned. "Of course I do. Your Aunt Hildy's a smart woman. She knows where it is."

She stopped and changed her demeanour. "Yes, of course, you're right. I know there's treasure. Did she say where it was?"

"It's everywhere."

"Everywhere?"

"She tells me where."

Juliet could hardly breathe she was so excited. "Really? Aren't you lucky? Where is it?"

"Oh, let me think." She tapped her cheek with her finger. "There's some in the birdhouse. There's some behind the kitchen clock. And then there's stuff hanging off the ceiling.

I'm sure she told me that. Or was it in the banisters? I get confused."

A tiny nerve in Juliet's left eyelid exploded, causing it to flutter uncontrollably. She almost smacked the demented old fool. Instead, she walked away without saying a word and slammed the screen door behind her.

She pounded up to the attic, where Faith was at her computer, as usual. Her sister looked up. "Well, it's about time."

"I couldn't have stayed with Robert one more minute."

"How are you, anyway?"

"Lousy. Fed up. Cranky. Miserable. Take your pick."

"Completely normal then."

"What a card." She put Kiwi down. "I nearly swallowed my tongue out there. Mrs. Noseworthy told me she knew where the treasure was. Turns out she's nuts. Treasure in the birdhouse. Really."

"There isn't. I checked."

"You checked? You're nuttier than she is."

Faith lit a cigarette. "You have to look everywhere if you're going to be successful." She took a long drag and blew smoke rings.

Juliet sat in an old armchair and watched her. "Wait a minute, you know something, don't you?"

"Maybe. Maybe not."

"Cut the crap. Out with it."

Faith crushed her cigarette and bounced out of her chair. Reaching for the garment bag that hung in her closet, she zipped it open, reached in and extracted the box.

Juliet jumped up and down. "I don't believe it. Why didn't you call me?"

She brought it to the couch and the two of them sat on either end of it. "I didn't want Robert to overhear anything."

"That was very good thinking," Juliet concurred. "Good for you."

Faith looked smug.

Juliet clapped her hands. "Come on, hurry up."

She opened it slowly.

"My God, look at this. It actually looks like treasure." Juliet reached out and grabbed a handful of jewellery. "It's beautiful. This must be worth a fortune."

"I know. I've counted everything. If we get top dollar for it, it'll keep us going for the rest of our days."

Juliet picked up a huge ruby brooch. "Imagine what we can buy with this."

"We can buy whatever we want."

"I'll buy a first-class ticket to Paris. And I'll stay at the Ritz."

"I'll go to Paris too. I'll buy a garret and drink wine and write in cafés. I'll be a bohemian. How romantic. All those gorgeous Frenchmen." Faith looked out the window and sighed. "I won't be lonely anymore."

"Of course you won't. You can have anyone you want when you're rich."

Faith sat back. "Some people get who they want without being rich."

"No one I know," Juliet sniffed.

"You won't tell Robert about this?"

"Not on your life. The way he spoke to me today, he can kiss me goodbye. You wouldn't believe what he called Kiwi, the big meany."

"How will we get this out of here? Who do we sell it too?"

"You leave that to me." Juliet put the jewellery back and closed the lid. "Maybe I should take it now, in case someone finds it here. I'll bring it to a jeweller I know. One of Robert's associates — he'll keep quiet though."

As she spoke, Juliet stood with the box in her hands, but Faith reached over and grabbed it. "I don't think so, Sis."

"What do you mean, you don't think so? Don't you trust me?"

Her sister smirked a little. "Not really."

"Faith, you can be so annoying."

"I'd rather be annoying than careless. I found it. If it goes, I go."

Juliet shrugged. "Fine. Whatever. Do what you want." She grabbed Kiwi and sat back on the couch.

"Don't get so bent out of shape. I didn't have to tell you I found it. You could've come over here today and found me long gone."

She pressed her lips together. "I suppose so."

"Let's enjoy this, Juliet. We found it and the rest of them didn't. We're the winners, not them."

"You're right. Hurray for us."

Later that afternoon Dahlia, Slater, Lily and Eli sat together on the floor in front of the fire in the library and tried to approach the treasure-hunting in a more organized fashion. They realized they were working at cross-purposes by doing everything separately. Four heads were better than two. Well, three heads really.

"Slater. There is no map. Why would she leave a map? She already told us it's here. It's not like searching a deserted island."

"Where there's treasure, there's always a map. It's treasure law."

Lily looked at Eli, who refused to look back at her, the coward. "Treasure law? What the hell is treasure law? Are you an authority on treasure law?"

Eli grimaced. "Lily, leave it."

"No, I want to know."

"Treasure law's awesome. It's the pirate's code."

"And you want to marry this guy?" she said clearly, looking at her sister.

Dahlia snuggled into him. "He knows all about pirates, don't you, Slater. Pirates plunder and pillage and kidnap women and have their way with them."

Slater grabbed her hair and pulled her into his lap. "I love plundering…" He cupped her face in his hand and bent down to kiss her.

The other two stared.

"Excuse me," Lily said. "There are innocent villagers here."

"Go get your own pirate, Lily," Dahlia murmured.

Eli got up and pulled her with him. "She's right. Let's get out of here. My timbers are shivering."

Lily pouted as she was dragged across the room. "So much for trea-sure hunting."

"Well, I wouldn't say that. I'm still searching for booty, baby, and I think I know just where to find it."

She giggled. They rushed out the door and nearly careened into Aunt Hildy.

"Sorry," they said together.

"That's quite all right," she said. "I'm only returning a book on astrology. It was a fascinating read. Excuse me."

Before the kids could stop her she pushed her way in, just in time to hear Dahlia say,

"Oh, Captain Kidd! Don't lash me to the mast. I'll do anything you want...just don't tie me up."

"I'll make you walk the plank if you don't obey my every command."

Aunt Hildy pulled the door shut quietly and leaned against it.

"I'll say this for them. They keep themselves amused."

Elsie couldn't wait to get home. She'd had a bitch of a day at work. Mrs. Abernathy had been in. In spite of the list (3 "come back"/42 "stay away"), she'd let Mr. Abernathy come home. A week later she'd found him and the cleaning lady under the covers on their king-sized bed.

To top it off, Elsie met Harry for lunch but they didn't stay in the café for long. He managed to persuade her to come back to his place. He said she deserved a little attention. Afterwards, she buttoned up her blouse and listened to him whistling in the bathroom. At least someone was happy.

Unable to cope with anything that night at home, she ordered three large pizzas and told the girls to divvy them up when they arrived. She had a monster headache and the usual chaos that swirled around her didn't help her mood any.

Graham banged on pipes downstairs. She hoped it was to fix the hot water tank, but since she'd been avoiding him, she couldn't be sure he wasn't just having a snoop around. Her sisters seemed to be up to something in the sunroom. Their heads were bent together over a travel brochure and when she tried to join them, they shut it and clammed up. The girls were baking cookies in the pantry — making a horrible mess to judge by the flour on the floor — while Aunt Hildy entertained the boys in the kitchen with her story of the time she was on a ship that almost sank off the coast of China.

Slater hollered, "I bet pirates sank that ship. I wouldn't put it past those dudes."

When he began to tell everyone about a code for pirates, Elsie did herself a favour and tuned him out.

She'd started for the stairs when the front doorbell rang. She went to answer it, Flower at her heels. That's when she noticed dog barf in the corner of the front porch. Perfect. She looked at Flower. Flower stared into middle space and pretended it wasn't there.

"Not to fret, Flower. I don't see it either."

She opened the door and Mrs. Noseworthy barged in. "I have frozen runner beans for your supper."

"That'll go well with pepperoni pizza. Thanks Mrs. ..." but the woman was gone, headed for the kitchen. Elsie almost had the door shut when she saw a subdued Robert approaching with a bouquet of roses.

"For me?"

"They might as well be, for all the good they'll do."

"Whatever it is, I'm sure it'll help. Women love roses."

He gave her a weak smile. "These are for Juliet, remember."

"That's true. Good luck. She's in the sunroom."

He schlepped past her and disappeared.

"Everyone's here," Elsie whispered to Flower as they trudged upstairs. "Everyone's always here."

Finally in her room, Elsie took off her clothes and wrapped her old bathrobe around herself. With Flower at her feet, she sat at her dressing table and held back her hair with her hands as she peered into the mirror. "I need to make some changes."

She sat for a bit. "Who's going to care if I do?" She sat for a little longer and realized her bathrobe really was in rough shape. "I can buy a new one. That's a start."

Flower pushed her thigh with a flat rubbery nose. Elsie looked down. "Do you want Mommy to get a new bathrobe?"

Flower gave her a low woof.

"That's what I thought. Now, if you'll excuse me, I'm in dire need of a bubble bath."

At the word bath, Flower tore out of the room.

Five minutes later, her hair held up in a big clip, Elsie eased herself into the heavenly hot water and closed her eyes. Maybe now she could cry. Maybe she could have one moment of privacy to let it all out.

There was a crash, followed by a bang, then a yell from downstairs.

Maybe not.

"If I ignore it, it will go away."

No such luck. It came to her.

Dahlia ran into the bathroom. "I need a towel." She grabbed one and took off.

Lily was right behind her. "I need gauze." She left.

Slater burst in. "Dee told me to get hydrogen peroxide." He looked around.

She pointed. "It's in the medicine cabinet."

Elsie started to cry — but of course, was interrupted. Faith wanted antibiotic cream.

Elsie had had enough.

"What in blue blazes is going on down there?"

"Stupid Robert tried to kiss Juliet and Kiwi went berserk."

"Good lord. Is he all right?"

"Once his ass is in a sling, he'll be fine." She looked around. "You don't have any of that sterile adhesive tape do you? And maybe a rolled bandage?"

Elsie sighed. "You may find some in my dresser. Bottom left-hand drawer."

She heard more drawers open and close than was necessary. "It's in the bottom drawer. On the left."

Faith returned. She held the music box.

"What's this?"

Elsie stammered, "Something Aunt Hildy gave me."

Faith nodded slowly. "Oh really? She gave you something, but not us. I don't think I believe you. I think you hid it. All that mealy-mouthed crap about having to share everything. You had no intention of telling us about this."

"It's not what you think. She gave that to me. I didn't ask her to. She just did."

"You're a liar."

Elsie leapt out of the tub. Faith screamed and took off. Quickly wrapping herself in a towel, Elsie made chase down the stairs. By the time they reached the kitchen, Elsie almost had her.

Everyone was gathered around Robert. Even Graham was there.

Aunt Hildy bristled and rose to her feet. "What's going on? This has got to be the most ridiculous family I've ever run across."

"And you're the head of it," Graham pointed out. He handed a glass of brandy to Robert-the-victim.

"Elsie said for all of us to share the treasure and look what I found in her drawer. Liar liar, pants on fire." Faith held up the music box for everyone to see. It glittered in the evening light that came through the kitchen window.

Mrs. Noseworthy hopped up and down. "We found the treasure. We found the treasure."

Juliet looked shocked. She turned to Elsie. "Is it true? You tried to pull a fast one?"

"Mrs. B would never do that," Slater warned her.

"Shut up. This is none of your business."

Someone knocked at the back door and Flower raised the alarm.

"Oh for the love of Mike. Who's that?" Graham grumbled as he headed for the door.

"Mario's Pizza." A kid pushed his way in with three large boxes. "Holy shit," he said when he spied Robert. He took a step backwards. "Ah…that'll be forty-two bucks."

Everyone patted down their pockets but no one produced anything.

"Do I have to do everything in this house?" Elsie crossed the kitchen in her bath towel, bubbles still clinging to her legs. She reached for her purse and took out fifty bucks, handing it to the delivery boy.

"Keep the change dear, because you've earned it."

"Thanks lady." He backed out the door as fast as he could.

Elsie turned to face them. "I don't give a monkey's uncle if you believe me or not. Aunt Hildy gave me that box. I didn't sneak up a heating vent or shimmy my way down the chimney to dig it out of the soot."

She adjusted her towel. "And since you're all here, I might as well tell you. There is no treasure, is there Aunt Hildy?"

All eyes turned to her. Even Robert straightened up.

"Tell them."

"No. There isn't."

Everyone screamed at once. Amid the noise and confusion, Faith banged the table to get everyone's attention. "You guys are idiots…there is treasure. And I found it."

Now there was complete silence. "I found it and I'm keeping it."

"Did you know about this Juliet?" Robert demanded.

She shrugged. "No…sort of…maybe."

Faith turned to her sister. "Don't be such a wimp. Tell them. Tell them I'm not crazy."

Juliet crossed her arms. "She's right. There is a box of treasure. We found it and possession is nine tenths of the law."

"There is no we," Faith shouted. "I found it."

Elsie looked at her aunt. "So you lied to me? I can't believe a thing you say."

Lily spoke up. "Faith didn't find treasure, did she Dee?"

Her sister agreed. "No, she didn't. She found our costume jewellery. We hid it behind the wall. Remember when you gave us that old junk jewellery when we were kids, Mrs. Noseworthy?"

Mrs. Noseworthy looked worried. "I did? I don't remember. Was that wrong?"

Faith panicked. "No. No. It's in a box. It's old and it's full of stuff. It was behind the wall. I'll go get it." She put down the music box and took off like a flash.

Graham shouted, "Why do you let this old woman wreck our lives, Elsie? Why has she come into this house and turned it upside down? No one should have to live like this. If this is a hoax, I wash my hands of this whole business."

"This doesn't concern you anymore, Graham," Elsie said quietly. "Go and live your own life. Aunt Hildy isn't your problem now. Neither are we."

Lily turned to her father and started to cry. "You always yell at Mom. This isn't her fault."

Eli took Lily in his arms and cradled her head. "This is very upsetting for Lily, Mr. Brooks. I don't think you realize the emotional turmoil your separation has caused. And I don't want to see her hurt anymore. I think she should come home with me."

Not to be outdone, Slater grabbed Dahlia around the waist. "Yeah, this sucks."

Dahlia nodded and looked at her father. "Big time. Everyone has ignored my wedding."

Graham pulled his hands through his hair, looking like he wanted to jump out the window. "How come no one else can see what's going on? We are all tap-dancing to a crazy woman's tune. She's unstable and yet you insist on believing every word she says."

"You've been looking for this treasure too," Juliet reminded him, "so don't get all holier than thou on us."

"I'm done. Do you hear me? Done."

Faith rushed back with the box and spilled it open over the kitchen table. Everyone looked at it.

Mrs. Noseworthy picked up a brooch. "I wondered where that went."

Faith looked at her aunt.

"I'm sorry, my dear. These aren't my things. This is not the treasure I referred to."

Juliet stomped her foot. "I don't believe it. How could you have been so stupid, Faith."

Faith looked stunned. The blood drained from her face.

Robert grabbed the table top, in an effort to keep upright. "Aunt Hildy, you just told us there's no treasure. So what treasure are you referring to now?"

Juliet walked over and picked up the music box. "I suppose it's this? Then why does Elsie get it and not us? How much is it worth anyway?"

Aunt Hildy gathered herself up to her full height.

"That music box was a gift given to me by someone I loved. I gave it to her in a spur-of-the-moment gesture. It's the gift she was to receive upon my death. As I've told you before, you will all receive a gift. And despite the ridiculous goings-on here tonight, you will still get those gifts." She paused and looked at Juliet. "I'm appalled that you would ask about its worth. Is that how you judge a gift?"

Juliet kept quiet.

"I've made very few mistakes in my life. And I have even fewer regrets. But I must admit, I do regret the mention of the word *treasure*."

Everyone looked glum.

"Oh my, what a bunch. You're all spoiled brats if you ask me. Fine. I'll give you one more clue, but that's it." She paused. "You've all seen it."

Juliet threw her hands in the air. "Here we go again. I can't believe this."

Aunt Hildy suddenly looked very tired. Elsie went over to her. "Let's go to bed. I think there's been enough fun and games tonight."

"Yes. Let's." She took Elsie's arm and gave them a brief wave. "Goodnight. Goodnight. Parting is such sweet sorrow…"

"Blah, blah blah," Juliet grumped. "We know the rest."

As Aunt Hildy and Elsie left, Juliet fell into a kitchen chair and looked at Faith, who was still in a state of shock.

"Snap out of if, Faith. Look at the difference. It's obvious." She held up some of the costume jewellery and put it next to the bejewelled box. "There's no comparison."

Faith nodded.

Mrs. Noseworthy pointed to her things. "Well, I think this treasure is nice too. I like it."

Dahlia gathered up the jewellery. "Why don't you take it home, Mrs. Noseworthy? It's yours anyway."

She clapped her hands. "Really?"

"Really."

"Oh goody." She picked up her box and ran out the back door.

"I've got to get out of here," Graham said.

Lily scowled at her father. "And leave Mom with everything, as usual. Go then. No one cares. Least of all, me."

Graham turned around and left.

The boys took the girls out on the porch swing. Faith, Juliet and Robert were left in the kitchen.

"What do we do?" Juliet asked no one in particular.

"Play Russian Roulette?" Robert suggested. "I'd find it more relaxing than spending an evening with this bunch."

"I'll never get out of the attic," Faith moaned. "My entire life is that hole upstairs."

Her sister frowned. "At least you have a hole. We won't even have that much, unless we find some money."

Robert rubbed his cheek. "You can have mine. I have more than enough."

"Oh, shut up Robert."

Elsie was much too weary to say anything to her aunt. She led her up the stairs and to her bedroom door. "Goodnight."

The final twist of the evening came when her aunt reached out and kissed her face. "That music box was a wedding gift to me from my lover. He died trying to get to me. He never saw my dress. Take back your man, Elsie, and spend the rest of your life with him. Do it for a woman who never had that privilege. Promise me."

Elsie's eyes filled with tears. "I love you."

"And I, my dear, love you."

Grabbing Elsie's hand, she gave it a final squeeze and closed the door.

It was the last time Elsie saw her aunt alive.

❦

Late that night, under a full moon, someone snuck into Aunt Hildy's room. Hildy woke with a start, and perceived a figure standing over her.

"Who's there?" She fumbled for her glasses but couldn't find them.

"Where's the treasure?"

"What?"

"Tell me."

"I have no intention of telling you," she said crossly. She squinted and saw a gun. "Well, that's a bit dramatic, don't you think?"

"Where is it?"

"Oh, I've had enough." Hildy looked into the dark. "Go ahead. Shoot me. I dare you."

Her last moment was one of surprise.

Chapter Ten

Slater wouldn't stop crying.

It was morning by the time the ambulance left and the police were done with their initial enquiries. But investigators still roamed the premises. Everyone else wandered around in shock. Mrs. Noseworthy hurried over when the police cars arrived and made coffee for everyone. Elsie called Crystal in the first hysterical moments after she found Aunt Hildy's body — when she'd run downstairs to get Graham and discovered he wasn't there.

Elsie went into the sunroom and put her arms around Slater. He laid his head on her shoulder and wept like a child. She'd grown to love this kind-hearted boy.

She patted his back. "It's going to be all right, sweetheart."

"This is like, totally…"

"She thought you were wonderful. I want you to know that."

He lifted his head. "She did?"

"Of course, she did. Because you are."

He bawled even harder. He finally took the tissue she handed him. "Why didn't she scream or something? I would've got them. I would've saved her."

"I know."

Dahlia sat on the couch, her arms wrapped around her knees. "Aunt Hildy lived through everything. How could she die right here under our noses, with all of us in the house? It doesn't make sense."

"I know it doesn't. I don't understand it either."

Crystal stuck her head in the doorway. "Elsie, there's some-one here who wants to speak to you. In the foyer."

"Thanks Crys." She gave Slater one more pat and left to see who it was. There were so many people in the house; she hoped it was someone she knew.

There stood Harry.

Elsie immediately started to cry. He came and put his arms around her.

"It's so awful," she whispered into his shirt. "I can't bear it."

"I'm very sorry Elsie. I only just heard. Here. Take this." He passed her a handkerchief and she wiped her eyes.

"I don't understand it Harry. How could she be killed in her own bedroom and none of us see anything?"

"No one saw anyone leave or run away?"

"No. I mean, I'm pretty sure we all heard the shot, but I was half asleep and thought it was a car backfiring. I didn't jump up right away, but when I heard Lily open her door and call for me, I got up."

"I know you've talked to the officers in charge, but is there anything you've forgotten to tell them?"

"Faith, the girls and I were upstairs."

"And who was downstairs?"

Elsie paused. She'd already been interrogated. She only want-ed a hug. "The boys. They were in the sun porch and my sister and her husband were in the family room on the hide-a-bed, because Robert had a bit of an accident and we felt it was best he stay here for the night."

"And Graham was in the basement, I take it?"

Elsie sniffed. "No actually. When I went to get him, he wasn't there. Which is bloody typical. He's never there when I need him."

Harry looked at her more closely. "Does he usually stay out at night?"

"I really have no idea. It's none of my business, is it?" She took a deep breath. "There was a bit of a family argument before bedtime. Maybe that's why he went out."

"Was your aunt's bedroom door open or closed?"

She put her hand on her forehead. "Closed. All I know is the girls and I were in the hall when Faith came down the attic stairs. We were frightened because she'd heard it from up there. So I knocked on Aunt Hildy's door and asked if she was all right and when she didn't answer, I went to check on her and that's when I found her…."

His arm went around her and the weeping started again. When she'd quieted, he said, "I'm not on this case obviously, so I'm not supposed to be here. I better go and let them get on with things. I just wanted to make sure you were all right. When I heard there was a shooting at this address, I…"

She looked at him.

"I'm sure they'll find whoever did this, Elsie. Whatever happens, I'm here for you. I'm not going anywhere."

"Thanks Harry." She put her arms around him and gave him a hug. He kissed her on the cheek and left.

Harry was a nice man who seemed to genuinely care about her. More importantly, he was here when she needed someone.

Graham wasn't.

❧

Lily's outburst the night before shocked Graham. He hadn't been aware the girls were so upset. They always seemed fine, but then again, he wasn't around them all the time. He only wanted the best for them, and it seemed to him the uproar Aunt Hildy caused in the household made their lives worse. He didn't want his children living in chaos.

Lily said he yelled at Elsie all the time. Maybe he did. He didn't know any more. All he knew when he left was how hopeless and lonely he felt. He had nowhere to go. No one to talk to. He found himself at Bunny's door. It probably wasn't smart, but he didn't care. He needed someone to need him, and she was there.

"Look who's crawled back. Are you here to apologize?"

"Yes."

"Come in then."

They sat on the sofa in her living room. "Before you say anything Graham, I want you to know that I'm tired of being jerked around. You can only have one woman at a time. That's the way it works."

"Elsie and I are finished."

"How do you know that?"

Graham looked down at his hands. "Because I'm the last on her list, and Elsie has a very long list. I can't compete anymore and I'm tired of trying."

"I'm not sure I believe you."

"I understand that. I'm sorry I dragged you into all this. I'd like to make it up to you."

She hesitated.

"Let me stay."

She reached for his hand and led him to the bedroom.

Graham woke up in the dark and didn't know where he was at first. The air was thick, and heavy with perfume. It was hard to breathe. The room was hot but his body was in a cold sweat. He thought maybe he was having a heart attack, because he couldn't breathe. He needed air. He got up and fumbled for his clothes by the bed, trying not to wake Bunny. He left the apartment door unlocked and ran outside, staggering up the street until he came to a park bench. He sat and took in great gulps of air. He needed to think. If he could only think, then he'd know what to do.

Bunny woke up and discovered him gone.

"That son of a bitch." She checked the time: it was three o'clock. Where the hell was he? She lay there for two hours and mulled over what this could mean. Finally she heard the front door open. She held her breath and pretended to be asleep.

He went into the bathroom. The water ran for what seemed like ten minutes. Finally, he came out, undressed and lay beside her. She wasn't sure whether she should confront him; he had come back, after all. Why rock the boat? She wanted him. She wanted him bad. So she stayed still and waited until his breathing became soft and even, then she too fell asleep.

At around eight o'clock, she opened her eyes and saw that he was awake.

"Good morning." She stretched her arms over her head.

"Hey."

She turned on her side and leaned on her elbow. "Last night was great, mister. I could do with more of that."

He smiled. "I'm happy to oblige. I know I've behaved badly. I'll try not to do it again."

She traced her nail down his chest. "I like it when you behave badly. I just need to know that you're not going to screw me over, okay?"

"I'm not. I promise."

She gave him a saucy smile. "It's okay if you screw me, though." She reached for him, but he held her off.

"Don't take this the wrong way, Bunny, but I've got to go."

She felt a familiar dread. She fell back on the mattress. "Fine."

He leaned over and gave her a long kiss. "I am grateful for last night. And I do like you. I'm coming back, okay?"

"Okay."

She watched him get out of bed and put on his clothes. He reached for his change on the dresser and put on his watch. His leaving so soon annoyed her.

"Where were you last night?"

He froze for a moment, then turned around and shrugged. "I couldn't sleep. I went for a walk."

"At three in the morning? That's not a very smart thing to do. You could have been mugged."

"I wasn't, was I?" He walked over and gave her another kiss. "I'll see you tonight."

"What happened?" Graham shouted as he came through the door. A cop stopped him.

"Who are you?"

"I'm Graham Brooks. I live here. Girls, what's going on?"

The family sat around the kitchen table, while Crystal stood and poured tea. They looked at him with sad eyes. It was Robert who spoke up.

"Someone shot Aunt Hildy last night."

Slater howled. Eli put his arm around his shoulder. "It's okay, buddy."

"Shot her? Is she dead?"

They nodded. Faith grabbed some napkins and gave half to Juliet. They blew their noses.

"Where's your mother?"

"She's upstairs," Dahlia said. "I think you should leave her alone."

He started across the kitchen. "To hell with that."

"Sir? Could you come with us to answer a few questions?"

Graham hesitated. He looked at the man in uniform. "Me?"

"Everyone who lives here has been questioned. I understand you didn't sleep here last night?"

He gave the girls a quick glance. They turned away from him. "No. I didn't."

"Where were you?"

"Could we go somewhere else?"

The man nodded. Graham led him into the living room.

"Look, officer. I've no idea what's going on. I just got home. I haven't even spoken to my wife…my wife. She'll be devastated. I need to speak to her."

"In a moment. Where were you last night?"

"At a friend's house."

"A female friend?"

Graham shot him a dirty look. "Yes."

"I'd like her name and address please. We'll have to talk to her."

"Oh God. This is insane. Neither of us knows anything about this."

"According to your wife, there was an argument here last night and you walked out."

"She said that? Am I being accused of something?"

The officer waited.

"It wasn't just her and I having an argument. It was the whole lot of them out there. They were here last night. Wouldn't they be more suspect than me?"

"We've spoken to each person in turn. And no doubt we'll speak to everyone again."

Graham rubbed his chin. "Look, I'll answer your questions, but can I just go see Elsie? Her aunt's just been *murdered*. I need to see her. I won't go anywhere."

"Fine. For a few minutes."

Graham took the stairs two at a time and opened the bedroom door. Elsie lay curled up on the bed like a little girl. He went to her.

"Elsie?"

"It's so unfair, Graham."

He sat and placed his hand on her back. "I know."

"How could anyone do that to her? She was an old woman. She deserved to end her days gracefully, not…"

"It'll be all right, Else. I'm sorry. This is terrible."

She sat up. "I found her. It was awful." She covered her face with her hands. "I can't get the picture out of my mind."

"Don't think about it."

She lowered her hands. "Just like that? My aunt was shot through the heart not fifty feet from here and you want me to wipe it from my memory? How does one do that Graham? Is it that easy for you?" She laughed. "What am I saying? Of course it is. You hated her anyway. You don't care."

"That's not fair. I know I didn't like her very much, but I'd never have wished this on her."

She looked down and sighed. "I know that."

"I get the feeling the police think I did it."

"They think we all did it, and who can blame them?"

"Why did you tell them we were arguing?"

"Because it's the truth. You think that wouldn't have come out?" Elsie reached for more tissue. "Think about it. Slater's downstairs. He's so upset he'd confess to shooting her if he thought it would make things easier for everyone."

"Elsie. I know things are bad between us. But I'll always…" He choked on his words.

"I know."

He couldn't keep the tears back. "The girls — they blame me for our breakup. Maybe they hate me."

"Of course not. Don't be silly."

Graham looked at his feet. "I can't seem to do anything right."

She held her own arms and rubbed them. "Where were you last night? I needed you. Were you with her?"

He nodded. "But how could I know this would happen?"

"I'm just tired of having to deal with everything myself. I nearly went out of my mind when I found her. I needed you." Tears fell down her cheeks. "Can you please stay away from her until this is over? I don't want her hanging around. I really need your support, Gray. I can't do this…I can't do the funeral and dismantle Aunt Hildy's life all by myself."

"I will. You have my word."

"I sure hope you mean it," she said quietly.

Graham looked at her pale face and the dark circles under her eyes. "Can I get you something?"

"I'm so tired."

"Go to sleep for a couple of hours, if you can. I'm here now. I'll deal with everything downstairs."

She nodded wearily and lay down. He pulled the duvet over

her and left the room. Standing outside the bedroom door, he realized he was in an awkward position. He'd need Bunny's help.

The first chance he got, he called her and told her what happened.

"The police want to talk to you," he whispered into his cellphone.

"Why me?"

"Because I had to tell them where I was last night."

"Oh damn. I can't believe it."

"Listen to me. All you have to say is that I was with you all night and I was, wasn't I?"

There was silence.

"I was, wasn't I?"

"Yeah. Okay. You were with me all night. That's what I'll tell them."

"Thanks a lot. I've got to go. I'll call you later." He was so rattled by what he'd just done, he forgot to tell her that he couldn't see her for a while.

Later that afternoon, Juliet and Robert went out on the back deck. They pulled their chairs near one another. Robert let out a groan as he sat on his cushion. Juliet looked around to make sure no one was within hearing distance.

"You didn't do it, did you?"

He looked horrified. "What are you saying? That I'm capable of murder?"

"SHHH. Pipe down. We have to keep our stories straight."

He gave her an odd look. "What do you mean keep our stories straight? Do you know something I don't?"

"I'm just being careful. Everyone knows I was at the end of my rope with Aunt Hildy. I don't want them to get the idea I pulled the trigger."

"Did you?"

She shoved his arm. "What do you think?"

"I think yes."

"You miserable…"

"Well, you let dogs eat people. You hate everyone we know. You knew about that so-called treasure chest, but you never told me. How can I trust a thing you say?"

"Robert, I'm a lot of things, but I'm not a killer. You could be, however."

"Are you nuts?"

"You need money, don't you? You never liked her. You hate my family. You told me yesterday we could all rot in hell. And I know for a fact that you got out of bed last night and were gone for quite a while. Where were you?"

"In the bathroom."

"For an hour?"

"I'm sore, in case you hadn't noticed."

She leaned into him. "You weren't in the bathroom, because I checked."

He became flustered. "I could ask you the same thing? Why were you out of bed?"

"Answer my question first."

"I can't."

"Why not?"

"Because."

"Because why?"

"Just because."

Juliet crossed her arms in. "I can keep this up all day." She stared at him.

"I was…"

"What? What?"

"I got stuck in the library with Slater and Dahlia, okay?"

She leaned back in her chair. "Excuse me?"

"They were playing doctor with the leftover bandages."

"With you in the room?"

"I went to get a book because I couldn't sleep. I sat in that comfy old chair by the window and they didn't see me when they came in. I had no choice but to stay after a few minutes because they would've been too embarrassed to know I was there. I was mortified."

"I shouldn't wonder."

"Now you tell me why you roamed the halls all night, since you knew I wasn't in the bathroom."

Juliet waved her hand. "Nothing exciting. I wolfed down a piece of pizza in the kitchen. No one had supper last night."

Robert counted on his fingers. "Okay. So let's consider the information we have so far. If I was in the library with the lead pipe and his girl, and you were in the kitchen stuffing your face, and Graham was occupied with the bimbo, that leaves only Elsie, Faith, Lily and Eli unaccounted for."

She strummed her fingers on the table. "Well, I can't see saint Elsie firing a gun since she refuses to kill ants and Lily and Eli can't keep their hands off each other long enough to hold a gun, so that leaves only one person who's capable of the dirty deed."

He nodded. "And she was pretty distraught last night."

She nodded as well. "I know. That's what worries me."

The kids retreated to their favourite meeting place, the porch swing, where they were the objects of their neighbours' curiosity. Mrs. Mooney came running out of her house when she saw them, carrying a plate of cold chicken and a Tupperware bowl of potato salad. She was stopped by the police tape. Lily went down the front steps and walked over to her.

"Thanks, Mrs. Mooney."

"Oh, no trouble, dear. No trouble at all. If you need anything, just let me know."

"Sure."

"Is your mother okay? Oh my, what a stupid question. As if she'd be okay. Do they know what happened yet? Do they have any suspects? Dear lord, the times we live in, when someone can just come in your house and shoot you in your own bed. We all feel so badly about this dear...it's not right…"

"I better get this in the house."

"Oh, of course dear. Here I am talking your ear off. Now don't forget, if your mother needs anything, she only has to call."

"I'll tell her."

Lily left in a hurry before Mrs. Mooney said anything else. She put the food in the fridge and went back to sit with the others.

Dahlia shook her head. "I can't believe it. The whole world is just going on with its regular activities. The garbage truck just went by. Mr. Mooney is over there cleaning his gutters. The kids two doors down are playing street hockey. Don't they know Aunt Hildy's dead?"

"That's the way the world works," Eli said. "It just keeps revolving, even though for us it's stopped dead."

"Dead," Slater sniffed. "I hate that stupid word."

Dahlia looked at the other three. "I feel like I'm floating. I'm not attached to anything, ya know?"

Lily hugged herself. "That's called disassociation. It comes with shock."

"What's shocking is how it happened," Eli said. "It doesn't make sense that no one saw anything. Did anyone hear anything out of the ordinary?"

Dahlia shook her head. "No. Nothing. We were in the library and I didn't hear a sound."

Lily rolled her eyes. "I'm sure you didn't. Except maybe heavy breathing."

"Well, where were you then, Miss Innocent?"

"We were in the…ah…dining room, for a while," Eli confessed.

"The dining room?"

"Well, where were we supposed to go? There were people everywhere. Anyway," Lily said with exasperation, "we didn't hear anything from the dining room. But when I went upstairs to go to bed, I thought I saw Faith come down from the attic. I never thought anything of it. I figured she was on one of her ten nightly trips to the john. You don't think she could have done it?"

Slater clenched his fists. "If she did, I'll massage her neck real hard. Real hard."

Dahlia patted his arm. "It's okay."

Eli spoke up. "You know, from what I've seen of your Aunt Faith, she's more depressed than angry. I can't see her shooting anyone, except maybe herself."

"Your dad was pretty angry with Aunt Hildy last night," Slater mused. "You don't think it could be him?"

"What a horrible thing to say!" Dahlia shouted. "How can you even think such a thing?"

Slater raised his hands, "Okay, okay. I'm sorry I said anything."

"Well, you should be. Gee whiz, I don't say stuff like that about your father, even though he's the meanest person alive. My dad is a hundred times better than your dad."

"You were mad at your dad last night too," Slater reminded her. "I'm not the only one who thinks he's been a real jerk to your mom."

Dahlia stood up. "What did you say?"

Eli saw that Lily was about to jump in, so he quickly grabbed her hand and pulled her in the house.

"It's true," Slater told her. "Your mom is the best and I don't think he should go around getting mad at her all the time and making her so unhappy. You've said the same thing yourself, don't forget."

Dahlia poked him in the shoulder. "I'm allowed to say it because he's my dad. Who are you to criticize him? He's only ever been nice to you."

"Your mom's nicer."

"How dare you!" Dahlia marched towards the front door, grabbed the handle and turned to face him. "Slater, go home."

"I am home."

"Not anymore, you're not."

She slammed the door behind her and ran into the library, throwing herself on one of the leather chairs. This was the worst day of her life. Her head ached and she just wanted to scream at someone.

Lily thought maybe she should go in there and speak to her, but Eli said that would only make things worse.

"How do you know?"

"I take psych too, remember. I'll talk to her in a few minutes when she calms down."

Eli knocked on the library door before he entered. Dahlia didn't look up. He crossed the room and sat on the ottoman in front of her.

"You okay?"

"NO."

"He didn't mean it."

Dahlia looked at the empty fireplace. "Why did he say it then?"

Eli took a deep breath. "He said it because none of us are thinking clearly. We're battered and bruised. Aunt Hildy was killed upstairs last night. We're all in shock, but especially the big guy. He loved that old woman. He's just trying to figure out who would do such a thing because it makes no sense to him. It was a random thought that meant nothing. And I think you know that."

Dahlia's face crumpled and she tore out of the room, blinded by tears. She ran all the way to the front door and threw it open, then down the steps, over the walkway, under the police tape and out into the street, trying to see his car.

When she realized he was gone, she knelt on the ground and put her hands over her face. She rocked back and forth. Her life was over.

Graham saw Dahlia first. He yelled for Elsie. They rushed out of the house. Her mother took her by the shoulders. "What's wrong, honey?"

"I told Slater this wasn't his home anymore. I told him to go away and now he thinks I hate him. I can't believe I was so

stupid. I know him. He'll throw himself off a bridge or something. He's so upset about Aunt Hildy and I do this to him. I
can't bear it."

Graham knew what to do. "Dahlia, get in the truck. We'll go find
him."

She gave him a startled look. "Okay."

Elsie kissed her. "Everything will be all right, sweetie."

"Where would he be?" Graham zoomed down the street before she had a chance to put on her seat belt.

Dahlia dried her eyes on her sleeve. "Check at his house first.
If his car's there, I'll go in."

"Don't worry, Dee. He won't do anything stupid." *I hope*, he
thought.

She punched her fists into her knees. "How could I have been
so rotten?"

"We often hurt people in a thoughtless moment." He gave
her a sideways glance. "We just hope if people love us, they'll
forgive us."

Dahlia nodded but didn't look at him.

He added, "Honey, it's been a terrible day. None of us can
think straight. Just say you're sorry and everything will be all
right."

"I hope so," she sniffed. "I'd die if anything ever happened to
him."

They pulled up to Slater's house, but his car wasn't in the
yard. "Never mind. There's no one home."

"How do you know? You haven't even gone in."

"There's never anyone there."

Graham realized he'd never asked about Slater's family before. "Why not?"

"He's an only child. His dad's a drunk and his mom's always out with one of her dozens of boyfriends."

"God, that's awful."

She started to cry again. "That's why he's always over at our house. That's why he loves Mom so much. She calls him sweetheart and that's why he loved Aunt Hildy, because he never had a grandmother. Oh my God. I have to find him."

Now Graham started to panic. "Well, where would he be? Do you have a favourite place you like to go?"

"The library," she sobbed.

"The library? Slater likes to read books?"

"Not that library. Oh, never mind." Then she brightened. "I know. Gus."

"Who's Gus? A friend?"

"No silly. Gus the Tortoise. Slater loves him. At the museum. Hurry Daddy, hurry."

Graham drove like a maniac. It was the one thing he could do for her and he didn't want to screw it up. By the time they got to the museum's parking lot, his stomach was in knots.

"I see his car!" Dahlia screamed. "He's here. He's here."

He stopped on a dime and she fumbled for the door handle, but not before she turned around and gave him a big smile. "Thanks Daddy." And out she went.

He watched her run up the stairs to the museum. She looked like her mother just then. Graham put his head on his hands as he gripped the steering wheel. How does everything go so wrong?

She ran until she saw him. He was with a bunch of school kids who were trying to entice Gus out from under one of the display counters.

"Slater!"

He turned at the sound of her voice. She ran right up and jumped in his arms. "I love you so much. Please forgive me. I can't tell you how sorry I am."

He gave her a big hug back. "I love you Dee."

"Please come home. We need you. Everyone loves you. It's not the same when you're not there."

Slater gave her his sexy blonde playboy smile.

"Sweet."

❧

Juliet and Robert happened to be in the living room drinking a cup of tea that Crystal made for them when Dahlia went tearing down the hall and out the front door. They munched on their chocolate digestives and watched the soap opera unfold from the window. Apparently Dahlia wanted to be run over by a car, because why else would someone kneel on the street? Thankfully she was rescued by her parents, before they actually had to go out and do something.

Once that died down, they twiddled their thumbs for a while, then went back to their discussion about what to do about Faith. They finally agreed Juliet should talk to her.

"If she confesses, what will you do?"

"How should I know? Have I ever done this before?" she snapped.

"Take a small tape recorder. Then if we get a confession, at least we have proof that you and I are innocent."

"That's not a bad idea, actually."

"I told you, I'm not stupid."

Juliet got up from the sofa and headed for the attic. Then she came back. "You are stupid. We don't have a tape recorder."

He snapped his fingers. "I think I saw one on the desk in the library."

They opened the library door. It was empty. They walked over to the desk and looked around.

"I don't see anything," Juliet grumbled. "You must have imagined it."

"I could have sworn there was something that looked like a tape recorder. It was a square box anyway."

"Maybe it was the treasure and you let it get away. I wouldn't put it past you."

Robert looked through desk drawers and searched on some of the shelves. "Do you ever have anything nice to say?"

"I would if you did something nice." She looked around too, but stopped when the sun came out from behind a cloud and shone through the window onto the chandelier that hung in the middle of the room.

"God, that's bright. I can't believe Elsie actually dusted it. She doesn't dust anything else in this house."

He grunted. "Oh, hell. I don't know what it was I saw... What's wrong?"

"Robert, look at those hanging crystals. Do they look too sparkly to be crystals? They look like diamonds!"

He looked up and gasped. "Oh, my God. I think you're right. Aunt Hildy said we've all seen it. That has to be it."

"Help me move the desk closer," Juliet ordered. They pushed and pulled at the heavy piece of furniture.

"I think we're scratching the hardwood," Robert wheezed.

"We'll buy them a new floor. I think we're close enough. Get the chair."

Robert hurried over and retrieved it, helping Juliet step up on the seat and then onto the desk itself. "Don't fall."

She steadied herself and reached above her head to grab one of the dropped crystals. She took it off its hanger and held it in her hand.

"Oh my God, if this is real, you and I are in the money," she squealed. "Here, take this and scratch the window."

She passed it down to him. He stood in front of his handy work.

"Say something."

He turned around, his face white. "It's a diamond."

They looked at each other and giggled like fiends.

Juliet gloated. "We did it. Let's get these down and get the hell out of here."

"And where would you be going?" a deep voice asked them. A policeman stood in the door.

Robert recovered first. "Nowhere officer. I just told my wife to get down from there. That's it's not necessary to clean everything before the funeral."

Juliet picked up the story. "I'm afraid I have a cleaning fetish. I've had it my whole life. Could you help me down, officer?"

The policeman went over and offered her a hand. She stepped down as if alighting from a carriage. "We know we aren't allowed to go anywhere without permission. The detectives made that quite clear. And we'd never do anything to jeopardize the investigation. I want the murderer of my darling aunt brought to justice and I won't rest until that's accomplished."

"Fine," the policeman said. "Just so we're clear."

"It's perfectly clear." Robert assured him. He walked over and put his arm around his wife. They stood there and grinned like idiots until the officer left.

Juliet and her Romeo grabbed each other by the hands and did a victory dance all around the carpet.

Chapter Eleven

Aunt Hildy's remains were cremated, as per her request, once the coroner finished her report. Elsie knew what to do because of the big black binder Aunt Hildy had handed over when she first arrived. Elsie hid it in the cedar chest at the end of her bed and reluctantly took it out the day after the shooting. The lawyers were called. It seemed those first days were nothing but men in three-piece suits who acted very business-like as they pored over documents. Elsie let them handle it. She needed only one thing from the binder, a thick envelope that was addressed to her and which she kept hidden until after the funeral.

Her aunt wanted no part of an organized religious affair. She requested that her ashes be scattered on the water by Point Pleasant Park, where she played as a child. She wanted only immediate family in attendance, and afterward, if they gathered by the fireplace in the old house and raised their glasses to a life well lived, she'd be very grateful indeed.

The night before the ceremony, Graham drove Elsie to Cruikshank's Funeral home to retrieve Aunt Hildy's ashes. The box was inside in a blue velvet drawstring bag, and Elsie hugged it to her chest as they drove home in silence. The ashes were still warm. That wonderful heat seared itself into her heart.

They put the ashes on the coffee table in the living room and by the end of the evening, it was surrounded with flowers, pictures and the music box.

The family had a hard time saying goodnight, knowing she would be alone with only Flower and the cats for company. They left a small light on. But Elsie couldn't close her eyes, and wandered back downstairs.

She need not have worried. Slater was fast asleep, curled up on the floor beside her. She tiptoed across the room and grabbed a chenille throw to put over him.

"Thanks, sweetheart," she whispered. She went back to bed and thankfully nodded off.

The next morning was cold and grey, a foggy mist in the air. It suited everyone's mood as they piled into the cars to go to the park, everyone in their dark finery. They gathered at the edge of the water, at the farthest end of the park. A loon cried in the distance, and two herons stood still at the water's edge, ready witnesses to this solemn occasion.

They told her they loved her, and would never forget her. Then Elsie opened the box and flung Aunt Hildy's ashes into the wind. They swirled upward and mingled instantly with the grey fog over the grey water and disappeared into the unknown, heading out on the next wonderful adventure.

The family gathered with their glasses of champagne around the fireplace when they returned. A toast was made "To Aunt Hildy." They took a sip, each lost in their own private thoughts.

Until Elsie spoke up. "Could you sit down please?"

All eyes turned to her as they seated themselves around the room.

"This isn't how I imagined this day. Aunt Hildy taken from us violently and the killer still at large. And it hurts to know the police consider us suspects. But quite frankly, I can't think of a soul who'd want to hurt her."

"Come on," Robert scoffed. "Everyone she ever came in contact with would've gladly wrung her neck, given half a chance. You know that. Don't make her out to be a saint, because she wasn't."

She held up her hands. "I refuse to talk about her faults, today of all days. I just asked you to be here with me, because she left me something."

"Another music box?" Juliet suggested. "I wouldn't be surprised."

"Will you let her finish, please?" Graham said impatiently.

Elsie went over to the secretary desk and took out the thick envelope. "This is a letter from Aunt Hildy. She wanted me to read it to you, after her death."

Slater bit his knuckles. "I don't think I can do this."

"You'll be all right, honey. We're all here," Elsie reassured him.

Faith rolled her eyes. "Can we just get on with it?"

Lily agreed. "Yeah, Mommy. This is too hard. Just read it."

Elsie took a deep breath. "Okay."

She sat on a chair and faced them. She took the letter out of its envelope and unfolded the creamy thick paper.

"It's dated a month ago."

"*Dearest Elsie,*

I have given you the job of reading this letter, as you are the mistress of this house. It pleases me enormously that you have done such a fine job, keeping the home fires burning as it were, and I hope you and your family have many more happy years under this roof.

"*I know my life is ending. I look forward to it, in the same way I've looked forward to all the adventures in my life. Because I know the journey is not over. I have spent my time here on earth uncovering the remains of past lives and know what peace there is in these sacred places. So do not grieve for me. I am where I want to be. And I am with the one I love. The one I'll be with until the end of time."*

Elsie had to stop because her tears made it hard to see the writing. She took a handful of Kleenex out of her pocket and wiped her nose. She didn't dare look up because she could hear sniffs, and she'd be lost if she looked at the girls. Besides, she knew from a stifled howl that Slater was on the edge.

She continued.

"Each of you will receive a gift from me. It is my personal thank you for gracing my life. The bulk of my estate, as you know, goes to the university. My personal effects, the cherished mementos in my room, can be divided among you. That is for you to decide.

"To Elsie…the music box that means the world to me. I know it will be in good hands."

She blew her nose and went on.

"To Juliet…a diamond tiara, given to me by a member of a royal family."

Juliet squealed. "Oh my God, are you serious? This is so exciting."

Everyone shushed her.

Elsie started to laugh. "There's more… *'I give her this so she can be queen for a day, something she's always wanted and strives very hard to achieve.'"*

"Hey, what does that mean?"

"It means Aunt Hildy was one smart dame," Graham smirked.

Elsie continued.

"To Faith…my journals. There are hundreds of rip-roaring good stories between the pages and I'm sure she will write a book I'd be proud to read."

Faith cried so hard Juliet had to go over and give her a hug.

"To Graham...my archaeological tools. I made my living with my hands and so does he. I admire that."

Graham got up and went to the fireplace. He turned his back on everyone and held on to the mantel.

Elsie read on.

"To Robert...a piece of real estate I've had for a long time. I think he'll be surprised when he finds out the address."

Robert jumped to his feet. "I can't believe it. I thought she hated me."

"Maybe she did," Lily said. "You don't know where it is yet."

"Lily, let me continue," her mother said.

"Sorry."

"To Lily...two steamer trunks full of clothes her great-grandmother made for her grandmother and me, as well as outfits I've collected over the years on my travels to many different lands. I believe they'll complement her unique personality and her fascination with the human condition."

Lily put her hands over her face.

"To Eli...my grandfather's pocket watch...from one gentleman to another."

Eli stared at his feet.

"To Slater...a donation has been made in your name to save the most endangered species in southern and East Africa. These include the black rhino, the African elephant, the mountain zebra, the cheetah and the leatherback turtle. I've opened a bank account in your name and I want you to use the money to go on safari and visit the places on this earth that have brought me much joy. I've also had a star named after you, so you can keep me company and make me laugh forever."

Everyone held their breath, sure that Slater would go berserk. He surprised them. He put his fist in the air as a salute. "Far out, Auntie baby."

Elsie looked down at the letter. She gasped and looked at Dahlia, who jumped up and started to tremble. "What?"

"To Dahlia…my wedding dress. Marry that Prince Charming of yours and live happily ever after."

Her hands flew to her mouth. "I don't believe it!"

Juliet looked confused. "Aunt Hildy never married. What wedding dress?"

Elsie put the letter in her lap. "She told me she was to be married, but her young man died trying to get to her and he never saw her dress. She's kept it all these years."

Lily sighed, "Oh my God, how romantic is that?"

Dahlia cried, "Remember when she told us she saw the most beautiful dress of all. It must have been hers. I can't wait. Where is it?"

Elsie motioned for them to sit. "The lawyers have everything in a vault. I'll make the arrangements to have it delivered. Anyway, I'm almost finished." She picked up the letter again.

"And so, I hope these gifts put a smile on your face, since I clearly made you miserable with the treasure business. The only thing left to say is that it's there. You just have to find it. I love you all. Aunt Hildy."

No one spoke for a few moments. Then Elsie folded up the letter. "What a woman."

"Let's go upstairs and divvy up her room," Juliet suggested. "That's what she wants us to do."

"Don't," Elsie said. "There's been enough of her given away today. I couldn't bear it."

Faith spoke up. "We've been given permission to go in that room. What's the harm? Let's do it and get it over with."

Lily nodded. "Why not Mom? I think I'd love to touch her things. I want to be near her."

Her sister agreed. "Lets do it together and then it will be over."

Elsie stayed where she was. "I'm sorry. You go ahead. I just can't face it right now."

The women trooped upstairs and Graham suggested the guys have a beer out on the deck. They readily agreed.

Elsie sat with her head against the armchair and watched the dust mites dance in the sunbeam that streamed in through the window, the fog finally rolling back out to sea. One of the pussycats lay in the spot of light, stretched out to enjoy the warmth.

It made her smile to think of Aunt Hildy as she floated through the air in the park and drifted out over the water. That's what she'd like to do too, when her time came. She didn't want to be buried. She wanted to be free.

She closed her eyes and tried to remember her aunt the way she looked the day she sat under the big tree in the back garden. It made her feel better. She started to relax and grow drowsy. That's when she heard Dahlia call her softly from across the room.

"Yes?" She kept her eyes closed.

"The terrible twosome are wreaking havoc up there. They'll take everything if you're not careful. Are you sure there's nothing you want? I can get it for you, so you don't have to go in the room."

She wanted to sleep. "Thanks honey, but no. I'm fine."

"Okay."

"Wait," she said, her eyes still closed. "I'd love to have some of her photo albums."

"That's a good idea. I'll make sure you get them."

"And Dee. Bring me her carpet bag. I always thought it belonged to a gypsy when I was a little girl. That's how I remember her best. Carrying that bag."

"Okay."

Elsie nodded off and woke up sometime later. There was a stack of photo albums on the piano bench and in her lap was the only other thing she wanted. She touched the velvet embroidery, worn away to a smooth sheen in spots, and rubbed it on her cheek. It smelled musky and old and wonderful. Just like her.

"I miss you."

Elsie unclasped the bag and looked inside. What a marvellous array of odds and ends. She pulled out her passport first and opened it. Aunt Hildy glared back at her. Elsie felt sorry for the photographer. Look at all the stamps. The Congo, Japan, Brazil. Iceland for heaven's sake! Why didn't she ever ask her about these adventures? They're gone forever now. That deep well of sorrow bubbled up and threatened to overwhelm her, just like the first time she thought, "I must ask Mom," only Mom wasn't there anymore.

She put the passport back and took out a comb. A few white hairs still clung to it, so Elsie wrapped it in a lace handkerchief she found at the bottom of the bag. There was a book, *The Screwtape Letters* by C.S. Lewis. A few practical items, an accordion plastic rain bonnet loved by little old ladies everywhere, a jar of Vaseline and a tin of Altoids. But what on earth did she need with a silver spoon? And a bag of clothes-pins? She even had a Swiss Army knife, a handy gadget, for sure, but did she carry it through customs?

Elsie was about to close the bag when she caught a glimmer of metal in a small pocket. She had a hard time taking whatever it was out because the pocket was very narrow and deep. After much manipulating, she freed a large, old-fashioned brass key. Now what on earth does this open?

Another secret taken to the grave.

It had been an exhausting day for everyone, so there wasn't much movement in the house that evening. Only the sound of *The Simpsons* coming from the family room, the ticking of the grandfather clock and the sound of a blowdryer upstairs.

Juliet and Robert asked if anyone would like to join them in the library for some tea and a game of Scrabble before they left for the night. There were no takers. Their plan had worked. They went to work quickly and quietly. Juliet picked the crystals off the chandelier one by one, and Robert scratched up Elsie's leaded windows. It turned out only three were diamonds, which was disappointing, but with the horde of goodies from Aunt Hildy's room, they'd still fetch a tidy sum.

Juliet hung the last of the crystals back up just as Faith walked in on them.

"Thought I'd…." She stopped. "I didn't know you were a domestic goddess. Perhaps you'd like to tell me what you're doing up there?"

"I'm not doing anything."

"You're not standing on a desk that's been pulled into the middle of the room, fondling the chandelier?"

Juliet got down. "No."

"What's up Robert?"

"You are an awfully suspicious woman, did you know that?" Robert answered.

"Is it any wonder, with the way you two sneak around?"

"I wouldn't be so quick to point fingers," Juliet scowled. "You've done your share, only you weren't terribly successful, were you?"

"At least I shared what I found with you. I have a suspicion that's not true in your case."

Robert went over to the hearth and gave the fire a poke. "Don't be so paranoid. We're allowed to look. Aunt Hildy did say it was still here."

"I think she gave us our treasure already," Faith said quietly.

Juliet crossed her arms. "Now you've gone all soft in the head. Why would she tell us it's still here if she gave it to us already?"

Faith dropped into the armchair. "I think she means we're it."

"What? We're it? What's it?"

"Never mind," Faith sighed. "It's probably too deep for you to understand."

Juliet took a step back. "What did you say?"

"I said you're too stupid to understand anything."

Robert put up his hands. "Now girls…"

"Too stupid, am I?" Juliet yelled in her sister's face. "I'd say you've cornered the stupid market in this family with Mrs. Noseworthy's cast-off junk."

Faith leapt in the air. "I could kill you sometimes."

"Oh really? Just like you made sure Aunt Hildy never opened her mouth again?"

"You miserable bitch," Faith gasped. "You think I could shoot someone?"

Juliet stood there and looked at her nails.

"The only person I'd shoot at the moment is you." She lunged at her sister. Juliet screamed and fell backwards onto the floor. Faith jumped on her and pulled her hair. Robert tried to separate them, but had trouble bending over.

"You're a shrew!"

"You're a hag!"

"Stop it, stop it." He flailed about and tried to grab an arm or a leg like some wrestling referee. That's when the door banged open and they froze. Elsie stood there.

"I…"

"I what?" Juliet yelled. "Spit it out."

"I wish I were an only child." She walked out and left them to it.

The fight raged on.

Elsie made arrangements for the lawyer to come to the house the next afternoon. She wanted everything settled. Only then could she move on. She invited Crystal and Mrs. Noseworthy too, as they had been so kind to the family in those first terrible hours.

Dahlia and Lily got themselves dolled up in anticipation of the unveiling of the "dress." Elsie put Aunt Hildy's music box in the middle of the coffee table, so a small part of her would be included in the ceremony.

Crystal admired the beautiful piece. "It's gorgeous."

"Wait until you hear it." Elsie turned the key and its melody filled the room. No one said anything until it wound itself out.

Dahlia dabbed her eyes. "That's the music I want for my wedding."

"That's a nice idea," her mother agreed.

Lily realized something. "Maybe Slater shouldn't be in here…you know…the dress and all."

Dahlia smiled over at the boy himself. "Poor Aunt Hildy never got to show it to the man she loved. I won't make the same mistake."

"Yeah, and I hope I don't die before I get to the church. That would be a bummer."

Juliet filed her nails. "I wonder how he did die?"

"The story's probably in one of her journals," Faith said. "I can't wait to get them all. I read the one in her bedroom and she referred to the time she smuggled maps for the Allies across the border during the war, under the guise of them being archaeological documents."

Graham looked at his watch. "What time have you got, Robert? They should be here by now."

That's when the doorbell rang and everyone flew to their seats. Elsie went to the door and the lawyer came through with a couple of men who brought the gifts inside. Once that was accomplished, the lawyer had Elsie sign a legal document to say everything had been delivered and Aunt Hildy's wishes fulfilled. He bid them adieu.

They took turns. Everyone knew what would be opened last. Juliet took the red velvet case that had her name tagged on it. She opened it up and, for once in her life, was speechless. A diamond tiara, as promised. She picked it up and took it over to the mirror above the fireplace. She put it on her head and everyone oohed and ahhed. Graham rolled his eyes.

Faith received twenty-eight old and very worn leather-bound journals, held together with twine. Juliet gave her a pitying look as she stood by the fire and looked for all the world like a duchess.

Robert took his deed and read it over. "I don't believe it. I now own the house behind you. Our backyards adjoin."

"On Beech Street?" Juliet yelled. "That old thing? It's been rented out to grad students for years. It's an eyesore."

"It's a house," he pointed out.

"Oh God," Faith moaned. "Not you two over the back fence. I think I'll move."

"Yippee," Graham mumbled.

Elsie gave him a look and passed him his gift. The tools were in what looked like two ancient doctor's bags. He spent a quiet time at the dining room table looking through them.

Eli received his pocket watch, a gold beauty that went perfectly with the dark suit he wore.

Lily opened the steamer trunks and clapped her hands in delight.

Slater looked at his bank book and visibly blanched but refused to tell Juliet and Faith how much it was worth. Elsie finally told them to leave him alone. He read the literature about the specific funds allotted for each animal and then opened a map of the heavens to seek his star.

Eli looked over his shoulder. "You were right, buddy. Every treasure has a map. It's the pirate's code."

Finally the moment they all waited for. They cleared the gifts away and left the large box wrapped with a satin ribbon in the middle of the room.

Dahlia stood and shivered. "I'm so excited."

"I hope moths didn't get at it."

Everyone gave Juliet a filthy look.

"Kidding. Geez, you people are a tough crowd."

Dahlia took the ribbon and untied it. She looked at her

mother and took off the lid of the box, then unfolded the yellowing tissue paper inside. She bit her lip and her eyes watered. As everyone gathered round, she said to her sister, "Take it out. I want to see it from across the room."

So Lily lifted it up and held it out in front of her. The dress was a sheath of ivory silk. Perfect in its simplicity. It was slightly off the shoulder, with long sleeves that came to a 'V' over the fingers. It had an empire waist and a skirt that fell to the floor in a pool at Lily's feet.

"It's so beautiful," Elsie whispered.

Mrs. Noseworthy fanned herself with a *Reader's Digest*. "That looks just like mine did. Isn't that amazing?"

Elsie smiled vaguely. "That's nice."

"There's something else." Crystal leaned into the box. "The veil's here too." She took it out. It was floor length with what were the remnants of a crown of white roses.

Dahlia whispered, "It's about the love, my dear. Nothing else."

❧

Harry didn't see much of Elsie in the days that followed the shooting. Not that he expected to, but he thought of her constantly. He was worried. She had looked so small and frightened the morning he went to see her.

He'd called the house a few days later, but Graham answered, so he hung up. If she didn't get in touch with him soon, he'd go to the house, Graham or no Graham.

As he got ready to go out on patrol, Harry overheard the discussion between the detectives involved in the Chamberlin murder. He pretended to go through some files to hear what they had to say.

"Every one of them tells the same story about the hours before the shooting," Detective Olson said, "We can't break them on that. And yet every one of them could have done it. An old auntie, eccentric from what I understand, worth a fortune. There are lots of reasons why someone would want her dead."

"There's no weapon, no obvious signs of a break-in." Detective Smith scanned his notes. "It looks like an inside job. But how would the killer get down the stairs undetected? It's a big house but there were people on every level apparently...unless they're all in on it." He paused. "And what's the husband's story? I can't believe he lives in the basement. Must be in the doghouse for sleeping with his lady friend. He was the only one out that night. Does his alibi hold up?"

Olson frowned. "So far. But I'm not sure about the girlfriend. She said he was with her all night, but she didn't sound very convincing. Maybe we should go rattle that cage again."

"I'd like to rattle her."

"Not me," Olson laughed. "The wife would do just fine."

Smith shook his wrist and whistled. "The daughters are something, too."

Harry had enough. He went up to Olson and stabbed a finger into his shoulder. "You judging a beauty contest? These people are in mourning. Keep your mouth shut."

"What's your problem, Adams? Suddenly develop a respect for women?" Olson laughed and Smith joined in.

"I won't tell you again." He gave Olson an extra poke and walked away before his temper got the better of him. He didn't want anyone talking about Elsie that way. His Elsie.

It was early on a Sunday morning when Olson knocked on Bunny's door. She flung it open, almost as if she were expecting someone.

"Oh."

"Detective Olson. May I speak with you again?"

She looked uneasy. "I guess so."

He waited for her to move away from the door but she didn't, not until he was almost on top of her. She seemed reluctant to let him in.

He walked into the middle of her living room. An unfriendly looking Siamese cat gave him the evil eye from underneath an end table. "I just have a few more questions."

"I've said everything I have to say about that night." She immediately lit a cigarette and blew the smoke in his face. Her hands shook a little. She'd been more together the first time he spoke with her. Why the change?

"When did Mr. Brooks arrive that night?"

"I told you already. Around ten, I guess."

"And when did he leave?"

Bunny paced back and forth and flicked ashes that weren't there. "Again. I told you all this. In the morning…about eight."

"And he was with you all night?"

She turned her back to him and looked out the window.

"Yes."

"Are you sure?"

"I said yes, didn't I?" She butted her barely smoked cigarette in the nearest ashtray.

She was a little too touchy. "You know it's a crime to lie to the police, don't you Bunny?"

She didn't say anything.

"Did Mr. Brooks ask you to say he was here all night?"

"No."

"Are you sure?"

She spun around. "Will you people leave me alone? I had nothing to do with any of it. I'm sick to death of having my life disrupted by that family. I just want you to go away and stop asking questions."

Olson took a step closer to her. "Tired of the runaround, Bunny? Does he always tell you what to say and do? He's not very loyal, is he? But then again, he's not stupid. All he has to do is get back with his wife and he's got it made. The old lady was rich. Probably left her money to the family. And Mrs. Brooks is a looker, isn't she? What man wouldn't want her? And that house. That's some house. Do you really think he'd come here to live with you?"

He looked around at the small drab apartment with disgust. He waited for his words to sink in. He could see she was on the edge, and wanted to set her off.

"Is he only over here when he wants…?"

"Shut up." She crumpled into a heap on the nearest chair and cried as if her heart would break. "You bastard."

He stood there and waited. He handed her a hankie and she took it. After a few deep breaths she looked at him.

"When I woke up at three, he was gone."

Olson's ears perked up. Pay dirt. "When did he get back?"

"Around five."

That was enough time to leave and get back. The old dame had been shot around 3:45.

"Did he tell you where he was?"

"I pretended to be asleep when he got back. When I asked him in the morning, he said he'd gone for a walk."

"Had he ever gone for a walk in the middle of the night before?"

She shook her head no.

Olson felt sorry for her. She looked pretty broken up.

"You've done the right thing. If he did it once, he could do it again."

She looked at him. "You think he'll come after me?"

"I won't give him the chance. If we can catch a few more breaks, I think we can nail Mr. Brooks."

She stared into space.

"By the way. Why would he want the old girl dead? Why not just wait for her to croak?"

"She told them there was treasure in that house. He wanted it so he could run away with me."

Olson nodded. This just got better and better.

"You're well out of it, you know."

"Yeah. Sure."

When Olson hurried off, Bunny got up and walked over to the mirror. She wore a smirk.

"Take that, Graham."

The Brooks gang sat in the sunroom and had their first normal breakfast since the shooting. The girls made pancakes for their men. Faith had her nose in a journal as she ate her toast. Elsie was enormously grateful that Juliet and Robert went home for a while, but she knew they'd be back. In their rush to get Juliet's share of Aunt Hildy's loot out of the house, they forgot Kiwi. Not that Elsie minded.

She and Graham drank coffee on the deck. It felt good to be outside, even if it was a bit chilly. They spent a lot of time together, comforted by each other's presence. The events of the past week put their differences into perspective — they didn't want any more drama. They recognized the need to present a united front for the girls and for themselves. Other matters could wait.

They looked at the house on the other side of the back fence and discussed the odds of Juliet being persuaded to live there. Elsie didn't think it would happen, but Graham said he wouldn't be surprised, the way their luck had run lately.

The words were no sooner out of his mouth than Detectives Olson and Smith came around from the side entrance and walked onto the deck.

"We rang the doorbell," Olson said. "You couldn't have heard it."

Graham stood. "No, we didn't. May I ask when this police activity in and out of our home will stop? Can it at least keep until a more convenient time, and not first thing on a Sunday morning?"

"Murder is never convenient, Mr. Brooks." Smith sounded unfriendly.

Graham backed off. "You're right, of course."

Elsie was uneasy with the way they looked at Graham. "Is there anything you wanted in particular, detective?"

"Yes, Mrs. Brooks. We want your husband."

Elsie and Graham looked at each other. She got up to stand beside him. "What do you mean?"

"Your alibi has unravelled, Mr. Brooks."

Graham stood stock-still.

Elsie shouted. "What? What's going on?" She quickly glanced over to the patio doors and realized her family was in the doorway.

"Miss Bunny Hopkins says your husband got out of her bed at three o'clock in the morning the night of the murder and didn't crawl back in until five. Which leaves plenty of time for him to run over here, kill your aunt and run back to his girlfriend with no one the wiser."

Lily ran over to her mother. "Mom, what's happening?"

"It's all right, Lily. Calm down," Graham answered quietly.

Elsie panicked. "That can't be right, you're mistaken. Graham would never kill anyone. I know him."

Olson gave her an impatient look. "He has no alibi and he has a motive."

Elsie yelled, "Motive? What motive? This is ridiculous."

Graham turned to her. "Call our lawyer. He'll know what to do and don't worry. This is a mistake. You know that, don't you?"

She nodded. Without further ado, they marched Graham off the deck, down the steps and around the corner of the house. They were gone as quickly as they had come. Everyone looked at one another.

Elsie held her hand over her mouth. "This can't be happening."

Dahlia shivered. "What do we do?"

Eli said, "You should call that lawyer. That's the first thing."

"Yes, of course." She rushed into the house.

Mrs. Noseworthy yelled from her porch as she hung out her wash. "Is everything all right?"

Lily smiled and gave her a wave. "Fine, thanks." Then she whispered to the others. "Quick. Get inside and pretend like we're normal."

They rushed at the door together, creating a bit of a bottleneck.

The first thing Faith did was pick up a cellphone and go into the hall closet to dial Juliet's number.

"You're not going to believe this," she whispered.

Chapter Twelve

Faith saw Juliet and Robert hurrying into the house.

"Is it really true?" Juliet said. "Graham did it? I never liked him."

Faith hit her arm. "I didn't ask you here to gloat over Graham's stupidity. We have to help Elsie. She looks terrible. I'm worried about her."

Robert gave a grunt. "Since when have you ever worried about anyone but yourself?"

"You're a fathead, did you know that? Don't ever move into that house behind the fence or I'll take a propane torch to it."

"Sticks and stones…"

Juliet slapped her thighs. "Refresh my memory. Why am I here? If Graham's guilty, he's guilty. We pick up and move on." She leaned towards her sister and said in a loud whisper, "It's not like he's technically her husband anymore, so good riddance to bad rubbish."

Faith held her head. "Why did I think you two could help? Just go home then, before you're inconvenienced any further. We'll call you when it's over."

"Well, I'm here now," Juliet hissed. "What do you want me to do?"

Her sister gestured them over to the far window. They bent their heads together. "I read detective novels. You're supposed to try and make people crack, catch them in a lie."

Robert pointed to his wife. "She's good at that."

"Thank you, I think."

"We should pay this Bunny Rabbit a visit. Ask her what she thinks she's playing at."

Robert folded his arms across his chest. "Maybe she's telling the truth. Have you considered that?"

Faith tsked. "If Graham were capable of murder, he'd have knocked off you two long ago."

Juliet looked at her with incredulity. "And leave you alive? I think not."

Faith tilted her head to look at the ceiling. "Please Lord. Why do I get into these conversations?"

"So you want us to pay this woman a visit, to say what?" Robert asked her.

"This isn't the story she told the police when it happened, otherwise they'd have dragged Graham off days ago. That means she's changed her tune and I want to know why."

Juliet sighed. "You watch too much *Law and Order*. Besides we don't know where she lives."

Her sister said, "I do. I went downstairs and looked it up in his address book by the phone."

"Why would she talk to us? And why do we want him out of this jam?" Juliet asked.

Faith said through gritted teeth, "Because like it or not, we're family."

Elsie called the lawyer. He said he'd meet her at the police station. She dressed quickly and hurried downstairs, ignoring the three musketeers in the living room and headed straight for the kitchen. The kids were around the table.

"Has anyone seen my black pumps?"

"I think they're in the front porch. I'll get them." Lily jumped up and disappeared.

"What should we do, Mrs. B?"

Elsie struggled to get her earring on. "There's nothing you can do at the moment. Just don't worry. I'm sure it's all a mistake. Dee, pass me my purse."

Dahlia reached over and grabbed it from the window sill. "But what if they ask us if Daddy liked her? We know he didn't want her here. He always said how nice it would be if she wasn't around."

Lily returned with the shoes. Elsie took them from her. "Thanks. Listen Dee, I said the same thing myself a couple of times. She was difficult. She drove us crazy, but none of us would've hurt her." She rooted through her bag. "Where are my keys? I can never find anything. Oh, here they are."

"But Mom, why would anyone else want her dead? Why wasn't it one of us that was shot?"

"Don't say that! I can't even go there."

Lily lowered her voice. "You don't suppose those three idiots in the living room did it?"

Her mother stamped her foot. "Oh, for the love of God, Lily. It doesn't help me when you say things like that. Now do I need to take anything else with me?"

It wasn't really a question for them. She looked around the kitchen. "I better go. I have no idea when I'll be home."

"Call us when you know something," Lily shouted at her retreating back.

Once the back door closed, Eli said, "I think those three clowns could've done it."

Lily nodded. "I mean, who else is there? They're so greedy I wouldn't put anything past them."

Slater looked down the hallway. "I can see them from here. They look like they're up to something. Maybe we should tail them."

"You watch too many James Bond movies," Lily told him.

Dahlia grinned. "He knows all about cops and robbers, don't you Slater? How they tie…"

"We know the drill," Lily groaned. "How they tie people up, use handcuffs and jump into bed with girls named Pussy Galore."

"Shh, she's coming," Slater whispered.

They were interrupted by Faith, who stuck her head in the kitchen door. "We have to go out for a bit. I don't know when we'll be back."

"Where to?" Lily asked.

"Groceries. See ya." She disappeared.

"There's something rotten in the state of Denmark," she whispered. "Faith's never bought groceries in her life and besides, Superstore isn't open on Sunday."

"What happened in Denmark?" Slater asked.

Eli slapped his shoulder. "Don't worry, buddy. It's been taken care of. Let's go and follow those nitwits."

They got up and snuck to the window in time to see Robert drive off, so they hurried out to the car.

"Maybe that's why they wear wooden shoes," Slater said to no one in particular.

Harry walked down the hall with arrest reports under his arm. When he turned the corner, there was Elsie. She sat in a chair all by herself outside the interrogation room, looking lost.

"What's wrong, Elsie? Why are you here?" He sat in the chair beside her so she wouldn't have to look up at him.

Swallowing a few times, obviously in an attempt to keep her emotions under wraps, she told him how the detectives had come to the house and taken Graham away for questioning. "Apparently his alibi fell apart. They think he killed Aunt Hildy."

"If they thought that, they'd have arrested him. If they're only questioning him, they don't have quite enough evidence against him," he said, trying to reassure her.

"Yes. That's true. Maybe it's not as dire as I think."

Harry didn't say anything because he knew it could turn serious, very quickly. "You told me Graham was out that night. Where was he?"

She stared at her hands.

"With that woman we met in the driveway?"

She nodded and looked at him with her big brown eyes full of tears.

"Elsie," he whispered. "Why does that upset you? You're going out with me. He's allowed to see other women, isn't he?"

"I'm not upset about that," she said quickly. "I'm upset that the father of my children is a suspect in a murder investigation and if he wasn't with that woman for two hours in the middle of the night, then where was he?"

Harry didn't know how to comfort her, so he said the first thing that came to mind. "Would you like to come to my place tonight?"

"I don't know, Harry. I'm a little pre-occupied at the moment."

"Of course, of course. Whenever you're ready."

"Thanks for the thought though," she smiled absently.

"I better go. Call me if you need anything."

"I will. Thanks."

As he walked away, he wondered if Elsie really liked him. She seemed awfully upset about Graham. But then she was always *something* about Graham.

Six people were in two cars parked outside Bunny's apartment building. The first carload wasn't sure how to approach her and the second carload waited for the first carload to do something.

Juliet and Faith argued about what they should say.

"I don't think it matters, because we won't be able to say anything. No one opens the door to strangers anymore," Juliet pointed out.

"I'll tell her I'm a political candidate and ask if could I have a moment of her time."

Juliet snorted. "A political candidate in jogging pants? You better go to plan B."

"I don't have a plan B...unless I say I'm selling Girl Guide cookies."

"You? A Girl Guide? She'd die laughing. Then where would we be?"

Robert turned the car off. "So you drag us over here for nothing. Let's just go in the damn place and knock on the door. If she answers then we'll ask her point blank. If she refuses, we'll go to No Ifs Ands Or Butts tomorrow morning and catch her in the office."

They agreed.

"What are those morons doing?" Lily shouted.

"Who's place is this?" her sister asked. "Do you think it's The Rabbit?"

Eli said, "Why would they go see her? If they did kill Aunt Hildy, wouldn't they be thrilled Bunny's thrown suspicion your father's way?"

"Maybe they're all in on it, and now they want to get rid of her before she rats them out," Slater suggested.

Lily chimed in. "Well, I hope they do kill her. The slag deserves it."

Dahlia shouted, "Look. Slater's right. There they go!"

"Don't be ridiculous," Eli said. "It's broad daylight. The three of them just went in the front door with their car parked right outside. No one would do that if they were bent on murder. Besides, we don't even know if this *is* Bunny's place."

Lily said, "We'll never know if we just sit here. I'm going in. I don't care about the rest of you." She dashed out the door.

"Me too." Dahlia banged the door behind her.

"Me three." Slater leapt out.

"Well, shit." Eli went after them.

The kids hurried into the building and snuck up behind their relatives. They peeked around a corner. Their aunts and uncle stood outside the door of an apartment on the second floor, arguing amongst themselves in loud whispers.

"Why don't they do something?" Lily wondered.

Just then Juliet hit Faith over the head with her Gucci bag and Robert wrestled it away from her.

"Oh, for the love of pete. Those twits are killing each other," Eli griped.

"They are? Let's see." Slater moved closer to the edge to get a better look and lost his footing. He fell into the other three, who went down like bowling balls in the middle of the corridor with a muffled THUD onto the carpet.

"Freaking heck, Slater," Eli groaned. "I think my ankle's broken."

The trio at the door whipped around at the commotion.

Juliet screamed. "What are you idiots doing here?"

"Ditto," Lily yelled from the bottom of the heap.

The apartment door suddenly opened and Bunny stood there in all her glory. "Are you here to collect for an idiot charity? If so, I gave at the office." Bunny stepped forward. "Let me guess." She took a drag of her cigarette and blew it at them. "The Brooks family."

No one moved.

"Save your breath. I told the truth. And I don't give a flying fig if you believe me or not." She turned to go and then stopped. "And another thing. You can tell him that if he ever tries to come near me again, it won't be just your precious Aunt Hildy with a hole in her heart."

She slammed the door.

Juliet huffed. "Well, this is what I get for doing a good deed. I swear, never again." She stepped over the kids in the hall.

"What good deed?" Lily said. "You didn't do anything except have a snit in front of her door."

"Button your lip, young lady. You're too mouthy for your own good. Come on you two," she said to her husband and sister. "Let's get a bite. I'm famished."

The kids were walked over twice more before they untangled themselves, sat up and looked at each other.

"This isn't good." Lily said quietly.

"You know what just occurred to me?" Dahlia whispered. "How did she know Aunt Hildy was shot through the heart? The papers never said."

The police had to let Graham go after a miserable afternoon of interrogation. When it came down to it they couldn't prove that he didn't just go for a walk. But the detectives warned him that asking Bunny to lie about where he was made him the prime suspect. The lawyer and Elsie met him as he came out, exhausted from the endless questions that were seemingly all the same. Graham and Elsie walked to the car and got in, Elsie behind the wheel. She didn't move.

"Tell me."

"Honestly, I'm sick to death of talking, if you don't mind."

"I do mind, Graham. I sat outside that office all afternoon. I deserve to know."

He gave a big sigh. "I asked Bunny to tell the police I was there all night and she did. But the fact is, I wasn't there all night and she knew it. She decided to tell the police the truth."

She looked incredulous. "Why did you do that? Don't you know how suspicious that makes you look?"

He hit the glove compartment with his fist. "I'm such an idiot. I panicked because she knew I went out but I had no explanation for why I went. I honestly went for a walk. I sat on a stupid park bench, which is a dumb thing to do in the middle of the night, but I needed to get some air. The evening was so upsetting, not only about the treasure crap but the girls being angry with me. Even their boyfriends looked at me like I was the world's biggest loser. I was humiliated and I couldn't sleep. I think I had a panic attack. But the fact is, no one can verify that I did sit on that stupid bench, so I'm stuck."

"But why did Bunny change her story all of a sudden?"

He looked ahead at the windshield. "I didn't see her for

awhile, what with the funeral and everything. It obviously pissed her off."

"She threw you to the lions, Graham, just to get back at you. What does that say about her?"

He lowered his head. "You don't have to point it out. Can we just go?"

She turned on the ignition and threw the car into drive, pulling out onto Gottingen Street a little too quickly.

"Don't get a speeding ticket in front of Police Headquarters," Graham said.

Elsie gave him a dirty look. Why didn't she let him take the bus home? She could've spent the day fretting in front of the television watching old movies. Instead, she sat in that stinking corridor counting the holes in the ceiling tiles.

"Stop chewing your bottom lip," he said out of the blue.

"If it's okay by you, I'll handle stress any old way I please."'

They sat at a red light on the corner of Gottingen and North Street. Elsie looked at the other cars, filled with people who didn't spend their day at the police station. They were probably going to Grandma's house for Sunday dinner. They'd have roast beef with gravy and Yorkshire pudding, topped off with warm strawberry-rhubarb pie and a dollop of vanilla ice cream for dessert.

The light turned green and the car behind them honked impatiently. Flustered, Elsie turned the corner and continued up North Street. At the next stop sign, Graham put his hand up to her cheek and rubbed a tear away with his thumb. He kept his hand there for a moment and she leaned into it.

They pulled into the driveway. Graham turned to her. "I can't face the kids right now."

Elsie took the keys out of the ignition. "They've been worried too. They'll want to know what happened."

"Just tell them whatever you want. There's something I have to do first." He started to get out of the car.

"What do you mean? Where are you going?"

He looked back at her. "I have to see her, Elsie. She can't get away with this."

"Let me go with you then."

"I don't think that's a good idea."

"She's upset my life and our children's lives as well, don't forget."

Graham let out a big sigh.

"Never mind then." Elsie slammed the car door in his face and walked up the back steps into the house. Graham watched her go. Then he too got out of the car, picked up his van keys and drove as fast as he dared to Bunny's apartment.

When she opened the door, she tried to close it in his face.

"I want to talk to you."

"Get lost, Graham."

"Please. I've had a bitch of a day and I need to speak with you."

"Oh, come in then and get it over with." She held the door and let him through. "You're not the only one who had a crappy day. I had your whole damn family here this morning."

"What?"

"Screaming in the hallway, bunch of lunatics."

He paced in her living room. "Never mind about them. I can't believe the stunt you pulled. I know I was wrong to ask you to lie about where I was. I shouldn't have done that. But to tell them I wanted the treasure to run away with you? Why? I just want to know why?"

Bunny looked at him as if he was mad. "I don't owe you any favours. That shit of a detective had it right. You're only here when you want a lay. You could care less about me."

"Well, I was stupid enough to think you did care for me," he yelled. "You told me often enough, flinging yourself on me day and night. But obviously I was wrong. The trouble is, your kind of revenge is deadly. There's a cloud of suspicion over me already because I don't have an alibi for my whereabouts that night. But now thanks to you, the police think I had a motive for killing Aunt Hildy."

"You're a selfish prick, did you know that? How was I supposed to know that you didn't kill that old woman? You were gone when she was shot. You snuck back to bed and obviously didn't want me to know you'd been out. Besides the fact that you never shut up about how much she ticked you off."

Graham took a step back. "You actually think I'm the type of man who would kill a defenceless old woman?" He pointed his finger at her. "You're sick, lady."

"You deserved it," she hollered in his face. "You treat me like trash. I took you in when you needed someone the other night. I gave myself to you. And just when I believed you really liked me…when you said you'd come back to me, you make one phone call and then nothing. Not a word for days. What did you expect me to do? Roll over and take it?"

"My wife's aunt was murdered. She was distraught. I needed to be with my family. Is that so difficult to understand? Someone was killed in my house. I know it's hard to believe, but that took precedence over you."

"Well, understand this, Graham," she said as she walked over to the door and opened it. "I want you to stay away from me.

You've used me once too often. And if your weird family ever come near me again, you'll be sorry."

He walked up to her. "You go near my family and you won't know what hit you."

He heard the door slam behind him. He got in the truck, fumbling with the keys because his hands shook. This was a bloody nightmare. The woman was sick. How could he have brought her into his home?

He needed a beer.

He opened his small fridge when he got back home, but he'd run out. So he walked upstairs and got one out of Elsie's fridge. He sat at the table and downed it.

She walked into the kitchen. "Did you see her?"

He only had the strength to nod.

She waited for him to say something. "Fine. Don't tell me." And out she went.

He could see Juliet on her hands and knees in the sunroom. She peered under the sofa. He had no illusions as to why — he knew it wasn't to help with the housework. "Do you ever go home, Juliet?" he shouted across the room.

"Do you?" she yelled back.

"Witch," he muttered. As he sat there, Eli came into the kitchen and grabbed four cans of Pepsi. These two characters ate Elsie out of house and home and she didn't seem to mind. Well, he did. People took advantage of her and he was tired of it.

Eli gave him a sympathetic look. "You must have had a hard day, Mr. Brooks."

Graham got up, took another beer from the fridge and sat back at the table. "Never mind that. What do you do, anyway, Eli?"

"I volunteer at various human rights advocacy groups, Amnesty International, that sort of thing. And I man the phones for a kids' hotline at the youth centre. And take a few classes."

He took a swallow of beer and leaned back in the kitchen chair. "I didn't ask about your extracurricular activities. I mean your real job."

"That is my real job."

He swallowed another huge gulp of beer. "Let me put it this way. How would you buy groceries if we weren't around?"

"Oh. My mom and dad sent me monthly cheques."

Graham finished the can. "They sent you cheques?

"Yeah. To help ease their guilt for never being around. They really don't care what I do or where I go. I've always sort of interfered with their lives."

"Interfered?

"Mom was forty-six when I was born. It's family legend that my father had to beg her to come in off the window ledge when she found out she was pregnant."

"I see." Graham went to the fridge and took out his third beer. "But Elsie told me you were brought up on a commune. How did the hippie thing happen if your parents were middle-aged when you were in diapers?"

Eli shifted the cold pop in his hands. "Personally, I think they both had nervous breakdowns and my grandparents shipped them off to the middle of nowhere until they were better."

"Your grandparents? How frigging old are they?"

"They're in their nineties. Last I heard they were on their yacht in Monte Carlo. They like to gamble. It's their hobby."

Graham pointed at him with his can. "Are you saying your family's rich?"

"Stinking."

"Give Elsie your next cheque. To buy groceries."

"No problem."

"How much do you get every month?"

"Twenty g's."

Graham choked. When he could talk again, he wheezed, "That should just about cover it."

Eli turned to go, when he paused and looked back. "You're lucky Mr. Brooks. Not everyone has a family like this one. I wish I did."

Graham sat for a long time after Eli left the room. Then he got up and downed his fourth beer.

What with the funeral and the treasure hunt and being mired in Elsie and Graham's problems, Juliet and Robert delayed making a final decision about their predicament. But now it was crunch time. Creditors breathed down their necks. Their only option was to sell the house to pay off their debts and move into the old barn across the yard.

Juliet was distraught at the thought of it, until her husband reminded her that they'd be able to sneak into Elsie's pretty much at will. There had to be more treasure than the three diamonds.

Luckily the Beech Street house was vacant of tenants and their place sold quickly because of the many amenities they'd acquired over the years, but handing the key over to the real estate agent wasn't easy. Juliet cried all afternoon.

It took a few days for their belongings to be packed up and the old house put to rights with the help of a cleaning company, so they bunked in with Elsie until the move was complete.

When the workmen were finished, they went over to see their new property. It was a cold day, a definite nip in the air. Naked tree branches waved against a steel-grey sky. The ground was hard, almost frosty. Kiwi strained at her leash, sniffing around in her tangerine-coloured wool sweater and matching booties.

As they started off, Juliet looked back at Elsie's house with a stab of pure envy. She'd hated the old dinosaur growing up. Couldn't wait to get out of it and into something modern and stylish like some of her friends in the newly developed end of town, full of split levels and bungalow-style dwellings with vinyl siding and brick inlay.

Now, of course, the family home was a beauty. She had to admit her little sister had done wonders. She was a messy housekeeper, probably due to the fact there were only so many hours in the day, but she had great taste in decorating and a natural style that Juliet tried to emulate but could never copy.

The flowers that edged the front walk to the wide surrounding porch were gone now, but the perennials stood bravely in the biting wind. The red maple her mother planted years ago had flourished on the front lawn. The shingles on the house were stained a gorgeous tint of mossy pewter, with a complementary cream on the trim and rich brownish rust on the front door, shutters and window boxes. Depending on the season, cattails, pussy willows or pine and holly were stuffed into the large milk cans and butter churns Elsie used as flower pots on her veranda. Only recently, a beautiful country screen door was added and it set off the house like a little jewel.

Juliet decided life was unfair and stupid. She set off at a faster clip, to get away from the perfect place.

"Wait for me," Robert whined. "I can't keep up."

She looked back at her husband. When did he get so old? His hair looked silver in the sun and his small pot belly hung slightly over his belt. To top it off, as far as she could make out, his posterior looked exactly the same as before. Perhaps there was no hope for improvement. The thought didn't add to her mood.

"It's only around the corner," she said impatiently. "It's not a marathon."

"I'm stiff."

She mumbled, "You're a stiff all right. Except where it matters."

"Thank you very much," he groused. "How am I supposed to perform? I've just lost all my money, my home, my job, not to mention the fact that my backside looks like a cheese grater. Pardon me, if I'm not in the mood to sweep you off your feet."

"Fine. Never mind. Let's just go and see if the cleaners have put a dent in the stupid place."

They walked to the end of the street, turned left, walked up the street, turned left again and walked halfway down the street to stop in front of a monstrous beast of a house.

It was the same vintage as Elsie's, but the bones weren't as aesthetically pleasing. There were no gabled windows and it was on a smaller piece of property. At some point over the years, it had been converted into three apartments, so there were multiple doors on the front porch, which looked awkward and confusing. It was in desperate need of paint and had an air of neglect. The only thing on the front lawn was grass, and even that was patchy and brown. It was definitely the black sheep of the street.

"Oh God."

"Let's go," Robert said. As they went up the stairs, Juliet tripped on a broken board.

"A new front porch wouldn't go amiss. Oh great. I just put a hole in my stocking."

They entered the largest apartment. At least the cleaners had taken care of the musty smell. They wandered around the large rooms. Their footsteps echoed in spite of the boxes piled everywhere.

"Yuck, what a horrible old house."

"It looks a lot better than when we first saw it," Robert said.

"How's one supposed to make a home out of a place that's been divided into three apartments? I mean, how many toilets do I have to clean?"

"One. If we rent two of them, that'll bring in cash."

Juliet looked around. "Are you kidding me? I'm not having a bunch of strangers in my house. That's disgusting."

"But they'll be on the other side of the wall. What do you care?"

"What if they cook cabbage all day? Or smoke and burn the place down? I'm not the sort of woman who becomes a landlady in the prime of her life."

Robert raised his voice. "You don't want to be a bag lady either, and you will be if we don't generate some income."

"But the money from the house and my car?"

"Juliet, I've told you. That paid off our debts. I can't find a job, at least not yet, and you refuse to work. So how are we supposed to put bread on the table?"

"We sell the diamonds and our share of Aunt Hildy's stuff."

"That would keep us for a year," Robert sighed. "Of course, if we sold your tiara…"

"No flipping way. I've given up too much already."

"Be realistic. Where will you wear it? To the movies?"

She wanted to punch the wall. Instead she took a piece of peeling wallpaper and torn a huge strip off. "I'll wear the damn thing everywhere. To yoga class."

"— we can't afford yoga class."

"To the tanning salon then."

"We can't afford the tanning salon."

"To the manicurist."

"We can't afford the..."

"AAAAAAAAAAAAAAAAAAAAAA."

Elsie came home from work just in time to hear the ungodly scream. Mrs. Noseworthy rushed over to the fence with her pruning shears.

"Oh dear, not another murder? I don't think I could stand another murder."

Elsie dropped her paraphernalia and ran across the back lawn, sure someone was in mortal agony, stopping as soon as she saw Juliet chase Robert out of their house with a hanger.

Elsie stood in the yard and shook her fist in the air. "Thanks a lot Aunt Hildy." Then she shook her fist at her sister and brother -in-law. "Don't think I won't call the cops on you for disturbing the peace, Juliet, because I will."

"Elsie, save me." Robert tried to climb the chain link fence between them but the cedars that grew over them were too thick and he couldn't get a good grip.

"Juliet!"

Juliet stopped and looked around in a daze. "What?"

"Put down that blasted hanger and stop making a spectacle

Lesley Crewe

of yourself. And go get ready for dinner." Elsie walked back to pick up her things.

Mrs. Noseworthy shook her head. "There goes the neighbourhood."

"Tell me about it." Elsie stormed into the house. She threw her stuff on the kitchen table and sat for a minute to try and think about what she had in the freezer. Then it occurred to her that Faith and Juliet had been in the house all day. Why wasn't supper ready for her?

She no sooner had that thought than Graham came home with a couple of buckets of KFC. It was as if he had read her mind.

"I could kiss you."

"Well, I assumed the great lumps hadn't made anything for dinner. I'll take mine downstairs."

"Don't. That's stupid. Let's just eat."

Everyone was at the table when Robert and Juliet walked in for dinner. Robert was mortified because — just to tick him off — Juliet wore her tiara.

Graham stood at attention. "Everyone rise. The queen is here." Slater stood.

Dahlia gestured with her fork. "Sit down. Dad's only joking." Slater sat.

"So. How are the new digs?" Faith asked her sister.

Juliet pouted. "Since it's a hole, that's a good way to describe it."

"I wouldn't look a gift horse in the mouth. She gave you a house for heaven's sake."

"She gave us a dump that needs to be fixed up."

Graham smirked. "I think she did it for fun…just the thought of Juliet in a tiara, sitting pretty on a porch the Clampetts wouldn't own."

"They ended up with the goods in the end, didn't they? Just like I plan to, so don't be so smug."

Graham reached for more chicken. "You'll never find any treasure, Juliet. You're a royal. You might have to work too hard."

Robert coughed and then gagged when he saw Juliet's face. He tried to get her attention because he knew she'd blab about the diamonds, but she ignored him. There was nothing he could do but pretend to fall off the chair and faint dead away.

Everyone jumped and ran to help him. Everyone except his wife.

"He's faking."

Elsie looked at her sister. "You're the world's meanest person." She knelt beside Robert and loosened his collar. "Maybe we should call 911."

"I know him," Juliet said as she reached for a roll. "He just wanted me to shut up."

"I've had first aid," Eli said. "Put something under his head and elevate his feet a little."

Lily ran to get an afghan off the sofa.

Juliet shrugged. "You can levitate him if you want to. He's awake." She leaned over the chair. "Aren't you darling?"

Robert was still.

"Stop with the games. I'm starving."

Robert stayed inert.

"Oh, you bloody man." Juliet huffed. "Tickle under his armpits. That always gets him."

Elsie was horrified. "You're a nut case. Leave the poor man alone. He's out cold."

"He's faking, I tell you. He does this to me all the time." She reached down and grabbed his pant leg to give it a shake. "Stop it, Robert. Stop it."

"Get away from him," Eli yelled. "Slater, get her."

Slater reached over and grabbed her. She let poor Robert's foot go and it fell to the floor with a thud. Suddenly Kiwi came out from under the table and started to lick his face. That revived him rather quickly.

"Oh look, he's coming around," Elsie cried. "Good work, Kiwi."

"What happened?" he whispered.

"You fainted, didn't you darling?"

"I fainted?"

"Yes, love. So I wouldn't tell them about the diamonds."

A hush fell over the room.

"Oops."

"I hate you, Juliet."

Elsie wished they'd all shut up. She left the squabbling crowd around the table and took a cup of tea in the living room, sipping it as she looked out the window at the neighbours. They went about their business, just nice normal families who looked happy while they washed their cars and played with their kids. Some even put up Halloween decorations.

Why was her life nothing but chaos? She was a normal person who strived to do the right thing and be there for her family, but nothing she ever did seemed to be enough. She had a sort-of husband she both wanted and didn't want, and two sisters who were so selfish, they'd never think to have supper on the table when she got home from work. Her girls were totally wrapped up with their own affairs and, certainly by the looks of it, had vastly superior sex lives in comparison with her own. She basically subsidized their young men. But worst of all, Aunt Hildy had been killed. Right under her nose.

Elsie looked into the fireplace and thought of her aunt. There was a woman who lived by her own rules and if someone didn't like it, that was just too bad. What would Aunt Hildy think of her, as she moaned and moped about her life but refused to change it? She had lots of advice for her clients, but none for herself.

She pulled her knees up and hugged them, rocking back and forth. Beside her the cats, Pip and Squeak, purred up a storm. Elsie leaned against them and closed her eyes. If only sleep would come.

But the gods were against her and the whole stupid family poured in, still screaming at each other over the injustice of treasure found but not shared. She let them scream for a while and wondered why they needed her opinion, but apparently they did because they stared at her and waited for an answer.

Elsie never planned what happened, so you couldn't say it was premeditated. It shocked her as much as it did everyone else and when she thought of it years later, she realized it was the turning point in her life.

She got off the couch, picked up the fire poker, and waved it around menacingly in front of her family. They backed up.

"I want you all to stay away from me, do you hear me? I'm sick to death of all of you! You're greedy and inconsiderate and never think of anyone but yourselves. All you do is fight and bicker over this ridiculous treasure. Well, none of you will get any of it because I'll make sure I smash everything to smithereens before you can get your grubby little hands on it."

She slammed the poker against a crystal vase filled with pink hydrangea. Glass shattered everywhere. There were horrified screams from Juliet and Faith.

"Mom, don't!" Dahlia cried.

"Dad, stop her," Lily shouted.

"Elsie, please." Graham held out his hand. "Stop this. It's alright. We can talk about it."

She walked toward them, still brandishing the poker. They backed up even further. "I haven't even started!"

Whipping around, the lamp was next, then the pictures on the wall, smashed and knocked to the floor. She swung the poker like a baseball bat and hit the face of the grandfather clock.

"Stop Elsie! Stop it now!" Faith screamed.

"Why?" Elsie screamed back. "This is my goddamn house. It's not yours!" She reached up and threw the poker at the mirror over the fireplace mantle. Shards of glass crashed to the floor as the large model of her grandfather's ship fell from its place of honour and broke into a million pieces on the hearth.

There was complete silence. No one moved a muscle.

Then Dahlia whispered, "What's that?"

"Oh, my god. It's Aunt Hildy's treasure," Lily whispered back.

Scattered amongst the wreckage of the wooden ship were diamond rings and necklaces, ruby bracelets, sapphire brooches and ropes of cultured pearls — hundreds of thousands of dollars' worth of jewellery.

The family looked at one another in shock, then back at Elsie.

She turned to face them. "I say, you guys are pretty pathetic treasure hunters. I say, maybe you should just relax and let the treasure find you."

She grabbed her car keys and left.

Lily and Dahlia burst into tears. Everyone else just stood there. Finally Graham spoke.

"And I say, we should clean up this mess for your mother. We'll gather it all up and put it in a garbage bag so we can look at it later. Then we'll do the dishes, make our lunches for to-morrow, and have everything ship shape for when she comes home." He cleared his throat. "If she ever does."

Chapter Thirteen

When Graham woke up the next morning, he tiptoed upstairs to make sure Elsie was there. She was sound asleep, thank God. He was almost surprised to see her. He wouldn't have blamed her if she left town. He looked at her and thought how beautiful she was. It occurred to him that he was the biggest idiot alive. What man lets a woman like this walk out of his life?

When he went back downstairs he was surprised to see an immaculate kitchen, with breakfast ready and the coffee on. The table was set with the good cutlery. There were even napkin rings. The girls were bright-eyed as they waited for their mom to come down and be impressed.

"Is she up yet?" Lily asked.

Graham shook his head.

Dahlia looked worried. "You don't think she really hates us, do you?"

He poured his coffee. "Would you blame her if she did?"

"What do we do with all the stuff Mom found?" Lily wondered. "I can't believe I feel this way, but I really hope we don't find anything else. Who needs more aggravation?" She took her napkin out of the ring, really looking at it for the first time. "Tell me they're not real silver."

Her sister looked inside for the mark. "Yep."

Lily was incredulous. "Why on earth is all this stuff here? Was Aunt Hildy some kind of kleptomaniac? Surely everything doesn't belong to her?"

"Maybe she was a smuggler," Dahlia suggested. "Maybe she robbed tombs and came back here every few years to hide more loot, so no one would know where to find it."

"That actually sounds like a reasonable explanation," her father said. "It's possible your Aunt Hildy was a master criminal."

The girls looked at each other. Lily said, "Maybe Aunt Hildy was killed by a rival. Someone who wanted their stuff back."

"They weren't very smart then," Graham laughed, "because they didn't take it. Not to mention, if they were Aunt Hildy's vintage, they'd be pretty darn old."

"That's true."

Faith wandered in to the kitchen. "Good morning. What's true?"

Dahlia buttered her toast. "We want to know why Aunt Hildy had so much stuff and how she hid it without anyone knowing."

Their aunt poured her orange juice. "She's squirrelled this stuff away for a long time, a veritable packrat. Think about it. She always travelled and never had a home of her own. She accumulated a lot of stuff over the years and probably used this house as a storage facility."

Graham took a sip of his coffee. "But there are storage facilities. Why not use them?"

"I know why," Lily almost shouted. "She said her whole life was a game of hide-and-seek. She found buried treasure all the time, whether it was bones or dishes. She'd love it if someone looked for it instead of just turning a key in a safety deposit box."

Faith drank her juice and put the glass on the table. "Either that, or the more likely theory: She was bonkers."

"That's my take on it," Graham said.

She turned to him. "By the way, two outlets in the attic don't work. Maybe I blew a fuse. Could you check?"

He got up. "First Elsie, now you." He started for the basement stairs, but turned back. "Lily, call Crystal and tell her your mom won't be in today. Say she has a sniffle or something. She needs her sleep."

"She needs a psychiatrist," Faith said.

"And you don't?" Graham went down the stairs to the fuse box and opened it. She was right. A fuse had blown. He replaced it and was just about to close the box when he saw something out of the corner of his eye. He picked it up and rubbed the dust off it.

He trudged back up the stairs.

"Look what I found." He opened his hand to reveal a large ruby ring.

Lily had a mouth full of Cheerios. "Now it's becoming kind of a bore, don't you think?"

The other three nodded.

❧

Elsie woke with a start out of a sound sleep, confused at first about where she was. She thought she heard a bang. But of course, since the shooting, she jumped whenever she heard something out of the ordinary. It was probably Faith in the kitchen. The kids would be gone. And Graham. Juliet and Robert were probably over at the house. So she lay in bed and thought about what happened last night.

For the first time in a long time, she felt powerful. When she left the house, she drove for hours. Then she found herself at Harry's door. She didn't even question why she felt the need to go there. She didn't want to think at all.

But she knew it was because Harry was uncomplicated. He didn't ask anything of her, made no demands. He only ever wanted to make her feel good, so she took what was on offer and surprised herself and him with her wild lovemaking. She wanted to feel something other than emptiness and he helped her for a while.

Now it was time to get up. She got out of bed and had a hot shower, scrubbed her skin raw. It felt good, as if a layer of her old self had been removed. As she dried herself off she heard another muffled bang. What was that? She put on her bathrobe and went into the hall. It was quiet. She walked over and opened the door to the attic.

"Faith? Are you up there?"

Only silence. She went downstairs and was nearly in the kitchen when Kiwi gave a high-pitched yip. She poked her head into the dining room. The little dog was barking in circles. He wouldn't come to her, so she continued on. Flower was standing in the middle of the kitchen floor growling at nothing.

"What's the matter with you two? Faith, what have you done to these dogs?"

She waited for a saucy answer, but none came. Since Faith wasn't in the kitchen, maybe she was in the pantry.

"Faith?"

Nope. No one there either. It felt like someone was home but no one was to be found. Out on the deck, she saw Robert on his back stoop, throwing boxes into the yard.

Elsie yelled over. "Are you feeling okay? No more fainting spells, I hope?"

"Nope. What about you? That was quite a performance last night."

"We're all entitled to go around the bend once in a while."

"Lucky for us you did!" he laughed. "You're a natural when it comes to finding loot."

"Is Faith over there?"

"Yeah. They're arguing. Naturally."

She gave him a wave and went back in the house. She suddenly realized it was a workday. She phoned Crystal.

"Social Work Department."

"Hi Crys."

"Hey, how are you? Lily called and said you were under the weather."

"No. I was under Harry all night. And get this. I trashed my house before I left."

"I'm sorry but is this Elsie Brooks, model citizen?"

"This is Elsie Brooks, wanton sex goddess."

"I hate you."

"And I love you. I'll be there in an hour."

"I won't be here. I don't work for a woman who gets some while I dry up like an old prune." She hung up.

Elsie looked at the receiver. "I love that girl." She hung up the phone and grinned, but stopped when she noticed Flower. The fur on the back of her neck stood on end while she stared at nothing.

Lily wanted to apologize to her mother, but she had to leave for school and couldn't wait any longer for her to get up. She didn't know exactly what she would apologize for, but she knew one thing: Last night her mom was frightened. And that scared her.

She had a weekly quiz and she was late for it. Eli looked up when she hurried into class. He smiled and gave her a thumbs-up.

She tried to concentrate but was struggling to finish the last five questions when tears welled up and the need to blow her nose became more important than anything else. She rose from her seat and took her paper to the front. The professor glanced at her but she didn't stop to explain. She left the classroom and ran down the hall as far as the Coke machine. That's where Eli caught up to her.

He took her in his arms. "Let's go to my place."

Eli snuggled her on the mattress and let her cry about her mom's fit of rage and her dad being a murder suspect and Aunt Hildy's death and finally Dahlia's leaving home.

She eventually cried herself out and once she did she felt much better — and hungry. As she stirred the Kraft Dinner, there was a knock at the door.

Eli smiled. "Guess who?"

"Mrs. Minelli?"

"Who else?" He went to the door and opened it. "Hey, gorgeous."

"Oh, you're such a flirt," Mrs. Minelli walked past him holding a CorningWare dish like it was a gift to the gods. "Pasta primavera tonight. Oh hello, Daffodil, how are you?"

Lily smiled and didn't bother to correct her. "Fine. Something smells divine."

"You two sit," she said. "I want to make this an occasion."

They set the table and sat around it. The cook watched them dig in.

"Are you sure you won't have any?" Eli said with his mouth full. "It's out of this world."

"Na. I make it all the time."

Eli took two more huge bites, then dropped his fork, startling them both.

"What's wrong?" Lily cried. "Did you bite your tongue?"

He shook his wrists and tried to swallow. "Eureka!"

Mrs. Minelli put her hand over her heart. "That good, is it?"

"I know what I want to do with my life!"

"It just came to you in a bolt of lightning?" Lily laughed.

"It came to me in a casserole dish." He turned to Mrs. Minelli. "You and I can open a little Italian restaurant. You'll be head chef. We'll make a million bucks and become famous."

Lily shouted, "Oh my god, what a great idea! This is like, the best food on the planet."

Eli slapped his hands together. "This is fantastic. I can invest in my own business with my own money. You won't have to do anything, Mrs. Minelli, except cook your little heart out. And, wait! We'll call it…Mrs. Minelli's."

The kids were so thrilled with themselves they didn't notice Mrs. Minelli hadn't said anything. They finally looked over expecting her to be all smiles, but instead she looked like she was going to cry.

"What's wrong?" Eli said.

She shook her head sadly. "Thank you Eli. It's a nice dream, but it won't happen."

Eli couldn't hide his disappointment. "Why not?"

"I came to tell you tonight. I have to move back to Italy."

Eli's face fell even further. "What do you mean?"

"I lost my job and I'm too old to find another one. Who'd hire me? I can't afford to live in my apartment anymore. I have just enough money to fly home to be with my sister."

"That's terrible," Eli frowned. "How long have you known this?"

"A little while. I didn't want to tell you." Mrs. Minelli pulled a Kleenex out of her sleeve. "I'm going to miss Canada. And you." She dabbed at her eyes.

Eli got upset. "You've been trying to save money and yet cooking all these wonderful meals for me. You shouldn't have done that."

"It made me happy," she sniffed.

"Well, you can't go and that's that. I'll pay your rent. I can afford it."

"No, bambino. I couldn't do that. It's too much."

Lily bit her lip. "I hate to say it but she might be right, Eli. If you have to pay for your rent and hers and try to open a restaurant, you might be stretched too thin."

"I have to try Lil. This is such a great opportunity, not only for me but for Mrs. Minelli too."

"You're like a son to me," Mrs. Minelli sobbed. "The son I never had."

Eli took her hand and squeezed it.

Now it was Lily's turn to have a bolt out of the blue. She jumped up from the table. "I've got it. I've got it. This will work if you trust me, Mrs. Minelli."

The poor soul looked like she was hanging by a thread. She clasped her hands together as if in prayer. "What? What?"

"I want you to come with us. My aunt and uncle just moved

into a big old house that has two extra apartments in it. If Eli moved into one of them, instead of staying here, you could stay with him until we have the restaurant up and running and then you'll be making so much money you can afford your own apartment!"

Eli yelled, "That's perfect, Lil. You're brilliant! What do you say, Mrs. Minelli?"

She put her hands over her mouth for a good ten seconds. She looked uncertain. The kids waited on tenterhooks.

"I don't think...I'll miss this place!" She jumped up and they ran around the table to hug each other.

❧

Elsie's sisters and brother-in-law spent the morning in the Beech Street kitchen re-hashing the night before. None of them had ever seen Elsie in that state before and they were rattled. Elsie had always been the "good" one. Who knew she had the capacity for such anger? Juliet reminded Faith that their sea captain grandfather was known for his temper. Faith pointed out it was a good thing he wasn't around, because he would've hit the roof at the sight of his precious model ship reduced to kindling.

After three hours of rolling paint on the ceilings, Faith had to take a breather. "Why did I say I'd do this?"

Juliet looked up from painting the trim around the windows. "You have no life?"

"We'll all have a life when that bag of treasure is sorted out tonight," Robert grinned as he wiped up spills that missed the drop cloth. "We don't need to worry about who gets what. There's more than enough for everyone. What time did Graham say to be over?"

"Dinnertime," Faith answered. "Although why he figures he's the boss is beyond me. He wants out of our family, so why do we listen to him?"

Juliet shook her head. "I can't believe those jewels are just sitting over there. There better be a babysitter in that house."

Her sister nodded. "Elsie's there. Graham got Lily to call her off sick."

"Hellooo. I think she proved that last night."

"And besides," Faith continued, "the stuff's been in the house for a million years, why would someone steal it now?"

Her sister tsked. "Because we conveniently found it for them, that's why."

They heard footsteps on the front porch and a knock on the door.

Juliet rolled her eyes. "I hope to God it's not some welcome wagon dough head."

Faith dipped her roller into the tray. "That's a neighbourly attitude. You'll make a ton of friends on this street."

Robert went to the door. Lily and Eli barged in, dragging along an Italian woman straight from the old country, with her rolled up stockings and hair in a bun.

"You've got to help us Uncle Robert," Lily panted.

Faith put down her roller. "What have you two done now?"

Eli put his hands up to ward off questions. "Just hear us out. This is Mrs. Minelli."

Mrs. Minelli smiled and bobbed up and down. "How do you do?"

Juliet looked down at her from the chair she stood on. "Do you have a first name?"

"Nella."

"Nella Minelli?

Mrs. Minelli shrugged.

Eli continued. "I'd like to rent one of your apartments. Mrs. Minelli and I are moving in together."

"Do you approve of this arrangement, Lily?" Faith smirked. "It's awfully open-minded of you."

Lily made a face. "Oh, hardy har har."

"Mrs. Minelli here is the key to a wonderful business venture that will make us millions of dollars," Eli boasted.

Robert rubbed his hands together. "How so?"

"With this." Eli took the spice rack Mrs. Minelli held close to her chest. "This is the best cook in the world and we'll soon be the owners of a Mrs. Minelli franchise of Italian restaurants. We might even let you in on the ground floor as investors. What do you say?"

Juliet surprised everyone with her authoritative instructions. "She'll have to pass a test first. Take her over to your house and get her to make dinner. We'll be over and judge the results. If we like what we eat, it's a go."

Everyone ran about. Except Juliet. She stared out the window. She'd always been able to smell a deal and when she looked at Mrs. Minelli, she smelled success, along with the pungent aroma of oregano, basil and garlic. There was something about the woman. Juliet knew this was it. Her ship had come in.

When Elsie went to work that same morning, she hit every green light. Her favourite song played on the radio. She had a good hair day. She won ten bucks on her lotto ticket and the grouch at the cash register in the cafeteria was off sick. Even the debit slip matched the amount in her cheque book. Things were simply wonderful. She floated all afternoon in the after-glow of her incredible night.

Only as she drove into the driveway that evening, did she take a moment to collect herself. She didn't know how she would explain her behaviour last night but she *would* defend it. She needed to be brave. She would demand things for herself. It was about time.

She got out of the car and walked to the back door. Mrs. Noseworthy raked a few leaves from under her hedge.

"Something smells heavenly, Mrs. Noseworthy. What's for dinner?"

"I wish I knew. It's over at your house."

"It is? Well, I must go investigate. See you later." Elsie smiled as she went through the door. It was probably the girls, trying to make amends to their poor old mom. But there was no one in the kitchen except a large woman with a moustache throwing spices in a huge pot of tomato sauce.

"Hello?"

"Oh hello Missus. Please. Sit. Eat. Everyone's in the dining room. I'll be right in with your dinner."

Elsie did as she was told because she didn't know what else to do. When she walked into the dining room, everyone was at the table. No one spoke. They were stuffing their faces and dipping their bread into the mounds of fresh pasta on their plates.

"Excuse me. Who's in the kitchen?"

Eli grinned. "That, Mrs. B, is a woman who'll be as famous as Aunt Jemima in no time."

The woman hurried in with a plate. Eli introduced them. "This is Mrs. Minelli. Mrs. Minelli, this is Mrs. Brooks, the lady of the house."

Elsie smiled at her. "It's nice to meet you. But aren't you eating too?"

Mrs. Minelli adjusted her bulk. "I never eat."

"Oh."

Slater held up his plate for more. "You wouldn't believe it, Mrs. B. Dahlia and I came home from work and this far out chick was doin' her thing in the kitchen and I say: Party on, Mrs. Minelli, party on!"

Graham looked at her. "Try it."

Elsie sat down and swirled a bit of spaghetti on a spoon with her fork. They waited for the verdict. "It's absolutely delicious."

Eli got up and hugged the woman of the hour. "What did I tell you?"

Mrs. Minelli beamed and shouted, "Tomorrow…ravioli."

A cheer went up.

The time came to sort the treasure. The dishes were done and the family assembled, which included the newest member if only out of politeness.

Graham rubbed his hands together. "I'll go get it."

"Where did you put it anyway?" Robert asked him.

"Ah ah. That's my secret."

Elsie had no interest in what she'd uncovered, so she looked out the window at the night sky. No one asked her to explain her behaviour, so she kept quiet. Maybe they were afraid she'd fly off the handle again.

They waited. And waited. And waited.

"That miserable man," Juliet griped. "He's doing this deliberately. I could strangle him."

Faith yawned. "That's what you say about everyone. If you strangled as many people as you say you'd like to, there would be no one in this room. Or on the block."

Graham entered the living room slowly. "It's gone."

Everyone but Elsie leapt up.

"If this is a joke, so help me..." Juliet warned.

"It's gone."

"Where?" Faith screamed.

Graham screamed back. "If I knew that, I'd have it, wouldn't I?"

Mrs. Minelli tiptoed into the kitchen.

"But that's not possible," Robert said. "It was here only twenty-four hours ago. No one knew we found it but us. Did anyone mention it to anyone else today?"

Everyone shook their heads.

"But Elsie was here today," he insisted.

"No. I went to work after lunch."

"What!?"

"No one told me I couldn't."

"Well," Juliet spit, "if you'd been here last night, you would've known that. We said we'd divvy it up tonight since some of us were upset by your hysterics. I knew we should've bloody well done it the minute you walked out the door."

"Where did you hide it, Daddy?"

"In the sewing room. In the big wardrobe."

"I don't trust you," Robert said. "You've hidden it."

"I refuse to justify that remark with a response."

"It wouldn't hurt for all of us to look," Lily said, and before the words were out of her mouth everyone but Graham and Elsie had dashed upstairs.

"What's going on in this house?"

"The usual nonsense," she said.

"Who'd take it?"

"McCasper, our friendly ghost?"

"Yeah, right." He held onto his head and then suddenly spun around. "You didn't dump it off a wharf, did you?"

"I should have, but no."

"Did you hear anything today, before you left for work?"

Elsie suddenly got goose bumps. "As a matter of fact I did. I heard a bang and I thought someone was in the house. The dogs growled but I didn't see anyone, so I figured maybe a skunk knocked over a garbage can."

"That's it then. Someone stole it right out from under our noses the same way they killed Aunt Hildy. But who?"

The family trooped back downstairs. "It's not there. It's not anywhere," Lily said. "This is nuts. I swear this place is haunted."

"Crazy man," Slater said. "Maybe Aunt Hildy's mad that we took her stuff."

Juliet threw herself on a chair. "She wanted us to take it, you pinhead. I can't believe my life. Just when something goes my way, the gods decide to have a shit-on-Juliet day."

"Right," Robert sniped, "you're the only one this affects. None of us had a stake in any of it."

"Well, someone in this room must be responsible, since only we knew about it," Faith surmised. "Which one of you is the liar?"

"Get a clue," Dahlia said. "Why would any of us hide it from anyone else?"

"Why did Juliet hide pieces of the chandelier from us? It's the same thing," Lily pointed out.

Everyone looked at Juliet. She jumped out of her chair. "You ingrates think I took it? When? Did I climb the fence and wander over here in the dark, or was it this morning, when I was up to my eyeballs in paint?"

"Since you're afraid of the dark that lets you off the hook for last night," Faith said, "but you could've sent Robert over the fence."

"My hind quarters wouldn't permit vaulting a fence," Robert said.

"So where was everyone in this room today?" Faith asked. "Juliet, Robert and I were painting the kitchen over in the new house."

"And Eli, Mrs. Minelli and I were at his apartment."

"And Slater and I were at the salon."

"And I was at work."

"And I was at work too."

Slater looked at Flower and Kiwi. They cocked their heads at him. "These amigos are innocent."

Juliet's mouth hung open. "Are you frigging Dr. Doolittle? Do you honestly think two dogs would cart off a bag of treasure? And then tell you about it?"

"Of course not. But it's only polite to include them. Faith asked where everyone in the room was today. They're in the room."

Juliet advanced on him. "Okay, Einstein, you might be on to something. Let's ask the cats." She whipped around, hauled poor Pip off the couch and held him up in the air.

"Where were you today, Pip? And remember. I'll know if you're lying."

"Meow."

"He might be guilty, I don't understand cat. Perhaps you could translate, Slater?"

"Hey, don't make fun of me. It's not very nice."

Elsie stepped in. "No it's not. You're acting like an idiot."

Juliet threw Pip back on the couch. "Me? That's rich. I guess you don't recall your little temper tantrum last night."

"You can argue about this later," Graham yelled. "Let's just try and figure out who might have done this."

"I've got a better idea," Elsie said. "Why don't we just call the police and report a robbery? Maybe they'll find fingerprints."

Just then, Mrs. Minelli stuck her head in the room. "I made some hot chocolate with tiny marshmallows and some ten-minute fudge. Would anyone like some?"

The herd stampeded to the kitchen.

There was a full house that night, as Juliet and Robert were forced out by paint fumes and Eli and Mrs. Minelli didn't have any furniture. Slater organized the linen closet detail as people lined up for their sheets and face towels. He also ran around and moved cots and generally helped out with everything. Mrs. Minelli protested that she didn't need the guest room, she'd be happy on a lazy-boy, but Elsie insisted. The old woman cried and kissed everyone over and over.

Everyone was up early the next morning, thanks to the smell of frying bacon and baked tea biscuits. Mrs. Minelli presided over the kitchen as if she'd cooked there all her life. Elsie was more than happy to let her take over. Her mood soured, however, when the doorbell rang and who was there but Harry and another officer, sent to investigate the robbery.

"What are you doing here?" she whispered to him as his colleague, Officer Fish, went into the living room ahead of them.

"Believe me, it wasn't my idea," Harry whispered back. "Because now all I want to do is take you upstairs and rip your clothes off."

"Stop it."

The family quickly gathered in the living room. Graham gave Harry a curt nod and Harry returned one. Elsie felt sick to her stomach. Of all the stupid policemen in the city, she got Harry. The rest of her family gave Harry big smiles.

Officer Fish started off. "So. You had a robbery here yesterday."

Everyone spoke at once.

"Hold it," Officer Fish said. "Perhaps you could fill me in Mr. Brooks, since you're the one who called us."

So Graham told them what had transpired. Elsie could tell he was on edge. He made a point of ignoring Harry. Fish asked Graham to show him around and told Harry to go upstairs and dust for fingerprints on the wardrobe in the sewing room.

"I'll show you where it is," Elsie said quickly. Graham gave her a look as he left with Fish.

Elsie went up the stairs ahead of Harry. When they were out of view, he pinched her bottom.

"Don't," she squealed. "Are you crazy?"

Harry followed her into the sewing room. "I sure am. Crazy about you." He grabbed her and whispered, "Just a kiss."

"No. Stop it." She tried to get out of his grasp.

"I won't leave until I get one," Harry smirked. "You were happy enough to give me plenty the other night."

"One. I'll give you one." She let him kiss her longer than she should have. She was trying to push herself away when in walked Graham and Officer Fish. Fish gave Harry a horrified look. "We're old friends," was all Elsie could muster.

Graham's expression was stony. Harry glared. Elsie was getting tired of the male sex. They were too much work.

That evening, as Mrs. Minelli made ravioli, a fight broke out between the two families as to whom she would cook for. Technically she lived with Eli, but he didn't have any furniture and Mrs. Minelli's belongings were still in her apartment. Eli and a buddy with a truck were going to bring it over one trip at a time. Why waste his investment dollars on a moving company? It made sense for Mrs. Minelli to stay at Elsie's with a fully functioning kitchen, but Juliet quickly pooh-poohed that idea, saying she had a perfectly good kitchen too and why did the Brooks family get to decide everything? The lady in question was oblivious to the tug of war that went on. She stayed by the stove, stirring and humming to her heart's content.

Since the warring factions could not come to an agreement, Graham went downstairs and stormed back up with a big pair of wire cutters. He marched outside, muttering about morons and boneheads. Everyone followed in his wake and wondered what he'd do. He soon set to work and cut a ragged doorway into the cedar bushes and the chain link fence that separated the property from Robert's.

"There." He pointed to his handiwork. "Mrs. Minelli can run back and forth between us. We'll have her Mondays, Wednesdays and Fridays and you get her Tuesdays, Thursdays and Saturdays."

Faith blew smoke above her head. "And what do we do on Sundays? Chop and sauté her in half?"

"This is cool," Lily cried. "The yard looks so much bigger." She ran towards the fence and slipped through to the other side. Dahlia and the boys followed her.

"That looks like fun," cried Mrs. Noseworthy. She ran from her porch to join them.

Elsie came home a little early with some paperwork to finish and did a double take when she noticed her family chasing each other back and forth between a jagged hole in the fence, with Mrs. Noseworthy galloping behind them.

She flew into the yard. "Will you numbskulls get in the house and stop this? Look at poor Mrs. Noseworthy."

The dear soul ran in circles around the yard whooping, "We're playing musical chairs, Elsie. Go get us some chairs and some music."

"We're just trying to make it easier for Mrs. Minelli to get back and forth between us," Dahlia explained.

"She's not!" Elsie barked. "Eli, you're the one who wanted Mrs. Minelli to come and live with you, so take one of your parental guilt cheques, and get your apartment outfitted properly. Mrs. Minelli is not our servant. She needs a home. Have you got that?"

"Yes, ma'am."

Mrs. Noseworthy looked unhappy. "Don't ruin the game."

Elsie stomped into the house, said a quick hello to Mrs. Minelli and ran up to her bedroom. She'd just thrown her briefcase on the bed when the phone rang. She picked it up. "Hello?"

Someone was breathing.

She was in no mood for a crank call. "Hello? Who is this?"

Still only breathing.

She hung up and started to take off her jacket. It rang again. "Hello?"

Nothing.

She hung up. Why didn't she have call display? It rang again and she let the machine get it. There was breathing but nothing else. Elsie unplugged the phone. She didn't need this crap today or to have Graham scowl at her when she went back downstairs.

"What's your problem?"

"I'd like to thank you for making me look like an idiot this morning. I'm sure you found it amusing to kiss Harry in front of me, in my own house, no less."

"Don't judge me, Graham. As you once told me, it's not all about you."

She turned around and went back upstairs, grabbed her purse and left the house, not bothering to tell anyone where she was going. She went straight to Harry's. She needed to prove she was an independent woman who could handle her own romances — and anything else life had to offer. It was no one's business but her own. Certainly not Graham's. That phrase was becoming her mantra.

Later that night, as she pulled into the driveway, she didn't see the car that followed behind and didn't know who it was that knew exactly where she'd been, who she'd been with, and what they'd been doing all evening.

Chapter Fourteen

For Faith, Aunt Hildy's journals were the portal into another world. Ever since she received them, she read and read and read. She'd stay up until all hours, carefully turning the fragile, worn pages. Her aunt wrote with a bold, sweeping hand, always in ink pen, the margins filled with little pictures or doodles. She jotted funny comments or observations about shipmates, co-workers and friends, but most were devoted to her lovers.

For a woman who never had a man of her own, Faith found Aunt Hildy's adventures a revelation. At first she was titillated, and then, of course, envious. But very gradually, Faith became disturbed and anxious about these recollections. More than once, Aunt Hildy's anguish leapt forth and grabbed her by the throat, to the point where she couldn't bear to read anymore.

Aunt Hildy had a dreadful secret and as Faith dug deeper and deeper into the journals, fragments of the mystery about the treasure and why it was in this house began to unfold. But the complete picture still eluded her. She kept the story to herself, not wanting to share it with the others until all the pieces fit together. It seemed that's what Aunt Hildy intended when she entrusted her with the diaries. Faith felt a great responsibility to get it right before she let the family in on what actually happened in this house so long ago.

She'd had another long day of helping Juliet and Robert organize their new apartment and was rather weary when she climbed the stairs after supper. All she wanted to do was sit on the window seat and watch the street lights come on, one after another. Gazing out the window through a veil of tobacco smoke, she tuned out the ruckus downstairs. How did Elsie manage with people trampling underfoot night after night? Did mothers just have a coping mechanism that switched on the minute the umbilical cord was cut? She'd never know.

Faith sat motionless for a long time, staring at the bedroom lights that turned on one by one in the surrounding houses. What did other people do with their time on this earth? Did they have heartache and pain, or was life happy and content? Who decides these things?

She must have dozed off because when she opened her eyes, all the bedroom lights were off, and stars twinkled in the sky above. The air in the room was stale, so she opened the window and let the cold night air creep in. There was something so soothing about night sounds, the far off whish of a car's tires on wet pavement, a dog barking and the rustle of leaves.

That's when it occurred to her. Aunt Hildy lived on in spite of her heartbreak. She decided to make her life meaningful anyway. She was a courageous woman, albeit a damaged one. Faith had scars too, but maybe it could be the same for her. Maybe Aunt Hildy would help her do it. She got off the window seat and went over to her computer, gathered up the journals and placed them near her. She opened a new document and titled it, "Aunt Hildy's Treasure, by Faith Spencer."

She started to type.

A day later, Eli, with the help of a friend and his truck, moved all of Mrs. Minelli's furniture into their new place. Lily helped and, amazingly, so did Juliet and Robert. They worked all afternoon and wouldn't let Mrs. Minelli lift a finger. She'd wave out the window at them from Elsie's kitchen from time to time and they'd wave back.

Saying they deserved a well-earned drink, Robert went into the kitchen and poured ice water into four glasses.

Eli couldn't believe the change in the Worthingtons. It was as if the piss and vinegar had gone out of the two of them. The lost treasure had been a hard blow for them both.

"Why don't you sit down?" Robert said. "We'd like to talk to you."

Eli thought he was hearing things. He and Lily exchanged looks as they sat at the kitchen table. Juliet gave Robert a quick glance and folded her hands together in front of her.

"We talked last night…"

"Hollered is more like it."

She sighed. "Will you pipe down and let me finish this?" She looked back at Eli. "You said you'd be interested in having us come in as investors for your Mrs. Minelli's restaurant and we'd like to do that."

Eli hoped Lily wouldn't make a face and ruin everything. "Well, that's great. Because it takes a lot of capital to start a business and I'm not sure even my bribery cheques will cover what we need to start up."

"Exactly," she nodded. "And that's why I'm about to make the supreme sacrifice and sell my diamond tiara to give you the money."

Eli looked at Lily, unable to believe his ears. "You. Juliet. Sell your tiara?"

"Will wonders never cease?" Lily cracked.

Eli gave her a stern look. She shut up.

"We think it would be wise to try and change careers," Robert said.

Lily interrupted him. "Juliet's never had a career."

"May I point out, young lady, neither have you?" her aunt said.

Lily shut up again.

Robert continued. "I'm interested in new business opportunities and I think that between rent from the two apartments and being part owner in a restaurant, our future looks good."

Juliet chimed in. "Robert has real estate experience and I'm sure he can find you a perfect location and, in case you didn't know, I'm a whiz at math and can do the books. Be your accountant as it were."

"Do you think we'd trust you after the chandelier fiasco? Maybe you'd cook the books." Lily suggested.

Juliet gave another great sigh. "Don't be an idiot. I want this to work as much as you do. Most of our capital will have to be poured back into the business, so why would I jeopardize that?"

Lily shut her mouth once more. Eli tried not to smile. He knew she had no idea what capital was or what could be done with it.

He sat back in his chair. "This actually sounds like a plan. I think it's a great idea. You and I, Robert, should scout out locations so we can get this show on the road. Why wait? We're losing money as we speak."

And so the four unlikely business partners stood and shook hands. Across the yard, their human treasure was waving yet again from Elsie's kitchen window.

While Eli and Lily cemented their business deal, Dahlia and Slater were in the library enjoying their day off. She flipped through another bridal magazine. He sat beside her and ran his fingers through her hair.

"It says here your parents are in charge of the rehearsal dinner."

Slater's heart skipped a beat. He'd been keeping a secret from Dahlia, and only he and Dahlia's mother knew about it.

It started the day Mrs. B. found him sitting forlorn on the back step. She came over and sat beside him. "You look down in the mouth. Anything I can do to help? I'm a good listener."

He didn't mean to tell her. He didn't want to worry anyone, but tears welled up and he couldn't help it. "When I went home today, there was a For Sale sign on my house."

"You're moving? Does Dee know about this?"

"I'm not moving," he said. "My parents didn't tell me."

The look on her face said everything. "What do you mean?"

"That's just it. They never said a word. When I asked my dad about it, he told me to grow up and get the hell out. I don't want Dee to know yet, because she expects them to help with the wedding, but I don't think they'll come now. I don't even know where they're going."

Mrs. B. looked away for a few moments, then sat up straight. "Slater, this is what we'll do. You go home and collect the rest of your stuff. You're a member of my family now. I want you here. This is your home until you two find a little nest of your own. No one has to know about it. Not even Dee. We'll worry about the wedding later. But I promise you, things will work out."

He hung his head then. "I love you, Mrs. B."

She grabbed his hand and gave it a squeeze. "I hope you remember that when I become your cranky old mother-in-law." She got up and gave his shoulder a pat. "Now go get your duds. Supper's in an hour."

So far, no one was the wiser, but now this.

Dahlia poked him with her elbow. "Did you hear me?"

"Yeah, I can ask them, but you know what they're like."

His fiancée made a face that said, "They're probably going to expect my parents to do everything."

Slater got up suddenly, went over to the window and looked outside. He stood there for awhile before he finally said, "You know what, Dee?"

"What?"

"I don't think I want a big wedding…so many people. They'll look at me and expect me to give speeches in front of a microphone and stuff. I don't want to mess things up for you."

She ran over and hugged him. "You could never mess things up."

He swayed while she held him. "I'm afraid my parents might. They'll get drunk or something and ruin it for you. I don't want to see anyone that day but you. And this family. My family."

She listened to his heart beat as she snuggled into him. Nothing else mattered but this boy and his heart full of love for her.

She looked up at him. "Ya know what?"

"No. What?"

She pushed out of his arms, picked up the magazine and threw it in the fireplace.

"I have you. I have Aunt Hildy's dress and we have this house. We'll get married in the back garden and Mrs. Minelli will cook up a feast."

Slater smiled. "Sweet."

❧

Elsie drove to work that morning down Oxford Street and turned left onto South. As she passed Sherriff Hall, she watched the skies. There was a weather system brewing. The wind howled as large rain clouds formed off shore. They rolled and rumbled over the city. She assumed that was the cause of her uneasiness, but as she sat in traffic with her windshield wipers swishing rhythmically, her mind returned to the liaison with Harry two nights before.

She looked at herself in the rear view mirror. "I enjoyed it," she said firmly. So why did she constantly feel the need to peek in the mirror to look at her own eyes?

She got drenched as she ran from the parking lot into the hospital. She had five umbrellas at home. She'd pick up her sixth at Lawton's during lunch hour.

Crystal grinned at her as she walked past into her office. "You look like a wet dog."

"Careful. I bite."

Elsie shrugged out of her trench coat and gave her hair a quick brush in the small mirror she took out of her drawer. Crystal stood in the doorway.

"See Harry lately?"

"Yeah, actually." She continued to fuss with her damp hair.

"Sooo…"

"It was good."

Crystal grunted. "That sounds enthusiastic."

She shoved the mirror and comb back in the drawer and closed it, then sat in her office chair and swivelled back and forth for a few seconds. "I have a sneaking suspicion sex isn't the key to my new independence. I mean it's fun, but something's missing."

"Yeah," Crystal pouted. "I told you. I'm not getting any. Well, when you tire of Harry, do me a favour and send him my way."

"Okay." She grabbed the end of her desk and pulled herself in. "I better get to work."

"Righto." Crystal disappeared.

Elsie checked her messages.

"I know what you did," was the first one. She couldn't tell if it was a male or female voice. It wasn't very clear. She checked the next one.

"You won't get away with it."

And the next.

"Where's the treasure?"

And the next.

"Watch your back or you'll join Aunt Hildy."

Elsie dropped the receiver in horror. Then picked it up again and called Harry.

Elsie and Crystal played the messages over and over as they waited for him. Crystal agreed with her — it was hard to tell anything about the caller.

Harry finally arrived.

"Thanks for coming," she said. "Listen to this." She played the messages for him. When it was over, he said, "It could be a crank, but to mention your Aunt Hildy makes it more serious. I can take this to the sound lab and see if they can pick out some background noise, something that may help figure out who did this."

"Do you mind if I speak to Harry alone, Crys?"

"Of course." She closed the door behind her.

"Hold me."

He reached out and took her in his arms. It made her feel a little better.

Elsie whispered into his shirt. "Why would someone do this to me?"

"There are a lot of weirdos out there. The murder was in the paper."

She held him tighter. "But to know about the treasure? And to say I know what you did. I think they mean us."

"Elsie, I don't want to frighten you, but do you think Graham could have made that call?"

She let go of him and walked over to the window. "Of course not. He wouldn't frighten me like that. I know he's upset about you and me, but he'd never threaten to harm me."

"I hate to point it out, but he doesn't have an alibi for the night of Aunt Hildy's murder. He left Bunny's bed in the middle of the night and his only explanation is that he went for a walk? No matter how you slice it, it's a feeble excuse."

She shivered at the thought. "The whole thing makes me sick to my stomach."

Harry came over and took her hand. "People don't want to believe someone they love, or loved, could be capable of something this terrible. But Elsie, you said so yourself, no one else would want to kill Aunt Hildy, except maybe one of your family, out of greed. Think about it. There was no one in the city she knew anymore. No one broke into the house. And even if someone was bent on murder, there were plenty of people who could've been shot on the first floor, not an old lady in a back bedroom upstairs. And I hate to say it, but the only way the killer could have run downstairs in the dark without being caught was if he knew the layout of the house very well and was able to get in and out quickly."

Elsie wrung her hands. "I know it doesn't look good, and maybe I am in denial, but I still say it couldn't be him."

He held her shoulders. "Don't be blind out of misplaced loyalty. You know what will happen if you're wrong?"

She shook her head.

"You'll be dead wrong."

When Elsie got home from work, she was confused. It was early evening, but there was no one there. A glorious aroma lingered in the kitchen so Mrs. Minelli had to have been there recently. Elsie looked in the microwave and found a plate wrapped with wax paper and a note. "To Mrs. B From Mrs. M."

Realizing she hadn't eaten all day, Elsie dove into Mrs. Minelli's veal Parmesan. She reached for the mail and looked for something other than bills. There was an envelope with no name on it, stuck between the other letters. That was odd. Probably some local kid advertising leaf-raking abilities. Taking a bite of her dinner, she opened the envelope.

She didn't want to believe it. Her stomach curdled and she spit her mouthful into a napkin.

It was a picture of her and Harry naked on the bed. The fact that someone would take a picture through a window was disgusting enough, but what really broke her heart was that it looked just like a photo in a dirty magazine.

She ran up the stairs, barely making it to the toilet before throwing up. All the horror of the day overwhelmed her and she had to get rid of it. She gagged until she had nothing left.

She reached for the sink and splashed cold water on herself, then brushed her teeth and tried to feel better.

She had to tell Harry. She went into the bedroom and saw them right away — two more pictures on her bed. She started to tremble, her teeth chattered as she picked up the first one. It was another shot of her and Harry.

"No."

Then she picked up the other, expecting the same thing, only this time it was a picture of Graham and Bunny.

She screamed.

Everyone was across at the other house. Mrs. Minelli refused to go over to see the new apartment until everyone ate. Then she refused to go over until the dishes were done. When there were no excuses left, she burst into tears.

Eli rushed to her side, terrified that maybe all this was too much for her. Dahlia ran to get her water and Slater got some Kleenex while Lily comforted her.

"If you don't want to go over to the new apartment tonight, you don't have to Mrs. Minelli," Eli said. "Maybe you'd rather stay here?"

She waved her hand around, blew her nose and continued to cry up a storm. The kids weren't sure what to do. Mrs. Minelli tried to explain through her hiccuping sobs. "I thank God for you kids. I bless the day you came into my life, Eli. You and your precious girl. Everyone is so nice to me. I never thought anything good would happen to me and it's like a dream. I'm afraid I'll wake up and you'll be gone."

The two couples surrounded her in a group hug and reassured her they weren't going anywhere. She kissed them, took a deep breath and said she was ready. Slater picked up her suitcase, Eli took her spice rack and the girls escorted her out the door.

They trooped over to the house and went up into Eli's new apartment. Juliet, Faith and Robert were already there.

Mrs. Minelli's hands flew to her mouth and she blessed herself. "I'm home! Oh, look at this!" She pointed to her solid oak sideboard, the one piece of furniture that nearly gave both Eli and Robert a hernia when they carried it up the stairs. "It looks so nice against that wall!" Then she pointed to the other wall. "And you even put up my pictures. Look, here's my Mama and Papa and that's my uncle Guido. Oh, and this one," she hurried over to another picture, "this is my sister Rosa and her son Umberto." She twirled around the living room once more. "Oh how can I say thank you!"

By the time Faith and the kids wandered home across the garden after the housewarming, a police car was parked outside the house.

"What now?" Faith wondered.

"Maybe they found the treasure," Eli said.

They ran into the house. Elsie sat with Harry at the kitchen table.

"Have you found the treasure?" Lily asked.

"No."

"What's wrong, Mom?" Dahlia asked.

Elsie sighed. "Look, I can't go into details but I've had some trouble at work with phone calls and things, and tonight when I got home, some items were left for me to find and I was upset, so I called Harry. It's nothing that won't be solved or figured out, but I can't discuss it right now."

Faith made a face. "Things were left? How's that possible? I know we were over at Eli's moving furniture, but Mrs. Minelli was here."

Harry asked them, "Did anyone check the mail today?"

Faith answered. "I brought it in this afternoon when I ran over here to get a screwdriver. I just put it on the table."

"Look guys, do any of you know where your father is?"

"Why?" Lily asked. "Has this got something to do with him? Tell me it has nothing to do with him."

"I didn't say that. I just wondered when he'd be home, that's all."

"Oh, okay."

"I haven't seen his truck all day," Faith said.

"I hope nothing's happened to him," Dahlia cried.

"I wonder if you'd mind leaving your mother and I alone for a minute," Harry said. "I have a few more questions to ask her."

Everyone looked at her and she smiled. "I'm fine. You go. I'll be along later."

When they left, she said, "So with everyone over at Eli's, someone had plenty of time to get in here."

"That's possible I suppose, but what about Mrs. Minelli?"

Elsie leaned forward. "They'd only have to sneak up the stairs to my room and back down again. Mrs. Minelli would never hear them. The kitchen's at the back of the house and she'd be banging pots around."

Harry looked at her. "Or, Graham could have done it in about two seconds after you left for work."

"Oh God. I can't believe it, but it must be him." Elsie held her arms across her chest. "He must have followed us. Who else would? And the picture of the two of them. That was cruel."

She put her hand on Harry's arm. "What should I do when he comes home? What do I say?"

"Tell him the police know about his little games and it won't help his status on the murder case if he continues to harass you."

"Thanks for the help Harry. You must think my family is nuts."

"I'll have *him* by the nuts if he doesn't let go of your hand," Graham said.

Both Harry and Elsie jumped. Graham stood by the back door. He was drunk.

Elsie let go of Harry's hand in a hurry. "God. You didn't drive home like that did you?"

"I took a cab. Just in time to see you and lover-boy from the back deck."

Harry stood. "Where were you today?"

Graham swayed. "Where was I? What business is it of yours? No wait. I've got nothing to hide. Wouldn't want to give the police any more trouble, now would I? I went to work and then I went to a bar, in case you didn't notice."

Elsie raised her voice. "Why are you doing this to me?"

"I'm doing something to you? You could have fooled me. I think this is the guy who's doing something to you. Isn't that right officer?" Graham tried to focus on Harry.

"I'd advise you not to make things more difficult for yourself. Do you know anything about pictures?"

Graham steadied himself on the kitchen counter. "Like the movie pictures? Now that's something I haven't done in a million years. Go to the pictures. Too busy at work, bringing home the bacon for an ungrateful wife and kids."

"Did you take pictures of me? And leave them for me to find?"

"Why would I take pictures of you? I know you. Or at least I did before Mr. Handsome came on to the scene."

"I've had phone calls and now photos of me and...and there was one of you and Bunny."

Graham blinked and pulled his head back, as if trying to see her properly. "What are you talking about? What about Bunny?"

Harry said, "Elsie found a compromising picture of you and Bunny. But you don't have a clue how it got there?"

"No. I don't have a clue. I don't have one clue. I'm clueless, get it? Clueless."

"How could you, Graham? How could you do this to the girls? Because all this will come out. Everyone will know what kind of man you are."

Graham suddenly stopped swaying and took a minute to focus his eyes. "I'm the kind of man who wants to be forgiven. I'm the type of man who wants to make it up to you. But you've decided you don't want me anymore. You'd rather have this guy, I guess, judging by the way you looked through that window." He shook his head, as if to clear it. "This is the guy you want now, isn't it, Elsie? This is the guy you go to bed with?"

She started to say something, but Harry held up his hand to stop her.

"How do you know that? Where's your proof?" Harry caught her eye. She looked at him and understood.

"Proof? She doesn't love me anymore. That's kick-in-the-head proof."

"You didn't follow Elsie in the car last night, did you?"

"Last night? Why would I follow her around? She doesn't

want me. I don't follow people who don't want me." Graham was turning maudlin. "Bunny said she wanted me but now she doesn't, so now no one wants me. No one at all."

He looked green by this point. He was fading fast.

Harry said, "Let's get him to bed." They took his arms and practically carried him downstairs.

"No one. No one wants me. What did I do? Why does everyone hate me? The girls hate me, Elsie hates me and now Bunny hates me. I don't understand. I'm a sweet guy. I'd never hurt a fly...except maybe Juliet. She bugs me."

They put him on his bed and Elsie unbuttoned his collar while Harry took off his shoes. She threw a blanket over him and, afraid he'd be sick, put a basin by the bed. She'd never seen him like this before.

As he nodded off, he mumbled, "Where's Elsie? Where are you, baby? I want my baby." Then he started to snore with his mouth open, looking about as pathetic as a person can look when they're three sheets to the wind. She leaned over him and brushed his hair away from his forehead.

Harry cleared his throat, and she turned around and left the room with him. They looked at each other.

Harry said, "Being that drunk is almost as good as a lie detector. It seems impossible, but I don't think he's lying."

"I don't either. And I should have known better. He'd have come through that window and punched your lights out instead of taking pictures of us."

Harry started to say, "So that leaves..."

"Bunny."

"She wants to get even for some reason."

"Graham stopped seeing her for a while, because of the

funeral and everything. That must have made her mad. Did you know she told the police he wanted the treasure so he could run away with her?"

"There's nothing like a woman scorned. And if she gave him up to the police, there's no telling what else she might do."

Just then they heard a creak on the stairs.

"Who's there?"

The girls crept down the stairs. Lily said, "We saw you bring Daddy down here. Is he drunk?"

"You could say that."

Dahlia confessed, "We just heard what you said about Bunny and…" She looked at her sister. "We think we should tell you something."

"Well, spill it."

She took a deep breath. "Remember the day the police took Dad for questioning?"

Elsie nodded.

Lily picked up the story. "Remember how we said maybe Faith and Juliet…"

"…and Robert killed Aunt Hildy. Yes, I remember and I told you not to be so foolish."

Dahlia continued. "So the three of them took off after you left and we thought something was up so we followed them. It was Slater's idea to tail them." Her sister elbowed her.

"Anyway, we followed them to Bunny's apartment."

"Bunny's apartment? Why were they there?" Elsie looked at Harry as if he knew why.

"We never found out because Slater tripped and we all fell down and everyone hollered and Bunny opened the door to see what was going on."

Harry said, "What has all this got to do with anything, girls?"

Lily said in a rush, "She yelled at us and said she told the police the truth and she didn't give a fig if we believed her or not. She said to tell Dad if he ever came near her, he'd have a hole in his heart like Aunt Hildy. But how could she have known that? No one knew but us."

Elsie was horrified. "Really? Why didn't you say anything? You accuse your own relatives and yet you keep a piece of information like this from us?"

They looked at each other. "Because when we thought about it, we realized Dad probably told her."

The wind went out of Elsie's sails. "That's true."

"I'm sorry we eavesdropped," Lily said, "but if Bunny's doing awful things, maybe she *did* kill Aunt Hildy and maybe we should have told you before."

They looked frightened and worn out. Their mother gave them a hug. "It's all right girls. I need to talk to Harry in private, so why don't you guys go over to Eli's for a bit, okay?"

They nodded and went upstairs. Harry and Elsie followed them and sat back at the kitchen table.

"I think it's probably a long shot that Bunny had anything to do with it," Harry said. "Why would she want to kill your aunt?"

Elsie shrugged. "The treasure? Knowing Graham, he probably mouthed off about Aunt Hildy more than once, so Bunny would've known about it. Maybe she just wanted to scare her into revealing where it was. I know Bunny wanted Graham bad and probably thought he'd leave town with her if she found it."

"Maybe."

"But what she didn't reckon with was Aunt Hildy, who would have told her to take a hike, God love her. And look what happened," Elsie moaned.

"It still seems unlikely she'd get in and out without anyone seeing her." Harry stopped. "But of course…"

"Of course what?"

He gave her a sympathetic look. "Graham had her over here. Maybe he gave her a tour of the whole joint when you guys weren't home."

"But Aunt Hildy was here. Of course she napped a lot. And Faith's here, but even she goes out from time to time." Elsie slapped her hand on the table. "Oh that miserable man. If they were in my bed, so help me. I swear, if that walking mammary gland is responsible for Aunt Hildy's death, I'll have those so-called tits of hers surgically removed and re-sewn on her fat backside."

Harry smiled.

"What? You don't think I'll do it?"

"No. I just think you're cute when you're mad."

She waved her hand. "Oh pooh." Her eyes suddenly widened. "And if she's hell-bent on hurting us maybe she got in here and took the treasure."

"She didn't know you found all the loot and she certainly didn't know where Graham hid it."

"No, but since she knew about it, maybe she had a quick nose around when she dropped the pictures off. The sewing room is next to our bedroom. It would only take a second to slip in there and the wardrobe would actually be the first place you'd look if you were in a hurry. She must have flipped when she found it."

"But no one saw her."

"There's no one at home on this street during the day. Even Mrs. Noseworthy plays bingo with her cronies at the church hall three mornings a week. Bunny took a chance and it paid off."

"How did she get in, do you think?"

Elsie cringed. "This is such a big house. Sometimes I forget to lock a window. I know I need a security system."

"You do. Get one."

"How can we prove that she did it?"

"The only way is to get her to confess," Harry said.

"I could ask her over here and say I want to talk about Graham. I'll tell her he's heartbroken over their breakup."

He laughed. "She won't believe that."

She pointed a finger at him. "I've seen her in action. She's out of her mind over him. That's why she's pulled all this crap. She'd jump at the chance if she thought she could get him back."

"You may be right," he nodded. "If that's the case, then you ask her over for a chat and we'll try to record your conversation in case you get something out of her. But I'll be here. If she's capable of these horrible stunts, I don't want you alone with her. I'll hide nearby. And for heaven's sake, don't tell your family this is going down. From what I've seen of them, things could unravel very quickly, so they need to be out of the house until it's over."

Elsie smiled. "Thanks for all this, Harry. I'm very grateful to you."

"That's okay." He grinned and gave her a big wink. "You'll make it up to me later, won't you?"

For a moment, she didn't know what he meant. But only a moment. She got up and went to the kitchen sink.

"Elsie?"

"Sorry. I just have a frog in my throat." She poured herself a glass of water and downed it. Then she turned and gave him a quick smile. "I'm tired. I think I'll turn in, if that's okay?"

"Sure. No problem." He got up, went over to her and tried to kiss her on the lips. She turned her face away slightly and he got her cheek instead.

By the time Harry left, Faith had turned in and the kids were still next door. She trudged up the stairs and got ready for bed, but couldn't sleep. So much had happened that her mind was awhirl with theories and what-ifs. She heard Dahlia and Slater come home, but not Lily. No doubt she wanted to be with Eli for awhile.

Elsie couldn't get over how much Lily had changed in such a short time. Eli brought laughter into her life. Lily had always been such a serious little girl, stuck in the shadow of a blonde pixie sister who made friends so easily. Boys called the house and always asked for Dahlia but never Lily. It broke Elsie's heart. And now this wonderful young man had taken her into his life. She hoped they'd be together forever, but thought it unlikely they'd ever marry. Lily would say, "Who needs a piece of paper to say we love each other?"

Elsie fumed again when she thought of Slater's parents. What kind of person would you have to be to let your child worry and wonder if you'd even be there when they got home at night? She vowed he'd always have somewhere to go.

She closed her eyes and was starting to get sleepy when she heard Dahlia say her final goodnight to Slater and climb the stairs. She knocked on the door. "Are you asleep, Mom?"

"No. Come in."

Dahlia crossed the room and sat on the bed. "We didn't have a chance to tell you our good news. Uncle Robert had the great idea of renting out the third apartment to me and Slater. What do you think?"

"Wow. Who knew Robert could be so clever? I never thought of that apartment for the two of you. I'm thrilled for you, honey." She turned over on her side. "But gosh, what will I do when you guys all leave me?"

"You can yell out the window and tell us to come over."

They laughed.

"And you'll be glad to hear this. We've decided not to have a big wedding after all."

Elsie got up on her elbow. "You're kidding?"

"Slater confessed he'd be nervous in front of all those people and he was afraid he'd let me down, if you can imagine. He only wants to see me and this family on our wedding day. 'His' family he called us."

Elsie's eyes filled with tears. It had been such an emotional day. The lump in her throat made it hard for her to swallow. She watched Dahlia wipe her eyes on her sleeve. "I told him we didn't need anyone else. I have him and Aunt Hildy's dress. Mrs. Minelli can cook a nice meal and we'll get married out in the garden."

Elsie reached out and stroked her daughter's beautiful hair. "I think that's perfectly perfect. I'm so glad sweetheart, because I know one thing. Even if you had surrounded yourself with the best of everything, no one, and I mean no one, will look at anything but you that day. And I'm so grateful that Aunt Hildy will be a part of it. You know she wouldn't have missed it for the world."

They cried then, mother and daughter together in each others' arms. It made up for every awful thing that had happened
earlier in the day.

They kissed each other goodnight. Dahlia got off the bed and
was almost at the door when Elsie said, "You know what, Dee?"

She turned to look at her. "Yes?"

"The money I've saved so far for the wedding — it's not an
enormous amount, but I'd like you and Slater to have it. Fix up
your little nest. It makes so much more sense to spend it so you
can enjoy it for a long time, and not just one day."

"Thanks, Mom. I love you."

"I love you more."

Elsie finally went to sleep.

Chapter Fifteen

Faith ran across the yard the next morning and salivated over the delicious smells coming from Eli's kitchen window. Mrs. Minelli waved a dish towel out of it.

"Good morning, Miss Faith. You're just in time for homemade waffles with blueberry sauce and fresh-brewed coffee. And I hope you like banana bread. I'll bring it down to your sisters and we can have a chat. Eli's trying to sleep."

"I was," said a tired voice from the next window.

"Sounds wonderful." Faith didn't know what to be more thrilled about, the food or someone happy to see her.

The three women sat at Juliet's kitchen table. They didn't know it then, but it was the start of a beautiful friendship. Mrs. Minelli had more than enough horror stories to keep the sisters enthralled — she was a real gossip and prone to exaggeration. And being a widow for the last twenty years, she missed having someone to confide in and chat with at the beginning and end of the day.

The sisters spent the entire morning saying, "What?" "I don't believe it," and "You're not serious?" while their new friend nodded sagely, saying, "I kid you not."

Finally, Mrs. Minelli glanced at the clock and said, "Mama mia. It's noon. I'll run and make us a Greek salad and stuffed pita. You girls will like that." She was off before they could say another thing.

Juliet punched her fist in the air. "Yes! Our ship has come in. The eagle had landed and the saints are marching, baby."

"I never thought I'd say this but: Thank God for those kids," Faith said. "If Eli hadn't thought of it, well, it just doesn't bear thinking about."

"Oh, I know. And Robert is so happy. I can't remember the last time he was this happy."

"It was before he met you, that's why."

Juliet gave her the finger.

"By the way. Where is the man himself?"

"He was up at five this morning and out the door at six. He wanted to look for properties."

Faith was puzzled. "Why isn't the boy genius with him?"

"Ro said if he found anything interesting he'd be back to get him. Thought he'd let him sleep. Lily was upstairs until at least four. I heard her leave."

"It must be nice to be so in love and have that kind of energy," Faith sighed.

"Actually, I thought I heard her crying. What happened over there last night?"

"We thought the police found the treasure because there was a police car outside the house. No such luck of course. Turns out it was Harry Adams. God that man is easy on the eyes."

"And?"

"Apparently Elsie's had trouble…phone calls and whatnot, at the office and now at home. She didn't go into a lot of detail, but she seemed upset. And then the girls told me their father came home drunk. I have no idea what's going on."

"But why would someone give Saint Elsie trouble?"

"Hey," Faith frowned. "It's her nature to be kind. And she's good to us, so don't you forget that."

"Yeah, yeah. Don't get sappy on me. I hate that. Now, before

I forget, how goes it with the journals? Any cracking stories in them?"

Faith had been afraid of the question and, with a writer's superstition, she didn't want to tell anyone about her work in progress. Not this time. So she shrugged. "I guess," then added, "I probably wouldn't do them justice anyway."

Juliet surprised her. "Sure you would. Aunt Hildy was crazy, but she wasn't stupid. She left those journals to you, not the rest of us."

"Gee, thanks, Jules."

They heard a key turn in the lock and Robert burst in. "I found it. I found it. The perfect spot."

Juliet bounced up and down on her chair. "Where?"

"Lower Water Street, near the farmers' market. It's a little pricier than I'd hoped, but a steal when you consider the location. And location is everything. That part of town is packed all day with shoppers and all night with university students. It was an old warehouse and it does need a lot of repair, but that's an incidental. With a bank loan or two, Eli's money and your jewellery, we might just swing it. There was a number on the For Sale sign, so I called and the agent said he could meet us there tomorrow. So what do you think?"

Juliet got up, bent Robert backwards and gave him a big wet one right on the lips.

"Don't think this will happen everyday, but for now...ya done good, Ro. Real good."

Robert was speechless.

Faith jumped up. "Let's go tell Eli and Mrs. Minelli." The three of them charged out the door and up the stairs to Eli's apartment.

To go from living the life of a bachelor to having a middle-aged roommate was taking a little getting used to. Eli and Mrs. Minelli only had one bathroom and already there were stockings hanging on the towel racks. On top of which, Juliet, Faith and Robert seemed to stream in and out of his place all day. And here they were again, just as he was trying to catch up on his lost sleep.

Once they spilled the news they were off again, chatting like magpies. Eli laid back in his bed and dreamed about his restaurant. He hoped he liked the location tomorrow. If it was as nice as Robert said it was, it would be just the ticket.

He heard more footsteps approach and groaned inwardly, but was delighted to see it was the one person he wanted. Lily came into the bedroom and shut the door. "Did you miss me?"

"No," Eli grinned, "You only left a few hours ago."

"I missed you." She bounced on the bed and cuddled up to him. "Our partners waylaid me on the front porch. Isn't it fabulous about the restaurant?"

"It sounds like it's a hole at the moment, so don't get too excited. But if it has any kind of potential I think Robert's dead-on about the location. It's the perfect place for a small ethnic restaurant. Just the cruise ship passengers alone will bring in a bundle."

She absent-mindedly rubbed his arm. "It's hard for me to see Uncle Robert as anything but a buffoon, but you know, I think this is his forté. He really seems happy."

"We need to keep him happy so promise me you won't piss him off with that razor wit of yours."

"Fine. From now on I'll keep my mouth shut."

He rolled her over. "I didn't say around me, did I? Come here."

She giggled and did as she was told.

❧

Earlier that same day, just about the time her sisters were making short work of Mrs. Minelli's waffles, Elsie had gone down to check on Graham. Her knees buckled at the stale yeasty air that hung like a cloud in his bedroom. She opened the small basement window and pushed it as far as it would go.

He was still out like a light. She gave him a shove, but he snored on. She'd give him a few more minutes, then it was hit-the-showers time. She left the door open so the breeze would blow through.

She went back up to the kitchen. Dahlia and Slater had gone to work, the remains of their breakfast left on the counter. She shook her head. Dahlia made her yogurt fruit smoothie in the blender, as usual. The loud whirring was everyone's alarm clock. Beside it were Slater's peanut butter and toast crumbs, with the cap off his bottle of Flintstone vitamins. Elsie always told him to take just one, but he insisted Fred and Barney needed to be together. She couldn't argue with him. A finer physical specimen you'd never see.

But the kitchen was quieter than usual and it suddenly hit Elsie why: Faith wasn't around with her journal, reading bits and pieces to her while she ate her toast. Elsie realized she missed her. She had a good idea where her sister would be. Faith was no fool.

Elsie went out onto the deck. She could hear the three women through the open crack in the kitchen window. The wind carried their voices across the yard. They were having a great time by the sounds of it.

It seemed implausible that Mrs. Minelli would take to Juliet and Faith, but maybe, having lived with the heartache of being a widow at such a young age, she recognized the sadness they carried around with them. Who knows why her sisters were like that, but Elsie had always sensed it. That's probably why she put up with so much of their nonsense.

It was time to shake Graham awake. She went back downstairs and eventually, after a lot of pushing, he opened his eyes. When he finally stumbled into the shower, he stayed there so long she thought he'd fallen back to sleep, but he eventually came out, a towel around his waist. He sat on the end of the bed and she passed him some painkillers and a can of Coke. He downed it and belched.

Elsie sat on the nearest chair and looked at him. He slowly turned his head toward her.

"I know. You don't have to tell me."

"I didn't say a word."

"I heard it anyway. How did I get home?"

"Taxi."

He put his hands on his head. "I feel like dying. Maybe I'll do you all a favour…"

"Stop it."

"Well, it's true, isn't it? I seem to screw up every relationship I have."

"That's not true. Your daughters love you and I love you. You've been my best friend for a long time. That's what I've missed the most."

Graham wiped his stubbly chin with the palm of his hand. "Christ. I look and feel like my old man. I vowed I'd never come home to my family in this state. When did I become a loser?"

"Now you're being ridiculous," she said sternly. "You're not a loser."

"According to your sister, I am."

"Which sister?"

"Take your pick."

She sighed. "I wouldn't worry about what they think. One's a hermit and the other gets her toes painted for a living."

"How did you become so normal?"

Elsie got up and wandered over to the bureau. She picked up a picture of the girls. "What's normal about going berserk in front of your entire family?"

"True."

She spun around. "Hey you." She walked back to sit beside him on the bed. "God. You have no idea how good it felt. If I ever set up my own business it'll be for women who need to throw a fit and are willing to spend good money to do it. I'd make a fortune." She laughed. "I'll sign up Mrs. Abernathy."

"Who?"

"Doesn't matter." She was quiet for a moment. "I hate to tell you, but you know the old Elsie? I think that lady's left the building."

Graham gave her the first grin she'd seen in a long time. "Oh, I figured that out pretty quickly. I think it was when you threatened your entire family with a poker. Or maybe it was when you trashed the living room. It's all a blur."

She looked at the man who had been her husband for so long. He seemed sad, or beaten down. She wanted to help, so she put her arm around his shoulders. "Graham, I want you to know that, despite everything, I'll always treasure the fact that you chose me. You and I were meant to have those two young ladies upstairs. We did that, together."

He put his fingers up to the corners of his eyes and hid his face. His shoulders shook up and down. A sob finally escaped his lips. Elsie stayed quiet.

Finally he said, "Thanks Else."

"You're welcome."

She told him to go back to sleep. He had dark circles under his eyes and there was no way he'd be able to cope with work. She said she'd call him off. He nodded and crawled back under the covers. He was out like a light before she shut the door.

She called Crystal first.

"I'm taking a couple of days off, Crys."

"Are you okay?"

"I will be. I can't explain now, but there's something I have to do."

"Does it involve those messages?"

"Yes, but don't worry. Harry's with me."

"I just bet," she laughed. "Your penalty for making me reschedule everyone is a big bottle of wine and a full account of what's going down."

"I'll make that two bottles. Wish me luck."

"Be careful, Elsie."

"I will. Bye."

The next order of business was to call Bunny. Elsie's hand trembled as she picked up the phone. It sounded easy when she suggested it to Harry; however, now that the time had come, her mouth was dry. But, she was determined. She had to know for sure if Bunny pulled these miserable pranks and, if possible, find out if she knew anything about Aunt Hildy. The surest way of doing that would be to sit face to face with the woman.

Elsie's career was reading people and it was essential to find out the truth. The one obstacle was the fact that she was emotionally involved and that made things more difficult. But it didn't matter. She owed it to her mother's big sister.

She dialled Graham's work number.

"No Ifs Ands Or Butts Plumbing."

"Bunny?"

"Yes."

"It's Elsie Brooks."

There was a long silence.

"Graham won't be in today."

"Good."

"Can we talk?"

"About what?"

"Graham."

"Tell him to go to hell."

"I think you should listen to what I have to say."

There was a long silence.

"He came home drunk last night and confessed he'd made a mistake about you."

"What do you mean?"

"That's what I'd like to discuss. Can we meet here at the house tomorrow at noon? Everyone will be out. Graham doesn't know I've called you. I'd just like the two of us to sit down and talk rationally."

"Why on earth would I want to talk to you?"

"Why not? We're circling the same man. I think we can solve our differences, if you give it a chance. There are some things you need to know."

"Are you social workers nuts? Do you think you can manipulate people at will? This is bullshit. If Graham has something to say, he should say it to me."

"But that's the thing, Bunny. He won't. It's too bad you've taken this position. I'd have given you more credit than that, but if that's the way you feel, I'll say goodbye."

"Wait."

Elsie waited.

Finally Bunny spoke. "What time again?"

"Noon. I'll be here."

Bunny hung up the phone.

Elsie put down the receiver and sagged into her chair, completely drained. She wanted tomorrow to be over. Her next call was to Harry.

❧

The following day the whole family was anxious to see the property, and disappointed when Elsie said she couldn't make it. Graham didn't want to lose another day of work, so he begged off as well.

The others piled into three cars and journeyed in a convoy with Robert leading the way.

At the waterfront, they piled out en masse. The salt water breeze whipped up the waves against the wharf. There were sailboats further along. From where they stood they could hear the sound of the sails — like sheets drying on a windy day. The sky was blue with streaks of white cloud and the sun sparkled off the water. Seagulls circled overhead and a buoy marker bobbed off shore, rhythmically clanging its bell.

The lampposts along the length of the boardwalk gave it a rustic charm. The hot dog stand made a killing with the lunchtime office workers, as did the small ice cream shop nearby. People meandered about as they carried their parcels from the small shops that lined the street.

"This is perfect." Eli gave Robert a high five. Everyone was thrilled, until Robert spoke up.

"Look. Our property isn't along this strip. We'd never afford a place down here. It's up one of those side streets, but it looks out over this bit because of the steep climb."

"If it's too steep, no one will want to walk up to get to us," Juliet said.

"Sure they will. This is a gorgeous part of the city. Tourists love it. The streets are narrow and lined with heritage buildings. It looks touristy if you know what I mean."

Mrs. Minelli clapped her hands. "Let's see it. I want to see it."

They followed Robert along the waterfront, chatting happily about the great view and the quaint atmosphere. But once they turned the corner, it wasn't nearly as developed. They passed some abandoned buildings, a few stores undergoing renovations, and a little book shop newly opened.

Robert tried to cheer them up when their voices dropped off as they walked along.

"Keep remembering, you have to think of this place as it will look. Once you have a business set up, more stores come in behind you and suddenly the whole street lights up. And if it's a restaurant, people will clamour to open a few more, which is great, because it becomes the street where you go to eat when you're downtown."

There were murmured agreements to that.

"There's the agent." Robert hurried forward to shake the man's hand.

The agent laughed. "You've got quite the crowd."

"Everyone. This is Mr. Petrie. Mr. Petrie, this is my family."

"Well everyone, if you'll follow me." Mr. Petrie walked to the building next to the one they stood by and put the key in the door. He went ahead and held the door open for them.

Everyone stood in the middle of the room and looked around. No one said anything. It was larger than it looked from the outside, with a wide deep porch that Robert mentioned could be knocked down for a terrace. Its high ceiling was crisscrossed with exposed pipes. There were large windows that looked out on the old wooden building across the street but the harbour was still visible at the end of their block.

The agent marched them out back and discussed where a kitchen could be set up and pointed out the large exit doors that were perfect for deliveries.

They went back into the main room and noticed for the first time the old wooden counter off to the side. It was massive and would make a great bar.

Still no one said anything. Everyone waited for someone else to go first.

Robert looked worried about their seeming lack of enthusiasm. "Listen, don't look at the peeling paint. Don't look at the damp patches or the missing tiles. The bones are good. If we get this place cleaned up it'll look like a million bucks."

Mr. Petrie jumped in. "I have two more interested parties scheduled for this afternoon. I don't want to pressure you —" Juliet rolled her eyes —"but I've been the one to sell most of these properties and I'm here to tell you that this place will explode over the next eighteen months. People want to take back their cities and are anxious to use these old buildings, because frankly it's become très chic to renovate. The old tenements five blocks down have sold like hot cakes to young couples with money, who convert them into lofts with waterfront views."

They looked at one another. Robert held out his hands toward them. "It'll mean a lot of work. A lot of sweat, but I think we can do it. Are we in?"

Slater spoke up. "What would Aunt Hildy do?"

"We're in!" everyone shouted.

At home, Elsie rehearsed what she thought she'd say, but in the end gave up, knowing it would be impossible to predict what an estranged wife and a girlfriend would say to each other. But she was in a different position than most wives. She wanted the woman in question put in jail, if indeed that's where she belonged.

Harry arrived just after the mob left. She blurted, "I don't think I can do this."

"Say to yourself, 'She's a big boob.' It will make you feel better."

"I don't think so. I'm going to be sick."

The doorbell rang.

Elsie shook. "Oh, God."

"Calm down. I'm here. Where are you going to talk to her? In the library?"

She nodded.

"Is there a place I can hide near there?"

She nodded.

Harry sighed at her. "You have to talk. You can't just nod at her."
She nodded.

They crept down the hall and she pointed to the closet near the library door.

"This might be too far away." The doorbell rang again.

"There's no time," Elsie panicked. So Harry opened the closet door, gave her a thumbs up and closed it. She took a deep breath and walked toward the door. Flower ran in from the sunroom to be with her. She was grateful for the show of support.

Elsie opened her heavy front door. There was Bunny, in all her glory, with her skirt up to here, her cleavage down to there, high heels and war paint. Elsie realized too late she should've put on some lip gloss.

"Come in."

Bunny didn't say anything as she walked through the door. Flower gave a little bark and jumped on her, as if they were old friends. Elsie realized with hate she probably was. That galvanized Elsie's resolve. Mess with my husband if you must, but stay the hell away from my dog.

"We'll go to the library." They started down the hall, when Flower sniffed the air and ran over to the closet door. She snuffled for all she was worth. "Flower, I told you no more cookies today." She looked at Bunny. "I have to hide them in there, or she eats them out of the box."

Flower barked. She took the dog by the collar. "Excuse me. I'll be right back." She dragged a very unhappy puppy dog into the back porch and shut the door on her, hurrying back to Bunny to escort her into the library.

"I made some lemonade." She pointed to the iced pitcher and glasses. "Would you like some?"

"Okay. Mind if I smoke?"

Elsie did mind, but what could she say? "I'll get you an ash-tray." She searched around, settling on a thick coaster — any-thing to get on with it. She indicated a chair for Bunny, poured lemonade and took the chair opposite, on the other side of the fireplace. Bunny blew her smoke in the air. "So what's all this about?"

Harry knew he'd have to get out of the closet. He couldn't hear a thing, so he peeked out. In her nervousness, Elsie had almost closed the library door. He figured he better move — he couldn't be sure how short and sweet their conversation would be. He quietly snuck out, eyeing two doors that lay down two corri-dors, trying to judge which one would be best. To get to the one closest, he had to cross the library door to do it. He decided to go for it.

He heard a cry. Damn. He'd spooked Elsie. He heard Bunny ask what was wrong, whether there was someone else in the house. He heard someone get up and walk toward the library doors.

He had to take the first door or all would be lost. He jumped into a small, dark closet, realizing too late that he'd locked him-self in.

Bunny looked out the library doors and went back to her chair. "I don't trust you. Why are you so nervous?"

"I could ask you the same thing."

"Are you sure there's no one else in the house?"

"I told you, no. This is between you and me. I guess I'm a lit-tle flustered. It's not every day a woman talks to her husband's girlfriend."

"He's your estranged husband. You live apart...kind of...and you're the one who wanted to talk. If you're so flustered, why do it at all?"

Elsie took a deep breath and grabbed the arms of her chair. "Because I want to ask you why you feel the need to terrorize me."

Bunny's cigarette froze on her lips. She slowly pulled it out of her mouth. "I'm not terrorizing you."

"You followed me and took pictures without my knowledge. What do you call that?"

"Why would I take pictures of you? You're not that attractive."

Elsie got annoyed. "Listen you. There's no one else I know who would want to take pictures of me."

"They might want to take pictures of your man."

"If you didn't take the pictures how do you know I was with a man?"

Bunny threw the cigarette in her glass of lemonade. "Okay, let's cut the crap. Yes, I took those pictures and yes, I phoned you. You deserved it. You're supposed to be separated but you keep your claws in Graham anyway because you can't stand the thought that he might want me instead. Why do you get to be with someone, but he doesn't? You're a greedy, two-faced cow."

"I'm not two-faced. I knew you were dating. I only asked him to stay away from you until I handled my aunt's funeral. The girls needed him and so did I."

"He wants to be with me, but the minute you crook your little finger, he runs back to you. Tell me you don't get off on that."

"You say you care about him, yet you lie to the police. A woman in love doesn't do that."

"I told the police the truth. That's the thing everyone seems to forget. I didn't make up the fact that he went out for a walk. He did go out for a walk, so when the police hassled me again, I broke down, that's all. I didn't tell them on purpose. It just happened."

"But why tell them he wanted to find the treasure to run away with you?"

"Because it's the truth," she spit. "He told me. He wanted us to go away to the Caribbean. We had it all planned."

Elsie blinked and stared at her rival for a moment. "Why should I believe you, Bunny? You're the kind of woman who sneaks around and takes pictures of other people, then breaks into their home to make sure they see them."

"I didn't break in. I have a key."

Elsie's mouth hung open. "Graham gave you a key?"

"So what if he did?"

Elsie was incredulous. "So what? Do you mean to tell me you've had access to my home all this time?"

Bunny shrugged.

Elsie stood. "So yesterday wasn't just a fluke? Well lady, if that's the case, I'd say you're a prime suspect for theft and murder."

Graham tried to concentrate, but it was impossible. He was halfway through the morning when he helped one of the guys load up the truck. His mind was a thousand miles away but screamed back to earth when his buddy closed the van door on his fingers. Cursing, he shook out his fingers. Back in the locker room, he kicked a cardboard box that was filled with nails — just his luck.

"Christ almighty, get a hold of yourself." He sat on the edge of the table that held the coffee machine and dirty cups and tried to settle down. The pulse in his fingers was his universe for ten minutes.

He remembered another time his hand throbbed like this. He even had a picture from that day. He took out his wallet with his good hand and rifled through the thick wad of school pictures of the girls, some dating so far back they smiled at him with missing teeth and messy pig tails. He found it. A friend took it, unbeknownst to him, the day their school had lost a big football match. Graham, the quarterback, had injured his hand on the field. His lousy throw had cost them that game. As he walked off the field with his head down, there was Elsie, her arm around his shoulder, bending down to smile up at him, trying to give him comfort. He'd kept that picture because he thought her legs looked great and he liked to show it off to his friends.

He looked closely at that sweet face. He'd seen it yesterday, exactly the same way, from the end of his bed.

Could he be a bigger jerk if he tried?

He couldn't get out of there fast enough. As he gathered the keys for his truck, a co-worker came by and smirked, "Going home to referee?"

Graham frowned. "What do you mean?"

"Didn't you hear? Bunny went to your house on her lunch hour. She told Wanda she'd wipe the floor with your missus."

Graham took off.

The happy gang was headed to Dairy Queen for ice cream. Sitting at several small tables, they talked about what they should do first.

"Go to the bank," Robert said.

Juliet spooned caramel sauce out of her plastic container. "Get an estimate from Graham about the plumbing."

"Hire a contractor," Eli shouted.

Slater yelled, "Watch *Trading Spaces*. I love that dude Vern. Not like Doug. I'd deck him the first day in."

"Go get paint brochures," Lily said.

"Pick out dishes and flatware," Dahlia suggested. "I'm good at that now."

Mrs. Minelli held up the remains of her ice cream cone. "Cook!"

Robert stood. "I say we go tell Elsie the good news."

Everyone agreed.

Harry couldn't believe it. He tried to pry the door open without making too much noise but the miserable thing wouldn't budge. Damn these old houses with their solid construction. If it had been a modern gizmo he'd have had it open in a jiffy.

He could just hear their conversation. Elsie was holding her own. But as soon as she brought up robbery and murder, they'd be in a different league altogether. If things took a turn for the worst, he'd bash the door in, but he didn't want to make his move yet. He'd wait a few more minutes to see what would happen.

Bunny gave her rival a filthy look, and Elsie became a little frightened.

"Just what the hell are you implying? That I killed your aunt?"

Elsie pointed a finger at her. "Think about it. You just told me you have a key. The house wasn't broken into that night.

Obviously you've been here before. Even my dog didn't bark at you today, so no barking the night of the murder. Graham told you about the treasure. You knew it was here and you were impatient for him to find it, because you wanted him to run away with you. So you thought you'd hurry Aunt Hildy along and get her to tell you where it was. Only you didn't know Aunt Hildy, did you? You didn't know that she'd never tell you in a million years. That's why you killed her."

Bunny stood too. "You're off your rocker, lady."

"And what about the bag of treasure that was stolen from us?"

"What bag of treasure?"

Elsie was coming to a boil. She tried to think clearly and remember her facts.

"Don't pretend you don't know what I'm talking about," she shouted. "You've come into this house lots of times, haven't you? You made the noise I heard the day the treasure disappeared."

Bunny grabbed her purse. "You've gone nuts. I won't stand here and listen to this bullshit."

Elsie put her hand out to hold her back. "And wait. Something else I remember. The girls told me you shouted that if their father came near you again, he'd have a hole in his heart, just like Hildy. But what you don't know is that the papers never gave out that information, so how did you know about it, unless you did it?"

Bunny ripped her arm out of Elsie's grasp. "No wonder Graham got rid of you. You're insane. I never killed her. Graham told me what happened to her on the phone that morning."

"Isn't that convenient? I think you're lying. Everything points to you. Everything." Elsie started to cry. "We were overwhelmed with greed, but no one in my family would've killed Aunt Hildy. She drove us mad, but that doesn't mean we'd ever kill her. It was you, I know it was."

"Get out of my way," Bunny screamed at her.

Elsie ran to the desk. "I've taped our whole conversation. I can't wait to tell the police."

Bunny's mouth dropped open. "You bitch. You're trying to frame me? I'll kill you."

She lunged at Elsie, just as the family spilled in the door laughing and talking over each other. Graham had been on the doorstep when they arrived home, and they were filling him in on their news. At the same time, Harry decided it was time to kick his way out of the hall closet.

Everyone screamed and ran about.

"What's going on?" Graham hollered. "Elsie. Elsie. Are you all right?"

The girls screamed for their mother.

"I'm in here!" she cried, as she held on to Bunny.

"Let go of me, you bitch."

"She's killing Mommy," Dahlia screamed. Slater flew past Harry in an attempt to reach her.

Twelve people scrambled about in a mini riot. Everyone hit everyone else. The only one who wasn't in the melee was Mrs. Minelli. Robert, frantic to protect his investment, pushed the poor soul down the hall and told her to run. No one could hear over the girls' screams and both Harry and Graham had a hard time pulling Slater's hands off Bunny's neck.

That's when the gun went off.

Chapter Sixteen

Everyone froze.

Harry said, "Is everyone okay?"

They all nodded.

Graham turned to him. "Jesus. Was it yours?"

"No."

"It was mine." The voice came from a sliding door in the panelling to the left of the fireplace.

A gun emerged from the wall. Mrs. Noseworthy followed.

"Nobody move. Isn't that what you're supposed to say?"

Frightened faces looked at the gun.

Elsie was the closest to her.

"Mrs. Noseworthy," she said quietly. "It's me. Elsie. You know who I am."

The old woman looked at her. "I know who you are. You're the girl who ruined the game."

"What game, dear?"

"Musical chairs. You told us to stop. That wasn't nice."

She moved around the room and pointed her gun at one, then another.

"That was mean. I'm sorry. We can play now if you like?"

Mrs. Noseworthy shook her head. "I don't feel like it. You people make me tired. You run around and scream all the time. You say you have treasure and then take mine."

Elsie continued to speak in a soft low voice. "Did we take your treasure, dear?"

"Of course you did. The girls even said so. But they only gave me back one box. I know I had more. Lots more. But you people are too greedy. Even Hildy said that."

Elsie turned her head to follow Mrs. Noseworthy around the room. "Did you like Aunt Hildy?"

"She was nice when she first got here, but then she got bossy. Always talking about treasure. But it wasn't hers. It was mine. I just wanted her to tell me where the rest of it was. But she wouldn't. She said, 'Go ahead, shoot me, I dare you.' Well, I don't know about you, but when I was a girl, a dare was a dare."

"Are you sure it was you?" Elsie asked. "That's a brave thing to do, get into someone's house and get back out with no one seeing you."

"You're stupid, Elsie. You're all stupid. Hildy told me about the secret passageway. I just went through the hidden door in her closet. Her father built it in his rum-running days. You didn't know that, did you?"

She approached the library doors, still waving the gun around. Elsie saw Harry nod at Robert. If Mrs. Noseworthy got close enough, Robert might be able to tackle her into the hallway. Elsie needed to keep her talking.

"No, I didn't know that. Why don't you tell me about it?"

Mrs. Noseworthy smiled. "No. You think you know everything. You think I'm a crazy old woman. I see those girls give me looks and Juliet twirl her finger at her head. I know what that means and I'm not crazy."

"Of course you're not crazy. I'm sure she didn't mean it like that, did you Juliet?"

"No. No. I didn't mean it. I'm sorry."

"Sometimes I forget. But I'm smart. I've been in this house

lots of times and you didn't even know it, that's how stupid you are."

"Did you find the bag of treasure in the sewing room?"

"So what if I did? It's mine."

"Is the treasure over at your house?"

Mrs. Noseworthy suddenly looked very cross. She reached out her arms and pointed the gun right at Elsie. "That's none of your business. I'm not talking anymore. I'm tired. You're giving me a headache."

She was almost to the library doors. Only a few more steps. Harry looked at Robert again and jerked his head. Robert nodded and got ready to seize his opportunity.

There was a quick bonk and Mrs. Noseworthy crumpled to the floor in a heap. The gun dropped beside her.

Mrs. Minelli held up her frying pan. "Now you're really going to have a headache."

Everyone jumped up at once. Elsie and Graham flew into each other arms and then to their girls, who were in the arms of the boys. Juliet and Faith grabbed Robert and Bunny made a beeline for Harry. A moment later, everyone ran to Mrs. Minelli.

The afternoon was spent in confusion. The police wandered about taking reports and the ambulance carted off Mrs. Noseworthy. Once more, the neighbours shook their heads at the goings-on in the Brooks household. Mrs. Mooney rushed over with two pans of squares, Queen's Lunch and Death by Chocolate. Elsie thanked her very much.

Elsie tried to apologize to Bunny, but she'd have none of it.

"You're an idiot," Bunny fumed. "This entire family needs to be locked up. You and stupid Graham deserve each other."

"May I have our keys back? The set you stole?"

"With pleasure." Bunny took them out of her pocket and threw them at her. Then she turned to Harry. "Officer Adams, I'm feeling so faint. Is it possible to get a drive home? May I lean on you? I think I twisted my ankle." As she bent over to caress her stockinged leg, cleavage poured out of her blouse. Elsie saw Harry's eyes bulge.

"Ah, sure," he stammered.

Elsie smirked. "Can I talk to you for a moment, Harry?"

He followed her into a corner of the living room. Bunny gave her a smug look.

"I want to thank you for everything, Harry. You were awfully nice to me when I needed someone. But you know this is over, don't you?"

"I know," he sighed. "I knew the minute you and Graham locked lips earlier…after the frying pan…"

She smiled. "But you'll stay my friend?"

He smiled back. "Try and stop me."

She whispered in his ear, "I think you've found a new friend. And I don't believe you'll ever need champagne to get her in the mood."

They looked at Bunny and laughed together.

It wasn't until later that night, as the family sat around the dining room table and ate Mrs. Minelli's homemade pizza, that everything fell into place.

"I saw you talking to the officers outside," Juliet said to Graham. "Did they say what they found when they went into Mrs. Noseworthy's?"

"It was a rat's nest, apparently. Everything everywhere. Some of the stolen items were in planters and in the dryer. Others were in the oven. The poor old soul's been losing her faculties for a while, judging by the state of the house."

"No wonder she'd never let us in," Faith said. "I just thought she was a private person."

"I should have known better," Elsie fretted. "I deal with people like her all the time and I let her suffer in that house all by herself."

Graham pointed his finger at her. "Don't be so hard on yourself. You were good to her. She loved to come over here and you couldn't have known what went on inside that house."

"Well, I should've guessed. I should have checked and made sure," Elsie frowned. "Most elderly people in the first stages of dementia don't take care of their personal hygiene, but Mrs. Noseworthy always looked pretty good. Maybe that's why I didn't tweak."

"What will happen to her?" Dahlia asked.

"It depends on what the physiologists determine," Graham said. "She's in the hospital tonight, exhausted and dehydrated apparently. She'll be placed in a facility."

"I hope I didn't hurt her too badly," Mrs. Minelli said. "I didn't want to kill her, just knock her out."

"You knock all of us out with that frying pan of yours, Mrs. Minelli," Robert smiled.

Everyone laughed.

Lily shook her head. "What I can't believe is the secret passage in my closet."

"Yeah," Eli winked. "If I'd known…." He glanced at Graham and didn't even try to recover. Graham downed his glass of red wine.

Dahlia looked at Slater. "Remember we said Aunt Hildy always seemed to be in the library? Maybe she used that secret passageway sometimes."

"She'd have loved that," Lily laughed. "Thinking she pulled one over on us. Although, I wonder why she told Mrs. Noseworthy about it, if she didn't tell us?"

Elsie smiled. "We tend to think of Aunt Hildy as someone who never put a foot wrong. But she was ninety-one. I'm sure she just got carried away one day out in the garden and spilled the beans inadvertently, while telling Mrs. Noseworthy a story. She took it all in, of course."

Robert fingered his glass. "So we've solved the mystery of where the treasure went, but we still have no idea what it was doing here in the first place."

"I know why."

Everyone turned to look at Faith.

"Well, for heaven's sake, fill us in!" Juliet shouted. "If you know, I can't believe you didn't tell us."

Faith leaned back in her chair. "I didn't know everything until yesterday, as it happens. And I didn't know about the secret passageway until today, obviously. Our dear aunt often used code words and there are still things I don't understand. She didn't write every day, in those early years, so there are great gaps. I've just pieced it together. Aunt Hildy's story spans decades, and it wasn't until the last bit of the puzzle was revealed that I was able to solve the mystery."

"So put us out of our misery," Graham urged. "What's the secret?"

She played with her napkin. "It's a heartbreaking story. But it explains why Aunt Hildy was so eccentric. Her sadness coloured her whole life."

Juliet slammed her wine glass down. "Out with it!"

Taking a deep breath, Faith started. "When Aunt Hildy was about seventeen, she met a young Norwegian sailor who worked on one of her father's ships. Nikolai came to the house one night with her father. He must have been helping bring rum barrels in through the secret passageway, because I could never figure out why her father would take home a lowly sailor. Anyway, Hildy and the sailor fell in love almost instantly." Faith stopped. "And of course! That's how she slipped out of the house to meet him. Through that passageway. It all fits." She took a sip of her wine. "Aunt Hildy knew her father would never approve of Nikolai as a suitor. He was a poor immigrant, but she didn't care. She made plans to marry him. They were going to run away together and start a new life. He was the one who gave her the music box. It was his grandmother's.

"Anyway, the night they were to be secretly married, Aunt Hildy's father found out about it and waylaid Nikolai on the dock. She waited at the church almost all night for him but he never showed up. Her father was in her room when she finally returned home. He told her he'd bought Nikolai off, had given him a large sum of money to leave town and that's just what he did. He told her she'd never see him again."

"That's so mean!" cried Dahlia. "You wouldn't do that, would you, Daddy?"

He shook his head. "Never."

"Aunt Hildy didn't believe her father and looked everywhere for Nikolai. For weeks she wandered around, asking everyone, but no one knew what happened. She slowly accepted the fact that maybe what her father had said was true. Her bitterness over these two men changed the rest of her life."

"What do you mean?" asked Elsie.

"She ran away and vowed no man would hurt her again. She took money from her father's cash box and went to Europe on her own, to start her new career."

"As an archaeologist," Lily prompted.

"No. As a courtesan."

Everyone gasped at the same time.

"Are you serious?" Elsie whispered.

"A courtesan?!" Slater shouted. "Aunt Hildy was a lawyer?"

"No, you idiot," Juliet said. "A prostitute. For wealthy men."

"You take that back," Slater yelled. "Aunt Hildy wasn't a hooker. No freakin' way!"

No one said anything, so Slater looked around. Finally he said, "For real?"

Faith continued. "She travelled in well-heeled circles. She was beautiful, intelligent and completely without conventional sensibilities. She did very well. Very well, indeed."

Juliet went pale. "My tiara…you don't think…"

Her sister nodded. "Very high circles."

Graham whistled.

"She was paid with 'treasure.' Our treasure."

"But why is it here?" Elsie wondered.

Lily's eyes got as round as saucers. She looked at Eli. "She wanted to rub her father's nose in it. It's classic passive-aggressive behaviour. He wouldn't let her have the man she wanted, so she had lots of men and surrounded her father with the fruits of her labour." Lily looked back at Faith for confirmation.

"You're right. That's just what she did. She'd visit her mother every few years but apparently never spoke to her father again."

No one said anything. Graham cracked open another bottle of wine and poured everyone a drink.

"It gets worse," Faith said.

"Worse? It can't get much worse than that," Elsie frowned.

"Her father was on his death bed and her mother begged her to come home. He wanted to see her before he died. The only reason she did come was because of her mother and sister."

Faith took a deep breath. "At her mother's urging, she went to her father's bedside. It was there that he begged to be forgiven for what he'd done. He didn't want to go to hell for killing Nikolai."

There was complete silence at the table.

"It's true," Faith said quietly. "Our grandfather went to meet him that night with the intention of buying him off, and the young man threw the money back in his face. He punched Nikolai so hard in the jaw that he went down, hit his head on the iron anchor mooring and fell off the wharf into the inky black water of the harbour. Grandfather dove and dove but couldn't find him."

"Oh my God," Elsie cried. "Poor Aunt Hildy."

"Before he died, her father returned the small gold band that he'd wrestled out of Nikolai's hand before the fight."

"What did she do?" Dahlia sobbed.

"She sat and watched her father die, without forgiving him. But she never told our mother and grandmother what he'd done. She spared them that heartache. She went back to Europe, got an education and started her career. She stopped giving herself away to men. Nikolai hadn't left her all those years before. He loved her until the end. That's all that mattered."

"No one would believe this story if it wasn't true," Lily sniffed. "All this stuff. All these things, hidden away. No wonder she was confused as to whether she wanted us to have the treasure or not."

"How so?" Robert asked.

"Well, think about it. A part of her was ashamed of it, and yet she was smart enough to know that it couldn't just sit here forever. It might as well be used by us. But she didn't want to explain to us what it was doing here. At least not while she was alive. It was too personal, and probably too hard to talk about. So she invented a foolish game to focus our attention elsewhere."

"But the story was in her journals," Graham said. "If she didn't want us to know, why not burn them?"

"Because all her life she was alone," Eli said. "She wanted someone to know her suffering. Wouldn't you?"

Lily agreed. "But she couldn't stand the thought of being pitied. It was there for us to find after she was gone. Back to him."

Everyone around the table nodded.

Faith turned to Slater. "She said you reminded her of Nikolai, a big blonde gorgeous man. She wrote that it amused her to think that maybe their son would have looked like you."

Slater folded his arms on the table and hid his face.

"Oh, this just stinks," Dahlia cried. "Why isn't she here? Stupid Mrs. Noseworthy."

"I can't get over Aunt Hildy," Eli said quietly. "Can you imagine staring down the barrel of a gun…"

"Yes," everyone interrupted.

Eli held up his hands. "Okay, okay, so we can imagine. But I don't think anyone at this table would have the guts to say, 'Go ahead, shoot me, I dare you.'"

"She was tired," Faith told them. "She longed to just close

her eyes and have it over with. She wanted to join her lover. She said he'd waited long enough for her. And she looked forward to the day when she would see him again." Faith cleared her throat. "I, for one, am glad Aunt Hildy didn't die a slow and undignified death in a hospital somewhere. That was her greatest fear. And knowing her, the way I've come to know her through her words, I think she saw an opportunity and took it."

Elsie looked around the table. "This house has seen so much sorrow and joy over the years. I've often thought that memories must live inside the walls of a house. I now understand why Aunt Hildy needed to come back here, and why she wanted to be in her old room. Just to be close to Nikolai again. To walk down that passageway, perhaps remembering a summer's evening when she'd slipped away to meet him in secret. If she had to die anywhere, her bedroom was no doubt the one place on earth she'd want to be."

There wasn't much more to be said after that. Everyone drifted away from the table, lost in their own thoughts as they took the dishes into the kitchen and thanked Mrs. Minelli for her usual great meal.

Elsie was on her third trip to the dining room to collect the tablecloth, when Faith and Juliet stopped her.

"That was scary today," Juliet said. "You made it better in there. You talked your way out of that mess. You used your people skills to make Mrs. Noseworthy calm down and I just wanted you to know that I'm proud of you."

Faith nodded. "Me too."

Juliet added, "You sounded and acted…"

Elsie smiled, "I know, just like Aunt Hildy."

"No. Just like Mom."

Elsie cried then. She hugged her sisters tight and blubbered, "That's the nicest thing you've ever said to me."

Juliet pulled herself away. "Well, don't get used to it. I hate sentimentality. It's a bore."

"You can't take it back, Juliet. You can get as bitchy as you want but I'll always remember you just said that."

Juliet did her famous eye-rolling thing. "Oh God. I've created a monster. Good night all. I'm off to soak in a hot tub." With that, she waltzed out the door.

"I think I'll go over and have a cup of cocoa with Nella," Faith said. "You and Graham have some talking to do."

Elsie smiled. "We do, don't we?"

"I could smack you," she sighed. "When am I ever going to find anyone?"

"Oh, you'll meet your sailor someday."

Elsie went out onto the deck. Robert and Mrs. Minelli said their goodnights and headed out across the garden with Faith, through the ugliest gateway in the neighbourhood.

The girls turned to their parents. "Do you mind if we go over next door? Mrs. Minelli's making fudge."

Graham quickly said, "No. We don't mind. Just save some for us."

When they too ducked their heads through the jagged fence, Graham mused, "That thing's got to come down."

"It does, doesn't it."

They looked at each other. Graham gathered her in his arms and they stood there, almost awkwardly. Then he pulled her closer and she leaned her cheek against his chest. He kissed the top of her head and whispered, "You were wonderful in there today. I was so proud of you."

"Thank you. My sisters just told me that too, not five minutes ago. You could have knocked me over with a feather." Then she laughed. "Of course, it's tempered by the fact that it took a gun to their heads to make them say it."

He laughed too. "Well, they did. That's the important thing."

"When I think of what could've happened today, my knees get weak," Elsie confessed. She squeezed him tighter. "Everyone I love was in that room. My whole family. It makes you realize how precious we are to each other and how quickly we can be gone."

"Today wasn't the first day you've helped save this family. You do it every day of your life and I've taken that for granted or ridiculed it. No more. Never again."

"Oh Graham, please forgive me for being so stupid. I've always made you think you could've done more with your life, if only you'd tried a little harder. I had no right to do that. You're a wonderful man, just as you are. Aunt Hildy loved a penniless sailor. It wasn't about what he was, it was about who he was."

"Did you know your father offered me money to get out of *your* life?"

She drew away from him and gasped, "No!"

He nodded. "I told him to kiss my ass. Now that I have daughters of my own, I can understand why he hated me so much after that."

She shook her head. "God. You never told me."

Graham looked at her. "I never told you because I loved you. You know what Faith said about Aunt Hildy wanting to be with Nikolai? Think about it. He's been gone for more than seventy years and she still loved him." He put his hand up and rubbed her cheek with his thumb. "That's what I feel for you. I know that even if something happened to one of us, we'd still be together. I've loved you my whole life. And I'll love you for the rest of my life Elsie, however long or short that may be."

She reached up and gave him a soft, sweet kiss. "And I'll love you right back."

Graham smiled at her and quickly glanced over at the Beech Street house. "How long do you think they'll be over there?"

Elsie laughed. "Just long enough, if we hurry."

He grabbed her hand. "Let's go then." They made a dash for the back door.

Later that evening, Faith was in bed and the kids were downstairs in the kitchen playing 45's. While Graham took a shower, Elsie wrapped her sorry old bathrobe around herself and snuck into Lily's room. She wasn't sure why she felt compelled to go through Aunt Hildy's passageway, but decided to trust her instinct. She took a small flashlight, and pushed Lily's clothes to one side. It amazed her that she never noticed the small doorway cleverly hidden behind three shelves, shelves that looked like they were nailed to the wall, but that were really just hinged, so they could be moved aside easily.

She opened the doorway and shone the flashlight down the wooden steps. They were old and worn and creaked as she crept down them. The passageway was narrow and the steps circled around once, twice, three times. Her flashlight picked up dusty cobwebs among the wooden beams. A big old spider hurried away, out of sight. As she followed the path of the spider, her eyes fell upon a dust-covered metal box shoved deep into the rafter. A metal box with a lock.

And I have the key, she thought.

A shiver ran up Elsie's spine. "Did you want me to find this, Aunt Hildy?"

Elsie pushed the cobwebs away and reached as far as she could, just managing to grab the small metal handle at the top of the box. She dragged it out, disturbing a few more spiders along the way, and quickly tucked it under her arm. Instead of continuing down to the library, she re-traced her steps and went back through the closet, tip-toeing to her bedroom. Closing the door, she placed the box on the side table by the old armchair and went to the closet. She reached for Aunt Hildy's carpet bag and brought it over to the chair. Opening the bag, she pushed her finger into the pocket as before and slid the key out.

Elsie's heart was racing. What was it that Aunt Hildy had hidden away and yet kept so close to her in the form of this key?

Fingers shaking, she put the key in the lock. She turned it one way, then the other, hearing the small click. The lid popped.

There were the letters from Nikolai tied up with a ribbon. This was his handwriting. Suddenly he was a real flesh and blood person. A boy whose life was ended before it even began. She couldn't bear to open them, so she placed them to one side. Underneath were a few black and white photos of them together. They were leaning on a fence, looking out over the water. They looked so young and in love. Were they planning their future that day?

And then Elsie saw the thin gold band. She lifted it out of the box. It was so delicate, probably all the young sailor could afford.

Elsie's eyes filled with tears. Her heart broke for the young girl who longed to wear this ring so many years ago.

When Graham opened the bedroom door, she was startled. He took one look at her face.

"What's wrong?"

"I've found Aunt Hildy's treasure."

"What do you mean?" He walked across the room in his robe and sat on the bed.

"Nikolai's letters, and photos of them together. And look, here's the wedding band." She held it up for him to see.

Graham shook his head. "What a waste."

Elsie nodded.

"What else is in there?"

She lifted out what looked like official documents. They were wrapped together with string. A letter was on top. Elsie opened it and started to read. Her eyes got big.

"It's from my grandfather to Hildy."

"What does it say?"

"*Dearest Hildy, I can never repay the damage I've done to you. Certainly not in my lifetime. I worry about you alone in the world and know that I am the reason you are alone. These stocks are for you, so you will never have to worry about supporting yourself in your dotage. I realize that at your tender age, you cannot imagine yourself as old, but believe me, the day will come. Promise me you will use this income and, if you can, please find happiness again. Father.*"

Graham and Elsie stared at each other.

"He must have given this to her on his death bed," Elsie said.

"And she never used them."

Elsie gave him a half-smile. "Well, she wouldn't, would she?

Graham shook his head. "No. She certainly wouldn't."

Elsie untied the string and unfolded the documents, leafing through them. "Ford Motor Company, Canadian National Railway, Bell and Howell, Kodak. These must be worth a fortune."

Graham gave a low whistle. "Imagine that. What are we going to do with them?"

Elsie sat back in the chair. "Oh god, I don't know. It's all too much." She covered her eyes, trying to think.

"As you pointed out, money can make even the best families go crazy. We have more than enough for all of us from the sale of the jewellery. We don't need this."

Elsie looked up. "Even if we did, I could never spend it. It's blood money, Graham. To appease the guilt of an old man. Maybe I should just put it back where I found it and let the past lie."

"Or you could use it for something good. Like a scholarship fund perhaps."

Elsie sat up. "You're right! That's just what we should do. Scholarship funds for Maritime girls who want to go to university but can't afford it. Or wait! What about using some of it to set up trust funds for women's shelters? I think Aunt Hildy would support something like that. Helping other women who've suffered."

"Sounds like a plan. And you certainly have the connections to see that it gets to the right people."

"Oh, this is so exciting! Wait till I tell the kids. Juliet and Faith may sulk for a bit, but I think they'll come around in the end." Elsie put everything back in the box and locked it. Then she sat back with a big smile on her face.

Graham laughed. "It's so good to see you happy again."

"I am happy. I'm happy that you're back in this messy bedroom where you belong."

He pointed at her. "Have you got anything on under that?"

She gave him a big smirk and rose from the chair. "Why, no

I don't Mr. Brooks." She slowly untied her robe and let it fall to the floor.

He reached out and grabbed her hand. "Get over here."

They fell back on the bed in each other's arms. Graham kissed her nose. "First thing tomorrow I'm taking you to the mall and we're buying you a new bathrobe."

"You're so romantic." Elsie laughed. She ran her fingers through his hair. "I love you."

"My sweet Elsie."

He kissed her then, the way he'd always kissed her. Totally, completely and with great skill.

Reader's Guide

The relationship between the sisters in *Shoot Me* is ongoing and mercurial, but their bond is a strong one. How are Juliet, Faith, and Elsie different? What are their similarities? Which sister is most like Aunt Hildy?

When the novel opens, Elsie and Graham Brooks' marriage is on the rocks. They come up with a unique way of handling the situation by having Graham live in the basement instead of leaving the house altogether. What does this arrangement signify? Is it a good decision?

Elsie Brooks is a chronic do-gooder. Her family certainly benefits from this desire to please, but they suffer because of it, too. How is Elsie's personality contributing to or hindering her life?

Faith is a woman who suffers from depression. She has no home of her own, no social circle, and no job. She dreams of becoming a novelist, but relies on Elsie to give her a roof over her head. Is Elsie's support helpful? What is the difference between helping and enabling someone? Will Faith ever write a book?

Juliet and Robert have a love/hate relationship. Their bickering masks underlying resentment. What are the causes of that resentment and do you think Juliet and Robert really love each other?

Aunt Hildy's treasure is at the centre of this story. She drives her family crazy with tantalizing clues about this so-called treasure and yet won't offer an explanation. At times she even denies its existence. Was it poor judgment on Aunt Hildy's part to involve her family members, or did they have a right to know about this dark secret? Can you think of other novels where family secrets play such a pivotal role?

Slater and Eli become members of the family by virtue of being the boyfriends of Elsie's daughters. They are vastly different in some respects. What do they have in common?

Throughout the novel, the characters are faced with decisions that could alter the lives of the rest of their family members. Knowing Juliet's personality, do you think she would have told the others if she'd managed to find the treasure first?

Finding Aunt Hildy's treasure is about more than just looking for loot. It involves the interpersonal relationships between family members, and their reactions to this bizarre quest will shape the rest of their lives. What are the lessons learned from this treasure hunting?

An Interview with Lesley Crewe

Shoot Me, your second book, is so different from *Relative Happiness*, your first. How did *Shoot Me* come to you? Did it start with one specific scene, or a character, or did the plot present itself?

A friend suggested I write a murder mystery. Well, I'm no P. D. James, but I thought I'd have a crack at it and *Shoot Me* is what I came up with. Aunt Hildy was the character I started with. She's based on an elderly woman who made a lifelong impression on me. She was the Brown Owl at a Girl Guide camp I attended with my mom when I was six (Mom was a counsellor). We went down to the lake at sunrise and Brown Owl was swimming in the calm water. She looked like an otter, and when she climbed up the ladder to the wharf, she was naked. She was absolutely at peace with herself and her surroundings, like she was one with the landscape. Even at such a young age, I knew I wanted to be that woman.

Is that writing process typical for you?

Yes. I take an image or an event that has somehow stayed with me and use it as a jumping-off point for a story. It could be a person or a house or a tree or something that stands out in my memory. It's not a story; it's usually just a fragment or picture in my mind.

Lesley Crewe fans all have a favourite book of yours. What do you think having *Shoot Me* as a favourite book says about those readers?

They can all relate to the craziness that goes on within families! We all have messy relationships and botched hopes and dreams, and yet it's usually our families who end up saving us in the end. Who else would put up with us?

This is a funny novel with some serious themes and issues. In your own life, do you tend to manage sadness with humour?

No. When I'm sad, I'm sad. But like everything else, wait five minutes and something ridiculous will happen that makes you laugh in spite of yourself. I've had a lot of sadness in my life, but I've also laughed a lot, and that tendency has saved me over and over again. It's very natural for me to weave humour and sorrow into a story. Life is not a flat line.

Do you have any favourite humour writers?

Roald Dahl is my favourite writer, and no one does humour better. He's brilliant. I grew up reading Erma Bombeck, and I love Elaine May and Nora Ephron.

Your main characters almost always have sisters—for better or for worse. What's your experience with sisterhood, and how has it affected your writing?

My younger sister Nancy has always been my best friend. A sibling is like having a reference library of your life at your fingertips. All you have to do is say, "Remember when…" and the two of you kill yourselves over silly things that happened decades ago…stuff that no one else in the world would know or care about. When I'm with my sister, I'm with my entire family, even though our parents are gone now. She remembers, and because she remembers, I'm not alone in the world.

I write what I know. I never had a brother, so it's simply a matter of comfort to be able to write about sisters. I *know* sisters.

The characters in this book are deeply flawed, in many different ways. But a lot of them are still very appealing. Which character do you most relate to in this novel? Is there any character you dislike?

I'm very much like Elsie. Actually, that's how Elsie got her name. I couldn't think of a name for her at the beginning so I wrote *L.C.* for the first couple of pages, and that got tedious, so I changed it to Elsie. Elsie and I share a deadly flaw, and that is that we can't say no to anyone. She tries to be all things to all people and spreads herself too thin. I think a lot of women do that in their everyday lives. We try to "fix" everything and end up wanting to shoot ourselves just to have some peace and quiet.

Juliet is pretty hard to like. She's a real pain. We all know at least one Juliet!

The shooting of Hildy is shocking to readers. Did you know from the start that she'd be shot?

Yes. I knew she was going to go out in a blaze of glory. Nothing else would have been sufficient for the old gal. Hildy would be the last person who would want to end up languishing in a nursing home. She died with her boots on, God love her.

At first everyone's under suspicion for the shooting. Did you ever consider anyone else shooting Hildy—were any of the other characters capable of it?

No. The family was full of misfits, but they weren't murderers. Juliet and Robert might have been selfish enough to consider it, but I doubt they'd go through with it. Juliet might muss up her hair.

Finally, let's talk about the book's setting. The big rambling house in *Shoot Me* is essentially a character of its own. What did you model it after?

When I attended Dalhousie University, I lived in residence at Sheriff Hall, in the South End of Halifax. I used to love to walk in the neighbourhood and look at all the beautiful old houses and wonder what was going on behind those windows and doors. I decided I'd write a story about one of them, since I'd love to live in a house like that, but I can't afford it! So I "borrowed" a house for a few months and lived in it while I wrote.

Nicola Davison

LESLEY CREWE is the author of ten novels, including *Beholden*, *Mary, Mary*, *Amazing Grace*, *Chloe Sparrow*, *Kin*, and *Relative Happiness*, which has been adapted into a feature film. A freelance writer and screenwriter, her column "Are You Kidding Me?" appears weekly in the *Chronicle Herald*'s community newspapers. Lesley lives in Homeville, Nova Scotia. Visit her at lesleycrewe.com.